shawn hopkins

AN EVIL FROM THE VERY BEGINNING IS STILL HERE

noahic

TATE PUBLISHING, LLC

"Noahic" by Shawn Hopkins

Published in the United States of America
by Tate Publishing, LLC
127 East Trade Center Terrace
Mustang, OK 73064
(888) 361-9473

ISBN: 1-9331488-9-6

I
An Orchestration Directed

PROLOGUE

1687

:::: *Morning*

The bow sliced through the warm Atlantic waters, the rolling waves passing beneath the keel and disappearing over the horizon past the stern. The bow's collision with the uneven sea raised the starboard side of the ship and suspended it in the air for just enough time to sink the stern deeper into the water. Once the wave lapsed by and released the ship from its elevated state, the starboard bow returned to the water with a thunderous impact. The see-saw effect sent warm ocean water splashing high into the air, the sunlight passing through the mist creating a temporary rainbow of colors. The waves came uninvited and left without farewell, continuing their everlasting sweep of the eternal seas, proving that there is no respect of persons with nature.

The sun was high and bright, blinding to look at. And the clear blue waters that stretched to the horizons only reflected that shining light in an arsenal of countless sparkling glimmers, making the water just as brilliant as the sun itself. The warm summer breeze traveled persistently over the ocean's surface, pausing only to rise higher than the occasional wave. The smell of salt water was strong in the air, as was the smell of fish- a regular part of a sailor's diet.

The *Sovereign Wing* was one of the fastest ships within his Majesty's service, hence its name. A war ship within the royal Navy, the *Sovereign Wing* had been through more than most ships that shared in her line of duty. She was a third-rate ship, meaning that she carried between sixty-four and eighty guns and seven hundred to seven hundred and fifty men. At one point in time the *Sovereign Wing* was a first rate ship, but the older she got, the more her parts and crew were assigned to newer, more reliable ships. What she was left with was still considered to be fairly grand, however she would, no doubt, be relieved of a few more possessions once port was reached.

The *Sovereign Wing* was made up of three decks. The lower deck housed the heaviest guns as they were set up to fire through the lowest line of gun-ports. The middle deck contained the medium sized guns, and the main deck held the smallest. Though the lower deck was where most of the sailors had their quarters, more recently they had moved to the main deck. The main deck was now, uncommonly, cluttered with pillows and blankets.

This book is dedicated to: Denise Hoagland (for continually prodding me on in this work and praying for me), Harvey Cola (for stimulating much of the spiritual discussion within these pages and helping create, in my mind, a main character that is a hero for eternal reasons), Dan Fackler (for encouraging me to write in the first place, all the way back in the 12th grade), and Uncle Michael (for providing the means and for cheering me on). To God be the glory.

"You can sleep topside, but you must clean off the deck at first light!" The Post Captain stepped over another pile of blankets. "We are still in the service of his Majesty! Get this stuff away lest we disgrace his image!" The sailors scrambled about, quickly hiding their beds out of sight. The main deck was cleared within a matter of seconds.

Post Captain White made his way past the cathead and to the figurehead. He grasped one of the huge ropes that ran from the foremast and leaned his body into it, causing the rope to audibly stretch. He removed his hat and let the warm ocean breeze travel over his face and pull at his long blonde hair, bleached from a lifetime lived under the intense sun. He stared down at the long bowsprit that stretched from the head and out over the waters.

Captain White was a veteran commander, having served since he was twenty. He had fought in two of the three commercial wars against the Dutch, and it was a battle he led that ultimately caused the Netherlands to drop out of the race for world commerce and American dominions. The *Sovereign Wing* had been under his command for nearly fifteen years. He did not enjoy watching its gradual recession, for it reminded him of his own. White was growing old, his sixtieth birthday just passing. He knew his day was drawing near, but dwelling on the thought was not a favorite pastime of his. He had made a reputation for himself and for his loyal crew over the years. The *Sovereign Wing* was a legend within the English navy. But that pride mattered little when so far from the sovereignty of England.

White watched as the blue waves passed by the bow. The mist that sprayed the air with every crashing wave dampened his face and bare chest. The long laceration that ran across his upper body began to sting from the salt. He reflexively placed his free hand over the wound while at the same time cursing his hasty instinct. Dry blood broke loose under the pressure of his hand, and new blood escaped the wound, beginning its dripping descent down his chest.

White wondered if it was even a rational idea, retiring. In fact, he now wondered if any thoughts given towards a future extending past this ill-turned journey were reasonable ones. He turned to face the stern and ran his thoughtful gaze over those working on the main deck. Most were wounded, some badly. The storm that had hit them the previous night left them in a position of extreme hopelessness. The *Savior's Song, Sovereign Wing's* sister ship had sunk under the enormous waves induced by the storm. She now lay miles below the surface of the next day's calm waters. Taking both ships into account, the death toll was somewhere near to nine hundred. White had yet to discover the peace of mind required for pursuing such a calculated statistic, so he settled with a near figure for the time being.

He took careful note of the condition of his ship. Both the mizzenmast and the mainmast were gone, leaving only the foremast. The foremast still had all of its sails save the fore royal, and that was due to the fact that the very top of the foremast was cracked and hanging off. Enough of the mizzenmast was left to fly the flag of England from the driver, but, besides that one sail, the mizzenmast was essentially gone and useless.

White watched the flag blow in the wind.

They were so far from England, so far from the place the banner represented. They were so far from home . . . and everyone was becoming aware that she would probably never be seen by them again. She was now only a distant reality, separated by countless miles of ruthless and unpredictable water. With each passing moment, the men aboard the *Sovereign Wing* watched their hope sink into the dark depths of the ocean below them, a place they knew they themselves would soon witness.

Most of the food stored in the orlop deck was destroyed due to a few leaks sustained by the ship through the fury of the storm. There were around five hundred people on board the *Sovereign Wing,* and nearly enough food to feed them all for more than a week. That would normally be fine if they knew where they were going or how to go about getting there, but since all of the navigation equipment, including charts and maps, were stolen by the madness of nature, the crew was left afloat. Even if they did know what direction they wanted to head in, they couldn't. When the mainmast came down, it crashed through the poop deck and destroyed the wheel. There was nothing steering the ship save the wind. The situation was bleak at best.

"We mustn't be traveling more than a knot an hour, what with the tip at the starboard bow."

White jumped at the sudden sound of the voice speaking over his shoulder. He turned his head just enough to learn the face from which the voice came. It was Lieutenant Winthrop, relative of the famous John Winthrop who was the first governor of the Massachusetts' Bay Colony.

"Yes, that is true. We shall be on this sea for some unknown length of time." Because the only remaining sails were on the fore-mast, which was forward rather than aft, the wind caught the sails and pushed the bow down into the water further than usual. When all the sails were up, there was an even distribution of air power, but now that the forward end of the ship was catching the wind only, the bow was lower than the stern, thus greatly decreasing speed.

"Any word on the prisoners?" asked White, still watching the flag blow in the wind.

"Let them be damned! We should just kill them!"

The *Sovereign Wing* had left England two months ago on a mission like no other- a mission that was sealed as 'classified.' Over the last two years, since King Charles II died and James II stepped quietly to the throne, there formed a group of men in a secret society called the *Community of the Beast.* Those who made up the society were against the Catholic presence that existed within England. Once James took the throne, they waged war on all Catholic persons. The community spent two years dwelling in the woods of England, killing patrols, travelers, and anyone else that might pass through the woods on their way to the castle. At first, the community was seen only as an annoyance. However, as the months increased, so did the number of deaths suffered at their evil hands. The number of deaths increased so rapidly over such a short period of time that King James II sent out a troop of one hundred soldiers to wipe out the *Community of the Beast.* When the army never returned, fear gripped the hearts of all those dwelling on the outskirts of England, and those who lived near the woods began traveling closer to the center of England. Before long, legend and myth had mixed with fact and, instead of men making up this evil community, it was spread around that Satan himself was this beast- the beast talked of in the book of Revelation of whom it was said by Daniel would make war with the saints and prevail against them.

King James II assembled a group of men to whom he gave the responsibility of attaining information about this cult. Those men, highly trained and specialized as spies, did not disappoint their king. They brought back terrible news of this beast.

"It is Satan himself, in the form of many men, who is leading this assault against the Catholic peoples of England and threatening her sovereignty!" The report continued to share the sights that the spies had subjected themselves to. They told of Devil worship and human sacrifice, rape and murder, and power like none they had ever seen.

It was the power of the men that confounded the King. He begged them to share detail.

"My King, I saw with mine own eyes the assembling of hundreds of men all chanting in unison the words from St. John, 'So they worshiped the dragon who gave authority to the beast; and they worshiped the beast.' This they did not say, my Lord, but the words said by them that worshiped the beast. 'Who is like the beast? Who is able to make war with him?' Then did they bring in a man of great natural strength and loosed him in their midst so that he tried to escape them. The men laughed at his attempt and before long overtook him by force and dismembered him with their own bare hands! The sight was awful as the poor fellow's blood soaked all those around him. And, my King, the most disturbing part . . . They enjoyed it. It was sport to them . . . The sight of the poor fellow's blood was the reason for their gathering and rejoicing!"

The King then learned of the involvement of the Tory and Whig leaders who were in support of this Catholic persecution.

King James II was expecting a child, and, of course, all kings wanted a male child to continue the kingship. Henry VIII had made that clearly known to the world and to his wives. However, King James knew that if he did have a son, that his own life, as well as his son's, would be in danger if the Tory and Whig leaders were able to use this community against him. He also suspected his daughter, Mary, and her Dutch husband, William of Orange, to participate in some way with his demise. He had to stop this secret society from existing if he had any hopes of living a long life and keeping England within the grasp of Catholicism.

King James then declared war on the *Community of the Beast.* This war was kept private and was not known by many outside of England, for no new taxes were made, nor was there any form of recruiting. This war was to be quick and quiet.

It was. King James had stamped out the devil worshipers within a week. They may have had supernatural strength imparted to them from the Devil, but strength did not compare to a battalion of rifle-carrying soldiers. Whenever an English soldier was unfortunate enough to get close to one of the members of the community, they were torn to pieces. But that was a rare occurrence in the battle. The entire community was destroyed.

Except for its leaders.

The King later learned that they had fled to New England. Fearing the same results in New England that England had suffered over the two years (or more so, the men returning to England at a later date and carrying out an assassination plot), the King had sent two ships to New England. They were to capture the leaders of the community and bring them back to England alive. If there was information to be had out of them, information about the Tory and Whig leaders and even information about his daughter, he would get it.

The *Sovereign Wing* and *Savior's Song* were sent out two months ago. After reaching New England, it took only a few days to find the evil leaders of the community, but it took a few more days to catch them. They were on their way back to England when the storm hit.

There were twelve prisoners chained up on the lower deck, which was why most of the sailors and soldiers preferred to sleep topside. Though the prisoners were chained, there were events that occurred since they set sail for England that could not be explained. One by one, the people aboard *Sovereign Wing* began to believe that the Devil himself was on their boat.

A soldier was sitting behind White and Winthrop on the cathead. He was concealed by a shadow cast by the fore mainsail, thus remaining hidden from the Post Captain's sight. He had overheard their conversation.

"Let them be damned! We should just kill them!" offered Winthrop.

The soldier spoke from the shadows, surprising both men. "I too, would support that idea." He stood, the sudden impact of light against his face causing him to squint. Both White and Winthrop were staring at him. "If I was sure that they would indeed die."

White could not tell of the man's rank for he was wearing only pants. His huge chest and massive arms told of his strength, his eyes declaring experience. White was aware that this soldier knew what he was talking about, though his statement sounded more than ludicrous.

"What is your name, Soldier?" asked White.

"My name is Peter Morgan. I was present during the battle against the *Community of the Beast.* These men, if men at all, are not to be troubled with. Our Majesty wishes to believe that the Tories and the Whigs are behind this community, or at least are in support of it."

Winthrop nodded. "Do you say differently, Soldier?"

Morgan continued, "The Exclusion Bill that was presented to Parliament not long ago was indeed to bar James II from the kingship. As you well know, King Charles prevented its passage by simply dissolving Parliament. The governing classes split into bitter factions. The Whigs favored the bill as the Tories opposed it."

Winthrop interrupted once more. "We are in no need of a history lesson, Good Soldier."

Morgan frowned. "I apologize, Lieutenant Winthrop. I merely meant to point out that there is no evidence that either the Whigs or the Tories, in fact, even know about any of this, much less be the source behind it."

White nodded. "Point taken. Are you a Roundhead?"

"Such names are foolish in origin. I am Protestant. I trust that answers the rest of your questions."

White nodded again. "Peter Morgan, I have no desire to debate theology here and now. The King may not be tolerant of your beliefs, but I am. There are more important things to discuss here and now."

Morgan agreed.

"So how fair the prisoners?" asked White.

Morgan looked him straight in the eye as he answered. White liked the soldier immediately. He respected a person who could hold the stare of another in higher authority. It showed confidence, strength, and, in this case, a union of knowledge.

"Two more soldiers died some time last night."

Winthrop cursed.

"How did it happen this time?" asked White.

"I do not know. The remaining guard had fallen asleep during the other's turn to watch. No one woke him up until he, himself, woke up this morning to find both of the other guards without their heads."

Winthrop cursed again.

"The prisoners are still chained?"

"Yes. It appears that they haven't moved. I can't explain it, but to attribute it to some damnable force of Satan."

White's eyes looked tired as his mind tried to think of a solution. "Would you try to kill them?"

Morgan let his gaze drop to the wooden deck on which he stood. "Captain White, when we engaged the other persons of their community . . . I cannot begin to tell you of their strength and power. I, myself, fired into the chest of a screaming man, yet he did not stop coming. I then ran my bayonet through his throat. He stopped screaming, but did not stop trying to tear me to pieces, which I had seen many others do to my fellow soldiers. Sir, I stabbed him through the heart with my sword as he began to eat at my flesh." He pointed to a group of scars. "It wasn't until I removed his head that he stopped breathing."

Winthrop began thinking out loud. "So if we take off their heads . . ."

Morgan looked over at Winthrop. "A musket ball at close range into the chest, a bayonet into the throat, a sword into the heart, and three swings to remove his head . . . " He looked over Winthrop. "You can go down there if you wish. But I have a bad feeling that if they wanted to get topside, they could. I do not want to give them a reason to. Do you?"

Winthrop's sun colored face began to grow pale. "If what you say is true . . . "

White looked at Winthrop. "Make sure they get some breakfast, lest they come looking for it up here."

Winthrop nodded and hurried off.

White looked back to Morgan. "Do you really think they could kill us all if they wished to?"

Morgan looked into the Captain's eyes. "Oh yes. I believe they can, and I also believe they will."

White stood motionless for longer than he thought. Morgan's large hand hitting him on the shoulder snapped him out of his bemusement.

"I don't believe it will do you any good, but if you wish to pray to Mary, you may as well get a head start." He began to walk away.

White reached out and grabbed him by the shoulder. "Hey! I am also a student of the Reformation, especially Tyndale's work."

Morgan smiled. "Catholicism is dangerous, my friend. You need only Christ to trust for your salvation. Anything more is an addition to the Word of God." He paused. "With that said, let us speak no more of theology. I told you what I believe is true, now I must concentrate on how we shall survive the terror that lies beneath these wooden floors." With that, Morgan turned and made his way back onto the main deck, leaving White alone to be terrified by the things recently uttered.

The young soldier suddenly thought of jumping off the ship. He would prefer drowning or being eaten by sharks rather than dying the way the prisoners killed people- at least according to rumor. George Fredrickson walked up the stairs towards the lower deck. His left hand was carrying a bucket of water and his right a sack of bread. He was coming from the orlop deck where he had been assigned by Captain White to feed the prisoners. He immediately felt sick to his stomach.

The prison was a closed off section of the lower deck. It was sealed by two locked doors on either side and was fitted with chains and cuffs. Three guards sat on each side of the prison, making sure nothing strange was happening and pretending that they could do something about it if there was.

Fredrickson walked to the guards and nodded towards the door.

One of the guards reached down and removed a large set of keys held together by a metal loop. He selected the right key and slid it into the lock that was fixed onto the door. The other two soldiers held their guns at the ready. The guard looked at Fredrickson as he opened the door, and the message sent from his eyes was not difficult to interpret. He simply felt sorry for the poor fellow that was chosen to walk into a room in which the Devil lay chained to a wooden wall.

Fredrickson's heart began to pound louder within his head. He began shaking, and water was sloshing out of the bucket and onto the floor. One of the guards gently pushed him from behind.

"Can't leave the door open this long." Then, to offer some glimmer of hope, he added, "It'll be all right."

With that, Fredrickson entered the darkness of the prison.

And the door shut behind him.

"Hey!" He turned around to face the closed door as he heard the metallic 'click' of the door being locked.

He heard a noise from behind him.

He spun around. The room was too dark to see anything, at least right away. Fredrickson was still trying to let his eyes adjust to the change. There were two small windows up in the corner of the room, but the sunlight that was allowed through only created more shadows in the areas the prisoners must have been chained, because Fredrickson couldn't see them anywhere.

Then he saw it.

An open cuff lay on the ground, its metal chain reaching up to the facets on the wall.

His heart was beating like a drum within his head as sweat began to soak his shirt. He began to slowly walk backwards, towards the door.

"We're hungry." The voice cut through the stillness like an explosion. Fredrickson jumped and his pants grew damp.

"Where . . . Where are you?" He strained to see where the voice came from, trying to decide whether to run for the door or to actually give the food to the prisoners.

"Over here."

Fredrickson spun around again, knowing that he heard the voice come from behind him. If there was a loosed prisoner in the darkness, then he knew he had little chance of surviving.

"Fredrickson . . . " The voice was low, emotionless, and yet eerily calm, as if it had the power to induce a trance.

Fredrickson looked around the room and was surprised and horrified to finally be able to see his surroundings. He was standing in the middle of the room, the prisoners chained on the surrounding walls. Fredrickson quickly looked away, not wanting to see their faces, their eyes.

"Fredrickson . . . " The voice was close.

Fredrickson let out a gasp. He did not even want to think about how the prisoner might have learned his name. Could he read his mind?

"No, Fredrickson. It was the others that were down here . . . " The voice was evil and perversely seductive. "They told me everything about you before they died . . . "

Fredrickson felt a blast of air rush by him. Whether it was a burst of air rushing through the small windows or whether it was someone running past him in the dark, he did not want to stay and find out. He ran to the door and pounded his fists into its wooden construction.

"Let me out!" He screamed repeatedly, but the door remained locked. Behind him, Fredrickson heard the sound of laughter erupt within the prison. He turned, placing his back against the door. His hand fumbled through his belt until it was able to grasp the dagger that he kept tucked into it. He pulled it out as he watched a dark figure rush towards him. Raising his arms up over his face, he screamed, waiting for the impact.

Fredrickson landed hard on the floor, the impact chasing the air from his lungs. He opened his eyes and, through the white spots, he could make out the three guards closing the door. They had apparently opened the door just as the figure was about to engulf him.

"Lock the bloody door!" yelled one of the guards.

"I'm trying!"

The two guards were trying desperately to lock the door, the third guard ready to fire at anything that might come through it.

"It's the wrong key!" The guard tore the keys from the other's hand and began to go through the many keys that were on the loop.

Then there was the noise.

Fredrickson was able to get himself to his knees, attempting to maintain a breathing pattern. He watched in horror as the two guards trying to lock the door froze in response to the sound. It was a hideous sound, coming from behind the door. It was so loud that Fredrickson couldn't hear what the third guard was saying. He was yelling about something.

The guards snapped out of their frozen state of fear and began to work on locking the door again. They found the right key.

Fredrickson watched as they fit the key into the lock. They were about to turn it when there was a huge impact against the other side of the door. The key was forced out of the keyhole and the whole set fell to the floor.

The two soldiers rammed their shoulders into the door, trying to keep it closed. "Get the keys!"

Fredrickson dove onto the floor and reached for them. There was another impact against the door and this time the door opened a little, forcing the soldiers to step backward. One of the guards stepped on the keys just as Fredrickson grabbed them. "You're standing on the keys!"

They didn't hear him.

"Get off the keys!"

The door began to open more, and the guard was forced to take another step back. His foot came off of the keys just as the door swung wide open.

The third guard, who was watching the whole event with his musket held at the ready, charged the door. He threw his entire body weight into the wood as Fredrickson tossed the keys up into the air. The door slammed shut as one of the other guards grabbed the keys out of the air and inserted the right key. The door was locked less than half a second after it was closed.

The noise stopped and it was silent once again, the only sound being the heavy breathing of the four English soldiers.

Fredrickson stumbled away from the door and made his way to the stairs. He needed to get topside.

The three guards stood looking at the door.

"What was that?" asked one of them.

"The Devil is on our ship . . . "

"Thank God for chains, locks, and doors." The guard was trying to find comfort in the wooden formation that separated them from certain death.

Another guard looked up at him. "I'll thank Him when I know that's enough . . . "

“I may not have seen the Devil with my own eyes, but I swear that I felt him!” Fredrickson was speaking to Post Captain White. It was mid afternoon now, and Fredrickson had a chance to rest and recover from the situation earlier.

White placed a hand on Fredrickson’s shoulder. “I wish you to keep this matter silent.” He looked over those working on the main deck. “If these stories reach topside . . . ”

“They’re not stories!” Fredrickson yelled. There were those around them that had started to take notice of their conversation.

“Lower your voice, I beg of you! If word of this reaches human ears, then we will have much more to worry about than what we should.”

“Captain, we need to do something . . . ”

“There is nothing that we can do, save pray the Lord have mercy on us all.”

Fredrickson cursed. “I’m not going down there anymore! You will have to find someone else to feed them if you wish to keep doing so.”

“You would dare disobey a direct order?”

“Captain, no fate that you could think up for me in form of punishment would be nearly as horrible as standing in the darkness of the lower deck.”

White nodded and then dismissed him. He looked up to the sky. The sun would begin to set in a few hours. He needed to get some sleep if he were going to stay awake through the night. Sleeping at night was proving to be a deadly habit as of late. He noticed that many others on the main deck had already managed to fall asleep.

White walked to the quarterdeck where he sat down, listening to the sound of the waves splash against his ship. He closed his eyes, praying that he would not have any dreams.

:::: *Nightfall*

White stood on the main deck, leaning over the side and staring at the moon’s watery reflection, its image distorted by the ripples in the water.

Behind him were most of the soldiers bearing arms. They were ready for the hours that were to come. White walked athwart ship to the other side of the main deck and looked over the side. He watched the dark waters roll by. Suddenly, he felt something rush by him. He spun around.

Nothing.

White looked around to the other soldiers and sailors, but they didn't seem to have noticed anything. They were still going about their business.

He felt it again. This time his hat flew off. Pulling the pistol out of his belt, he aimed it into the darkness before him. He looked frantically to the left and to the right, but still he could not see what it was or where it was.

A soldier laughed. "It's only the wind, Captain. Relax, that happens all the time."

White felt foolish for a second, and he replaced the pistol into his pants. But then he thought about it. He was a veteran in the Navy, and the wind had never felt like that. "How long has it been going on?"

The soldier shrugged. "Since the sun dropped and the wind picked up."

Since the sun dropped . . .

White ran forward to the starboard bow where he found Winthrop asleep. He pulled on his shoulder trying to wake him up. Winthrop was sitting on the deck leaning against the foremast. White couldn't understand how Winthrop could have managed to fall asleep.

"Wake up! Winthrop! Wake up! Where's Morgan?"

There was no response.

White pulled Winthrop away from the mast and immediately took two steps back. Winthrop's body was limp and there was blood on the mast. White looked around, searching the deck. He saw Morgan coming from below the deck, and he started running towards him.

Morgan took a mental note of the near full moon as he noticed Captain White running towards him.

White could hardly see where he was stepping, the moon offering barely enough light in which to operate. Then he tripped.

Morgan ran over and helped White get to his feet. "What is it?"

White pointed back from where he had run. "Winthrop is dead."

Morgan immediately knew what the news meant, and no great length of time was needed for him to formulate a plan of action. He quickly turned away from White and ran to the quarterdeck. He gathered a few men and then descended down to the lower levels and out of White's view. No one had ever died topside before.

The hallway was pitch black. Morgan and the five soldiers walked cautiously towards the prison. There was a candle lit outside of the door, used by the guards. The little flame sent shifting light all over the hallway, creating weird and distorted shadows racing about the walls.

"Hello?" Morgan was calling to the guards. He heard a small commotion of noise as the soldiers snapped to attention. One of them walked into

Morgan's line of sight, blocking the light from the candle. Morgan could only make out the man's silhouette.

"Sir, we're here."

Morgan and the others joined the three guards that were positioned next to the door. Morgan looked over everything, his eyes absorbing every detail. "Did you fall asleep?" he asked.

"What?" The guard recovered. "No, Sir."

Morgan believed him. "Any noise coming from in there?" He signaled towards the prison door.

"No, Sir. No noise tonight. They must be asleep."

"Thank you, Soldier." He turned to walk away, relief enabling him to breathe once again. The other five soldiers filed in behind him.

Then he stopped dead in his tracks.

"Open the door!" He shouted at the guard as the other two watched in confusion. At first he thought that White might have been hasty in attributing Winthrop's death to the prisoners, but something suddenly hit him.

"Sir?" The guard looked confused.

Morgan pulled a pistol from his pants as he grabbed the candle off the wall. The other four soldiers that he brought down took their rifles off of their shoulders- they were actually going into the prison after nightfall.

Morgan entered first. The flickering light that danced on the candle's wick was tempted to blow out due to the speed in which he was moving. He held the candle up, allowing the shifting light to wash over the prisoners that were chained to the wall. They were all there. He grunted and, once more, turned to walk back through the door.

Then he saw it.

There was a set of open cuffs lying on the wooden floor. There was a stain on the floor and Morgan knew that there had been a person chained there not long ago. His eyes wide, he brought the candle up high into the air. The pistol followed his eyes to every corner of the room. The soldiers behind him held their rifles against their shoulders, ready to fire.

"Can you feel it?" whispered a soldier from behind him.

Morgan looked behind him. "What?"

The soldier's face went pale. "I didn't say anything, Sir." He swallowed. "None of us did."

Then the candle blew out. And they were engulfed by darkness.

White was pacing nervously on the main deck, waiting for Morgan to reappear. His worst thought was that he wouldn't reappear. White didn't know what he would do if Morgan did not come back. Maybe lead the rest of the soldiers down there and fight to the death. What other option did he have? Then he saw Morgan come running onto the deck being followed by eight soldiers. White knew that three of them had to have been the guards. *Oh Lord, they're coming up!*

Morgan ran to White, ignoring all the commotion that suddenly erupted on the deck. White gave out a loud order for the men to keep silent. Morgan looked different as he approached. Something had happened. Morgan looked . . . scared.

"One of them is loose!"

A sailor nearby overheard the report and immediately got to his feet and started to scream to the others. White gave a nod and a nearby soldier grabbed the man's mouth from behind, silencing him as he smashed his head with the butt of his sword. The man fell, unconscious, to the deck.

"We mustn't let that word spread or we'll have a ship full of sailors jumping overboard."

Morgan nodded.

"Is there anything we can do?"

Morgan turned to look at one of the soldiers that had been following him and pointed at the lower foremast. The soldier immediately ran to the mast and began climbing it. He climbed into the fighting top and held his rifle at the ready. He wasn't able to see much, but it was a bird's eye view.

Morgan grabbed the soldier next to him. "Go get Johnson, Francis, Henry, and Philips." The soldier ran off into the darkness. Looking at White, he continued, "We'll walk the decks. Back and forth."

White nodded.

The soldier that was sent by Morgan returned with the others he was sent to find. "Sir?"

"I want groups of two's. You'll walk forward to aft and back again. Two groups on the main deck and two groups on the middle deck. Go." They ran off.

The sharpshooter that was positioned in the fighting top saw it first. He called out to the two soldiers that were the closest. They were walking straight for it.

The two soldiers stopped and raised their muskets. They walked slowly into the shadows beneath the foresails and the jibs. Their hearts pounded and sweat stung their eyes. They couldn't see anything.

The sharpshooter was able to get the attention of the other group that was walking aft. They ran towards the forecastle.

"Do you see it?" His voice was barely audible.

"No . . . "

They looked back up to the sharpshooter. He was pointing to their left. They continued to walk to the spot, though they could still see nothing.

The other group was running as fast as they could, nearing the forecastle.

"I see it." His voice was stoic. He pointed.

"I still don't . . . " He squinted, his eyes straining. "Wait . . . "

The figure that was hiding in the shadows burst from its cover and ran straight at the two frightened soldiers. They fired as they fell onto their backs, the blasts capturing the attention of every person on the ship.

The soldiers all converged at the same spot, the two fallen soldiers in front of them. They all looked around.

Morgan asked, "Did you see something?"

One of the soldiers that had fired got to his feet. "Yes, it charged at us."

"Where'd it go?"

"Sir, I don't know." The group of soldiers all stood on the forecastle, searching the night. They were all terrified and confused. It would be a long night.

:::: *Next Day*

Morgan rubbed his weary eyes. It hurt to keep them open. The sky was no longer dark but painted with a beautiful assortment of colors. The top of the sun could now be seen breaking the surface of the water.

"Get some sleep." White looked down from the damaged poop deck. "I'll keep a watchful eye."

Morgan waved his thanks and quickly made his way to a comfortable spot on the quarterdeck. He sat down, closed his eyes, and was asleep within seconds.

Morgan opened his eyes as he felt someone pulling on his arm.

"Wake up! You must see this!" The soldier was pointing over the side of the ship.

Morgan managed to get to his feet. How long had he been asleep? The sun was high in the sky, and the heat of the day was at its strongest. "What is it?" He was still waking up.

"Look! Port quarter!"

Morgan strained to see what the soldier was pointing at. He suddenly realized that he must be the last to see it, because everyone else that he could see was staring out into the distance.

It was another ship.

"Where's the Captain?" asked Morgan.

"He's up in the top." He pointed at the foremast.

White put down the looking glass and noticed Morgan running to his position. He sighed, suddenly deep in thought.

"Captain!" Morgan's voice interrupted his flow of thought.

White began to climb back down to the deck.

"What is it?" Morgan asked before White even got to the deck.

White hopped off the mast and put a hand on Morgan's shoulder, leading him away from the other sailors that were watching. "Pirates."

"Pirates?"

"Or a fishery . . . "

Morgan laughed. "Let me see the glass." White handed it over and Morgan looked through the eyepiece. "They are Pirates." He noticed the flag that flew from their driver.

White screamed to his men. "Battle stations!" He then looked to Morgan as hundreds of people ran about the decks getting into position. "We need to take that ship."

Morgan knew immediately what White was thinking. It was the only logical way out of their situation- and away from the prisoners. He put his hand out in front of White, stopping him from giving any further orders. He had a plan.

Pirates were one of the most feared threats upon the ocean. Until 1640, the English Migratory Fishery was plagued by pirates known as the Sallee Rovers. This group of pirates was made up of renegade seamen from all nations. They attacked trade as their target, cruising the coasts of Portugal and Spain, waiting to intercept merchantmen that converged in the market ports. The power that the Sallee Rovers possessed was so great that they even sailed into the English Channel, knowing that neither France nor England possessed navies capable of effectively challenging them. Once war erupted in those waters, the pirates were not so eager to patrol the coasts. However, they were still there. And they were here now.

"Do you think they are the Sallee?" asked Morgan.

"Too hard to say for sure. It depends on where we are. We could be in Pacific waters for all I know." White looked through a gun port on the middle deck. The pirates were coming up on the port quarter. "Do you think we have a chance?"

Morgan looked to the stairs that led down to the lower deck. "We have a better chance with those pirates than we do with those prisoners." As if to emphasize his point, there was an ungodly scream that came from the deck below. Morgan just looked at White. *This has to work.*

The ship was smaller than the *Sovereign Wing* and there were clearly fewer men aboard. The pirate ship came in close. It looked as if they would attempt to jump from their ship onto the *Sovereign Wing.*

"Are you ready?" asked White.

The powder man looked back and shook his head. Nine men were gathered around the huge iron cast cannon. The powder man, captain, 2nd captain, handspike men, assistant sponger, sponger, assistant loader, and loader hustled about, trying to prepare the cannon for firing.

"Hurry." White's eyes added, *or else!*

"Yes, Sir."

Morgan leaned over the canon that was fixed next to the one that was being prepped. He looked out the gun port and could see the Pirate's ship coming up along side the *Sovereign Wing.* He looked back at White. "We're going to miss it!" The ship was almost completely along side of them now.

White looked to the gun crew just as the captain of the gun screamed, "Ready, Sir!"

"They're coming." Morgan could see the pirates hanging from the ropes that stretched up to the sails. They were getting ready to jump onto *Sovereign*'s empty deck. They had swords tucked into their belts, knives held in their mouths, and rifles slung over their shoulders. They were ready to come.

"Fire!" yelled White.

The flintlock produced a spark and fired the charge. Black smoke poured out of the gun port as the round shot flew into the middle deck of the pirate ship, destroying a canon and killing its crew.

White watched as the canon recoiled violently but was restrained by the breeching ropes that were attached to the carriage. He then looked out a gun port. The loudness of the explosion sent all the pirates diving to their own deck.

Morgan pointed to a group of soldiers and shouted. "Go now! Go! Go!" The soldiers went running up the stairs to the main deck.

The five soldiers ran, crouched down, to the first canon that they came to. The canons on the main deck were smaller, and they didn't offer much cover. The five English soldiers immediately drew fire from the pirates.

"Can we risk another shot without sinking the ship or damaging it too badly?" Morgan wanted to draw the pirates' attention away from the soldiers on the main deck.

White held up his hand. "Wait."

The five soldiers managed to discharge the canon. Black smoke erupted from the barrel and filled the space between both ships so that visibility was almost zero, but the soldiers knew that the shot was effective. The screams that filled the air testified of a successful shot. Discharged from the canon was a case shot, twelve small round shot in a metal can. When fired, it broke up and scattered shot over the deck of the enemy ship. The soldiers went to the next loaded canon and fired.

More smoke. More screams. It was working.

"One more, one more." Morgan held his musket tight, waiting for the chance to run topside and start fighting. He looked back and noted that his soldiers also looked ready.

The final loaded canon exploded and filled the air with more black smoke.

"Go! Go! Go!" Morgan led the charge topside.

As the smoke cleared, the deck of the enemy ship could be seen. It was covered in blood and decapitated pirates. Morgan and his soldiers started firing at the pirates that remained alive.

The pirate ship began to move away from them.

Morgan knew that they would be finished if the ship drifted away any further. He threw his rifle over his shoulder and ran to the edge of the ship. He jumped off the Sovereign Wing's railing and sailed through the air, closing the spreading gap between the two ships. His hands caught the rail of the pirate ship, and he was able to lift himself up and onto the main deck. Immediately, a pirate ran at him with sword raised. Morgan knew he couldn't get his musket up in time, and he closed his eyes and waited for the pain. A shot sounded, and Morgan's face was suddenly wet. He opened his eyes and saw the pirate lying dead on the deck. He wiped the blood from his face and un-shouldered his rifle. He ran for the poop deck.

The pirate ship's main deck suddenly exploded with pirates, and they began firing at those on the English war ship.

Morgan pulled his sword from out of a pirate's back and took his place at the wheel. He steered the ship back along side of the *Sovereign Wing*'s. As the ship came closer, the English soldiers were able to jump aboard the pirate ship, and the fighting changed from firing across decks to that of hand-to-hand combat.

Morgan was still concentrating on keeping the enemy ship up close to the *Sovereign Wing* when he heard something from behind him and turned. A group of pirates had begun to wonder why their ship was being steered into harm's way. They drew their swords as they found their answer standing at the wheel.

"Johnson! Get up to the top!" White was still standing on his deck, issuing orders and directions to both soldiers and sailors. His men were trying to use ropes to keep the two ships together, but those attempting to do so were being cut down by the pirates' rifles.

Johnson climbed up to the fighting top where he had a bird's eye view of the entire enemy ship. He leaned three rifles against the rail and aimed the fourth. "Give me some help!"

White grabbed one soldier before he could join the fight on the other ship and told him to climb up to the top. The soldier obeyed.

Johnson watched as a pirate drove a sword through an English soldier's back. He fired and the same pirate fell to the deck. Johnson handed the gun to the soldier just as he reached the top. The soldier began reloading it while Johnson grabbed the second rifle. He fired, and another pirate fell to the deck.

Morgan deflected the first blow with his own sword while pulling a pistol from his belt and discharging it into the stomach of the same attacker, doubling him over and dropping him to the deck. Morgan then charged the other pirates, cutting down the first and, spinning around, brought his sword up and then down, cutting down the next. By now, the two remaining pirates were able to recover from the momentary shock of Morgan's suicidal attack, and they moved in to confront him. The first pirate swung crazily at Morgan's head, and Morgan ducked while blocking a simultaneous blow from the other pirate. Stepping hard on one of the pirate's feet and throwing an elbow into his chin, Morgan knocked one of the two remaining pirates to the deck. He continued to fight with the other.

Johnson grabbed the reloaded gun from his new assistant and followed a pirate that was running across the deck and sneaking up behind an English soldier who was leaning over his fallen friend. Johnson fired, but he was leading the pirate too much and the musket ball passed in front of him. He threw the musket to the ground and grabbed the next one out of the soldier's hand. There was no ball loaded into it yet, so Johnson just rolled one down the barrel. There was no time to use a ramrod. He brought the musket up to his shoulder and fired just as the pirate's blade sunk into the soldier's back. The pirate flew forward and slid off the deck and into the water below. Johnson cursed.

The fighting began to slow as pirates continued to fall dead. It seemed to be a victory, ropes now holding the two ships together. White knew that they were lucky they had not been attacked by more experienced pirates. This battle was easy. White could only count about thirty of the English soldiers dead and about seventy of the pirates. He looked up at Johnson who, alone, was responsible for probably ten kills. He watched as Johnson fired again and saw another pirate fall to the ground. Then he tried to find Morgan. It took him a little while, but Morgan was in a sword fight with another pirate and they had moved onto the quarterdeck. It looked to White like Morgan was having trouble. He called up to Johnson.

Johnson followed White's finger and immediately knew his orders. He aimed the rifle at the pirate's back and squeezed the trigger. The musket exploded. Johnson fell to the ground screaming, hands covering his black and bloody face. His assistant finished loading a rifle and nervously stood up to fire at the pirate. Despite his deafening heart beat and the sweat that stung his eyes, he fired.

Morgan was surprised at how well trained the pirate was. They moved back and forth on the quarterdeck, blocking high and blocking low, but it could not go on forever, and it was the pirate who was exhausted and thus desperately tried for a finishing blow. He grasped the sword with two hands and swung with all of his might at Morgan's head. Morgan ducked under the attacking blow and brought his sword up and into the pirate's stomach. The pirate doubled over just as a shot rang out from the *Sovereign Wing*'s fighting top. The background caught Morgan's eye, as if time had suddenly slowed down. Within that one instant, he saw the smoke pour out of the barrel and even noticed the look on the soldier's horrified face before he felt the impact. The English musket ball ripped through his chest, shattering his sternum.

He collapsed to his knees.

White watched as Morgan's blow doubled the pirate over and knew that the shot would now strike Morgan instead. White screamed to the soldier in the top but the shot had already been fired. He watched Morgan fall to his knees clutching his chest. He turned away, but Morgan's voice suddenly cut through the air.

"Captain!" Morgan's voice was weak.

White turned back to face Morgan. He was pointing past him and to something behind him. White turned and only caught the shadow of a person run out of sight. He looked back to Morgan but Morgan had already died. White called out to everyone that was on the ship. "Now! Let's get off this ship!" About three hundred sailors and a few soldiers started running for the pirate ship.

:::: *Two hours later*

Captain White sat on the rail of the pirate ship and waited for his sailors to finish transferring all the equipment and food over from the Sovereign Wing. White figured that with what food remained on his ship added to that of the pirates,' they would have enough food and water to last until they arrived on land. The loss of men only helped the situation. Previously, all the dead bodies had been thrown overboard, and it was not an easy experience, having to watch Morgan's body disappear beneath the clear rolling waves. White lifted his eyes from the water, trying to forget. Soon after, a soldier approached him.

"The transfer is complete, Captain."

White looked at the young soldier. His face was cut open, and he was trembling. White placed a hand on his shoulder. "Untie us." The soldier nodded and turned away. "Wait!"

"Yes, Captain?"

White really wanted to know about the prisoners. "Have someone go to the lower deck and check on the prisoners."

"What are you thinking, Sir? Surely they could not have . . . "

White cut him off. "I do not know."

"Yes, Sir."

White turned and set his gaze out among the countless waves. The sun was beginning its descent and the reflection painted across the ocean's surface was beautiful. "Humanity . . . a dark, out-of-place, stranger within this lovely creation."

"Captain, with all due respect, have you forgotten the previous night?" A sailor had been listening.

Captain White looked down at the man. "Tell me, Charles, do you think that nature was so cruel within the Garden?"

The man managed a smile. "No, Sir. I reckon there wasn't any of that."

White looked back across the ocean. "A strange reality that does exist, Charles. The beauty of God's creation and its solitude and peace mixing with man's nature and his hate and violence. Yet you feel as if nature herself does not notice the evil that inhabits her, for the sun never ceases to set. Nor do the birds cease to sing in the morning. No matter what we men are doing to each other, nature just keeps on, ignorant of the harm she entertains."

"Sir!"

White sighed and responded to the call. "Yes, Dear Soldier?"

The soldier had a look of fear in his eyes. "The prisoners are gone!"

The *Sovereign Wing* could barely be seen now. The sun was almost completely set, the sky dark above. White had debated sinking his ship but decided against it. He hoped that he wouldn't later regret his decision. He walked across the deck of the pirate ship and took note of the injured sailors being cared to. He noticed Johnson. His face was blackened from gunpowder and the burns were blistered under dry blood.

"Fredrickson, did you notice what language the pirates were speaking?" White had been thinking about that for a while now.

"No, Sir. But we found these recordings below." He handed White a logbook.

"I don't recognize this language," stated White as he thumbed through the text.

"Sir? What kind of pirate ship is this? I mean, it's not like any that I have seen from a fishery or any of the Sallee Rovers."

White had been thinking about that as well. "I do not know."

"Sir, how do we know that they were pirates?"

White had never thought of them being anything other than pirates. Morgan was sure that they were, and he trusted Morgan. "I suppose they could have been adventurers coming from America." But White knew that whoever they were, they were not at all familiar. That only meant one thing: they had no idea where they were.

Captain White opened his eyes and looked up into the sky. The English flag was waving proudly from the alien driver. That was the first chore ordered by White upon settling on the confiscated ship, making it identifiable now as an English ship. Fixed high and above the flag was the beautiful full moon. Its glow graced the waves with a silver outline. It was very quiet, everyone else still sleeping. He stood and stretched, looking around the deck. All of the men he could see were, indeed, asleep. He walked down the stairs and onto the main deck, his boots making the only noise, other than the ocean, as they walked across the wooden deck. He intended to walk past the wounded.

He stopped.

There was a wounded soldier that was missing his head. White walked over to the man, suddenly confused. As he walked closer to the man, he noticed that none of the wounded men had their heads. White's heart began beating violently within his chest as his eyes searched the deck. There were so many shadows cast by the moonlight that he couldn't tell if there was anyone still alive. He ran over to another group of soldiers. They were all dead. White heard something coming from beneath the deck. Someone was walking up the stairs. He grabbed a musket from the hands of a dead soldier and waited.

"Captain?" It was Fredrickson's voice.

White released the breath that he was holding, suddenly relieved. He stood and walked to Fredrickson. "Over here."

"Captain, there's something strange going on . . . "

"They're all dead." White swept his hand over the deck.

"Really?"

White couldn't suppress the chills that ran down his spine and looked more closely at Fredrickson. He watched as Fredrickson stepped out from a shadow and into the moonlight.

It wasn't Fredrickson. It was one of the prisoners.

:::: *TWO WEEKS LATER*

The water splashed violently against the huge, ancient old rocks. The force of the impact did not move the algae covered boulders, but only succeeded in filling the air with water as the waves collided against them. The waves pushed themselves up and onto the beach before retracting back into the deep. The amount of broken wood was growing as the tide gave up what was not hers. The remains of the ship and crew were washing up onto the beach in piles.

The pirate ship had finally been carried to land but was unable to avoid the rocks that littered its terrain. It only took twenty minutes before the ship was totally destroyed. Much of the crew probably wouldn't have survived the traveling distance from the ship to the shore, the waves too rough and the rocks too sharp, but none were given that chance. The crew had already been dead for weeks.

The jungle's canopy allowed little light through to the ground, but what little light was allowed could be seen stretching down through the mist. The prisoners continued walking through the jungles of the uncharted island, looking for any sign of life- human life. For if human life were to be found, then there would be means to sustain their own and continue the lineage that had created their most sacred community.

ONE
2003

Rain fell through the early morning sky and splashed against the glass windows. The sun had previously begun its climb into the sky, but the countless number of heavy rain clouds shielded the display. Upstate New York's warm summer air had been painted with rain clouds for the past week, wetness defining the lifestyle of all who lived under those dreary clouds. Due to the sluggish moods that usually accompanied the rainfall, things within the wet vicinity were unusually quiet. Parks and playgrounds had been abandoned, basketball courts and baseball fields were vacant, and the usual loitering on the streets non-existent. Within this somber atmosphere, fighting against the invasions of boredom, many found entertainment at the movies. Others made use of the downtime to incorporate some family participation into a game of Candy Land or Go Fish. Of course there were the occasional children that still hopped and skipped across the wet concrete, searching for signs of lightning, and jumping at the perilous sound of thunder. But those young ones were the minority of all the kids within the area. Not that all upstate New Yorkers were "Partridge Families," but within this certain location, the overall consensus proved it to be a highly moral and pleasant place to live.

Though many will reject the thought of a pleasant rainy day, there are a few that find days like this very peaceful. The gray sky hugging the trees whose leaves blow upside-down in the warm breeze, the thunder clouds looming over the earth muffling the noise of creation as with a pillow, and the lethargic mood that the rainy weather brings with it, slowing down the pace of life just enough to induce reflection. This stillness, this quietness, is felt by a few as a comfort to be enjoyed while it can be. This New York sky was found as a curse to some, while being a blessing for others, and it was under this same sky that the Streen family lived.

The bedroom was dark, yet not utterly dark, the raindrops on the windows casting their watery shadows onto the tan carpet that covered the floor.

James Streen lay in the king size bed with his eyes open, watching the rain fall against the windows. He watched the drops of water as gravity pulled them down to the window's base, leaving behind them a thin trail of water as they slid. Some drops rolled faster than others, and those caught in the path of the quicker were only captured and merged into the same body, thus doubling the size of either drop. James had always subconsciously thought of the display as a race of some sort. The smaller drops that seemed to get stuck, or halt for some reason, half way down the window crying out for help lest they never reach the safety of the windowsill. So, naturally, it was an act of selfless heroism when the larger drops picked them up and carried them the rest of the way.

Taking his attention off of the sight, he tuned his sense of hearing to the sound of the rain hitting his house. It played like soft music, tempting him to fall back asleep. Glancing at the clock that sat on the shelf next to the bed, he was able to make out the glowing green figures that read 5:58. Almost determined to rise out of his state of rest and comfort for the day, a soft rumble of thunder suddenly provoked new thoughts of staying in bed for another hour or two. Feeling this relaxed was not logged into his recent memory, and he wished to gain the most out of it while he could. He rolled over, facing the other side of the bed, and dropped his gaze onto his wife. She was sleeping soundly, a peaceful expression painted across her beautiful face. Studying had never been more pleasurable for James, and it was due to times like this that he was able to recall every curve, every depression, every tint, and all other features on his wife's body. He instinctively reached over and gently brushed a strand of hair away from her eyes. The alarm clock was set to go off in ten minutes, but seeing it as a crime to disturb such an image of beauty and peace, James decided to simply turn it off now. The sheets pulled as he rolled back over and made sure the alarm would not be disturbing his wife.

Reality began walking to center stage as he moved to sit up. Bare feet touching carpet, James sat on the edge of the bed, resting his head in his hands and rubbing his eyes. There was another loud rumble of thunder, and he smiled.

"Honey?"

James looked over to his wife, disappointed that her sleep had been disturbed.

"Can we swim now?"

The smile that spread his lips was due to the realization that she was still sleeping. He leaned over her, hoping his shadow across her eyes wouldn't wake her but taking the chance, and kissed her forehead. Her head was warm and smelled good, this being the reason for the length of the kiss. He then put his hand under the covers and gently rubbed her large stomach. She was due to have their second child in three months. He pulled himself away from his wife and out of the comfort of his bed. Surveying the world from his window, James stifled a yawn while he stretched.

James Streen was a handsome man, 6 feet tall, 195 pounds of pure muscle, and a face that could easily land him on the cover of GQ. His two years spent at community college was enough time for him to figure that out, though he had little patience for girls who only wanted a boyfriend to promote their own selfish image. After graduating with an associate's degree in liberal arts, he decided to join the Marines, which he did at the age of twenty. By the time he was twenty-four and serving his last year, he had fought in the Gulf War, an experience that had changed him forever. Once his previous three years were finally put to use in actual combat, he found that his training had evolved from routine exercise to instinct. He was good at being a soldier- good at staying alive, good at keeping those around him alive, and ultimately an expert at killing the enemy. He was so good at it that it scared him, and he left once his time expired. But it was too late, he had already acquired a taste for that line of work and nothing would ever be able to drive it out of him. The four years spent in the Marines made him a Marine, period. No matter how much he wanted it all to go away, it never would- it never could. After a couple of years spent chasing ideas, trying to put the war behind him, he finally found himself wearing a badge. A good compromise, he thought. Serve and protect, uphold the law, save lives . . . Saving lives; it was a mindset easier to live with, an excuse to exercise the soldier within him, justifying his skill. Rather than the focus being centered on taking lives, as it seemed to be in the war, now it was centered on saving lives and, with this new outlook, he could live with himself and be who he was scared of at the same time.

The SWAT team was a perfect match. He loved it, and he was really good at it. As a member of Special Weapons and Tactical, he could satisfy the beast within, created by the Marines, and yet not indulge its person so as to become him.

Of course marrying Kirsten helped keep that beast in the coffin as well. After joining the police force, James had decided to take some classes at a local college. Since becoming a Christian in 1991, he fell in love with the Bible and its doctrines and theology. Since the night he gave his heart to Christ at that little Baptist church that sat on the corner of his street, he had taken up theology as a passion. Others would call it a hobby. He loved the word of God; it was the most important thing in his life. When he opened the Bible, it was as if he was being transported to a place unfamiliar with pain, doubt, and fear, and to a place familiar with only God's grace and mercy. He loved to study the Scriptures inductively, analyzing and researching every word. His faith, his study, proved to be the centerpiece of his life. So when he found opportunity to audit some Bible classes at this college, he didn't hesitate. He met Kirsten in one of those classes. She was twenty-two, almost done with her social work major, and he was a twenty-eight year-old cop auditing theology classes. It seemed kind of strange at first, to fall in love with someone so much younger than himself, but as they began to date, it felt even stranger to think of living life without her. They dated for two years before getting married in 1997. Their daughter Jessica was born three years later. Yes, the James Streen that was a Marine, or at least the James Streen the Marine was becoming, was not fed or nurtured during the years Kirsten was in his life. Even though there were times in the SWAT that he had to kill people, that beast still refused to reveal its existence as long as Kirsten was present in his life. She was a prayer answered, a perfect gift. She was James' whole life. Though he loved the SWAT, he loved his wife more, infinitely more. He would do anything for her. Nothing got in the way of their relationship, because God was first and she was second. As long as he kept himself out of those two spots, their marriage was better than his best dreams. James looked at her again, still not able to comprehend such an amazing gift.

After a few minutes of watching her, James walked across the bedroom and into the small bathroom that was in the corner of the room. He made sure the door was completely closed before turning on the light. Looking into the mirror, James ran his hand over his scruffy face and reached for his razor.

Kirsten Streen reached over, but her efforts only left her to feel warm sheets. The absence of what she knew ought to be there caused her to open her eyes. Immediately, the light coming from beneath the bathroom door attracted her vision. Looking at the clock, she realized that James must have turned off the alarm before it was set to go off. She smiled and closed her eyes again, thunder sounding as was water from the shower in the bathroom.

James stepped into the warm water, steam quickly filling the room and fogging both the mirror and the window. Standing under the water, the thoughts concerning the days ahead began to formulate within his mind. First to be formulated were his priorities this day, which would begin upon his arrival for work at nine. As long as nothing big happened, the workday would end early. But it was too easy for his mind to simply glance over his priority for the day when such abnormal plans were only two days away. It was these plans that had taken the spotlight both in James planning and imagination. In two days he would be leaving for Bermuda in a desperate search for his brother, Steve, who had traveled to Bermuda on a business trip and never returned. That was two months ago. James had personally seen to it that every arm of investigation was exhausted in the search but still there were no answers, only little clues found here and there. The trip would cost him more than he could afford and most of his vacation days, but when weighed in the balances, it seemed a small price to pay for the safety of his brother.

James poured the coffee into a glass mug, and steam exploded from within as if it were an atomic blast. Carrying the mug back up to the bedroom, he walked to the window and sat on its ledge, staring out into the morning sky. He watched the rain fall as he drank his coffee and read from the open Bible that rested next to the window. Leaning his head back against the window, James closed his eyes.

The hand placed on his shoulder startled him and almost made him spill his coffee. Reflex demanded that he look up, and he quickly obeyed. Standing over him was his wife wearing a warm smile, a smile that induced one of James' own.

"Hi." Kirsten wrapped her hands around her husband's head and brought it against her body. She leaned down and kissed his head, his hair still damp.

James looked up to his 5'7" wife and looked into her blue eyes. "Hi." He then looked down to her stomach and kissed it. "How do you feel?"

Kirsten sat down on the other side of the window and reached for James' hand. "I feel good."

James looked her in the eyes and could see his own blue eyes in the reflection of hers. "It's going to be okay."

She smiled. "I know." They both looked out the window for a while, enjoying the weather while each rowing through their own cognitive worlds. Kirsten had been a little worried about James leaving for Bermuda, but she offered no objection, knowing that he had to go. She only wished that she could go with him, but she was aware that wasn't possible with her being pregnant.

"Come on." James stood and led her back to the bed. They climbed in together and snuggled under the covers. James opened another Bible and began reading scripture while he ran his fingers through Kirsten's blonde hair. Her head was resting on his chest, and she could hear his heart beating, a sound that she appreciated very much.

The clock read 7:00.

Jessica lethargically made her way down the stairs and into the kitchen where her dad immediately embraced her.

"Good morning, Sweetheart." James lifted her into the air. Never deterring from sucking on her thumb and keeping hold of her blanket that was slung over her shoulder, she put her head against James' chest and closed her eyes.

Jessica was only three years old, but she showed remarkable maturity for that age despite the blanket and thumb-sucking habit. James and Kirsten were trying so hard to raise her right, and thus far they could not complain.

Jessica opened her eyes and looked up to James. She, like her parents, had blue eyes. “Are you going to work?”

“Yes, I am, but I’m going to come home early to see you.”

She smiled and quickly put her head back against his chest.

“Do you want me to bring you home anything?” That drew her eyes back to his face.

Before she could answer, Kirsten walked through the doorway.

“Good morning, Honey.” She walked over and gave her a kiss. She then looked up and kissed James, a very different kind of kiss.

“I have to go.” James sat Jessica into a chair that was positioned at the kitchen table. “I should be back at one. Take it easy today, okay?” He rubbed her stomach again.

“You be careful.” She gave him another kiss, this one a bit longer, and Jessica covered her eyes.

“I will be.” He grabbed her hand and walked towards the door, not letting go until the distance was too great and her outstretched hand dropped from his. James paused only to glance at the picture of his brother that hung on the wall by the door, resisting the urge to meditate on a thousand different memories. He opened the door, stole another glance at his wife, and told her that he loved her. He then stepped out into the rain, closing the door behind him and making sure it was locked. His black t-shirt and jeans began to absorb water immediately.

Jessica looked to Kirsten. “Mommy, I forgot to tell Daddy what I wanted . . . ” The sadness that bent her lips communicated her disappointment.

“Oh, don’t worry, Honey. I’m sure he’ll surprise you with something.” She wiped the blonde hair from her face as she got ready to make breakfast.

James turned onto the next street and looked at the clock that was part of the dashboard. The gas pedal grew closer to the floor due to the increased weight that was being placed on it, and the silver ’99, series 7, BMW reached sixty-five miles per hour. The windshield wipers moved back and forth trying to keep up with the rate in which the rain was falling, as the morning news sounded over the radio. The roads were not too slippery, the oils being washed away weeks ago, and the tires hugged the road with ease. James rounded the corner with the same ease and began to slow down as he neared a stop sign. His cell phone rang as he completed his stop. Holding the wheel with his left hand, James reached down and removed the cell phone from its holder. The caller ID told him that it was his team leader, Jed. He was already two minutes late.

"Hey, I'm almost there."

"*Don't bother, we have a situation.*"

"What kind of situation?"

"*Hostage.*"

James sighed, *So much for a quiet last day.* "Status?"

"*Police are on the scene. They say the guy has already killed two people. He's holding some people hostage.*"

"Where?"

"*The 'New York's News' building.*"

A quick sharp turn onto a side street and the gas pedal to the floor set James in the right direction. The BMW's engine whined with power as the car shot down the street.

"*We're almost there. Jack is on the way, the rest of us got in at eight.*"

"Okay. I'll see you there." He hung up the phone and concentrated on driving.

Under the blanket of clouds that reigned sovereign over the morning sky, police cars were scattered about with their lights flashing in the rain. Reporters ran about trying to get a better shot of the action, as the police were constantly telling them to move back. Yellow warning tape and police officers sealed the surrounding area. All eyes were looking up to the middle floor of the huge news building. Occasionally, the suspect would walk in front of the window, sending the camera crews into frenzy.

Arriving at the scene, James pulled up just as the SWAT van was unloading. He got out of his car and grabbed for the bulletproof vest that one of his friends was handing him. They were already dressed, wearing their BDU's, tactical vests, and PASGT Kevlar helmets. Their hands were covered by flight gloves and were grasping MP5's.

"Can you believe this weather we're having?" He asked as he put the vest on.

"And I hear it's only supposed to get worse," came the reply.

James looked up to the building. "Do you know what's going on, Joe?"

Joe was one of the three entry personnel on the eleven-man team. "No."

James looked past Joe and started walking towards his team leader. James was, himself, the assistant team leader. "How's the wife, Jed?"

Jed laughed. James' reputation grew from moments like these. In the midst of stress and chaos, James was the only person whose heart rate maintained a normal beat. "She's doing good. How's yours?"

"She misses me. And I miss her." He tucked his Beretta into his tactical holster. "So why don't you tell me why this guy wants to keep us apart."

"All I know is that this guy went into an office this morning, pulled out a semi and started shooting people. He's up there right now." He pointed.

"How many hostages?"

"I don't know. At least a few. George is right over there, he's already given us the green light for anything we deem necessary. So, as usual, let's end this thing as soon as we can." George was the police chief and their close friend.

"No hesitation, no worries. Just do it."

"Right. George will cover our backs."

James turned away from the team leader, who was more like James' counter-part rather than superior and watched as the scouts ran towards the building. The scouts were fast, wearing only the standard soft-body armor with a load bearing harness. They reached the building in only a few seconds. The snipers also began running towards high ground. James surveyed the front of the building and was able to just catch the suspect walk by the window. "Fred!" He called to one of the snipers as he ran towards an adjacent building.

"What?" He was slightly irritated, the verbal exchange costing him valuable time.

"Set up here."

The sniper ran back over and set up his .308 Remington. The bipod rested on the hood of a police car as he worked the bolt-action.

James pointed towards the window. "He's in that one. Two rows below the flag, fourth one from the right."

Fred looked through the high-quality optical scope, and the window suddenly appeared so close that he could bring the crosshairs over one of the many water drops that sat on the glass.

A police chief made his way through the mess of personnel and over to the team leader. "The suspect said he would shoot a hostage if he saw one officer enter the building. He also is looking for tear gas and flashbangs."

The team leader called into his radio. "Scouts, do not enter front of building. Go around back."

The radio crackled. *"Already there, over."*

"We can't tell how many hostages he has or how many he has killed. We can't get a guy close enough to that office without him knowing."

The team leader sighed. “We can get into the ceiling with cameras.”

The chief shook his head. “I looked at the floor plan already, they’ve got pipes and all kinds of junk up there. It’s impossible to fit up there.”

“Elevator shaft?”

“Too far away. It’s on the other side of the wing. We could get close enough to throw a few flash grenades, but he insisted that he would open fire on the hostages. I believe him.”

“Is there a negotiator?”

“Yeah, he’s right over there.” The chief pointed to a man that was sitting on the hood of a car and talking very fast into a radio.

“What’s he doing out here?”

“The man said that if there were any attempts to contact him then he would shoot a hostage.”

“What does he want?”

“No one knows.”

“Great.”

James just watched the window.

“Come on, man! Three hours have gone by, and he still hasn’t established contact. This guy is crazy! Let’s just take him out.” A police officer was speaking freely to his superior.

James felt the same way, though he understood the risk it would create. The rain had only begun to fall harder in the last hour, and he was growing weary of it. He looked at his watch and sighed. Kirsten was expecting him home in just an hour.

Suddenly, and without warning, shots were fired from the upper window of the news building. Bullets streaked down to the mass of law officials and media personal. They thunked as they pierced holes into police cars and cracked as they shattered windshields and lights. Glass exploded into the air and police officers everywhere dove to the ground, seeking shelter behind their vehicles. A few officers were hit and the water on the street began to mix with blood.

Fred watched through the optical lens as the man fired a semi automatic from the upper window of the building. When he ran dry, he only inserted another clip and continued to spray the ground below with deadly fire. Fred looked over to James who was leaning his back against the same car he was set up on. “That guy is nuts.”

James turned to face the building and brought up a pair of binoculars. Fred’s comment was briefly confirmed. “We need to take that guy out.” He called into his radio. "Request permission to take subject out with clear shot, over."

"*Negative. Hold fire.*"

"Fred, when he stops to reload, shoot him."

"Come on, James, you heard the order."

James looked around for Jed, but didn't see him. He returned his eyes back to the window and watched as the subject left its view. A few seconds later, he returned with a hostage. This sight caused half of the policemen to stand to their feet in horror.

Fred called into his radio. "Sir, I request permission to fire on subject!"

"*Request denied! Stand down!*"

James looked over to Fred, the voice on the radio unfamiliar. "Who is that? Where's George?"

Fred shrugged.

James looked around the area he was positioned in and noticed a few officers wearing blue rain jackets. Written on their backs in big bold yellow letters were the initials: FBI "You've got to be kidding me."

Just then a shot fired and the hostage fell from the window. Fred and the other sniper called into the radio. "I have a clear shot!"

"*Negative. You have my order!*"

Fred cursed. "Where's George?"

James spotted him talking to the FBI, and he didn't look happy. Despite the obvious tension that was being manifested between the FBI man and the police chief, James was able to briefly establish eye contact with him. Never dropping the rate in which he was arguing, George was able to sneak James a head nod. That's all James needed. He then rested his hand on Fred's shoulder. "Do it."

Before Fred put the crosshairs over the man's forehead, he spotted Jed trying to get his attention. He was signaling for him to take the shot. So he began to squeeze the trigger.

The man opened fire on the crowd again and bullets streaked across the car that Fred was positioned on. The bullets chased him and James back to the ground.

"That's it." Fred brought the Remington back up and onto the bullet-riddled car. Suddenly, there was a loud rumble of thunder that seemed to perfectly emphasize the newest situation- another hostage being held in front of the window.

"This is ridiculous!" yelled James. He yelled into the radio, trying one more time to operate within the parameters of official orders. "Sir, request permission to take out target before he kills another hostage!"

The voice that came back was stern. "*You will do no such thing! That is an order!*"

"An order from who?"

"*That is an order!*"

James was hoping that there would be no response to his inquiry and was overjoyed when his hope was satisfied. He looked back down to Fred. "Take him out, Fred."

"James . . . The guy has a loaded gun to that girl's head. If I shoot him. . ."

James looked through the binoculars and could see the girl. She was soaking wet and the wind was pulling her hair across her face, but he could still make out who she was. He knew her from a couple of interviews he had done with her. She looked terrified, not ready to face the death she obviously knew was coming. Then the target squeezed the trigger.

Nothing happened.

"Take the shot!" yelled James.

Fred began to squeeze the trigger, but the man had pulled the woman directly in front of him. Fred cursed again.

James wiped the water off of his face and off of the lenses of the binoculars. He could see the man drop the semi and pick up an automatic pistol. "Give me the rifle." He reached for the sniper-rifle.

Fred was uncomfortable. "James . . . "

"Give it to me, now!"

He hesitated once more before handing it over. "Oh man, I hope you know what you're doing . . . "

James looked through the optical lens and brought the crosshairs over the man's head.

He pulled the trigger.

The silencer that had been fitted over the barrel made it impossible to determine exactly where the shot was fired from, but everyone saw the man let go of the woman and fall away from the window. The woman screamed and fainted, falling uninjured to the office floor. The masses of police and reporters were suddenly a mess with confusion, everyone wanting to know what had happened and yelling to find out.

Fred watched as the police, FBI, and SWAT all stormed into the building. "James, we could get into a lot of trouble for that." His face revealed his concern.

James smiled. "Don't worry about it." He glanced at his watch. "Shoot! I'm going to be late."

Fred couldn't help but to laugh. "You're crazy, man." He stood to his feet. "But I love you, anyway." He slapped him on the shoulder. "You're sure everything's going to be okay? I don't have to make plans around losing my job?"

James slapped him back. "Come on, you just start working with us today? You know how it works. George will take care of it."

"I hope so."

James noticed the FBI guys screaming at the police chief. "Hey, George."

George walked over to them. "Did you take that shot?"

James shrugged.

"Great shot." He looked back towards the FBI. "Let's get out of this rain."

Before leaving the scene, James exchanged a knowing look with Jed who was some distance away, busy with some police officers. The look communicated said, "Good job, I'll see you later. Good luck with your brother. Now get out of here, your wife is waiting for you." James and Jed had been working together for some time now, and many times their lives depended on them being able to read each other's eyes. James was given the chance to lead his own team, but he declined. He liked working with Jed, and Jed liked working with James. They were a team and each respected each other and trusted each other with their lives. James nodded his message in return appreciation.

The FBI agent screamed into James' face. "Have you any idea what you did?"

James held a steady gaze, refusing to be drug into a shouting match. "I ended the situation cleanly and quickly."

"You shot a key witness that was to testify in Federal court!"

"I shot someone who was killing innocent people and who fired on me and my fellow officers."

"You have no idea the mess you created!" The agent was pacing back and forth.

"With all due respect, any mess that exists was created by your department and the lack of security offered your witness. He should never have been able to access a weapon let alone carry it into a building."

"The man sucker punched his guard and jumped out a window . . . "

"I don't care."

The agent put his face up close to James.' "You disobeyed a direct order."

"You're not my commanding officer, nor did you identify yourself as such."

"That man was the only witness to a mob related murder! The murder of an FBI agent!"

"A friend of yours?"

"Yeah, he was! Why?"

"Because only someone with a personal attachment to such a case would justify these kinds of means to your end. Is that all?"

"Oh, that's far from all . . . "

James grabbed him by his jacket. "I know that girl he was going to kill, and I was not about to watch her die to meet the needs of some Federal agenda."

"You could have killed her . . . You were lucky that he didn't squeeze the trigger as a result of the shot."

James turned to leave. "He had the safety on." He walked out of the office.

"James!" George caught up with him.

"I'm late, George."

"I know. I just wanted to tell you that I appreciate your work."

"And I appreciate you cleaning up my messes." He smiled and looked back to the FBI agent who was now speaking angrily on a cell phone.

George's face dropped. "Yeah . . . Good luck with your brother. I hope you find him."

James forced a smile. "Thanks. I'll see you in a week or so."

The rain had begun to let up in its relentless bombardment and the clouds looked as if they were thinning out. Though James loved the gray sky and the tranquility the rain seemed to bring with it, he couldn't help but think that a little bit of sunshine would do some good. His BMW had two bullet holes in the front hood and one through the windshield. He was thankful that there was no interior damage to the engine.

He turned the key in the ignition and the car came to life as the engine rolled over. Catching the image of the FBI agent yelling at George in his rear-view mirror as he pulled away from the police station, only spread his lips into a smile across his face.

Kirsten watched from the kitchen window as James pulled into the driveway, and she noticed the bullet holes right away. Bringing her hand up to her open mouth, her eyes released a few tears that began to descend down her, paling face. Her husband shut the car door and disappeared into the garage. When he reappeared, he was holding a role of electrical tape. Kirsten watched as he covered the hole in the windshield, attempting to prevent the falling rain from entering into the car.

James closed the door behind him and took off his wet shoes and socks.

Standing in the rain for four hours made absolutely sure that there was not a dry spot on his body. He pulled the wet t-shirt off of his body and scooped up his socks. They soon found themselves flying down the basement stairs where they would wait to be washed. James closed the basement door and made his way into the kitchen, the tile floor cold beneath his bare feet, and the air conditioned atmosphere making thousands of goose bumps on his bear chest.

Kirsten looked up from the chair she was sitting on. "Are you okay?"

James saw the tears and his heart sank like a millstone in the ocean. "Oh, Honey . . . " He walked over to her, and she didn't hesitate to wrap her arms around him.

"I saw you on the news . . . "

His fingers ran through her hair as he thought of what to say.

"It was live."

"It's okay, Sweetheart. I'm fine . . . "

"I saw that guy shooting at you. I thought . . . "

Holding her chin and looking into her eyes, James smiled sympathetically. "Hey, it's okay."

"Did you shoot him?"

Though James knew that Kirsten was aware that he had killed many people in his line of work, he had always wondered if that was something that bothered her.

"Yes."

She held him tighter.

"I had to."

"I know you did."

She released her grip and stood. She then threw her arms around his neck and embraced him again.

"So how'd I look?"

Darkness hid the clouds that remained fixed over upstate New York, but the rain continued to fall nonetheless. Lightening would flash occasionally, giving the dark clouds a silver outline and providing moments of illumination. Thunder followed close after.

The sheets were cool, the air conditioner doing its job. The lights were out, and the Streen couple lay in bed holding each other, watching the lightening outside. James kissed her forehead as he spoke. "Are you sure you're okay with me going?"

She answered in a tired voice that James had always found attractively cute. "Yeah. You need to look for Steve."

Thinking of his brother had proven to be a stressful practice, yet essential in the process of trying to locate him. James knew that the situation was not good, but he didn't mention that to Kirsten.

"It'll be good, too, to be with those guys."

James knew that Kirsten wasn't going to last much longer, she was practically asleep already. "It'll be strange . . . " A rumble of thunder rattled the windows soon after a flash of lightning lit up their bedroom. "Wow, how close do you think that was?"

She was already asleep.

She lay, sleeping soundly and peacefully, in the protection and shelter offered by her husband. She also lay under the gaze of his loving eyes. More nights than he could remember, James, unable to sleep, found enjoyment in watching her sleep. The peace and security that her face revealed only reflected back onto her own thoughts of him. That proved to be James' entire ego. No reputation earned during war, no uplifting and boastful talk by others, no other heroic image that he could possibly find himself ascribed to was comparable or as desirable as being the man that could be responsible for the look on Kirsten's face as she slept. He thanked God for the strength to be that man and prayed that he would only grow stronger as that man.

James looked at the clock and unset the alarm. Sleeping in tomorrow was irresistible. He closed his eyes thinking of the reunion he would be having with some old friends, but that reunion was quickly erased by the more troublesome thoughts concerning his missing brother. He prayed that he was still alive.

TWO

Once upon a war - time

The NVA and VC consider the area secure. Charlie patrols the area regularly. The Secret Zone is dense jungle, wet after the three-day rain.

He walks ahead of the team, his eyes intensely searching, studying, and even expecting. The olive color fatigues that cover his body are uncomfortably wet from both sweat and rain. His right hand grips the handle of the M-16 tightly, his left occasionally flexing around the bottom of the M-80 grenade launcher that hangs from the barrel. He walks soft, his body low to the ground and his automatic rifle held ready to fire. The jungle stretches out before him. He listens for its voice.

Snap.

His eyes race through endless jungle as his fist goes quickly into the air. The rest of the team stops dead- waiting. The American M-16 follows his eyes to a shaking branch. Yes, the jungle is speaking to him.

Black pajama pants . . .

His chest and throat tighten as adrenaline courses through his body. He watches, through the stinging sweat that drips into his wide eyes, as the jungle comes to life with little men carrying AK-47's and wearing straw hats. He signals to the team: retreat. He slowly takes a few steps backward, M-16 held steady in front of him. A half-circle followed by a direction is the next signal to his team: retreat into the jungle, skirt around the enemy.

The distinct crackle of an AK-47 comes from behind. He turns in time to see his team- his friends- being violently jerked in involuntary reactions to the bullets that puncture their bodies. A few screams of surprise and pain escape into the jungle's sky before its floor is splashed with more American blood.

He squeezes the trigger and two Charlie are immediately thrown, mangled, to the ground by the M-16's bullets. His heart is beating like drums in his head as he desperately tries to formulate a plan. Reality attempts to grasp at his mind, but it operates purely on reflex and instinct. Slowly, reality does begin to set in, bringing certain fear with it. He begins to run through the jungle, weaving back and forth between trees and bushes. Sticks and other unseen objects tear at his face as he runs blindly through them. He knows that Tactical Operations Center is not going to be able to get him out of this.

A barrage of machine gun fire tears through the atmosphere, hot lead searching for his body. Splinters of wood fill the air around him as enemy bullets strike trees, barely missing his flesh.

Snap.

He knows the noise and closes his eyes. The explosion opens him into a hundred pieces and he sees himself land, like rain, in the mud . . .

James Streen exploded from beneath the sheets and snapped to a sitting position, trying to catch his breath. He looked around the room, trying to discern the dream from reality. The dark corners of the bedroom slowly faded in as the jungle's trees faded out. And the rain that was pelting the jungle's trees slowly morphed into rain hitting the sides of his house. He felt a hand touch his shoulder and he quickly turned, knocking it away. But Kirsten's face triggered something within James' mind, and reality had found a foothold. He began to relax.

"James, it's okay. It was only a dream." She held his soaked face, trying to get his eyes to lock with hers. His eyes were wide, an intense glare looking right through her and into the distorted world of dreamland. The sweat that was dripping from his face told of the convincing reality his mind had created and entertained. Finally, she could see him trying to regain control as his eyes began to slow down and focus.

He reached over and held her tight.

"It's okay . . . " It was the only thing she knew to say in these situations. "Was it the war again?" He was so tense, his muscles ready to tear through the skin that seemed to be constricting them.

James squeezed his eyes closed, and he nodded. The pain, the emotion, the fear, the smell, the noise, the faces, the blood . . . It was all too real in the dreams. In the early days of their marriage, James was terribly embarrassed by his reaction to his nightmares, and Kirsten was easily scared by them, not knowing how to help. She would watch her husband sit, soaking wet and shaking, in the bed until he was able to fall asleep again. Those experiences were not missed. Over a period of time, Kirsten was able to learn how to best help in the situation, but that period was not pleasant for anyone. The embarrassment that plagued him also shut him down to her. It was pure humiliation that had kept her on the outside and unable to help. But that changed, as she was able to comfort him and assure him that he had no reason to be humiliated. The nights he woke up screaming were nights he later fell asleep in her arms.

"I'm sorry if I scared you," he sighed as he ran his hands through his wet hair and lay back down onto his back.

"The anticipation of seeing your friends from the war must have triggered those old memories."

His lungs let out a big breath of air. "Yeah . . . " But he never told her which war it was that he dreamt about. She assumed that it was the horrors of the Gulf War, but it wasn't. It was a nightmare taken out of the seventies and misplaced, finding a different soldier from a different era. Whoever was in charge of dreamland had misplaced this one. And yet, it was too real to be simply fiction, it had to be memory. But how could James have memory of something he never experienced? He was only three years old when his brother Steve went to Nam, and he had no recollection of Steve coming home and sharing stories.

His eyes searched through the darkness of the room, confusion and fear taunting him. It was so real . . . He couldn't even remember how long these Vietnam nightmares had been going on. Forever, it seemed. At least this time he hadn't seen the image and the crosses. After making up his mind that he was in New York and that he was crazy, he looked down into his wife's concerned eyes and forced the words, "Thanks."

"For what?" She was so sincere.

"Well . . . " He took her hand in his. "For putting up with this and for helping me through it."

She smiled. "There was a time when you wouldn't let me help."

"There was also a time you didn't know how to help." In those days, James didn't even know how to cope with the dreams himself, let alone handle someone else's emotion on top of it.

"What could I . . . "

He cut her off with a finger over her lips as he smiled. "I know. I was embarrassed." He smiled. "What a way to kick off the honeymoon."

"Well, I must admit that I was a little concerned when you woke up screaming."

The door to their bedroom creaked open, letting the light from the hallway sweep across its floor. "Mommy?"

Kirsten sat up. "Oh, Honey, why aren't you sleeping?"

She walked into the room. "I'm scared of the storm."

James quickly kissed Kirsten before Jessica climbed into the bed and found shelter from all the evil in the world. The lightening that flashed and the rain that continued to pelt their house could not reach Jessica now, not while in the safety of mommy and daddy's bed. She fell asleep immediately, lying between husband and wife. James and Kirsten shared a locked gaze that was fixed only on each other as they held hands over their sleeping daughter.

"I love you." Kirsten's eyes said as much as her words.

"I love you." He held her hand tighter. "Goodnight, Kirsten."

She was already asleep.

But James still couldn't enter into that place. Not yet. His dream was still having its effect on him, the after-taste. He was afraid to close his eyes, afraid that this time he might see it. This Vietnam dream had always troubled him, he couldn't understand where it came from and why. At first he thought it was from his own war experience combined with a Vietnam movie he saw, but some of the images he saw were reoccurring, and he knew he had never seen them before. And now, since Steve disappeared, the dreams had gotten worse and more frequent than ever. Coincidence? James wasn't sure.

James' parents were married when they were still very young, his mother only seventeen. Steve was born in '51 and James was born fifteen years later when his mother was thirty-three. He had a couple of sisters in between, but he was the youngest, Steve the oldest. Steve was drafted into the army when he was eighteen, leaving for the jungles of Vietnam along with so many other boys, but James was too young to even remember that. From what he could remember, Steve was over there until after the war was over. He never asked why or what he was doing, because Steve never seemed to want to talk about it. But now, lying in his bed next to his wife and child, on a stormy night, and after the millionth Vietnam War nightmare, James wished he could ask. For some reason, he felt it was important to know, as if the answer could help explain his dreams. Hopefully, he'd get the chance to ask. That was another issue entirely- finding his brother. He set his mind on that, and, without knowing it, sleep captured him.

Surprise was not something that came regularly into James' world, but as he opened his eyes only to be forced to close them again, he found himself pleasantly surprised by the sunlight that was pouring into his room and across his face.

The clock read 6:50. He slowly slid out of bed, not wanting to wake up his wife or daughter who were still sleeping quite soundly. He slid his hands under Jessica's body and gently lifted her into the air. When he entered her bedroom, he was more disappointed than surprised to find a tree branch growing through the window. There was glass on the floor, gathered around the window's base, but it was contained to that area. He could also tell that the carpet was wet. He laid Jessica into her own bed and pulled the covers over her little body. A warm breeze found its way through the broken window and into the bedroom. It blew Jessica's hair across the pillow and rattled a few posters that were pinned to the walls. The breeze reminded James of the beach, and he suddenly remembered that he would be in Bermuda the next day. Though he was not too excited about going, due to the fact that he had to leave his family behind, the warm breeze across his face helped balance the scales just a little.

Before he started thinking about his day, James decided to give it to his Lord. On warm days like these, James loved to sit on the back porch with a cup of coffee and an open Bible as the sun was lifted into the sky. And that was where he found himself this morning.

Kirsten had worked very hard on the plant life that grew around the porch, hoping it to resemble a sort of oasis. The two weeks of rain had helped a little too much. It now was in danger of taking over the house, let alone the porch itself. The feeling now was that of being swallowed by vegetation. James leaned back against the chair and closed his eyes, letting the sun warm his body. The sound of the birds communicating to each other only added to the environment in which he was having a hard time staying awake. He closed the Bible and set it on the table next to his half-empty cup of coffee. His mind probed the words just digested. The words of Psalms chapter five floated through his mind, different phrases at different depths. "Give ear to my words, O Lord, consider my meditation. Give heed to the voice of my cry, my King and my God, for to You I will pray. My voice You shall hear in the morning, O Lord; in the morning I will direct it to You, and will look up . . . I will come into Your house in the multitude of Your mercy; in fear of You I will worship toward the temple of Your holiness . . . Make Your way straight before my face . . . But let all those rejoice who put their trust in You; let them ever shout for joy, because You defend them; let those also who love Your name be joyful in You."

The screen door behind him slid open, and a pregnant shadow glided across the deck. Kirsten put her hands on James' shoulders, forcing him to open his eyes. "How'd you sleep?"

James held her hand and swung her around so that she was in front of him. "You mean after I woke up screaming?"

She smiled while her fingers brushed through his hair. "You didn't scream this time."

"Oh, no? Well I guess that's an improvement." He pulled her into a sitting position on his lap.

"It must have been so awful, to effect you this way. I mean, I can't imagine an experience that would give me consistent nightmares from that day forth."

"I suppose a lot of people have them though." Again, he wrestled with the words she said. Wouldn't dreams that consistent usually be based on a past experience and not some random, made up, fictitious story of the imagination? But there was no experience, and the closest thing to the experience was his brother, not himself. So why would he dream about Vietnam? He couldn't even remember ever dreaming about the Gulf War or any situation he would face in SWAT. He didn't understand it, and it troubled him more than he would care to admit. As he looked into her eyes, he suddenly felt bad for keeping the truth of the dreams from her, letting her believe they were Desert Storm nightmares. Realizing he wasn't sure why he never told her, he thought about finally explaining the phenomena to her. But just before opening his mouth, he decided against it. He wondered why. Never before had he kept something from her. But that was beginning to change, he thought. Regretfully, he was withholding some information about his trip to Bermuda. But he didn't want to think about it now. He smiled and waited for her to change the subject.

When she finally did, it was with a trick question. "What are we doing today?"

James could tell that she was in a playful mood so he figured she already knew the answer to her own question. "You tell me." She stood and pretended to think about it, but James knew she already had something in mind.

"Well . . . We could play a game or two before lunch, go out somewhere after lunch, drop Jess off at Steve and Deb's, get a movie . . . " She was trying to seduce him into the idea, her face suggestive and pleading at the same time. "And a pizza. And we can sit in front of the fire . . . "

James stood up in front of her and took her hands in his again. "Whatever you want to do is what I want to do." He laughed. "I am yours!"

She chased him into the house.

He almost ran through the kitchen without noticing. Turning, he smiled at Kirsten. "You tricky little girl."

She smiled a guilty smile and accepted his thanks as they both sat down to the unusually large breakfast she had secretly made. James wondered how he could have missed the smell of bacon. And then he realized that he had probably fallen asleep for a while.

"Daddy!" Jessica came running around the corner and slid into the kitchen.

"What is it, Jess?"

"A tree fell into my room!" The wide-eyed expression and the sound of unbelief in her voice came across as humorous.

"Really?" Kirsten obviously thought she was just playing along to her daughter's joke.

James laughed as he picked up Jessica and sat her in the chair next to him. "She's right. I forgot about it."

"What?"

"Yeah, last night a tree branch broke through the window in her room."

"Are you going to fix it, Daddy?" Jessica asked.

"Yeah, don't worry. But don't go near the window until I do fix it."

The game of Checkers was dominated by Jessica, whose feelings of supremacy now conquered her behavior. Of course, mom and dad ignored the 'must jump' rule, but Jessica wouldn't learn of that for a number of years. James and Kirsten played the sad loser, trying to win the sympathy of their child. When that attempt failed, a large wrestling match ensued. Finally, a long kiss between James and Kirsten sent Jessica diving, face first, into the couch, and she was out of the match.

"Ewww . . . "

Suddenly, Kirsten's eyes widened as her hand went to her stomach. "James . . . "

James wasn't fond of those emotional shockers. "What?" His mind had already raced through all the different scenarios of something being wrong. They'd have to take Jess with them to the hospital, which wasn't a big deal. But his trip planned for tomorrow could present a huge problem. And more importantly, where were the keys? Did he have enough gas? A thousand concerns made him panic.

"She's kicking. Here, feel this." She put his hand over her round stomach.

James sighed, relieved that he didn't have to race to the hospital. He touched his wife's stomach, her skin smooth and tight beneath his fingers. She felt like she would pop, and she was only going to get bigger! And then he felt her kicking . . . "Wait a second. What do you mean 'her'?"

Kirsten shot him a wiry smile.

"Oh, no! I'm not going to be the only man around here. Honey, I just won't allow it this time. You're having a boy and that's final."

She smiled again. "I'll try." She knew that James had always wanted a boy and couldn't help but feel a little sorry for him that their first wasn't. But she also knew that James wouldn't trade Jessica back for a boy if he could. If their next child were a girl then James would love her the same as he loved Jessica, but she hoped that it would be a boy. That was something that she looked forward to seeing anyway, James and his little boy.

James called for Jess. "Hey, come feel your little brother."

Kirsten couldn't hold back the smile. How could she? Here she found herself sitting on the floor of her house, with child, and being surrounded by her loving husband and daughter. She was the center of their world at this moment, and she would cherish the instant for a long while. She realized, at that moment, that her youthful dreams were realized. She had what she had always prayed for, and she could never cease to thank God for that blessing.

The action within Kirsten's womb settled down and everyone went separate ways, at least until lunch. Kirsten went into the kitchen to make up some sandwiches, and Jessica went to the living room to play with her dolls (Dad told her that she couldn't play in her room until he fixed the window).

Walking up the steps to his room, James planned on taking a shower. He entered his room, still surprised at the sunlight illuminating the same room that had been dark for so long. Picking out a pair of clothes parallel to the mood he was in, he began to walk to the bathroom. But his vision picked up the luggage that was sitting against the wall, and he stopped walking. The bags were packed and ready to go, Kirsten doing most of the work there. But there were still things that needed to be packed, and James thought that now was the best time he would get to do so. He listened for the activity that came from the floor beneath before getting started.

The closet door glided open on the floor track and clothes on hangers were pushed aside. James inserted the key into the safe that was part of the closet wall and opened it. Reaching inside he removed the weapons from the gun rack. One sniper rifle, one shotgun, one submachine gun, and two assault rifles. He broke them all down to their basic components before burying them beneath his clothes in his suitcases. He quickly covered them with his clothes and shut the cases, locking them immediately. Going back to the safe, he pulled out a large duffle bag and a smaller duffle bag. Opening the smaller one first, he made sure it was empty before transferring equipment. Out of the large bag he took out a flashlight, a knife, a gas mask, a multitool, a couple rubber doorstops, a ten-foot roll of duct tape, four flashbangs, four flex cuffs, and two cyalume lightsticks. He put them into the smaller bag, along with a few boxes of ammunition and loaded clips. He tucked the small bag into his previously packed large duffle bag, but to do so he had to take out some of the clothes Kirsten had packed for him. He tucked them into the back of his drawer. Closing the safe and locking it, James once again regretted the secrecy and the deception he was handing to his wife. But he needed to bring back his brother, and he didn't dare tell Kirsten of the situation he was entering; at least not until he was home safely. He prayed that everything would go the way he and his friends planned it out, but in the back of his mind a voice taunted him, *how often do things work out the way they are planned?*

Before taking a shower, James decided he would get the mess in Jessica's room cleaned up first. He cleaned up the glass, threw the tree back outside, and covered the window with plastic. That would have to do for now. As he was walking out of her room, he stopped in the door way and looked around. He had never taken the time to observe his daughter's room and dwell on the thoughts doing so would induce. Three years old. That's how old she was now. James couldn't believe it. Where did the time go? Thinking of time brought with it another thought never before processed, and that was what Jessica's room might look like in another ten or twelve years. It was almost too much to comprehend, knowing that just as he stood in her doorway now, looking at her dolls and all the things one would expect to find in a three year-old's room, he would also lean against the same door frame, years later, and observe a completely different room. This moment that he was in right now would then only be a distant memory, its reality gone and aged into the teens. Thinking of that day made James a little sad. He knew that the next ten years would go by just as quickly as the last three, and he hoped that when he looked at the make-up, the diary, the hidden boy pictures and love letters, and (God forbid) the phone, that he would still be able to say, "It's all good. My daughter is still my little girl." He smiled, anticipating the years to come and all the ups and downs that were part of the deal. He only hoped that time took its time and that he wouldn't take it for granted.

He then went to take his shower.

The weatherman pointed to a busy area on the map, isolating the hurricane. "It's a big one, predicted to hit the Bahamas then move up into Florida and travel up the sea coast." The weatherman tried to make a few quick jokes but soon gave up. James wondered if the camera crew was making obvious the flatness of the attempted humor. "So enjoy the sunshine, because it's not going to last past this week."

Kirsten was in the other room, playing with Jessica. James turned the television off, not wanting Kirsten to hear anything about a hurricane. With her being due in three months, James figured it was best to keep her away from as much stress as possible. James thought about his brother again as he walked into the room his wife and daughter were playing in, and, again, he hoped he was still alive. His relationship with his brother was something he had taken for granted the last few years, and now that he was missing, he realized how much he wanted Steve to be part of his family's life. He wanted Steve to be there while Jess grew up. It wasn't the same without him, and he just hoped the realization didn't come too late.

The ransom note that he had received in the mail said he had three more weeks before they would kill his brother. Of course, no one other than himself knew that such a letter existed. Whoever was holding his brother was not an experienced kidnapper and for that James wasn't sure whether to be happy or worried. James was pretty sure that some cartel was holding him, though ransom notes were not typical of any cartel. This only worried him more. Because the actions of the people holding his brother were so abnormal, they would not fit any profile. This made the enemy unpredictable.

"Daddy, do you want to play dolls with us?" Her question interrupted his thoughts.

The answer came out somewhere between the laughing. "Only if I can play with the guy doll."

The phone rang, and James left to answer it. "Hello?"

It was Joshua, his friend from the service. James lowered his voice and quietly closed the door that led to the other room. "Hey, is everything looking good? Great. I packed five long guns. Yeah, I got a sniper rifle. Good. Do me a favor? See if you can contact the authorities down there. Yeah. No, that's fine. Oh, we'll have plenty of time to sit on the beach. Okay, don't forget your own personal stuff. Okay, good. I'll see you tomorrow. What? No, she doesn't know what's going on. I know. All right, see you tomorrow. Bye." He hung up the phone and rejoined his family.

Kirsten found herself staring at the bullet hole in the windshield and quickly turned to look out the window, focusing her attention, instead, on the houses that flew past the window of James' BMW. James pulled the car into the pizza shop and left the car. Kirsten sat waiting.

"That'll be 21.50."

James stole a glance at Kirsten and smiled while muttering, "My goodness, you sure are hungry these days." He smiled and waved. In exchange for the money, he received the food and began to walk out the door.

Kirsten noticed a few kids walking over towards the car, and she locked the door.

"Hey, you forgot your change."

"Oh, sorry." James turned back to get it. When he turned around again, he saw three kids standing next to the passenger side of his BMW. He walked out the door and to his car. "Can I help you guys?"

Two of the three kids obviously didn't like being there, and they started to back away from the car. The third kid, the leader, James guessed, decided to act a little tougher and older than he actually was. "Yeah, maybe you can. How 'bout some pizza?"

James shrugged. "Sure. We got pepperoni and plain." He walked to the passenger side and stood next to the three kids. Holding out a box of pizza, he gestured, "Help yourself."

The two kids were begging the third to leave, but the leader didn't like being humiliated like that. James had yet to acknowledge that this kid was dangerous or serious.

"Maybe you should give me your wallet too!" He pulled a knife out of his pocket.

James couldn't help but to smile. It was sad, and he was angry that the kids were turning out the way they were, but he couldn't keep from laughing at the pathetic picture in front of him. I mean, it was amazing to him how stupid kids were getting these days. The kid just pulled a knife on him in broad daylight in a relatively populated parking lot. He looked to the other two kids. "You guys get out of here." They hesitated. "Go on, get out of here!" They turned and ran. "Now what are you going to do? You just lost all your moral support."

The kid held the knife out in front of him in a threatening manner, challenging James.

"Now what?" The kid charged James, but James dodged the blow and caught the kid's extended arm. James used the kid's momentum and spun him into the car so that the kid's face was pressed up against the glass. James blew Kirsten a kiss. He then pinched a nerve in the kid's wrist that made him drop the knife with a yelp.

"Kid, that was so stupid. What are you thinking? You have your whole life ahead of you and you want to trade it all for some pizza and an empty wallet? Now I'm gonna' make you sit somewhere for a long time, and I want you to think about what I just said, and then I want you to ask yourself if it's worth it. If it's reasonable."

Kirsten reached into the glove compartment and retrieved a pair of handcuffs. She rolled down the window and handed them to her husband who quickly put them on the wrists of his attacker.

"Oh yeah, you see that beautiful woman right there?" He turned his face so that he was looking through the window at Kirsten. "That's my wife." He stepped back a little. "Oh! Did I tell you I'm a cop? Oh, stupid. I should have told you that before I started going off on my little speech, huh? Well, I'm a cop, and that's my wife. And . . . that's the knife you tried to stab me with. Do you see how bad this situation is looking for you right now?"

Silence.

Just then a police car came into the parking lot and pulled up next to James.

The officer got out of his car and headed for the deli that stood next to the pizza shop. As he stepped up onto the walkway, he recognized James. "Hey, James."

James gave a wiry smile. "Hey, Bob."

Noticing the painful expression on the kid's face and the manner in which James held his arm, he asked, "What's going on here?"

"I'm not sure, Bob. This kid appears to have been bothering my wife. I offered him some pizza, and he attacked me with that knife over there. If I knew that he felt that strongly about pizza . . . "

The officer walked to James' car. He leaned forward and peaked over James shoulder, waiving to Kirsten. "Hello, Mrs. Streen."

She waived back with a forced smile. She suddenly felt a little vulnerable knowing she was going to be without James for a while.

The officer helped the kid get into the police car as James opened the passenger door and handed Kirsten the pizzas. As he was walking around to the driver's side, Kirsten could hear the police officer mumble as he shook his head, "And he never put down the pizzas." He then bit into the hot piece of pizza topped with pepperoni that James had offered him.

James closed the door and started the engine. As the BMW left the parking lot, the police officer waived goodbye, clearly content to have both a piece of pizza and a kid on the way to the station.

Kirsten found it odd that James was wearing a smile. "Are you okay?"

"Huh? Oh, I'm sorry. Are you okay?"

She smiled. "You really like that sort of stuff don't you?"

He nodded. "Oh, yeah."

"You're so weird."

Credits rolled up the screen, and a closing song set the mood for the sad ending. Kirsten's cheeks were damp. She always cried during movies. James had woken up just in time to catch the last scene, but he wouldn't tell Kirsten that. He wasn't a big fan of chick-flicks. He had given them up early, tired of having his emotions played with so much.

A conversation concerning the next two weeks started as the tape rewound. The conversation ended with a kiss and James leaving to pick up Jessica. As he walked out the door, Kirsten said, "Don't keep me waiting."

James turned away from the image of his wife, not wanting to laugh out loud at the sight of her stomach rising from beneath the sheets. He thought that it resembled a volcano about to erupt. He let his mind drift to those he would see in Bermuda in just a short time. The thoughts of his friends brought back a lot of mixed memories. The experiences that came within the Middle East deserts were becoming fresh on his mind, and he had to try very hard to keep from letting those memories change him into what he once left the service to keep from becoming. He didn't want to go back to being the James Streen of the past, but nonetheless, he was becoming familiar with that feeling once again. It scared him. He had been so close to going over the edge before, he did not want an excuse to cross it now. He feared that if he crossed it, he would never be able to return to the other side. He'd seen people like that in the war, people that had gone past the point of no return. People that loved the killing, loved the rush, the smell of death . . . Once James engaged in combat, he felt that door beginning to open. There was one time in particular where he had put one foot over. At that moment, with dead bodies scattered at his feet, adrenaline pumping through his veins, and the overwhelming feeling of invincibility, he knew that he could go either way. It was his choice and he had to decide. Would he spend the rest of his life satisfying a blood lust, loving the possibility of death, yet knowing the possibility would only feed his excitement? Or would he get out while he could, put this behind him and live a normal life? Perhaps most soldiers were mentally tough enough to never cross that line, to serve their country for the sake of serving her alone. But not James Streen. For him it was different, and he chose to get out while he could. The difficulty was living a normal life having already tasted something he was excellent at. It still tugged at him, called to him. That's when he joined the police force.

He hoped that his time in Bermuda with his old friends wouldn't encourage the feelings of the past to influence the present. He also hoped that he would be able to sleep tonight without traveling through the jungles of Vietnam. He was sure that if he had been in Vietnam, he would now either be dead or still serving. If his nightmare was made a reality, he would have to cross the line just to survive. He hoped he would never have an experience that dramatic, an experience that would turn him into the complete machine the Marines had trained him to be.

The James Streen that was a Marine in Desert Storm was not a nice person. He was a person committed only to survival, and he was one of the best at it. He only hoped Kirsten never had to meet him.

THREE
A REUNION

The ground reluctantly released the sun to its everyday chore of rising into the sky, and as its climb grew higher into the early morning atmosphere, the curtains of night were retracted. For the Streen family, this was another day that was begun with faithful prayer. Though all of their days were set off with prayer, this day's prayer contained a shadow of uniqueness, for this day held an uncertain future.

Kirsten was very good at masking her feelings. She normally evaluated her emotion with an unbiased rod of reason, and though the emotion would not simply flee at the sight of reason, this did help her to formulate a proper raison d'être and bend her actions according to logic. This was a personal attribute that her husband came to appreciate from the beginning, a reasonable sound wife. However, this was one of those rare times of circumstance in which she couldn't hide her emotion. Nailed tight and sound were the walls around her fear, but truth always had room to seep between even the smallest of cracks. And it was a matter of truth that she was scared, and perhaps she couldn't suppress that fear with reason because it was a reasonable fear. In any event, James spotted the leaking emotion and was able to identify it right away.

James knew his wife. He knew her better than perhaps even himself, and he knew that when fear got a hold of her heart, there was usually good reason for the emotional war. This only added an extra thread of worry to the rope that had already been hung over his mind. It seemed to hang down his throat and into his heart. That would explain the sick feeling in the back of his throat and the difficulty his heart seemed to be having pumping his blood. These feelings were the center and focus of their prayers on a morning in which the coming night seemed questionable and uncertain. But the end of the internal debate was their belief that God was in control. Coming to grips with the belief was an issue altogether separate. It was this issue they were presently speaking of in their address to God.

James walked through the kitchen, luggage in hand. He had decided to dress in a white t-shirt and loose fitting jeans, relaxed but ready for adventure should it arise. One could never go wrong with jeans and a Hanes t-shirt, at least that was his thinking. On his way to the front door he stopped beside his bookcase. His bookcase stretched the entire length of the wall, and there were no bare spots to be found. The shelves were fit with books that were packed cover to cover, forever to be squeezed and tortured in the small space. The books that were forcibly crammed into the shelving space were books on history, theology, and law. Mostly. There were the occasional best sellers that must have committed some horrendous act of sin to gain access into the midst of factual debate, like a man's biography next to a sleazy romance novel. James had a couple of those too . . . biographies, not romance novels.

One of James' passions was to read, but a larger passion of his was to buy books that he thought he wanted to read. Standing there, bags in hand, trying to find a suitable book to take (should time permit such occasion), he realized that he had yet to read half of the books that filled this wall of his house. His eyes moved back and forth along the sides of the hardbound books, processing titles and authors. A novel would be a nice getaway from reality, but seeing as he was preparing to enter into reality, he decided against it- maybe on his next trip to the tropics. Law? Too boring for a flight and a beach. History was the same, it just didn't fit the sound of waves crashing against the beach and rolling up his bare feet. His eyes raced over his books on theology, realizing that he was running out of time. His finger traced over a few books, some he had read and others he couldn't even remember buying. And for some unknown reason he sighed and pulled out a book entitled *Angelology*. He had to pull hard, and he could almost hear the books on that shelf scream out in relief as they were given some room to stretch and breathe. In any case, it would make for interesting reading. James was a realist. He knew that he would not get any time to read, but he was also an optimist, hoping that he would find some small amount of time that the future would forget to use. A smile spread his lips. An optimistic realist? He wondered if there was such a thing.

He stuffed the unread and forgotten book into the inside pocket of his windbreaker jacket. It settled awkwardly, pulling that side of the jacket down much further than the other. A heavy book, literally.

Before James continued walking to his car, he rested his eyes on a familiar book. It sat on the bottom shelf, three books away from the end. It was a book that he and Kirsten had bought together right after their honeymoon. It was a book about marriage, one of those workbook kinds for both mates, the kind with the questions that you have to answer and your spouse gets to see how you really feel about something. The smile that spread his lips was a bit different than the previous one. This one was a smile induced by memory, and he suddenly found himself worrying about the trip again.

Feelings were strange things, sometimes too strange to even be interpreted. At times they could refer directly to reality, correctly informing of a valid situation; love, danger, stress . . . And at other times, they could stand directly opposed to knowledge and reality. The most remarkable thing in this situation may be that even though a person can be consciously aware of the irrationality of the feelings, those feelings can still have the power to influence. James was convinced that many people enjoy spitting out the philosophies that they think are so brilliantly developed within their realm of experience- philosophies like, "trust your feelings" or "follow your heart." But, as far as James could tell, they only sounded good until the time came to put the philosophy to action, because he knew that human beings don't have a heart that is capable of determining what that best thing is for them. Instead they rely on their minds and their intellect to logically discern what decisions to make. But then that power is limited as well, for who knows the future and can plan around it? And it is that uncertainty that the feelings of fear come to wed. James knew many people that feared the unknown, the future. He did not blame them. But he had a belief that others didn't have. He believed in a God that was in control and Who worked all things for him (whether good or bad) into good. And though he believed this with his whole being and knew it as fact, those fearful emotions still danced around his heart. Unreasonable feelings, James called them. Feelings that were not in tune with reality. As if the feeling of being watched influenced one to close the blinds, even when it was established as fact that there was no person or thing watching him, that feeling then was useless and not in accordance with reality. Yet the feelings were still real, and, as in most cases, fear dominates reason. Of course, one can learn to submit to logic and reality, as James had. Within the deserts of Iraq, you couldn't react to the feelings of fear that ran through your body. If you did, you died. Only those who learned to live with fear, and not by it, survived. But even in this case, leaving his family, James found it hard to pull his mind away from the hint of fear that defied reason. He knew that his family would be okay. Whether they had a great time or whether they were to die, James believed that they would be okay. He figured it was more of a selfish fear rather than a genuine one. After all, if Heaven were real- as James believed it was- then the best thing that could ever happen to his wife and daughter would be for them to enter through its gates. To leave behind the sorrow of this world, to forget what it is to cry, to not know any kind of pain, to be in the presence of God . . . Yes, it was most likely a selfish fear- the fear of living this hard life without the support he thought he needed from those he loved the most. And yet, there was something more to this fear . . . He almost wanted to relate it to a warning of some kind.

But that thought was elusive and quickly forgotten, only the strange impact of it left to tug at his mind. He didn't know what to expect in Bermuda but as he looked into the mirror that hung next to his bookshelf, he found that he was talking to himself. The words spoken seemed to be from his conscience to his brain, or his soul to his body. He watched his lips move as they formed the words and felt as if he wasn't looking at himself anymore, but at someone who knew more than he did. A tingle raced up his spine as he heard himself say, "I have a bad feeling about this."

The airport was as crowded as usual. James allowed a small amount of observation to lead his eyes, and his surroundings were realized with a glance or two. The people that filled this place . . . no wonder America was called the Great Melting Pot. James, history-loving James that is, found it remarkable at how far America had come over the last 300 or so years. So many different countries from all over the globe were being represented all around him. This line of thinking would have lingered longer had it been given the time, but something else pushed its way into James' mind. Standing in front of him was a middle-aged man wearing a very expensive suit talking on a cell phone. The man obviously had no other concern than to speak into the little piece of plastic he was holding so fashionably to his mouth. The expensive gold watch he wore dangled loosely from his wrist as he moved his hand around in the air, punctuating his sentences. The guy was standing in the middle of the floor; his bags sprawled carelessly at his feet. The crowd of people that was walking past James was coming too fast for him to make a merge into the on-coming traffic and get around the talking man. So, he was stuck staring at this man who had no thought in the world other than to be speaking to the President. That's who he had better be talking to anyway. Self-centeredness stabbed at James' patience like nothing else could. He could not stand people who only existed in their own realm of concern, people that could be holding up hundreds of others, but didn't even think about that when their cell phone went off or they participated in some other selfish activity. No one else on the planet existed in those seconds of personal interest, and as James watched a little girl trip over one of the man's bags, he was tempted to remind the man of the world he was holding up. This idiot was making a mess of his attempts to reach the baggage check-in terminal.

Kirsten noticed the flustered look and calmly rested a hand on his arm.

Taking a deep breath, James forced himself to relax. "I'm okay." He wanted to get the check-in over with, and every prolonged second was torturing him. Of course, Kirsten was not aware of the small arsenal hid in his luggage. He walked past the man, leaning his shoulder into him hard enough to send him scrambling for balance. The man turned and cursed at James. Though he wanted to hit the man in return, instead he smiled when he heard him trying to explain his comment to the person on the other end of his connection. "No, not you, uh . . . What? Hello?"

James reached for his wife's hand and continued his way to the baggage claim where he would set his luggage on the conveyor belt and watch it glide away from Kirsten, hoping it wouldn't spill open in the process. That would be a bad note to leave on. A really bad note. Of course the chances of that happening were nearly impossible, but that's how people think when guilt is operating from deceitfulness.

The check-in went by smoothly, James showing his badge to the staff that took his bags just in case. He prayed they wouldn't say anything in front of Kirsten, that they wouldn't even check his bags. They didn't.

Now came the most difficult thing, saying goodbye. Though James had the foresight to know that once in Bermuda he wouldn't be so concerned with the distance between them, that he would be 100% focused on his brother, it still didn't help the awkwardness of the initial wave goodbye. It never sat well with him. He felt like one of those chocolate bunnies, the hollow ones that you eat at Easter. After all, he couldn't be too sure exactly what it was that he was getting himself into. Sure the little pieces of intelligence picked up here and there painted some kind of picture, but it was a very general picture. They could find his brother in the first few days and it could be a clean operation, or things could get very heated. The bad feelings that James told himself were unreasonable were starting to make more sense, and he wondered if he had misinterpreted them from the start. He had a quick thought flash through his mind tempting him to be reasonable and cancel his foolish mission, but James was beyond those thoughts now. He sat, higher than the intellectual argument, understanding all that reason was saying. It wasn't as if she had to convince him, looking at his wife he believed her now, knowing that he was probably doing something really stupid by leaving all that he ever wanted behind to go chase shadows in another reality. That's why there was no use entertaining those thoughts now; he had already made up his mind that he was going, whether it was reasonable or not. Yes, he had a very bad feeling about this, but it was too late to turn back now. He was Steve's only chance, and reason was going to have to take a walk for a little while.

"Okay, Sweetheart, I want you to be a good girl for mommy." He leaned forward and kissed his daughter's head. She hugged him in return.

The directions to board his flight came through the loud speaker and had a strange tense effect on James. He was suddenly in a situation from the past, yet present. It was a situation he was in when he was thirteen, and it involved a pit bull that happened to be chasing him. James ran to the edge of the river, a fifty foot drop before reaching the water and safety. He turned to see the pit bull bearing down on him. It was decision time. The reality of that split second hesitation hit him now as he debated one last time if he should go. Stay and let Steve die, or jump and hope I survive? The look in Kirsten's eyes was tipping the scales. She embraced him as hard as her large stomach would allow before pulling his head down and kissing him. James knew at that moment that he was crazy for leaving. "Look, Kirsten, if anything were to happen to me . . . "

She covered his lips with two fingers, and after a few seconds of awkward silence, she leaned forward and lightly kissed him. There was nothing else to say, the kiss had said it all. An entire conversation wouldn't be able to cover all the details of what their kiss communicated. Put simply, the message was: everything was going to be okay, I love you, I'll be praying for you, and you better come back to me.

"I love you." His lips brushed against hers one last time and his hand traced her stomach. And then he turned and left.

James turned, smiled, and waved to his family before disappearing down the boarding ramp.

Kirsten stood, arm around her daughter and hand on her stomach, as a tear escaped from the corner of her eye. The tear was a waterfall of scared emotion rushing over pores and microscopic hairs. The bad feeling she had about this trip suddenly hit reality's bulls-eye, and she could no longer pretend. The tear was proof of her fearful feelings. In that split second, she knew that she might never see her husband on this earth again.

Another page was turned, and the new number in the top left corner of the page read 43. Fifty pages had been turned since he started reading. For some reason, some books count the index, publishing information, copy right materials, and blank pages as part of the total page count for the book. This book was one of them. Finishing the first paragraph on the new page, James looked up from his book in an attempt to relax his eyes. The theology of angels was an area that had not received much of James' attention, and he wondered if he had ever studied the subject before. If so, it had been a while ago. Demons . . . He had heard many a sermon on those hellish creatures, yet the teachers liked to attribute names to those demons that James had yet to find in this book. "The Demon of Wealth, or of Sickness, or of Lust, or of Sneezing." James had heard them all before, and, with those names, it was too easy for him to simply laugh at this un-seeable enemy. But this book was different. It used Scripture to enforce its statements, and, as of yet, the author had not mentioned any of those silly names. In fact, the demons described by the Bible and interpreted by this author were not as laughable as those granted silly names- if laughable at all. Instead, a strange reality was starting to sink in as he read over Bible verses discussing those warriors that fought in the spiritual realm.

A pocket of turbulence rocked the plane just enough to make James look out the window. He wiped the condensation off of the cold transparent surface, trying to assess his outside environment. He was shocked at the density in which the clouds were gathered around the plane. The person that was sitting next to him leaned over to look at this as well.

"Looks like we aren't rid of that rain yet." The older woman looked to be in her mid seventies, and James wondered if her skin could even handle an atmosphere like Bermuda's. He also wondered if he would be able to ignore the sounds that kept coming from her nose.

"No, it doesn't look that way." James was trying to be polite, though the woman leaning over him so that his face was smashed into her perfume soaked sweater tempted him to open the window. The mental picture of the old lady being sucked out the window made James chuckle. She mistook it for something else.

"How old are you, Son?"

James didn't like the devilish grin that she was sporting and asked, "Why?"

She began to move her shoulders in a sexy way- sexy if she had been fifty years younger. "You want to party with me in Bermuda?"

James covered his mouth and turned to face the window. "Oh my goodness."

Hands grabbed his shoulders and tried to move them back and forth in unison to the beat she was humming.

"Look," James put both of his hands up but didn't know what to say.

"You are one handsome devil!" She batted her eyes at him.

"Excuse me." Trying not to crush her fragile legs or even to touch her legs, James made his way into the isle. Just as he began walking to the bathroom, the seatbelt sign lit up and a stewardess blocked his path.

"Sir, you are going to have to return to your seat."

"I need to use the restroom."

"I'm sorry, Sir. The captain wishes that everyone remain seated for the next few minutes."

"Look, help me out here." He nodded towards his seat and the stewardess was able to see the old lady watching them and blowing kisses to James. Her smile was a blend of sympathy and amusement, but neither was enough to change her mind. James made his way back to his seat, watching the old lady light up the closer he came. "Lord, I don't think this is funny . . . " Just then the plane dropped a few feet and the lights flickered. Now the captain's voice came over the speaker commanding everyone to stay in his or her seat. Glancing at his watch, James hoped that the next hour would go by much faster than the last ten minutes.

Ignoring the old woman proved to be one of the most challenging things he had ever attempted to do. Though his eyes were closed and he was thinking about his family and the upcoming uncertainty concerning his brother, the sounds coming from the seat next to him were tearing apart his brain. The fact that he could feel her eyes set on him did little to sustain any little amount of comfort that survived the obnoxious noises. The smell of her strong perfume was like leftover torment. The flight was only two hours long, give or take a few minutes, but he could have been on a plane to Germany for all he knew.

The plane started to descend, James' stomach testifying to that fact. He wasn't sure if he wanted to risk opening his eyes or not. The old lady thought he was asleep, and if he looked out the window she might see that he wasn't. He decided to risk it and quickly opened his eyes. But the only thing he could see was the old lady's face peering down at him. He screamed in horrible surprise, his eyes growing horrifyingly wide as he tried to push himself through the back of his chair and away from her.

"Hello, Dear. You were sleeping like a log." There was that smile again.

His heart trying desperately to slow down, James clenched his teeth and looked out the window. "Psycho Granny . . . " He could see the blue ocean waters below and the tropical islands of Bermuda. Even from that altitude they were beautiful.

"So where are you staying?" asked the lady.

"Where are you staying?" James shot back, expecting the worst. He did not recognize the name she gave and this unfamiliarity relieved a sigh.

"I'm coming back on Saturday too."

"What?"

"I took the liberty of looking at your ticket while you were sleeping."

"You- you took that liberty did you?" Patience was making its way out of his reach.

"Yep. So if I don't see you under the sun, at least we can tell each other all about our trip."

"Oh, no."

"It must be fate, my Dear. I leave the same time you do."

"It must be that." Then he realized that it probably was. This test of patience, love, and sympathy was ready to make James beat the plane to the ground below. He realized that he had probably failed any test in the situation, but all he wanted to do was get away from it now. His wife and all his friends would have never let him live this one down, and he was grateful that none of them were present.

He continued to watch out the window as Bermuda came closer and closer, bringing with it a reality yet to be discovered.

:::: *Bermuda*

The two hours that it took to fly from New York to Bermuda was not enough to permit jet lag, yet James still found himself feeling a little disoriented in the midst of his new surroundings. If it weren't for the dark sunglasses, those lost feelings would have been evident to any passer-by who would take the time to notice. His huge army bag was thrown over his shoulder and across his chest, and his two arms held the suitcases off the ground. His short sleeve shirt wasn't hiding the form of his strength, and he caught a few people noticing. James smiled behind the secrecy of his shades. Some people use the darkened tint of the lens to hide what they look at: the girl walking away, the girl bending over, the girl swimming . . . it was a means to indulge in both curiosity and lust without appearing immodest or rude. But James liked that the tint hid his eyes for another reason. He liked that he could watch people watch him. Usually when two strangers make eye contact they quickly and awkwardly avert their eyes to the ground. But what if their stare was not met in return? James enjoyed observing the looks he received, mostly because those staring had no clue he was watching them. Did he like the looks he got? Sure he did, it was the most sincere compliment. As far as it being his pride or ego, James had decided that it was his humanity, that internal bent towards wanting to be closer to perfection. And though there were those who said his weight training was a vanity, others thanked him for saving their lives. It complimented his job- to be strong. There was nothing sexual about how he took those compliments, he couldn't care less about what any other female thought of him, but any gaze proved that he was nearer what he was striving for. Not that he worked out for appearance sake, far from it, but still . . . something was there.

He continued walking through the civil air terminal and towards customs. Along the way he met some more people that liked to stop and wallow in self-awareness to the exclusion of any other. He mentioned something to a man and a woman who suddenly stopped to make-out and cause at least five people behind them to bump in to each other. James almost tripped over their' suitcases, and he made sure that the couple knew so. But he flashed a charming smile as he walked away, easing the embarrassment of the couple while still reminding them of those around.

Finally standing in the customs' line, James looked through his brochure another time, trying to make sure he knew exactly where he was going. As the line drew shorter, so did the time between heartbeats. It sure had been a long time since he saw his friends, and an unrelenting excitement was beginning to remind him of that.

Feeling a hard and obnoxious push on his shoulder, James held his breath and turned to see what the problem was. The airport was packed with tourists, both coming and leaving. The chaos that loomed about made James itch for open air. Seeing the old woman from the plane standing next to him also made him itch for open air.

"Well, can you believe this?"

James stared away from her and simply stated, "No."

"Well, come on James, brighten up! We're on vacation!"

Bermuda was vibrant in very unique ways. The streets were small, sharing only two skinny lanes, pink and purple houses jutting out from behind green plant life spilling over chest-high, white, concrete walls. Palm trees swayed back and forth in the breeze, mopeds and motorcycles speeding past the 25 mile an hour speed limit. Taxis were parked all over, their drivers studying newspapers, waiting for a tourist to interrupt them and give them business. Immediately, one could see that tourism was Bermuda's greatest source of income. Souvenir shops and little cafés lined most of the streets near where tourists would be entering the island. The mood was laid back, relaxed. Boats tied to docks were drifting in the moving waters, visible from many parts of Bermuda's cities. It was a vacation heaven. Wave-runners moved back and forth through the wakes of cruise ships and tour boats while tropical birds and fish darted above and below.

The taxi pulled away from the curb, leaving the old lady to only wave desperately at the departing vehicle. She had come very close to sharing the cab with him, but James gave the driver an extra tip for leaving without her. James didn't bother to turn around and see her waving, and he hoped she wasn't chasing the cab. The next couple of minutes he took to relax, enjoying the scenery that passed by his open window. As the warm tropical air blew through his hair, he suddenly had to remind himself of why he was here in order to justify the moment. There was no point in feeling guilty about being in such a beautiful place when his time spent here would not be equally as beautiful. Focusing his attention to the driving and to the front of the car, he noticed the driver's eyes watching him from the other side of the rear-view mirror.

"Sir? Where to?"

"Oh, sorry. Southampton Princess Hotel."

The rear-view mirror showed the Bermuda native's white teeth through spread lips. "That is a good place. Very pretty."

It better be, James thought. It wasn't exactly cheap. "What's your name?" asked James.

The driver turned and looked back over his shoulder. He looked to be in his mid-forties, some white hair beginning to weave itself in with the black curls. His dark features mixed well with his native/British accent. "Hop. H-O-P."

James shook the outstretched hand. "I'm James."

"Nice to meet you, James." Hop nodded before turning his attention back to his driving.

A few seconds of silence went by in which James noticed a Bible sitting between the two front seats and a 'new-believer's guide' in the pouch on the backside of the driver's seat. "Are you a Christian?" James boldly asked.

Hop's eyes looked into the mirror. "Yes."

A smile spread across a curious face, and James added, "I was just noticing your Bible."

"It's the best book to read," stated Hop matter-of-factly.

"It sure is. I'm a Christian too."

"That's great. What denomination?"

"If you had to tag me as something, I'd say Baptist."

Hop frowned. "I'm Pentecostal."

James laughed. "You're still okay by me, Hop."

Some more silence passed along with the beautiful scenery.

"If you look to your left, you'll notice . . . "

The blue flag that was waving from the antenna attached to the car's hood told James that the car he was in was a bonnet- a cab driven by a tour guide. Suddenly, Hop's commentary became relentless, never slowing down or fading out. Hop wasn't like those tour guides back in the states that could drone on for hours just repeating boring facts while their demeanor revealed it the whole while; rather, this man talked with genuine emotion.

"The hotel you will be staying at is on a sixty-acre estate." He paused, indicating that he was about to ad lib from his script. "So what brings you to Bermuda, James?"

"My brother went missing . . . " He caught the sudden glance into the mirror made by Hop.

"So you come to find him? I wish you luck, James. It will not be easy."

"Why not?"

"Well, he could be anywhere. He could be on one of the many islands, or he could be-"

James cut him off. "Tell me about the crime down here."

A nervous laugh escaped from the driver's seat. "What do you mean, Friend?"

"How does it work down here? Drugs, money, girls . . . Who's in charge of all that?"

"You talking organized crime?"

"I'm talking gangs, cartels, or just very wealthy business men."

"I know what you are thinking, Friend. You are thinking that your brother was kidnapped by someone, yes?"

James nodded.

"That stuff is not normal here. Your brother is more likely to have gotten lost somewhere, or maybe he had an accident."

"But drug traffic can get pretty heavy down here, can't it?"

"Of course, Bermuda is the most expensive place in the world to buy cocaine. That fact alone draws many suppliers here."

"Didn't customs and police seized over 17 million dollars worth of drugs last year?"

"Much more than that, I would imagine. Over 11 million worth of cocaine was found on a plane in one instance."

"I imagine that some of the police down here are dirty."

"Quite an imagination you've got." He was shaking his head.

"Is cocaine the main drug?"

"Cocaine, cannabis, and heroin. Crack was big in '86."

"What about dope rocks?"

"Moon rocks? Bad news. If people were smart, they'd at least stay away from them."

"Why? What's the difference?"

"It's crack mixed with heroin sold for fifty bucks a hit. The effects are not pleasant, and people who think they're buying crack are not happy with the results. Many seek to get their money back and, of course, these can only be violent confrontations. It's rumored that moon rocks have taken off with the drug cartels in the states."

James knew all about that. It was a successful drug because it was doubly addictive. The crack created a psychological addiction while the heroin caused a physical addiction. Crack addicts were attracted to this because the heroin allowed them to calm down after the initial crack high and helped combat intense paranoia. "So who runs the drugs around here?"

"You want names? I don't think so, Friend. I can tell you where to meet them, but that's the best I can do. If you want my advice, stay away from the whole thing. It tends to get messy real quick."

"I'm only looking for my brother."

Hop sighed. "Look, most of the crime down here is centered around the tourists. Purse snatching, rape, theft . . . Why do you think that your brother may have been kidnapped by drug lords?"

James shrugged. He wasn't going to mention the ransom note. James wasn't too sure that drugs or money had anything to do with his brother being kidnapped, but he had to start somewhere.

"Your brother would never have been able to get into the company of any ring, not if he was just a tourist. Besides, those kinds of people don't kidnap buyers. If they have a problem with a buyer, they simply kill him."

The cab pulled over next to a curb that wrapped around a huge beautiful hotel. James leaned forward to pay Hop the price that was advertised on the meter, adding a little extra tip for a brother. "Thanks, Hop, it was a pleasure to meet you."

"Look, this guy may be able to help you." Hop handed him a piece of paper, and James quickly stuffed it into his pocket. "Take care of yourself, James. I will pray for you."

"Thanks." He closed the door, and the taxi pulled away and disappeared down the street.

The blue sky brushed atop the nine-story hotel and did much to create a pleasant welcome. The tropical breeze that blew through the nearby trees tugged comfortably at James' hair and his loose-fitting clothes. As he walked to the lobby, he took one quick look around. Though he couldn't see the ocean, he could hear it, and that sound alone was enough to get his mind off of his grim problems. On top of Bermuda's highest point, on one hundred lush acres, surrounded by ocean and bay, James absentmindedly began to plan his week around the beauty of his surroundings.

"Can I help you, Sir?"

In the short distance between the front desk and the main entrance, James somehow let his mind walk through whatever doors it opened. Daydreaming already and he hadn't even put down his luggage yet. The sudden sound of the man's voice was enough to bring James to attention, and he passed on his name.

"Sir, if you would follow that young man over there, he will show you to your room."

"Thank you." James made his way over to the young man who had just been pointed to.

"Hello, Sir." He reached for James' luggage, and James handed over his duffel bag. The boy then struggled towards the elevator, prompting James to follow.

The elevator door slid open, and James followed the boy out into the long hallway. Surrounded on both his left and right were two endless rows of doors. The numbers that identified the rooms, carefully placed on the pieces of wood that ensured privacy, were reaching into the four hundreds.

"How many rooms are in this hotel?" asked James, more or less for conversational purposes.

"Six hundred, Sir."

"Six hundred?" James played the surprised part, again for conversational purposes.

"That is correct, Sir. We have five junior suites, six honeymoon suites, two duplex suites, and two penthouse suites. Also, we have twelve one-bedroom suites and nine two-bedroom suites."

"So what suite am I in?"

The boy began walking slower and nervously looked at the key he was holding. "Sir, I'm sorry, but . . . "

James cut him off with a laugh. "I'm only joking." If only he could afford a suite. "So tell me about my room."

"Well, all the rooms have a private balcony with either an ocean or bay view."

"Sounds good, Sam."

The boy looked at James questioningly.

"Oh," James pointed to the boy's chest. "Your nametag."

The boy looked down at the tag, forgetting that he and his friend had switched nametags. "Right . . . "

The conversation had carried on long enough, and James was grateful when "Sam" opened a door and invited him in. Catching the number out of the corner of his eye as he passed the open door, he realized that he wasn't sure of where his friends were staying or how he'd find them. The muscles in James' arms cried out in relief as they let down the heavy suitcases. He flexed his arms a few times to keep them from stiffening while he surveyed his room.

"You have A/C, radio, TV, phone, private beach and beach club, six restaurants and bars, indoor and outdoor pools, golf course, eleven tennis courts, fitness center, and, if you're interested, a beauty salon."

Smiling, more from the mental picture created by the suggestion rather than by the actual suggestion itself, James shook his head. "No thanks."

"Sir, are you alone?"

Scanning the room with careful eyes, he replied, "I sure hope so."

"If you are interested, I have a friend that knows some beautiful women . . . "

James cut him off in mid sentence by holding up his ring finger. "No thanks, Sam."

"Sorry, Sir."

"James."

"Excuse me, Sir?"

"My name is James. You can call me James."

The boy flashed a smile. "Okay, James. You let me know if you need anything."

"Will do." James politely kicked him out by directing him to the door. As the boy passed through the doorway, James handed him a tip. "Thanks, Sam."

"Thank you, James!" He hurried down the hallway, anxious to count his tip but trained not to do so in public.

The door closed behind him, and the stillness that was sustaining the peaceful atmosphere in the room lulled him to the neatly made bed. But before falling victim to its clutches of comfort, he opened a window, allowing the sound of the ocean and its breeze to contribute to the comfortable atmosphere within his room.

The room had a very nice sober mood to it. The furniture was made up of light colors, as was the carpet. The walls were a darker shade of wood, huge windows with long cream-colored curtains in their midst. From his present position, lying on his back atop of the bed, he could see the blue ocean waters. The optical illusion made the sea level appear to be above his room's windows. The oceanic view was superb from his location, the highest point in Bermuda. Clouds hung gently above the still blue waters as the sunlight danced across both the sky and water. Closing his eyes only made him feel that much more present within the tropical islands. James was well aware of his imagination being provoked to wonder by the relaxing noise and air that traveled through the open window, but he was willing to be manipulated by the natural peace that was pulling him deeper and deeper into sleep. Lying spread eagle, the soft bed conforming to his weight and shape, relaxation had met its destination, arriving at the peak of such experience. The waves crashing against the shore of the private beach transported James to its location. Though he had yet to see the beach, his mind had no trouble painting the image for him and placing him there. Besides the occasional sound of a motorcycle or car passing on the street separating the hotel from the beach, the sounds were conducted perfectly in order with the shore program. Before long, he was floating on his back in the crystal clear waters, the sun warming his body, and the gentle waves massaging his back. Dreams- how real they could seem, especially when placed in certain environments or situations.

Drip. Drip. Drip . . . A pool of water collected in the leaf's center, though too much to be contained within the depression created by the weight of the water. Little droplets flowed from the center pool and to the tip of the leaf, the added weight bending it towards the ground. There the droplets hung on for dear life until gravity ultimately had its way and the drops of water plunged to the ground below. The dirt that covered the jungle's floor had long since been turned to mud, the constant rainfall transforming a world of dry stability into a flooded mess. Though this was nothing new in the Mekong, it was new to those American soldiers who were trying to establish any certain degree of normalcy within delta life. Wetness seemed to equal misery, discomfort, and lethargy. Though cold and wet, while taking a break from the normal patrols and missions, some were able to find the noises created by the rainfall peaceful and relaxing. The random pitter-patter of water smacking leaves and landing softly in the wet mud, the sound of the heightened delta rushing past their position, and the occasional rumble of thunder all played like music to the ears of a few.

Drip. Drip. Drip . . . Boom! The explosion interrupts the natural scene with such sudden and extreme contrast that the surprised American soldiers can only allow a short passing of time to elapse before moving to action. Those that are too shocked and remain stunned for too long are the victims of the second explosion, their blood spilled and mixed with the wet jungle floor. Gunfire erupts from many unseen positions and more confused soldiers fall to the ground. Few have the presence of mind to seek cover by diving into the mud, but those who do also manage to return fire, though insignificant compared to the amount of fire they are taking from the enemy. Water and mud splash high into the air as enemy bullets sink deep into the earth. Pieces of the jungle stream from the sky, broken and mangled, falling like rain. The American M-60 fires until the barrel is white-hot, mowing down jungle and hoping desperately to find the enemy it's hiding. The eighteen year-old firing the automatic weapon is shot through the head, and the relentless bombardment put forth by his weapon ceases as it falls to the ground along with him. Charlie would win this battle.

The mortar fire began, signaling the end of the American platoon. Trees, dirt, metal, and flesh are mixed together in the air as the explosions rock the position the American platoon had chosen to take a rest.

Dreams, how real they could seem . . .

Upon opening his eyes, James immediately realized two things. The first thing was registered more by his subconscious than any sense of awareness. The darkness that stained the air outside told him that he had been asleep for far longer than he had intended. The second realization was the more dominant one, for he found it staring him in the face and realized that it may have been the cause for him waking up in the first place. Leaning over him was a familiar face. It had been two years since James saw Joshua, and the sudden appearance made him doubt the reality of his presence. He squeezed his eyes shut and attempted to apply his mind to the situation. Dreams were very real to

James, and he wasn't certain if this was just an exceptionally real one. Joshua's lips were moving but nothing audible was transcribed, thus James believed he was still dreaming. He closed his eyes.

The force in which he was shaken erased the remaining cobwebs of fatigue and restored sense to his mind. James sat up, suddenly very awake, and shook Joshua's hand.

The next few minutes were moments in time that came very rare and at much expense. How two years could remind someone the value of a friendship . . .

An experience like this cannot be fit within the curves of letters or even the structures of sentences. Words were poor communicators for moments such as these. James looked around the table at his friends, wondering how he would attempt to describe how he felt. This was, no doubt, one of those 'had to be there' situations. The laughter and the smiles were the products of a happiness that had been void for far too long.

The restaurant in which they sat was in their hotel and was exceptionally pleasant. The atmosphere created was perfect and though none may have been cognizant of such awareness, the atmosphere did help the overall outcome of the scene.

Those who sat around James, the help he had summoned, were guys he had missed more than he realized until right now. Allowing his eyes to absorb the features of those who sat around him, James was pleased at how well they had taken care of themselves. Brian, John, Edward, Joshua, and Chris- what a group of guys . . . James knew Joshua from the Gulf war. Though Joshua was Special Forces and not a Marine, their paths had crossed and they became friends immediately. Their friendship lasted for only a couple of months before orders moved them in separate ways, but they met again once more before the war was over. That time, they saved each other's lives. After the war, the friendship was kept alive through annual visits, frequent mail, and telephone conversations. Joshua was one of the toughest men James had ever met, the kind of guy that you'd expect to dry shave with a hunting knife or kick box with broken feet. This SEAL was still in perfect shape, every muscle in his body ready to erupt into action if the situation called for it. He was a quiet man, confident in his abilities and reasoning; he had nothing to prove to anyone. Very intelligent, Joshua could have done many other things with his life, but his mental and physical toughness had always pointed him in the direction of the armed forces. He was one of those guys that James was afraid of becoming, though strangely enough, he found himself admiring Joshua for it.

Chris was a fellow Marine who served with James the entire length of his armed forces career. The two of them had been through a lot, had even gone through boot camp together. Fighting back to back and trusting each other with their lives had rooted their friendship deeper than most earthly friendships could grow. Chris had stayed in the Marines for seven more years so communication was not always consistent between them until he retired from the Marine Corps and moved back home to New Jersey. He was now head of security for a major corporation that was paying him a figure that reflected the success of that corporation. Chris was the same age as James and was still in just as good shape. He looked excited for some old school action with James and Joshua. And it was action that he thrived on. His time in the Marines, though very professional, some called haphazard. He seemed to be very happy, though James thought he saw a glimmer of hopelessness behind the excitement his face tried to sell. Fast women, fast cars, fast boats, dangerous climbs, dangerous jumps, intense clubbing . . . these seemed to be the things that provided amusement within Chris' life. The war years seemed to have had little effect on him, though he never did take danger seriously. He said he was 'living life to the fullest.' But James just thought of the U2 song, "Still haven't found what I'm looking for."

Then there was Brian, or as James had always called him, 'Uncle Brian.' Brian was 6' 3," black, and strong as an ox. In spite of his age, he was the best for the rescue job. It would not be the first time that he would rescue Steve. Brian was a Vietnam vet who had been in Steve's platoon. Though they never talked of Nam, James didn't have to guess to know that they had endured hell together, and when you passed through hell with your mind still intact, you were a warrior. When Steve finally came back from Vietnam, Brian was regular company and for a while was like another older brother to James. It had been some years now since James had seen Brian, but the difference in appearance was slim. Perhaps it was his big white smile that kept him looking young, but at the age of 52 he could pass as 35. Being with Brian again was like being reunited with family.

John was also in Steve's platoon and like family to James. Though John's appearance did not hide the transition of years, he still had that look in his eye. His hair was lined with gray, and he had lost a significant amount of the body he had prided himself in, but overall, he was still in pretty good shape. John had been the platoon leader in Vietnam, and the authority that came naturally to him then was still resonating from his face. His eyes were serious, even as the rest of his face was laughing. Those eyes had been responsible for detecting any possibility of danger in an environment that liked to totally conceal it. It was no surprise that the training carried, habitually, over into the rest of his life. His eyes also spoke of confidence, the confidence of a leader. That the look in his eyes hadn't changed indicated to James that what was behind those eyes hadn't changed either. In John's case, James knew of the tragedy he had endured since Vietnam. While he was fighting for his country, his fiancé was killed in a car accident. The loss could still be seen around his eyes. He had never married, never able to truly move on. It was hard to watch him those years ago, fighting the pain. Whenever there was a smile, it always seemed hollow and forced, the true source of what he used to smile about taken from him. He was successful in his business, working hard, taking his mind off his would-have-been wife.

Finally there was Edward, the jokester of the group. He had served with both Steve and James, his age splitting the difference between the two. He had only worked with Steve for a year or so and had climbed his way pretty high through the ranks by the time James had joined. Unlike the others, Edward had not kept in touch. There were a few written letters, but nothing more. His life was often too stressful for such relationships to last. He had gone through several divorces and a custody battle over his only child, coming from the first marriage. He worked hard, trying to ease the pain with keeping himself too busy to think of it. It was obvious that the years spent working away the memories had much affect on his mental and physical frame. And though his story was a sad one and he often wallowed in misery, he had always been a loving kind of guy, friendly, going out of his way to make someone happy. This often made him vulnerable, and he wasn't too good at foreseeing disappointment. He was one of those guys who "wore his heart on his sleeve." But he was smart too. His street smarts had saved the lives of his team more than once. If a grenade had been thrown in a friend's direction, Edward would be the first to jump on it. He was a true friend with a large heart and a street smart mentality. It was a shame that he had gone through such trial. Fighting in the last year of the Vietnam War, continuing to serve his country for many years after that, and then to be left by his wife, not only once, but three times . . . He was good at hiding it in public, but the eyes told all. At least, James thought, he was happy to be back together with some old friends.

"Yo! What are you doing? I'm allergic to this stuff!" The waitress looked confused as everyone else erupted in laughter. "That's not my dish! I could swell up like a puffer fish! You ever seen a puffer fish? They got those spiky things on them, it ain't pretty. I mean, could you see this gorgeous face swellin' up like that? It would be a crime, wouldn't it?" Edward was back to his old tricks again, and, as usual, everyone was laughing. Except the waitress, of course. The joke just happened to be on her. James did feel bad for the waitress, the confusion on her face begging for clarity, but seeing and hearing Edward up to his old tricks was like turning back time. For the length of the joke, they might as well have been back in the service, together out on a weekend night. For those two minutes, nothing seemed to have changed. But

James knew that the comedian act, though part of who Edward was, was also a cover-up for the pain he had.

"James?" Joshua leaned over and whispered in his ear.

"Yeah, Joshua?"

"You sure about these guys?" The question was sincere. Both Joshua and James had shared enough experiences where one person's un-preparedness got them into a lot of trouble.

James decided to just be honest. He whispered back, "I hope so."

Joshua smiled. "You know I love a challenge."

Though John, Ed, and Brian knew each other, and Joshua and Chris knew each other, the two groups seemed to have no difficulty in getting along together. The loud table attracted the eyes and ears of other tables that surrounded them in the dimly lit room. The stories of heroism and bravery were being recalled and were capturing the attention of all that were within earshot. Their table might as well have been under a spotlight and positioned on a stage, for they turned out to be the center of attention that evening in the Bermuda restaurant. That none of them were aware of this only added to the amusement of the scene.

When everyone was finished eating, James decided to steal the airtime. "Guys, I just want to thank you for coming down here to try to help me. I can't tell you how much it means to me."

Edward laughed. "Yeah! You really had to twist my arm! Free trip to Bermuda, a reunion with my brothers . . . " He looked at his hands as he tipped them as scales.

"Besides all that, we owe it to Steve." Brian managed a smile. "It's the least we can do."

Chris jumped in. "I may not know Steve, but I owe you, and if you need my help, then my help you have."

During the happy reunion, Joshua had noticed a man sitting, by himself, in the back of the restaurant who had been watching them since they sat down. But when the man's sudden desire to leave seemed to have been triggered by Brian and Chris' statements, Joshua knew that something was amiss. He slowly pushed his seat back, watching the man exit the room. "Excuse me for a second." He then walked across the room and out the doors that were still working on closing from the last person who had walked through them.

Joshua found himself standing outside of the hotel alone. The lights that surrounded the hotel helped much to illuminate the night around him, but he did not see the man whom he had followed. He ran around the corner of the building just in time to see the man from the restaurant speed off on a moped. Joshua suddenly realized that what James had asked for help in accomplishing was much bigger than even James was aware of.

FOUR

QUESTIONS

"What?" asked James.

They stood in the midst of James' dimly lit hotel room, both he and Joshua. After departing from the restaurant, the rest of the guys had gone off to enjoy either Bermuda or sleep, something that James had planned to partake of as well. Preventing this from occurring, Joshua had confronted James and asked to speak with him alone. James, in turn, offered Joshua coffee within the privacy of his hotel room.

The hot liquid that had long since been poured into hotel-provided mugs still sat cold and untouched. James was pacing around the room scratching his jaw, which was now shaded with stubble, his intense scowl indicating the seriousness of his thought.

"Look, I don't know for sure if there even is anything to this." Joshua tried to ease the paranoid response provoked by his observation made during their time spent at the restaurant.

"No, don't try to go back on your impression just to quiet me down." James stood still long enough to release a long breath of air his lungs had been holding and in a defeated manner offered, "I don't know what's going on." He scratched his forehead, the puckered brow on his face trying to help make sense of things. "So the guy sat watching us the whole time? Did he order anything?"

Joshua thought about it, searching his memory. "He had a drink or two, but I don't think he had anything to eat."

"And you're sure he just wasn't bored and found interest in our conversation?"

"Hey," he held up his hands in a defensive manner. "You're the one that told me not to go back on my impression."

"Yeah," he sighed. He trusted Joshua's observation and the deduction made from it- a practice that had proved healthy in time past. "That wouldn't explain why he suddenly left at the mention of my brother anyway."

Joshua eased himself into a chair that faced James, who was presently standing with arms crossed and gaze locked into the night. "James, we'll find your brother."

Looking down into the eyes of his old friend, he stated, "You don't think he's still alive."

Joshua shrugged. "No, I think he could be very alive. If the man in the restaurant is involved with your brother then . . . "

James cut him off and continued his thought, finding hope in the words that were formulated over his tongue. "Then perhaps my brother is alive. If they had just killed him and made his body disappear two months ago, then why would they even risk spying on us? The fact that they were spying on us only indicates their present occupation with Steve."

Joshua could only offer a shrug. "Could be. There's still too much to be discovered at this point. It could be any way."

"You're right." James sat into the chair that faced Joshua's and leaned his head back so that it was facing the ceiling. "You know, there is one thing that was discovered for sure tonight."

"What's that?"

"This is a lot more complicated than my brother just hitting his head and suffering from amnesia."

Joshua stood to his feet and walked to the door, stopping alongside of James long enough to rest a hand on his shoulder. "You knew that before you came." He paused in thought. "Can I see the ransom note?"

James answered with disgust. "I forgot it."

"You forgot the note?"

"Yeah, and I just hope that my wife doesn't find it."

Joshua's face suddenly grew concerned. "James, are you sure you know what you're doing? I mean, did you think of your wife and kid when you came up with this crazy plan?"

Only the sincerity in Joshua's eyes communicated the care that he had for his friend. James knew that Joshua was not married, and to him the thought of having a family and risking their welfare was probably seen as stupid and possibly ungrateful.

"I mean, I know Steve's your brother, but is all this worth trading the rest of your family for?"

These were the words that James found himself struggling with from the moment he stepped into the airport to leave his family. He could only answer, "Hopefully, I won't have to find out."

Pausing for a few seconds, partly in reflection and partly to allow for a transition in mood and subject, Joshua asked, "So no one else knows about the ransom note?"

James was tired, and the stress of the situation did not wed well with his fatigue. He just shook his head. "I knew that if I gave it over to the police or to the FBI or whoever, that they would maybe open an investigation, but they'd fail. I mean, in a month nobody has been able to come up with squat. After the case is left unsolved, they'd all know of my reason for coming down here and what I was planning on doing, including my wife. But if I do it this way, I'm able to get you guys and not have any eyes over our shoulders. If anything happens, then it can all be swept under the Bermuda carpet and left behind. Hopefully, we can avoid anyone ever even knowing of a kidnapping. We just bring my brother back after doing whatever it takes to free him. Also, the Feds probably would have urged me to pay the money, but I don't trust these people. I'm not giving them a cent. And if they won't give my brother back, we'll take him back." He yawned. "And the note also said not to tell anyone about it."

"It just doesn't make sense."

"I know." James managed to get to his feet.

"Well, tomorrow we begin to find puzzle pieces."

James yawned again, this time his eyes watering. "Tomorrow . . . "

Joshua walked over to James and wrapped his huge arms around him. "It's good to see you again, James."

And it was. James only wished the reunion had been under different circumstances. "I missed you."

Joshua released his hold and stepped back before again laying his hand on James' shoulder. "It's okay that we don't get the time we want to catch up. We all know why we're here. After the mission is accomplished, then, perhaps, we'll start thinking about getting all caught up."

"Thanks."

"James, we'll find your brother."

A tired nod sent Joshua to the door. "Goodnight, I'll see you tomorrow morning."

James was already headed to the bedroom.

"Hey James," Joshua stuck his head in the door before closing it completely. His eyes searched the room as to emphasize his words. "Keep an eye out will you. Places like this have a tendency to conceal the danger. Just watch your back." He then closed the door, leaving James to collapse into the clutches of scared confusion and his bed. The fact that Joshua had included a definite article in his sentence bothered him. Had he said, "Places like this have a tendency to conceal danger," he would have taken it as a simple warning: "There could be danger hiding here, so keep your eyes open." But he said,

"The danger" implying that it wasn't a question whether or not danger was present- it was, and it was concealed.

The phone was dropped onto the floor, James too tired to climb out of bed and replace it. Kirsten's voice had sounded exceptionally pleasurable, a complete contrast from his current unpleasant situation. A cool breeze blowing through the deserts of his mind, he longed to indulge within the snow-covered relief that being with her would bring. Home began to seem as if it were a mere dream that could only escape the cruel reality he sought to uncover, rather than the reality he had lived for so long. James Streen, after only his first night in Bermuda, lay on his back already wondering if he truly had the will to follow through with the search for his brother. Aware of this thought, he realized that things were going to be more difficult than foreseen. Wondering what he was thinking when he planned this mission and wondering why he thought it would be a success, he suddenly questioned what he was even doing here. Joshua's words, "Is it worth trading the rest of your family for?" echoed through his head, each time making his heart pound hard, giving the echoing words a terrible rhythm. It was a song that he did not want stuck in his head.

As he drifted into an uncomfortable sleep, his hand found the paper the taxi driver had given him, and plans for the morrow began forming and wedding the imagination as sleep offered its temporal relief.

Are demons the same fallen angels that were thrown from heaven along with Lucifer? The angelology book that rested within James' hands tried to settle that dispute. Looking up from the heavy pages to allow some free thought form into the beginning stages of an opinion, James imagined what it would be like to be able to see into that spiritual realm. The beauty of tropical Bermuda would, no doubt, do little to hide the horror of the demonic forces that raged in the unseen. James figured he would probably have a heart attack if subjected to that awful scene. After the imagination was through toying with the facts just read, his eyes retreated from the morning sun and the waters beneath it and settled again onto the printed words contained in his book.

The clock read 7:14 am. Previously established were plans to meet up with Joshua at 8:30 in the lobby. An early morning phone call had succeeded in arranging a meeting with the taxi driver's friend who was boasted to have information. James would take Joshua alone to this meeting. He left the others with instructions to go down to the beach or something, and that provoked no strong argument from any of them. James and Joshua would meet up with the rest of the guys over lunch, where they would discuss their findings and theories. After lunch, the search was to become exhaustive and the lone priority for all who were there on the search. After all, James only had a week.

Finishing the mug of coffee and closing the book after completing a chapter, James made his way to the bathroom, stretching along the way. The shower's hot water steamed the air as it splashed against his face, serving to wash away any remaining cobwebs of fatigue. While James stood under the falling water, he offered up a prayer. His prayer echoed the same words he had been offering for the last month- for wisdom, safety, and success in finding his brother. If Joshua was right about the previous night, then the situation could be more dangerous than James was aware. Hoping that he didn't invite his friends here to die, James prayed for them as well.

James and Joshua split up even before entering the bar, the location of their meeting established by the person who was to sell information. It was due to this fact that Joshua had entered the bar ten minutes before James and quickly began studying every person within the dimly lit room. Every sound, every facial expression, and every movement registered within his mind. Because of the event he had witnessed the previous night, Joshua did not trust anything about this meeting. He wanted to be sure that James wasn't being played the fool. Taking a seat in the back corner of the room, he ordered a drink. Though he was concentrating all of his attention on those within the room, he was able to notice the cool breeze generated from the ceiling fan that hung above him. The cold drink that he ordered also helped to defend his body against the attacking heat that sought to enclose him. By habit, Joshua could categorize everyone that was within the bar into two groups: threatening and harmless. The facts that he observed about each person were such things as body weight, attitude, composure, and even style of clothing. All these things mixed together and helped Joshua to quickly formulate profiles on every person in the bar. Of course, he could not always be right.

Joshua's eyes settled on James as he entered through the doors. James looked around the room but made careful effort not to let his eyes settle on Joshua. With eyes that missed little or nothing, Joshua took in every person's response to James' entrance. Searching for any sign of intent aimed at his friend, he concluded that James had been received as a tourist and nothing more. Now he was to find out whom this 'contact' was that they were to gain information from, and perhaps he could learn a thing or two about him from afar.

Unknown to Joshua, there was a man who was much better at this game than he sitting across the room. The man had already picked up on Joshua's presence, and he continued to watch him closely as he read a magazine and worked on a drink. Unlike Joshua, this man had been there for almost an hour. His cover was already perfectly established due to the level of alcohol consumption he had endured. The amount of consumption was just enough to make obvious its effect. Joshua's eyes had swept over him, and he was processed and categorized with the rest of the bar's normal occupants. Camouflage.

As James walked through the bar, he passed tables of talking men, mostly men with a degree of sunburn. No doubt it was the discomfort that kept them from the tropical shores and the sight of much female skin. This fact was quickly discovered to be true as conversation from a few tables fluttered past James' ears. How sad it was to see so many lives reduced to vain pleasures. No sense of reality or truth would settle within those drunken brains any time soon. Continuing to move through the bar, James waited for his contact to spot him and wave him over. As he reached the bar, avoiding the stare of the bartender and thus letting him know he was there for one reason only, his sight caught hold of a raised hand. He redirected his composed steps to intercept the man who had signaled him. The appearance of the man became clearer as James closed the distance between them. He was a younger man, probably in his mid-twenties, his clothes nice- almost business like, and his face was stern. As James sat beside the man, he looked into his eyes.

Looking into his eyes transferred a lot of information. The well-known saying, "The eyes are the windows to the soul" was true in many a case, and James was sure it was true in this instance as well. Noticing the man's bored eyes and set jaw, James was able to determine the man's normal exposure to such situations. If the man was nervous or excited, it did not show.

"So you're looking for information, my friend?" The man's voice was dressed intriguingly well with an accent one would expect from the British island, it was also calm and contained a hint of confidence, the kind of confidence that was backed by a certain degree of power. James knew that kind of confidence all too well. He had seen it in enemy soldiers, mob bosses, and even within himself. It stemmed from an immortal mindset, the feeling that you were too powerful to be touched and that everyone else had only reason to fear you. That this man was so young was reason to believe his confidence was built upon quick success. The kind of quick success that yielded that kind of confidence and power was usually illegal success. The man's mannerisms were that of a confident businessman, yet with the cold power of a money collector.

James had no great trouble matching the man's demeanor. Though it meant nothing in the grand scheme of things, there was a measure of confidence, not to be helped, that had been born from the training he had received while serving his country within the armed forces. Even in the midst of this man's portrayal of confidence and power, James did not find his present situation intimidating. If need be, he was fully aware of his ability to quickly kill the man with his own bare hands. The only thing that was threatening about the overall situation was the thought that this man represented a group of more powerful men. That would be a scenario that James would like to avoid. More men meant more money and more money meant more power and that usually led to lots of guns. He answered the man's question after he casually ordered a bottle of water. "Yes. Can you help me?"

The man lit a cigarette that dangled lazily from his lips. After exhaling the smoke into the warm atmosphere of the bar, he answered, "I can."

James found it amusing, the acting game that was taking place. The scene attempted to prove who was the baddest of the two. Who could display the most confidence and maintain a cool composure? It was all an act, James knew, but the fact that this man was playing the tough guy role did not sit well with him. There was something not right. "Why are you so sure that you can help me?"

The man's lazy eyes took their time in finding James' but when they did they offered a warning. "Don't play shrink with me. You want to know something, you ask me straight out." He took a long drag.

"All right." James leaned back on his chair and quickly surveyed the bar. He spotted Joshua in his peripheral vision as he continued to speak. "I want to know how it is that you're able to come by 'information.' What is it you're involved in that grants you access into otherwise restricted areas? In short, if you're sharing the same illegal positions with those I'm seeking to find out about, how I can possibly trust you?"

Looking around the bar, the man finally came to settle a testing stare on James. "I seem to be confusing the facts . . . was it I who came to you for information or was it you who came to me?" The boredom that was carried with the words impressed James. The man was either good at pretending, or he was a professional.

"You're right," James decided to meet the stare with his own. "You owe me nothing, but I would be a fool to simply take your words at face-value."

With that the man stood to his feet. "You don't like what you see at face-value? Then get your information somewhere else."

"Okay." James held up his hand, even more impressed. The fact that James was not needed and that there was business to be found elsewhere completely managed to remove the man from any sense of care concerning Steve, thus proving him as a business interest only. At least that was what the act was supposed to portray. "What's your name?"

The man sat back down, most likely feeling a sense of victory. That his bluff was not called only showed them both who really needed who. "You can call me Lance."

"Okay Lance, let me tell you why I'm here."

"You're looking for your brother. I already know this."

Not able to hide his look of surprise, James countered by taking a drink of his water.

"I know everything that happens around here."

"I'm impressed. So then you know what happened to him?"

"That's information that could get me killed. You better believe it's going to cost you something." *Ahh . . . the businessman emerges at last.*

"How much?" James didn't have that much to give, and he hoped the price named would be reasonable.

"Two hundred." He looked around the bar again.

James had a subconscious thought concerning the price named. Either this man was stupid or the information he was giving wasn't life threatening. No informant that James had ever heard of, especially one this businesslike, ever sold deadly information for a mere two hundred dollars.

Joshua watched from his table in the corner of the room as James handed the man some cash. He quickly scanned the bar but no one else seemed to notice the exchange. He continued to study the informant's facial expressions and mannerisms to determine if what he was saying could be taken as sincere.

Learning all that he needed to know, the man spying on Joshua stood to his feet. He noticed Joshua's eyes pick him up and follow after him as he staggered past James and Lance and out the door. However, while passing through the doorway, he glanced up into the mirror that hung fixed above the doorframe and could see Joshua return his focus back to the two men talking at the bar. The study had been completed undetected.

"Your brother, Mr. Streen, has gotten himself into much trouble with dangerous people. These people are not people to be taken lightly either. If you have come here yourself to save him, you might as well go home right now."

James brushed off the warning or the threat, whichever it was. "Keep talking. I want my money's worth."

"You see Mr. Streen, the rumor is that your brother tried to steal a large quantity of narcotics from a certain cartel . . . "

James cut him off. "Is he alive?"

The smoke that rose from the end of the cigarette seemed to rise in slow motion as Lance delayed his answer. "You're brother is alive, of course."

"Do you know where he is?"

"He's on one of Bermuda's islands. I'm not sure which. Many people talk, and many people will always say different things."

Not letting relief govern his choice of words, James continued to search for answers. "Why would a cartel keep my brother alive on an island? It doesn't make sense."

Lance stood to his feet to walk away. "I don't write the script, Mr. Streen. I just sell the information." With that he casually exited the bar, flicking his cigarette to the ground.

As Bermuda's beautiful scenery blurred past the left rear window of the taxi, by which James sat, he found it a complicated task to actually appreciate the paradise in light of the reality it shared. Things just weren't adding up to any logical sense, and the harder James tried to arrange the puzzle pieces, the farther the image got from becoming any kind of intellectual creation. His brother, to the best of his knowledge, would never do something so absurd. It was true that he had been deep into the world of drugs, but that was a long time ago. Not married, no kids, a pretty nice house, and a good government job (which took a lot of help from high-sitting friends); Steve didn't come off as one who would find himself involved with his past. Suddenly, that good government job struck a note with James. He was now an IRS agent, something that James had never placed into the equation. Perhaps this had something to do with the IRS, but if that were the case the U.S. would be all over this thing trying to find him. But stealing from a cartel? That wasn't Steve, and James didn't buy it. And since when did drug lords write ransom notes to the families of those caught stealing from them? This was the one thing that bothered James the most. He didn't care so much about the stories surrounding the reason for Steve's abduction; he was concerned with how he was going to get him back. The ransom note was only proving to interfere with that process. That was a piece that seemed to be as foreign to the rest of the puzzle as was the whole puzzle in comparison to that one piece. How all its distinct and separate parts could compliment the whole, working together to form the complete picture, James had no clue. Nothing seemed to make sense. Of course, James knew, the whole thing could be attributed to quick juvenile ideas. His brother could have been taken by some thugs and then held for ransom. It wouldn't be hard to get information out of Steve concerning those in his family who were most likely to get a hold of money. In fact, as James thought of it, perhaps that was the genius of Steve. Hoping against hope that James would be able to use his connections to either rescue him or pay the ransom, he would have given the men holding him James' name. At that realization, James wondered if he should have brought the ransom note to light within the scrutiny of investigators. The sudden panic that rose from his stomach was attributed to his belief that he had made a crucial mistake- a mistake that may cost more than anyone could afford to pay.

But another thought came just as quickly. If these were amateur criminals holding a hostage, why hadn't the local authorities or the FBI been able to find them? The fact that they were able to operate untraced indicated at least some level of professional skill. James could only pray that all would work out without human casualty. Feeling the effects of such thought pound against his skull, he forced himself to think of something else for a few seconds. Now traveling into the sight of his mind's eye was his family, and it was these thoughts that served to bring back some sense of awe to the scene outside of his window.

"James . . . " Joshua called him back to attention.

Sighing and pulling his eyes away from the window, James looked to his friend that was sitting beside him.

"Do you believe him?"

Turning to face the window again, he answered, "Well, like he said, I came to him. I guess I really don't have a choice."

"So what do you want to do now? Obviously we can't search each of Bermuda's islands."

"Yeah, I guess we need to find his captors. If they're the only ones who know where he is, then we need to get them to talk."

"That might take too much time. Somebody's got to know where he is, or at least what happened to him."

Choosing to ignore the last part of his friend's statement, James reached up and tapped the driver's shoulder. "Can you pull over up there?"

A look of confusion glazed Joshua's eyes. "You okay?"

James made a poor attempt at a grin. "Just hungry."

Exiting the tiny restaurant, the two Americans concentrated their efforts on waiving down a cab. As they waived down an on-coming taxi, intent on returning back to the hotel, James spotted a man that looked somewhat familiar to him, though he couldn't place why. The cab was now stopped alongside both Joshua and James, and Joshua had started to open the side door when he noticed James' diverted attention. "What is it?"

James began to walk towards the familiar face. "I know that guy." His voice did not hide his confusion. Joshua followed James, shutting the door and waiving the taxi driver off. The taxi left the curb and pursued another tourist.

Hop spotted James as they came nearer to him, making their way through a crowd of people. The look on Hop's face changed abruptly, a very serious expression and almost fear coloring his dark features. Walking quickly towards James, he closed the distance twice as fast. "My friend-"

James cut Hop off in mid sentence. "I talked to your friend," he blurted out.

"Oh good! Good!" Hop said, relief heavy in his accented voice. "I was hoping you had gotten the chance."

Puzzlement tainted James' keen eyes yet another time this day. "What are you talking about?"

"My friend was murdered." His eyes fell upon everyone that walked past him. The tourists were flooding this area of Southampton, probably on their way to an event that James was unaware of. For some reason, Hop must have suspected one of the tourists to be someone other than the tourist they were posing to be.

Shaking his head in response to the off-guard statement, James asked, "When?"

"Last night. He was killed in his house."

Joshua exchanged a troubled look with James. After tearing wide eyes from the stare of his friend, James was able to set them upon that of Hop's. "I called him last night to set up the meeting. I met with him an hour ago . . . " The people that were flocking past him managed to bump him a few times and their loud voices were coming off as obnoxious. Trying to think in the midst of that environment was proving to be far more than irritating, and it showed on his face.

"That's impossible. Who you met with was not my friend." He began to back-peddle away from James and Joshua, his eyes frantically searching his surroundings. "I'm sorry, Friends. You have more trouble than I would like to find out about. God go with you." With that he turned and ran into the crowds of tourists and shoppers.

Joshua's voice did little to hide his emotion. "James, 'our trouble' is beginning to look professional."

The confusion that had tainted James' face since he had arrived the previous day was now mixing with the beginning stages of worry. Both men stood in the center of the crowd hoping their stillness would provoke breakthrough ideas, and Joshua was the first to break their silence.

"Definitely not an amateur kidnapping."

Somehow, able to think through the recent course of events, James evidently had a slight revelation. He turned his gaze away from the crowds and the direction in which the man disappeared and looked to Joshua. "I have an idea."

Though it was mid-afternoon, the hotel room was significantly dark. The long shades that hung over the windows were positioned to prevent the sun's unyielding rays from filling the room. Using his fingers to separate the blinds, Joshua peeked out into the bright light, surveying the ground below. Brian was saying something to Edward from the center of the room, something about things being a bit bizarre. Though Joshua's brain picked up the conversation between the other five guys, his mind dismissed it as simple background noise. His mind was too busy trying to sort things out for himself. The reason he found himself looking out the window was due to the incident that had occurred the previous night at the restaurant. If they were indeed being spied on, which now seemed very plausible, then the spy obviously knew what they looked like. Joshua, being the one who closed the shades in the first place, did not want to grant the enemy, if an actual enemy at all, any easy surveillance opportunities.

As the conversation bore on from the room's center, James now filling the rest of the men in on recent events, Joshua was still finding himself distracted from the topic of conversation. There was something about the window that was drawing his mind away from all else. The feeling he couldn't shake, he realized, was the feeling of being watched. Hate usually was the word he used to describe such feelings- intolerable, distracting, and uncomfortable. After studying the ground below, he knew he had no evidence to support that feeling so he tried to let it go. He turned from the window, the shades snapping back into place as he removed his fingers, and walked to an empty chair in the midst of his conversing comrades.

James noticed the distraction in Joshua's eyes as he sat down across from him, and he knew exactly what Joshua was thinking. He kept talking, catching everyone else's expression, trying to attain a general consensus of feeling within those he brought to help. Surprisingly, there wasn't much of a response to the news of the previous night. They simply seemed to take that information in stride. However, when James told them of the events learned earlier that day, the response was a bit different.

"Say that again." Brian leaned forward as if it would help him grasp the reality of James' speech.

"The person that I met with today was posing as the informant he knew I was supposed to meet."

The room became silent as each person tried to figure out what that meant.

After an appropriate time of silence passed, Chris broke the hushed atmosphere with a question. "So what are the possibilities? What could Steve have gotten into?"

"Could this be IRS related?" asked John.

James honestly didn't think that it had anything to do with Steve's apparent kidnapping, but it was beginning to seem as if he was the only one who shared in that line of thought. "I didn't think so."

Edward asked, "Why not?"

Joshua leaned back into his chair, suddenly deep in thought. He hadn't known that Steve was in the IRS.

Running a hand through his gray hair, John tried to set things in some kind of order. "Steve works for the Federal government, comes down to the lovely islands of Bermuda and mysteriously disappears, and when his brother and some friends come down in search of him, they are spied on, a murder takes place, and-"

Joshua returned to his previous position of leaning foreword before interrupting John. "James, this could put a whole new spin on things. This could be a Federal case, even a conspiracy."

"Do you have the ransom note?" asked Chris.

James simply responded, "No."

"Can you fill us in on everything the note said?"

James began, "There's a deadline by which a certain amount of money must be dropped off at a certain location."

"The deadline?" asked Edward.

"Friday, four o' clock."

"And have you checked out the location yet?" asked Chris as his eyes went back and forth between James and Joshua.

James answered matter-of-factly, "No. I don't even have the money to pay the ransom. I have no intention of meeting these people's demands. I plan on being with my brother before the deadline even expires." That was news to them. They figured James would pay if they couldn't find him. The fact that he hadn't even brought the money seemed to put a little more pressure on their situation.

The faces that surrounded James were faces full of bewilderment. Each mind worked to make sense of the facts, to put them into some categorized alignment that led to a form of logic. But all were coming up far short.

"This is what I want to do," began James, breaking the silence of thought. "The man who sold me the information doesn't know that I'm onto his game. As far as he knows, I'm still in need of much information from this 'contact' that the taxi driver told me about. Since there are over a hundred islands that we would need to search before Friday, assuming the man was speaking the truth, we are left with nothing more to act on than what we came with.

"I want to set up another meeting with him, here. I want to make him take us to my brother." He looked around the room trying, through the darkness, to find a reaction.

"There could be more than one of them," offered Joshua.

"That's why I want it here. We'll set up an observation post, a sniper for worst case scenario, and when we grab the 'contact,' if others reveal themselves, we'll grab them too."

"It's the only way," Joshua sighed. "They're the only ones that may know where he is, we need them to take us to him."

James stood, walked out of the room and into the bedroom and returned with a phone in his hand. Before dialing the number he asked everyone, "Is everyone okay with this?"

Chris spoke for all. "We may not have a clue what the heck is going on around here, or what it is that Steve went and got himself into, but we're here to help him."

Brian, Edward, and John all nodded their consent. "He'd be here looking for us had the roles been reversed."

"Okay then." He dialed on the phone pad.

Once in a while reality can be seen naked, without the guises that hide it so well. The result of such events is often more than a mere mental revelation but almost a visible one as well. It's as if one's perspective of the world, viewed through a looking glass, is focused, the subject of reality being sharpened while all else is blurred away. It is during those brief times of clarity that things become certain. With the new pieces recently discovered, James was starting to see the whole of the puzzle. It was due to this new insight that James' visible view of the tropical environment around him seemed to change ever so slightly. In light of the truth that the tropics were holding, a new perspective had been discovered. For a brief second, Bermuda was no longer beautiful but seen as a mere mask only hiding its true identity. This place made good on concealing the evil that lived in its midst, its beauty blinding and distracting- like that pretty girl that happens to bump into a guy in a crowd and lock eyes with him, hypnotizing him with that beautiful look. Meanwhile he's just watching her walk away with his wallet. Remove the beauty of the location and the evil would surface as if it was New York City. The illusion had served to dull the senses to this present danger, and, for a split second, James was able to grasp a small degree of reality. He compared it to one's eyes being opened to the spiritual realm, an event he had recently decided he would not envy nor enjoy. Reality as he knew it was what was seen before him, but true reality comprised of more than what mere eyes could detect. Behind the fuss of everyday life, there raged an unseen war all around. That most people were ignorant of this war only complimented the comparison to his quick revelation. But just as quickly as the new perspective came, it was gone, leaving him to only reflect back to what he had learned. The knowledge, though, would not be as quickly forgotten as the experience which brought it about. But how hard it was, thought James as he looked up into the blue sky, to associate evil with such a beautiful place. As his mind ran through the island and its people, he recanted from some of his more harsh conclusions. Bermuda was nothing like New York City, most of her people warm and friendly, the environment relaxed and at ease. The crime was real, the drugs were real, the evil was real . . . but in comparison, the twenty-three mile long islands were a small taste of paradise when compared to major cities around the world.

The water rose and slapped him in the face again, washing away the deepness of his thought and bringing him to a more present disposition. James was kicking his feet to keep his head from sinking beneath the ocean's surface. The waves were a little rougher than normal, the rate in which he had to empty his mouth of salt water proving the fact. The tropical waters that surrounded Bermuda's some 180 islands (by definition, there were many islands in Bermuda, some of which were so small they'd be hard to spit on) were Atlantic waters, the same waters that touched New York. 650 miles from the coast of North Carolina, the fine coral sand that stretched pink across the beach amplified the differences between the east coast states and the British Isles. The vivid blue-green water, in which James swam, threatened to prove any other beach experience back home as unsatisfying both in time past and time future.

Water was an element that had amazed James since he learned to swim as a boy. When his mother took him to the public pool on the summer afternoons, James had found that he rather enjoyed swimming beneath the water's surface. While all the neighborhood kids splashed about the surface, wrestling and being whistled at by the pretty lifeguard, James would be seeing how long he could hold his breath at the bottom of the pool. This created somewhat of a problem for the lifeguard. After jumping in to save him on three different occasions, only to learn that he needed no saving, she decided to let him spend the whole day down there. Between keeping a watchful eye over all within the pool, to picking up the stares of the older boys, the young woman who sat up high in the white chair, lotioned skin sizzling in the sun, kept a careful eye on James. She would allow two minutes to pass from the time James dove beneath the water before she started to stand to her feet. Of course, James would always return to the surface for air as soon as she reached the bottom of the tall chair. She felt stupid for more than one reason, as she was well aware of the whistles and the eyes that followed her up and down the chair whenever James would test her judgment.

H20- water. It is the most abundant molecule in living organisms, thus essential for very life, and here James found himself swimming through it. The physical property of water was as complex to him as was space and time, yet because of its simplicity. How does one describe water- its taste, its feel? Here we have this clear, colorless liquid all over the planet that exists in huge expanses of land, falls from the sky, makes up close to 60% of our own body weight, and is absolutely essential for the survival of the planet. And this basic principal of life actually serves to cleanse us, cool us, refresh us, and entertain us as well as keep us alive. James had always considered himself strange for finding so much astonishment in water, but as his arms moved against the water that surrounded him and he shot forward, he knew why he loved it so. If he had the spare time, James would have taken up water ballet. Something about how he could make his body move- as if he were suspended in space. He dove beneath the surface and, with a few strong strokes, came to the ocean's floor.

It was another world beneath the water's surface. The sky of this world was not oxygen but water itself. It was within this liquid environment that everything seemed peaceful, still. Perhaps the feelings came from the amount of water in his ears; regardless, he decided that it was indeed more peaceful at the ocean's floor. Here, the trials of life, the hardships, all the stress that plagued mankind did not exist. There were only the colorful fish, the creatures that lived within the coral, and countless other oceanic life forms, some yet to even be discovered. Possibly, it was the simplicity of life within the water that attracted James, the casual crawl of a crab, the graceful gliding of the shark . . . Graceful, maybe that was the word he had been looking for. Water's performance was always naturally graceful. From the splashes to the crashing waves, from the waterfall to the brook, and from the rainfall to the raging river, there seemed to be a sort of graceful movement attributable only to water. On top of that, it seemed as though all that traveled through the wet world struck a perfect ten on the graceful performance charts.

James' head broke the surface, and though he wished he could stay longer among the fishes, reality taught him that he needed oxygen to keep alive. But that need was only met with as much time as it took to dive back beneath the rolling waves. Spreading his legs, he pushed down with his arms. The resistance moved him into a suspended position within the water world, and he reached out with his arms and, with powerful force, brought them back to his sides. As he shot forward from the great thrust of his arms, he brought his legs together so that he was in a pencil position. He then rotated his shoulders and let the rest of his body follow the turn. He twisted into a couple of complete rotations, trying to slide through the water as gracefully as possible. He had always been amazed at how well the fish were able to move and operate in water, how they could go from practically no movement whatsoever to what seemed like 100 miles an hour in no time at all. The way the stingrays could simply float through the water as if they were gliding among the clouds, the way the dolphins could turn and spin ever so gracefully . . .

There was but one pang of misplacement within the calmness of the Bermudan waters, one thing that did not sit well within the activities of James' mind. It was more of an absence rather than something present being amiss. If Kirsten, his wife, were along side of him, swimming in one of those bathing suits he had bought her the previous summer, especially that black one, then all would be perfect. The sudden thoughts of his wife brought with them the reality that existed on the other side of the water and his true reason for being there in the first place. Though he could swim all day with the tropical fish, searching for strange beautiful shells in the coral sand, and daydreaming about his wife, he knew that if he wanted to see her again on this earth and perhaps transfer some of his daydreaming into reality, he had better have a well-made plan for the next day.

His head broke the surface of the water, and his lungs gasped for air. Being there to meet him was the hot afternoon sun and a complimentary wave that managed to get much of itself within James' mouth. After recovering, James let himself float atop the water, hoping that he would not be some shark's lunch. The scene on Horseshoe Beach was post card material, the huge boulders looking like they were sporadically dropped from heaven. The rock formations that stretched into the water gave the beach a Robinson Crusoe feel to it, and the tree line behind it all helped. The area was void of humans, save the presence of James and his friends.

The beauty of creation . . . How wonderful it will be to finally see the Maker of such beauty, James thought. A sudden yell distracted his thoughts and directed them towards its source of origin. He should have figured that it would be Edward. He was running across the hot sand, waiving his hand frantically through the air, a crab swinging from it. Obviously, laughter began to erupt as Chris, Brian, and John fell to the sand in uncontrollable fits of amusement. It was a funny scene, a classic Edwardian scene. James remembered the story Steve used to tell of Edward in Vietnam, when he had come back from taking a leak in the woods with a huge snake around his shoulders. Edward hadn't detected the reptile's presence until he was standing in front of an audience of American soldiers. James had no trouble imagining the scene, and he laughed. He wondered, though, if the amusement was nervous amusement, or amusement that was aroused due to the unfriendly future. There were many times during the war that James found himself partying. There were girls, drinks, music, and a whole lot of laughter. But when the only thing that separates the party from the war is a thin wooden wall, the party is usually fueled by a subliminal fear of dying. And now, floating in the tropical Atlantic waters, James was wondering if the laughter he was witnessing was nervous or excited laughter.

A brush against his leg erased all thought of such an idea. Just as panic began to set in, Joshua's head broke the water's surface beside him.

"Hey," he was smiling, knowing that he scared his friend.

"Not funny," responded James. They both dove beneath the ocean's surface and enjoyed the little time that the future had forgotten to spend. In Vietnam, Steve used to call times like this, "change."

Joshua followed James back into the beach, where they would come up with a plan. *And,* thought Joshua within the confines of his own mind, *it had better be one real stinkin' good plan.*

It was late. James left the company of his friends to make a call to his wife. He was beginning to miss her a lot, especially in light of the mission he would be spearheading the next day. If anything went wrong, Mrs. Streen could easily find herself a widow, and that was a thought not very pleasant. James longed only to hold her, but for now, hearing her voice would have to do. He walked past the front desk on his way to the elevator before suddenly stopping in his tracks. He backed up a few steps and made his way back to the counter. "Excuse me," James tried to capture the attention of the person behind the counter. Though he never planned on even seeing the drop off point, he just decided that maybe he should at least know where it was- just in case. He was also suddenly curious. He asked the man behind the counter how to get to the location that was written on the ransom note he had received.

The man shrugged, a confused look on his face. "I'm sorry, Sir. Never heard of it."

"What do you mean?" James leaned onto the counter, his whole demeanor changing. Had he confused the name on the note? Not very likely, he knew.

"I never heard of those streets or the place."

"Well, is there anyone here that might know?"

The man disappeared through a door and was gone for a few seconds. He came back out with two other guys, all wearing the hotel's uniform. The taller one spoke up first. "Where is it you are looking for?"

"Lucy's on St. Stephen's street."

Both men shook their heads. "Sorry, Sir, no such place."

"Are you sure?"

The Bermudian flashed a patient smile. "Bermuda isn't that big, Friend. Those of us who live here know pretty much every street on the island and every place that sits along side of them. I am sorry."

James stepped away from the counter before slapping his hand on it. "Thanks." He tapped his hand a few times, his eyes set locked into the unseen, before continuing to the elevator. He overheard the three men talking as he walked away from them. One was laughing, "He must have gotten stood up." The words caught his ear and sunk into his heart like a stake. More like 'set up.'

The answering machine had picked up. James almost didn't recognize the voice that preceded the beep, even though it was his own. Another strange feeling swept through him as he found himself, once again, listening to himself . . . yet a different himself. The James that recorded the message on the answering machine in his house in New York, in which he lived with his wife and daughter, seemed so distant from the James that was now in Bermuda looking for his brother. It was as if there were two James,' one living the normal life back in New York, and one trapped in a bad mystery movie, only he knows he's trapped in a mystery movie and can't get out. He laughed at himself.

He sat in a chair looking out the window and into the night sky. He wasn't really looking, more like staring into nothingness, his brain running wild and untamed within his skull. He knew what the note had said, and the more he thought about it, the more he couldn't make sense of it . . . any of it. From the note itself, to the location it named not existing, to being spied on, and everything else that had happened during only his first two days in the tropical world. Well, whatever was going on, James would find out tomorrow- assuming that the mission was a success and that Lance was able to be captured and made to talk.

James sighed. What was he doing here? He adjusted his gaze to pick up his reflection in the window. He said to his reflection, "You're crazy."

FIVE

The Triangle

Crosshairs dissected the face of James Streen into four quadrants, the optical scope making a possible shot unbelievably accurate. Had the trigger been squeezed, the .308 Remington would have put a hole right through his head. But the rifle swung to the left a few inches and the crosshairs fell over Brian Smith's dark face. Brian was sitting at a table holding a magazine. With a slight dip of the wrist, the optical lens settled on the title of the magazine he was pretending to read.

Joshua continued to survey the ground below him with the sniper rifle; ever making sure the safety remained in the 'on' position. Fitted onto the barrel of the weapon was a silencer. Though the silencer would disrupt the perfect accuracy of the rifle (if it needed to be used), it was a must. The sudden panic that would be brought on by a shot ringing through the Bermudian sky was certainly not favorable. In retrospect, Joshua would have preferred darts to bullets, but there was no way he could have planned ahead for something like this. Bullets would have to be used, and people might have to die.

The scenario did not list up among his favorites, though he had been in much worse. Lance would only meet in a populated area- he wasn't dumb. James had already anticipated that. So, Joshua found himself aiming the Remington out of his hotel room's window and down at the pool and surrounding area which was crowded with innocent people and lots of witnesses. James wanted the plan to unfold at the hotel for a few reasons, one of which was so that they could get Lance into a hotel room as quickly as possible. Just grab him and drag him. The second reason was so that they could establish positions around the area, controlling it the whole while. At least that was the plan. The very reason Joshua was aiming through a high powered scope that sat fixed to a high powered rifle revealed the possibility of things carrying out a bit differently than planned. Joshua knew that if he had to pull the trigger, James and company would have to move fast to clear the scene before the police showed up. They had neither the time nor the affordability to get caught up in an investigation. Edward had a taxi waiting just in case things hit the fan and they needed to get away fast.

Joshua ultimately believed all would move smoothly, however he still had a feeling in his gut that disagreed with his conclusion. That feeling was whispering a message that what they were up against was a lot larger than what they were ready for. The feelings then flashed pictures of the man spying on them in the restaurant, and the image would not leave the shadows of his mind.

James looked at his watch and whispered to himself, "Two minutes late . . . " Perhaps Lance was just running late, but James doubted it. This was all a game, an act. Every gesture and every event was scripted to produce an effect desired by the actor. What message being late was supposed to send, James wasn't sure. Did Lance want him waiting on him, sweating a little bit, afraid that he might not show? Lance, no doubt, sought to amplify James' feeling of dependency on him- simply another act of 'who needed who.' James' thoughts were interrupted by a girl that walked close by him, flashing a warm smile among some other things, and he had to divert his eyes. As his eyes fled from the buffet of tan flesh, they came to settle on Chris, who was actually trying to pick up some women. James could tell that it was a sincere effort on the part of his friend, and he had trouble understanding the intelligence factor. True, very little of anything was taken seriously by Chris, and obviously this situation ranked with the less serious, but this time James had a sudden desire to discharge his Beretta into his friend's butt. He returned his eyes to their present uninterrupted position and found Lance walking towards his table. He was wearing tan khakis and a white polo shirt, the top few buttons opened so that all could see the silver that sparkled around his neck. He proudly walked through a group of people, his hand finding a hold on a woman's half-bare bottom. He continued walking, not looking back to the surprised face of the woman he had just sexually assaulted. If James were back in the states and not trying to maintain a cover, he would have *physically* assaulted the man who was approaching his table with such pride that it made him sick. With the new knowledge attained since their last meeting, James would have a much harder time maintaining his composure. He still wanted to get more information out of him, maybe get him to slip in his story. He then would stand up, everyone else coming out of position and circling the table, and they would escort Lance into the hotel.

Simple.

Joshua didn't miss the little encounter that James had with the near-naked girl as she walked by him, basically offering herself to him. He also didn't miss the fact that James willfully diverted his eyes from her and looked toward Chris. As strange as the thought even was to him, Joshua realized that he admired the commitment James just showed to his wife. Joshua was not so committed and found his scope following other things. But there was a sudden revelation that James was different than when Joshua had served with him, and strangely, Joshua suddenly felt guilty about his own actions. He let the woman walk out of his line of sight and instead found Lance making his way over to James. Joshua saw Lance's little move on the woman and her embarrassed reaction- or pleasant surprise- Joshua couldn't tell. He figured any girl wearing that skimpy of an outfit wanted that kind of attention, so while she may have showed embarrassment, inside she was probably gloating. However, that didn't excuse Lance's actions, and the arrogant smirk he wore on his face tempted Joshua to blow it off. He put the crosshairs over Lance's forehead as Lance sat down at the table across from James.

"50,000 dollars is a lot of money," remarked Lance as he settled into the chair facing James.

"Sometimes things are worth more than money." James tried to appear as relaxed as his enemy by folding his hands.

"And what is it that you think I can give you that's worth that much?"

The warm tropical air was complimented by a slight breeze as a few gray clouds began to move in front of the sun, casting a slight shadow over their table.

"The name of the island, the reason why he was taken, and by who."

Lance let his eyes follow a woman who walked by the table, again telling James that he owned the situation. Without taking his eyes off the woman he asked, "If you had to pick an answer to one of those questions, which answer would you pick?"

"Well," he started as he took a drink of water from his glass. "I already know who."

Lance's head spun back around so fast that he had trouble recovering. "Been that busy have we?"

James stared into his eyes, letting him squirm in the awkwardness.

Joshua lifted his eyes above the rifle, taking in the whole scene below him. The girls that Chris was trying to pick up so desperately had moved on to other interests, leaving Chris alone with only one woman whose attention he still had. Joshua looked back into the scope, bringing it around onto Chris and his new friend. The crosshairs rested over a whole lot of exposed skin, and

Joshua's feelings flashed a warning through his brain. Chris was talking to the same partially-dressed woman that had walked by James attempting to get his attention. Why that bothered Joshua, he could never explain, but he quickly looked over all the faces that were present below him and, not to his surprise, spotted another familiar face. The man that he had seen spying on them their first night in Bermuda, the same man he had seen speed off on the moped, was walking around in the crowd below drinking a beverage. It was the classical spy-counter spy scene, even down to the sunglasses that he was wearing. Joshua noticed a bulge in the back of his white pants, a bulge he knew to be a pistol.

"Great." His jaws moved slower, suddenly not caring about the mint flavored gum he was chewing. Any cover that had been established by Brian, Chris, and John was now shot, and the situation had just moved farther from their grasp of control.

The man wearing the shades was walking towards the back of James' chair, and Joshua cursed out loud in the solitude of his hotel room, the only connection between him and the scenario below being the high powered rifle he was aiming at the back of the approaching man's head. He tried to signal Brian by waving his hand, but Brian seemed to have already noticed the man approaching James' back.

There was no doubt that Chris liked what he was seeing. The girl in front of him was beautiful, and she was hardly wearing anything to hide the fact. He longed to give her his full undivided attention, and he found the temptation almost unbearable. So there was no surprise that Chris swore when Brian stood up- which was only supposed to happen if trouble was detected. The woman, in an effort to keep Chris' attention, suddenly reached foreword with both hands and grasped his head, pulling it to her own. She kissed him, and he undeniably loved it. But he was also aware that he was being played the fool. His hands being strategically placed by the seductress, Chris was not able to prevent the blow that dropped him to his knees. A man dressed as a waiter hit him in the back of the head while at the same time swinging a plastic lawn chair under him to catch his fall. The waiter quickly moved past Chris, continuing on as if nothing happened. The woman leaned foreword on the chair's arms, kissing Chris' unconscious lips. Nobody even noticed what had happened.

Except Joshua. His concern grew as the situation began to slip off their fingertips and into the enemy's will. He was surprised to say the least, now more certain that the opposition was nothing near amateur. True, the advantage was still theirs as long as Lance remained ignorant of their intent, but as he watched the ease at which Chris was so quickly taken out of the equation, he wondered how narrow that advantage was.

He switched the safety to the "off" position.

"My friend, if you want to play games with me, then I suggest you know what the game is that you're playing and how deadly it can be."

James smiled at the threat. "Do you want the money or not?"

"You think I'm joking?" Lance seemed to be growing annoyed.

"I think you're an idiot."

Lance paused and looked around, his face growing red. "You dare insult me? Mr. Streen, if you want to guarantee your brother's death, then by all means keep at it, because unless you know someone else that can help you, I'm all you've got, and I'm not sure you want to risk your last resort." He pushed his chair away from the table. "Forget it, Mr. Streen. Find him yourself." He stood to leave.

"Sit down," demanded James.

"Excuse me?"

James pulled his Beretta out of his pants and placed in on the table in front of him. "I said, sit down."

Lance was completely shocked to see James pull out a gun, and he frantically looked around for some sign of help. He noticed the man in the sunglasses making his way to James' back before sitting back down. "Mr. Streen, that is not necessary."

"Isn't it?"

Though neither John nor Brian witnessed Chris' attack, both found themselves quickly making their way to James. The man in the white suit wearing the sunglasses had attracted their attention, and it was clear his destination. Brian and John had little time to reach the man before he reached James, and they both knew he had a gun.

"Now I'm going to tell you what we're going to do," said James. He had Lance's full attention. "We're going to walk into the hotel where you're going to tell me exactly where my brother is, and then you're going to take me to him."

"Mr. Streen, I'll give you one chance to recant your most recent decision."

"My, we are confident aren't we?"

Lance smiled. "We both know that the gun is an idle threat since you wouldn't dare shoot me in a public place like this. Though you did rattle me a bit by the sudden change in direction, I'll give you that, the only thing that you've accomplished was to make matters worse for yourself."

Now it was James' turn to smile. "How confident would you feel if I told you there was a high powered rifle being aimed at your head right now?"

"Again, I'm the only one who knows where your brother is, so naturally, you would be killing your hopes of finding him while killing me."

"Clever. But nonetheless, you're coming with me."

"I don't think so. It was nice doing business with you, James."

For a split second his eyes focused on something behind James, and it did not go unnoticed. James turned just in time to see a man wearing white pull out a pistol and bring it up.

Joshua squeezed the trigger.

There wasn't enough time to evade the shot, and James was left with nothing else to do but to brace for the terrible feeling of hot lead piercing his body.

Time seemed as if it lost aspects of its property, slowing down enough to allow James to actually think of a hundred different things in that half-second moment of time. Thoughts of Kirsten, his daughter, brother, and even the friends he brought with him raced through his mind like lightning flashing through the sky. *So this is it?* He knew he would see God in glory, but he also foresaw Kirsten's reaction to the truth she would no doubt learn. But the painful feeling he was expecting never came. Instead, the man who was about to shoot him was shoved forward into the air, his chest releasing a shower of blood. The momentum that he had built up in his sprint caused him to fly head first some distance before landing awkward and twisted on the concrete, sliding forward a few more yards.

Had James enough time to stand and watch the man's white suit turn red and the concrete under him do the same, he would have realized the sudden turn taken by his sense of reality. But such time was not to be had, and he quickly turned his head away from the dead attacker and to Lance.

But he was gone.

Brian was in hot pursuit, chasing Lance through the labyrinth of recliners and plastic chairs that surrounded the pool, and by now he had to weave himself through screaming tourists as well. What little hope there was of catching the young man was beginning to fade as Lance seemed to be getting farther and farther away rather than closer. Even now his lungs were burning, and the cramp in his side threatened to double him over and drop him to the ground. But he kept on running.

The whole situation exploded and chaos erupted from the flames. Guys were pulling their girlfriends, mothers were dragging their children, and the only noise that was registering into James' brain was that of loud screaming. For some reason, screaming always took a situation and multiplied its stress amount ten fold, and James had to force himself not to react accordingly.

Calmly, but quickly, picking the Beretta up off the table and sticking it back into his jeans, James took off after John who was following hard after Brian in the pursuit of Lance. James was always fast, even from when he was in grade school he was known for his speed. He passed John with ease and came up just as quickly on Brian who looked like he was about to fall over. James' legs carried him past Brian and close to Lance who was taking a wider angle to the hotel than he was. Just as Lance reached for the door handle, James threw himself through the air and tackled him from behind. There was an explosion of glass as both he and Lance went through the glass door and slid across the hotel's marble floor. Their slide ended with showers of broken glass raining down all over them.

James was the first to recover, getting himself to his knees. Grabbing the silver chain hanging from Lance's neck, James pulled him up off the ground and threw a punch that sent Lance's head back into the hotel's marble floor where it bounced once before resting in unconsciousness.

Brain and John ran up beside James as he was getting to his feet.

"Come on, we gotta' move!" yelled John as he bent down to pick up Lance with Brian. They continued to drag Lance to the front doors and out to the waiting taxi.

"Yeah . . . " James stood in a daze, watching the tourists running around the lobby. Everything seemed to be in slow motion. The people that were coming into the hotel for the first time in a while had no idea what had happened, and only curious, paranoid eyes watched as Lance was drug out to the curb. But the sirens that could be heard in the distance told James that the situation was about to get much more complicated if they didn't get out of there now. He slowly began to walk towards the door, taking his eyes off the people whose lives he just introduced to fear and panicked confusion.

"James!"

James turned to see Joshua run off the elevator. His back was loaded with duffle bags, and his arms carrying the covered Remington.

"Come on James, let's go!" One of Joshua's bags hit James as he ran by, and it helped to snap his sense of reality out of the slower speed. He chased Joshua out of the hotel.

Edward opened the door so that Brian and John could throw Lance into the back of the taxi, which they did. Edward had all the luggage already loaded in the trunk and was waiting for exactly this moment. The frantic tourists, the confused employees, and the sound of sirens growing louder told Edward that things didn't go over as planned. He jumped into the middle seat, Brian, John, and Lance in the back, as Joshua came running over to the front passenger side of the mini-van like taxi. The taxi driver looked very confused and hesitant, even a bit scared, but the amount of money he was offered served to over-ride any thoughts of changing his mind.

James came running out onto the concrete just as Joshua jumped into the front seat, and everyone was yelling for him to hurry. But their cry for him to hustle changed into a cry of warning as they began pointing at something behind him. Catching the reason for their warning behind him in the taxi's window, James threw himself to the ground just in time to avoid being shot by the man who had knocked out Chris. The two shots that cracked Bermuda's peaceful skies harmlessly pierced the taxi's side, as James hit the ground pulling out his own pistol simultaneously. As he slid on his side, he brought his Beretta up and fired three shots- all of them striking the man wearing the waiter's outfit. He dropped to his knees before falling over, a look of disbelief on his face as his pistol fell from his lifeless hand. They always made that face when they realized they were about to enter a world they were never ready to consider before.

James ignored the splattered blood and dove through the door Edward was holding open from inside. "Go! Go!"

"Wait!" John was looking out the window and through the masses of people that were running and screaming. "Where's Chris?"

A few curses filled the atmosphere of the taxi, and the sirens could now be seen in the distance. The taxi driver looked anxiously at Joshua, wanting some kind of direction fast.

"We can't wait! He was knocked unconscious before anything even happened, he'll be fine! We gotta' go now!" screamed Joshua.

Just then a knock on the glass window captured everyone's attention.

"You weren't going to leave without me were you?" Chris stood beside the taxi smiling and rubbing his head. But the two bullets that suddenly whizzed by his head and cracked the window around him wiped the smile off his face and dropped him to his stomach. "Crap!" The girl that had seduced him was now shooting at him.

James didn't like shooting women, and the split second hesitation gave Joshua enough time to bring the Remington up to the passenger window. Finding the trigger through the bag's vinyl material, he shot through the taxi's window, and the bullet knocked the girl's left leg out from under her, and she landed hard on her face and chest- screaming in pain.

Chris struggled to his feet and stumbled to the door where James grabbed him and pulled him into the taxi as the driver floored the gas. The full taxi sped off the scene just as the police came skidding up in front of the hotel, their flashing lights washing over everything.

Eight people and luggage were cramped tight in the six person taxi that was racing down the small streets of Bermuda, dodging tourists on mopeds. "Well, this is working out quite nice," remarked Edward who was sitting next to Chris and James in the middle seat.

Brian looked at Chris. "Man, what the heck were you doing with that chick?"

Chris shook his head. "What? She couldn't help it. Just look at me."

Disgusted, mad, and yet slightly amused, he answered, "You're unbelievable."

James touched his head which had suddenly begun to hurt, and when he brought his hand down his fingers were wet with blood.

"You got a lot of glass in you," Joshua told him. And he did. Though he couldn't see it, the blood was running from his head, face, and neck. His hands were pretty cut up too.

James turned to get a glimpse of Lance who was sitting behind him. Lance had gone through the door first, so James expected him to be worse, but Lance looked to be unscathed. "Figures . . . "

The taxi driver cut a corner a little too sharp and the taxi went over the rounded curb. John yelled as his head smashed into the ceiling. "We are in a hurry, but it matters little if we aren't alive to arrive." The cab driver looked into the mirror. "Sorry, Sir, it's just that there are two cars that are chasing us. And I think that they would like to kill us all."

"What?" Everyone turned their heads to look out the back window, and, sure enough, two black cars were in hot pursuit.

"What the heck is going on?" screamed Brian. Chris echoed his confusion.

James put a new clip into his pistol.

The two black cars roared up close to the taxi, one of them carelessly taking out a girl riding a moped. Both the girl and the bike disappeared down a cliff that met the fringes of Horseshoe Beach below. As one of the cars got closer, a man leaning out the window opened fire with a sub-machine gun. Bullet holes lined the side of the taxi with metallic *ting* sounds and made sure everyone inside kept their heads down. The taxi driver put pressure on the brake and the car began to pass them in the opposite lane, he then slammed on the gas, turning the wheel hard right, and rammed the front of the taxi into the back left side of the car causing it to spin off to the outside of the road. The taxi took off past the spinning car.

The back window shattered and some bullets flew through the van and out the front windshield, breaking the rear-view mirror off and sending it flying through the van in the process. James tossed John his Beretta.

"Watch your ears," John said as he peeked over the back seat and began to aim through the broken glass. The black car was getting closer, and John waited until he could see the driver's face before firing. He fired four quick shots, all of them putting holes through the windshield. But the passenger's automatic sent John back down behind the seat.

"Hold on!" The taxi driver screamed even as he made the turn. The taxi screeched on the pavement, going way too fast, and came very close to going over the edge and into the ocean below. John aimed James' Beretta out the window and waited for the black car to come flying around the same corner. Sure enough, the car had taken the turn too fast and it struggled to stay on the road, its back tires actually sliding onto the dirt. John fired at the car, aiming for the front tires. It was as the car's front tires began to straighten that one of John's shots punctured the left tire. The car flipped over and rolled on its side and off the road. The speed at which it had been driving sent the car sliding right off the cliff.

The speed limit in Bermuda is 25 mph and James knew that going 70 on her roads was not a very wise action. Tourists weren't even allowed to drive cars because of Bermuda's road conditions: narrow, winding, and sharply twisting.

Joshua wasn't sure if he wanted to look out the window, and, as a pink bus came around the corner veering into their lane, he had made up his mind. The taxi driver turned the wheel to the left, trying to avoid the bus, but there wasn't much room on the left. The taxi's tires came close to the edge, and the bus just fit by. A few honks were exchanged before the taxi was back in its lane, resuming its illegal speed of 70 mph.

A few rain drops splashed against the windshield. James leaned up and placed a hand on the driver's shoulder. "It's okay, you can take it slower now."

But just as the driver released his foot on the gas, the remaining black car sped past them on the inside lane, shooting out all the side windows in its pass. The ominous black car then swerved hard in front of the taxi, getting out of the way of another on-coming bus. The taxi driver saw a man in the car's back seat aim a gun through the slightly tinted window, and he turned right into the opposite lane to avoid the stream of bullets that would have killed him. The rear of the taxi clipped the rear of the passing bus, and the driver struggled with the wheel to keep from spinning out and flipping over.

While the taxi driver was struggling trying to gain control of the van, the car pulled into the opposite lane, cutting off an on-coming car and some mopeds behind it. They all swerved into the next lane and were faced with the struggling taxi. The car turned hard left, trying to make it through the narrow gap between the black car and the taxi, but the gap closed too fast and the car's rear was hit by the front, right side of the taxi, spinning the car onto the side of the road and into the rock wall. The mopeds had even less options. One was hit head-on by the taxi, the driver being catapulted high into the air, another pulled off to the side and skidded into a guard rail, flipping its driver over the cliff, and two others were able to barely make it through the dangerous congestion.

James opened the sliding door on the side of the van as John tossed his Beretta back to him. James inserted a new clip and aimed it out the open door. Rain was beginning to fall at a steady pace, and he had to squint to keep it out of his eyes. The driver of the attacking car slammed on the brakes, and the van shot past the car, but James threw the door shut just as the car passed along side them and riddled the van with bullets once again.

"How much longer 'till we're there?" asked Joshua who was holding on for dear life. He wasn't used to driving on the wrong side of the road, much less on Bermudian roads in the rain, going 70 mph and dodging on-coming traffic with a rock wall to the right and the Atlantic a hundred feet below on the left.

"Five minutes at this speed," answered the driver.

The black car came along side of the van and rammed it, forcing its left tires onto the dirt and close to the edge. The driver struggled to keep the van on the road. He turned the wheel hard right and rammed the car in retaliation. James slid the door open just enough to aim his pistol at the car, but the car rammed them again and James was thrown backwards.

John reached over the back seat and opened one of the duffle bags they had brought. He pulled out an Uzi and fired it out of the broken window next to his back seat. James joined in the assault by firing seven consecutive shots at the car. At first it seemed as though the driver of the car was hit, the car swerving off the road and almost slamming into the rock wall, but it regained control and came right back at them.

The rain was falling even harder now, mixing with the oils on the road and making it slick. The clouds blocked the sunlight, and it was turning out to be a gloomy day all around.

The upcoming turn was a sudden turn around a yellow house protected by a concrete wall, a few trees behind it obstructing all view of anything that might be just around the bend. But the driver could see two faint beams of light bouncing off a thousand different rain drops, and he knew that a bus was coming around the corner. He slammed on the gas, forcing the ensuing car to keep up, bringing them both closer to the sharp turn. By the time the driver of the car saw the lights, it was too late. The taxi rammed it further into the opposite lane right before the bend. The struggling car tried to take the turn wide by slowing down and swerving back into the left lane behind the taxi, but the taxi driver slowed down too, and the car hit the taxi, just bouncing further into the lane of on-coming traffic. It was trapped, no where for it to go. It went around the corner simultaneously with the bus, and there was no time to do anything but slam on the brakes- which did nothing on the wet concrete. The car slid, the driver managing to turn it sideways, straight into the face of the on-coming bus. The bus was only going about 15 miles an hour around the corner, but the car had been going much faster and it was destroyed by the impact. Even after the bus stopped, the car was still fastened to its broken front. The taxi continued on its course.

Innocent casualties were something that most of the men were familiar with, but in this case, it seemed a bit harder to swallow than in times past. James could only hope that his brother's life was worth the exchange, as feelings of guilt tugged at his innards while the taxi fled from the carnage and to the waiting plane. "Forgive me," he muttered.

The taxi was quiet; each person in his own world of thought, attempting to break down the last half hour in his own way. It was almost too much for them to swallow, simply because the reality of it had a hard time finding grasp without reason as its hands. The taxi driver slowed down and continued cautiously through the rain.

"Are you okay?" Joshua asked the driver.

The driver looked over to Joshua. "I'm alive. I don't know how much longer I'll be alive, but I'm alive now."

"Do you know who those people were?"

"Not for sure, no. I could take a few guesses, but I don't know for sure. It seems to me though, that you really upset them. What did you do?"

"I guess we stepped into their bees wax."

The skinny taxi driver obviously didn't get the 1st grade meaning.

Edward was surprised at how well the taxi driver was holding up, astonished actually. And Edward had to admit to himself, the taxi driver from Bermuda was actually holding up better than he was. He was trying to mask his fear and uncertainty, but how good of a job he was doing he wasn't sure. It had been a long time since he was involved in something as dangerous and mysterious as these last few days. Not since Vietnam did he have no clue what to do, where to look, what direction the next gunshot would come from, or even why . . . why anything. He looked around the taxi at the others and wondered if he was the only one that was having these thoughts. James seemed concerned, his jaw set and his eyes serious. He was probably more concerned with finding his brother than with his own health. Edward next looked up at Joshua. Joshua looked confident, in control, a little shaken from the passenger seat's view of the previous action, but ready for what was next. Obviously, he was used to this sort of stuff; he looked to be in his element. Chris seemed okay, possibly trying to mask his fear by taking a light mood, unless he was actually having fun. John looked like he was trying to make sense of all this, trying to create a story line that would answer all the questions. Brian was looking around for more black cars. He looked more alert and expectant than scared. Edward sighed.

James heard him, and suddenly wished that he hadn't asked Edward to come. Not because Edward wasn't a help, but because of all he had gone through already. To invite him to more troubled mess just didn't seem fair. But perhaps, in the end, it would turn out for the good. James would have to wait and see and hope that the end would come soon.

"Where are you taking me? The sudden sound of Lance's voice attracted all other eyes.

James turned and looked him in the eye. "You're taking us to my brother, where do you think?"

"I told you, your brother is on an island."

"So you're going to take us to that island."

Lance answered, "You have no idea what you're getting yourself into."

Everyone had already figured that out. "So tell us."

Lance only averted his eyes to the window.

❧❧❧

The taxi pulled off the dirt road and onto the wet grass. Laid out in front of the short field was the Atlantic Ocean, its waters rougher than normal. Bobbing up and down in the water was a Dehavilland Beaver DHC-2, the seaplane's skis keeping the plane above the violent waters. Joshua had gone out for a while the previous night and had come back with keys to the plane. He wouldn't tell James how he got them, and James figured he probably didn't want to know.

The taxi doors opened and everyone piled out. Lance was handcuffed by John and pushed roughly towards the plane. Joshua, Brian, Chris, and Edward loaded themselves up with the gear and luggage and followed Lance.

"Thank you so much." James was handing the taxi driver a lot of money.

"No problem, Friend. I just hope you have better luck."

James shook his hand. "Listen-"

The taxi driver held up his hands, cutting him off. "Hey, whatever it is, it's none of my business. I got paid and those guys that were chasing us are most likely dead. The only thing is a beat up taxi and a few extra gray hairs."

James smiled. "Okay, I just don't want you to get the wrong impression about all this."

"Whatever. Like I said, your business. But if you're planning on flying somewhere, you better leave right now." He was looking up into the sky.

"Right, thanks." James turned and ran after the others who were loading into the plane already. He noticed the sky on his way to the seaplane, and it was getting significantly darker. The wind tugged at his clothes harder and harder, the rain mixing with his wounds and thinning out the blood, creating much more of it. He ran through the uncut grass that was being smashed against the ground by the same strong wind.

"You still remember how to fly this thing?" James asked Joshua as he was climbing in.

"You'd better hope so." Joshua was running through the checklist, preparing the DHC-2 for flight.

"You sit down." John pushed Lance down into a seat. "And stay there." Everyone strapped themselves in and prepared for the short flight.

As the engine came to life and the propellers started turning, Joshua look back over his shoulder to Lance. "So where are we going?"

Lance smirked. "I don't know."

After being seduced, shot at, and almost driven off the road into the ocean, Chris was beginning to lose his cool. He grabbed Lance by the collar and pushed him against the wall of the plane. "Listen, I'm sure that one of your buddies back there is still alive. So I want you to understand, you're not that important! If you don't tell us then we'll find someone that will."

Lance began to laugh, at least until Joshua turned around from the pilot's chair with a gun pointing at his face. "You know, I'm sort of hoping that you can't help us. I'd love to put a bullet between your legs."

"Yeah, right." Lance foolishly decided to play what he thought was a bluff, but without hesitation Joshua lowered the weapon and fired. Lance doubled over grabbing his leg and cursing. "You idiot! I'm going to kill you!"

Joshua shot him again, and he screamed some more. "Where are we going?" Lance spit the directions out between clenched teeth, and a few minutes later the plane was racing over the water. Joshua pulled back on the controls and the plane's skis slowly separated from the Atlantic Ocean. Seconds later, the islands of Bermuda were only a distant reality below.

The Beaver was cruising at 142 mph along the coordinates Lance had given them. James was sitting next to Joshua in the cockpit, everyone else behind them. "Why don't you try and see if you can find out what's going on."

It was a suggestion that didn't need to be made, but James nodded before turning around and facing Lance.

"As much as this doesn't make any sense to me, Lance, perhaps the thing that makes the least sense is why you sent me a ransom note demanding a certain amount of money be dropped off at a location that doesn't exist."

Lance looked up from his wounds. The two shots merely grazed his thigh and calf. "Yeah . . . "

James' eyebrows sunk closer to his eyes. "Yeah, what?"

Lance looked from the window to James. "Are you kidding me? Why would we write a ransom note?"

"I don't know! You tell me!" James was growing very impatient with the whole issue.

"I don't know what you're talking about!"

"What?"

Chris and John exchanged a glance as things just seemed to become more and more confusing. "Did you write a ransom note to James?" Chris screamed.

Lance shot an insulting look at Chris. "Shut up, Fool."

Chris lunged out of his chair and grabbed Lance by the neck, throwing him to what little floor there was inside the tiny plane. "If you don't tell us what the heck is going on, I'm going to kill you!"

James walked over and patted Chris on the back. "It's okay." Chris turned and sat back down next to Brian, giving Lance a look that said, '*I want to kill you*' in the process. They were *all* tired of searching for answers to questions that didn't make sense. They were all ready to know what was going on.

Lifting Lance back into his chair, James looked him in the eye. "You know nothing of a ransom note?"

"No. Do I look like some dumb kidnapper to you?"

"If you didn't write that note, then why did you expect us? You were waiting for us."

"We were told you were coming to look for your brother."

"By who?"

"I'm not sure, you'll have to ask my boss." Lance's tone was just a little sarcastic, and James slapped him for it.

"Somebody sent me a ransom note, which is the *only* reason why I'm here!"

"I don't know anything about a ransom note!"

"Then what do you want with my brother?"

"Your brother's an IRS agent! We couldn't have him connecting dots down here."

"What dots?"

"You name it. We have a nice little thing cooking here, and nobody's going to come down here and stick their nose into it. Especially some stupid American."

"Drugs?"

"No, when drugs get involved everything ends up a mess. Anyone who gets into drugs is . . . removed from the business. I guess you could think of us as an extension of your mafia, only without the publicity."

Just then there was a huge blast of lightning and an even larger crash of thunder. The small seaplane shook as rain pelted it without remorse.

John leaned up and looked out the canopy. "Where the heck did this come from?" A bolt of lightening cut through the air right in front of them.

Lance's lips spread into a grin at the sound of worry in John's voice. "It's only a mild thunderstorm."

Ignoring the comment, John asked Joshua, "Can you even see anything?"

"Not much, and it's getting worse. This is no thunderstorm."

"Speed, fetch, and time." Chris seemed to be talking to himself.

Chris won Brian's curiosity, and he asked, "What?"

Turning to face Brian, Chris answered. "The only things necessary for a storm to become a violent hurricane are speed, fetch, and time."

Edward's whine escaped from the plane's rear. "What? We're in a hurricane?"

"No, we're not in a hurricane," answered Lance.

Chris added, "We're in a meso-meteorological storm."

Edward looked confused. "Is that a bad thing?"

Turning his eyes to Lance, Chris answered, "Yes."

"Wonderful."

The plane shook violently and the lights flickered as another bolt of lightening and immediate thunder exploded in the stormy sky.

Joshua made eye contact with Lance. "We've been in the air for ten minutes. I don't see any islands."

"Just keep on course," Lance answered impatiently. He then added, "I can't believe you shot me. Twice."

"Why'd you take my brother to an island?" asked James.

Lance shrugged his shoulders. "I don't know. Usually we'd just kill him, especially if he was some jerk from the U.S. thinking he even has business being here."

"Like you killed the person I was supposed to meet for information."

"Yeah, but for some reason my boss didn't want your brother killed."

"So you stuck him on an uninhabited island?"

He laughed. "No, of course not, that would be too dramatic. The island is technically uninhabited, but not really. One of our centers of operation is housed there."

"So let me get all this straight. My brother comes down here poking his head around as an IRS agent. He's endangering your operations, your very way of life, so you have him thrown into some cell on an island that only you really know about. Then, I get this ransom note in the mail, two months after Steve disappeared, asking for a ransom, which nobody knows who wrote. So I call up some of my friends to help me go bring back my brother, only the people that took him are waiting for us. Why are they waiting for us? Because 'some guy' told them we were coming." He paused. "Does that sound about right?"

"Not entirely."

The plane shook again, and Joshua's visibility was approaching close to zero. "I don't know how much more we can take up here, James."

Lance looked at his watch and then looked out the window. "You should start your descent now." He looked at James, and, for the first time, James saw honesty in his eyes. "The place is heavily guarded. I don't know what you're planning, but I can guarantee you that they'll kill you all."

"We'll see."

"Start my descent to what?" asked Joshua.

"You should see the island down to your left."

"I don't see anything."

"It's there."

"There's nothing there!"

Lance leaned forward to see for himself. "Well, you must have flown off course."

"Hey, I flew the coordinates you gave me! Maybe we passed it."

"No, you can't just miss an island. We're not flying that high."

"We *are* in the Bermuda Triangle," said Edward.

A few amusing looks were shot his way.

"No, I'm serious. The 80th meridian runs right through the Triangle."

"The agonic line?" asked Lance.

Edward shook his head as thunder sounded. "Yeah, it's one of the two places in the world where true north and magnetic north are in perfect alignment."

Chris frowned. "And this is a bad thing?"

"In short," started Lance. "You can easily end up a few degrees off course."

"And it doesn't help that we're in an electrical storm." James studied the view from the cockpit. Lightening flashed and gave the clouds a silver outline, as the same light bounced off a million raindrops. There was suddenly a loud banging noise all over the plane.

"Hail." Edward was looking up at the ceiling.

"I've never had this problem before. It has to be induced by the storm." Lance looked to his left and out the window. It may as well have been night.

Joshua tapped the instruments with his finger, but they remained unmoved.

"What now?" Even as he asked, Brian was sent crashing into the side of the plane by a huge gust of wind.

After the recovery, Joshua answered, "Visibility is almost zero, we could get struck by lightning any second, we have no idea where we are . . . "

"Turn around," said Lance.

"But if the instruments are useless . . . "

"If you keep on this course, we'll run out of gas over the middle of the ocean."

The small seaplane made a wide turn and headed back in the direction it came.

"What's the name of the island?" James was thinking ahead now. Obviously they weren't going to get to the island today. His flight back to New York was in two days, and without the deadline for the ransom, he could work something out from New York- if he made it back onto solid ground.

"I can't tell you that."

"What?"

"I have family that they will kill without hesitation. I'm only thinking about them."

James exploded, "Were you thinking of *my* family when you took my brother?"

Lance's disposition had changed dramatically since his capture. He was not the arrogant, proud man gleaming with power that he was during the meetings with James. Now, he was just a man faced with an unknown future, evaluating the things that mattered the most to him. His heart was still black with evil, but it was being softened by reality's grip. Or, he could be one good actor. He was about to speak when another huge burst of wind shook the Beaver, almost flipping it end over end.

"What was that?" asked John.

"These winds must be fifty miles an hour!" exclaimed Chris.

Brian turned away from the window, his eyes wide. "That wasn't wind."

"What?" James looked out the window for a glimpse of whatever Brian saw.

This time they all saw it- a quick flash of lightening providing the light needed.

A face in the clouds was rushing towards the canopy. It was a face out of a nightmare, its mouth opened as if it were going to swallow the plane.

The second was over, and the sky turned black again.

"Tell me I'm not the only one who saw that." Chris' eyes were wide with horror.

"Oh no." Lance was looking out the window, and for some reason everyone turned towards him; perhaps because, for the first time, his voice was 100% honest. There was no acting in his voice this time. It was the first time during any of this that Lance sounded afraid.

Outside the seaplane and in the raging violence stood a twisting and weaving waterspout. It wiggled back and forth, pulling tons and tons of water from the ocean and carrying it straight into the clouds. It seemed to be moving towards the seaplane.

"Hold on!" Joshua fought with the controls, trying to evade the huge tornado.

"How can this be happening?" asked John to no one in particular.

"It's called the Devil's Triangle for a reason." Edward tightened his seatbelt as the plane shook more and more, threatening to simply fall apart and to the raging sea below.

Suddenly, another waterspout twisted up and into the sky. The two twisters seemed to be dancing across the water's surface, sliding back and forth, wiggling at their centers.

They looked to change direction and move away from the Beaver.

"That was close," breathed John.

"Yeah, but now we're completely lost," said Lance.

Then suddenly, the two waterspouts changed direction again and came straight at the seaplane. Joshua yelled as he pulled hard on the controls, but it was no use. The waterspout swallowed the Beaver and shot it straight into the sky, introducing it to a new world of chaos. The last thing anyone saw was the nightmarish face looking at them, and for some reason, they all knew things were only going to get worse.

SIX

When reality sleeps... and dreams

The streets were clear, except for the parked cars that lined the curb. Street lights glowed, depressing yellowish light being cast down onto the dark asphalt. It was a warm night in New York, and the sound of air conditioners could be heard humming from anywhere in the neighborhood. Most of the houses were dark, the late hour seeing everyone to sleep. Only a few midnight owls still moved about with a light on. All seemed normal on this New York night . . . and then a few cats darted from their comfortable positions and their favorite trash cans. They ran as far from that street as they could.

Kirsten was sound asleep, a comfortable expression painted across her face. The room was dark, the air conditioner humming soothingly, a music CD playing softly on repeat. It wasn't her normal habit to fall asleep to music, but it made James sleep better, and anything that made her feel like James was there would help her too. It's funny, the things people do for a familiar feeling. Her lips spread into a smile, her eyes still closed. One could only imagine the movie that played on the other side of her eye lids.

Something in the house crashed.

The loud noise was enough to bring Kirsten's consciousness nearer to reality. Though the sound did not cognitively register in her brain, the result of the noise still caused her to reach over for her husband. Her hand found his warm body, and her lips spread into a smile again- until the touch set her consciousness on fire. Something was wrong. Her hand probed the warm body of her husband, while her mind tried desperately to grasp the problem.

James was in Bermuda.

Her eyes snapped open. There was nothing there. She sat up in the darkness, staring at the empty bed beside her, still horrified. At first, she laughed at herself. But then she wondered why that would scare her in the first place . . . a dream about James sleeping next to her? Why would that make her sit up, horrified? Unless, it wasn't a dream. And the person wasn't James.

Crash! Something downstairs exploded with the sound of broken glass. Shaking, she jumped out of bed and picked up the phone.

It was dead.

A million horror movies that she had flooded her mind with as a teenager came rushing back for the first time in a long time. She dropped the phone and ran to the light switch.

Nothing happened.

She realized that the power must be out but then noticed the sound of both the air conditioner and her CD, which was skipping. Running to the chest that stood next to her bed, she fumbled through the drawer. She pulled out a small .22 pistol and made sure it was loaded. She then slowly made her way to the door of her bedroom and out into the dark hallway. The pistol wavered in her shaking hands, her wide eyes trying to see through the darkness.

Her feet began to move down the stairs, taking her closer to where she heard the noise. She moved quietly, too scared to breathe. Reaching the doorway of the kitchen, she stood still, listening for any kind of movement. She didn't hear anything.

She went in.

The room filled with light as soon as she hit the light switch, and her eyes darted to every corner of the room, but there was nothing broken or even out of place. *Then what was that noise?* She leaned against the wall, attempting to recover from the false alarm.

And then she heard more noise.

She walked back into the living room, this time noticing that the television was on. She laughed at herself again and walked over to the TV which was casting flickering light across the room. As she reached down to turn it off, a series of chills suddenly raced up her back.

The television wasn't on when she first came down. She wouldn't have had to try so hard to see into the darkness had there been light coming from the TV. She stood still for a long moment, afraid to move. Her eyes were locked on the old black and white movie that was playing. It was one of those classic shoot out scenes between the good cop, who was wearing the trench coat and a hat firing his six-shooter over some crates, and the mobster sporting a Tommy-gun. The angle changed and showed a close-up view of the cop's back as he was kneeling behind the crates.

The picture flickered a little, and Kirsten watched as James slowly turned his head around to face the camera. She would have screamed, but her voice disappeared somewhere in her stomach. The cop in the movie, her husband James, seemed to be looking straight at her. She fell on her knees and grabbed the television with both hands, trying to read his moving lips- he was talking to her. She turned the volume all the way up, but there was no noise.

She couldn't understand the message. Just then the picture cut back to the mobster who was firing the machine gun, but when the angle returned to the cop, it was still James Streen. The bullets from the Tommy-gun ripped through his body and the sound suddenly cut back in, the silent atmosphere exploding with the sound of loud machine gun fire. Kirsten screamed and jumped from the sudden sound and quickly fumbled through the buttons until finding the mute button. When she looked back at the screen, the actor playing the cop was lying dead behind the crates. But it wasn't James. Kirsten covered her head with her hands and began to cry. *What is going on?* She reached down and turned off the television, covering the room with darkness again. She stood and walked to the light switch. This time it worked, and light filled the room. She looked around, but, again, everything seemed normal.

"This is crazy." She went to turn the lights back out and go back to bed, but she noticed something on the light switch.

Blood.

She brought her hand up and noticed a drop of blood on her index finger. Slowly and cautiously her eyes went back to the television. And then, before she was even aware of it, her feet began moving her towards it. She looked at the 'on-off' button and could see some red liquid that seemed to be seeping from the cracks between the buttons. She ran her finger over it. And then the blood began to flow from every crack, little drops of blood also coming out of the screen and running down the picture. It was dripping onto the floor. Kirsten started to back away from the bleeding television and then turned away from it.

She bumped into somebody.

Standing in her living room and in front of her was a man. She screamed and pulled the trigger. The sound of the blast and the kickback caused her to blink, and in that small fraction of a second that it took her to blink, the man she had shot at was gone. Again, Kirsten Streen stood alone, everything around her seeming normal. The television was not bleeding, the lights were on, there was no blood on the light switch, and there was no man in her house. But there was a hole in her wall and a casing on the floor next to her feet. She ran up the stairs, praying out loud the whole time. After checking on her daughter, who was still asleep somehow, Kirsten walked back into her room. The lights were on, and her CD was not skipping. And yet, there was an indentation in the sheets next to where she slept- as if someone had been sleeping next to her.

Climbing back in bed, and leaving the light on, Kirsten tried to erase the image from her head- the image of the man who had been standing in her living room. Because the man she saw . . . was Steve Streen.

That bothered her.

II
POWERS AND PRINCIPALITIES

SEVEN
ARRIVAL

:::: *FIRST LIGHT*

The sun was almost fully visible now, most of its circle reaching above the water and creating sharp reflections on the ocean below. As if the ocean was a diamond come to life, it sparkled and gleamed from every angle as the morning light bounced from its surface. If it weren't for the early morning breeze that pushed ripples into the water, it would be hard to discern that the ocean wasn't, instead, a sea of glass.

There were few clouds invited to the birth of the new day, but those that were had been given a glorious welcome, the red glow that outlined them their honor. The morning was perfect. A painter or photographer could earn a living off of the scene if captured the exact way it appeared, for not a person in love with nature would be able to pass up such an image. It was awe inspiring to say the least. A few birds glided above the water, cutting through the still-life and offering some drama to the portrait. A few dolphins leaped from the water, their grace only adding to the completion as they blocked the rising sun in the background with their playing.

But something changed.

The birds suddenly stopped gliding together. They dispersed in chaotic fashion, beating their wings as hard as they could, flying to nowhere in particular. The graceful moves of the dolphins were replaced by agitated spasms as they began to swim hard out to sea. All of nature seemed to hold its breath.

A dark shadow appeared in the sky and began to move, erasing the beautiful colors. The shadow swept over creation, its origin too far away to be seen. There was nothing in the sky to block the sun's light, yet darkness consumed the sky. Night invaded the morning and slowly replaced it, as if it were black oil, alive and devouring the early day. As the shadow swept across the land, every living creature fled from its pursuit. Crabs scurried to the ocean, birds erupted from the jungle's trees, turtles pulled themselves into their shells, and fish dove deep into the ocean's depths. The darkness destroyed the perfect scene as if God had accidentally knocked over a bottle of black ink across His masterpiece. But God is not accident prone, and what was stretching through the morning sky was not of Him.

Salt water reached up onto the sand again, this time traveling further onto the dry earth. Chris Roberts lay unconscious in the sand, his face covered with seaweed. The strength of the ocean finally reached Chris, and salt water washed over his face and entered his nasal passage. He opened his eyes. Completely disoriented and only half conscious, Chris watched, his face still in the sand, as something made its way towards him. He blinked, trying to awaken his mind and senses, but nothing was clicking. The shadow swept over him, and he froze. Covered by darkness, he managed to turn his head in the other direction and could see five others sprawled unconscious along the shore line. In that direction was a beautiful sight indeed. The tropical sunrise, the warmth . . . But the same shadow that had swept over him continued to erase the fixating beauty. The darkness engulfed his unconscious friends one at a time and before long there was no light whatsoever. It was complete darkness, darker than the darkest night. Chris rolled onto his back and stared into the sky, but the sky was indistinguishable, and if it weren't for the feel of the ground beneath him, he would have no concept of any direction. Vertigo toyed with his senses until, at last, he was able to gain some of them back. And he quickly wished that he hadn't. Never in his life had he experienced such utter cold. He never imagined that anything could be colder than the icy water he fell into when he was only ten, the shock of it still chilling; but he was wrong. He had been so cold then that he could hardly breathe. But this new cold felt different, felt . . . evil. It wasn't an external coldness like he had experienced before. This harsh numbing feeling was inside him, as if a hand made of ice had reached inside and gripped his very being.

And though he was convinced that his eardrums were frozen with everything else in his body, they still managed to work. But the beats were making very little sense to his numb brain. What he thought he heard were a million different voices all speaking at the same time, in the same language, in a low whisper. And that noise, heard in total darkness, was not an inviting sound. He curled up into a ball and closed his eyes, hoping his heart would be able to continue beating despite the hand of ice that was squeezing it. He couldn't think, he couldn't move, he couldn't speak . . . but he could remember the face that came out of the sky and swallowed them all, and that memory seemed to be telling him more than he was able to understand or comprehend. He only knew that whatever it was, it was bad.

The whispering grew louder, and now he thought he could feel things moving past him. With all of his consciousness and might, he forced himself to reach out into the sand until his fingers brushed over a rock. With strength and awareness dying fast, he used what remained and smashed the rock into his head, sending him back into a world of dreams and ignorance. It was his only option to escape the knowledge of hell.

James Streen stumbled across the beach and through the shallow surf. It appeared to be mid-afternoon, the sun reigning high in the sky and its heat pulsating everything below it. Walking closer to his friends, he tried to ignore the pain that coursed through his legs with each step. He looked around, surprised that they were still alive, and wondered why he didn't see the seaplane anywhere, or at least pieces of it. "God . . . "

He collapsed next to Brian who looked pretty banged up. A long contusion traced his forehead, and he had some bruises on his neck. James gently shook him. "Brian." He called his name until Brian's eyes flickered open and his pupils retreated at the sudden light.

"What happened?" Brian's lips barely moved as he struggled to regain awareness.

James stood and began walking away from him and over to Joshua. "I'm not sure . . . "

Joshua lay flat on his back, his face red from sunburn, a clue as to how long they had been unconscious. He bent over and attempted to wake up Joshua.

Joshua came to his senses much faster and immediately sat upright. His eyes worked fast to take in all that was around him, but James could tell his mind had a little more trouble putting the sights and sounds to sense.

James slapped him on the back and went to wake up the others.

"So where's the plane?" asked Brian. With the surf in front of them and the nearby trees behind them, James, Joshua, Chris, John, Edward, and he stood together on the hot sand, trying to figure out where they were.

"And where's Lance?" asked John.

Edward looked out to the ocean. "Maybe he didn't make it."

"Doubt it. Those tracks are probably his." Joshua brought attention to a set of footprints that stretched from the shoreline into the jungle.

"Where do you think we are?" asked Edward to no one in particular.

"An island in the Atlantic, I guess. Where else could we be?" John then began to think a bit harder about his question.

"Wherever we are, I'd like to know how the heck we got here," added Brian.

Chris' voice seemed a little frightened, still shaken by his untold experience. "Did anyone else see that thing before we went into the spout?"

They all looked at each other, each in silence until, finally, they all agreed that they had seen it.

"What do you think it was?" asked Chris.

Nobody had any suggestions.

Joshua looked into the sky. "We probably have a few hours of daylight left, why don't we start walking. Maybe we can find the plane or at least find out where we are. Who knows, maybe this is a populated island."

As they all began to move along the beach, Chris looked into the jungle and muttered, "Somehow, I don't think so."

James asked Joshua, "Do you think we should follow Lance? Maybe he knows where we are. Why else would he head into the jungle?"

Joshua's gaze swept over the beach first then over the tree line. "Yeah, we can always walk the beach at night. If we're going to go into the jungle, I'd rather do it in daylight. This place bothers me."

"Second that," added John as he began walking to the tree line.

Lance's tracks seemed to go straight into the jungle, so that's where the team went after him. They walked through the tropical woods, John out in front just as he was in Vietnam. They had been walking for about half an hour before anyone said a word, each trying to compute their situation within the privacy of their own minds.

Brian broke the silence. "James, do you believe Lance?"

"About what?"

"About Steve being held on an island?"

"I don't know. Doesn't seem to matter much now, anyway."

Chris quickened his pace, bringing him up along side of James. "James. . . "

James didn't miss the tone in his voice. "Yeah?"

Chris lowered his voice. "There's something not right about this place."

"I know. I can feel it too."

"I saw something . . . "

James looked him in the eye, and there was definitely fear there. "What did you see?"

"I don't even know how to describe it. I woke up before anyone else, and I saw this black sheet being unrolled across the sky. Only it wasn't a sheet, it seemed more alive, like oil."

James nodded. "Could you have hallucinated from the trauma of the crash?"

"I would rather believe that. The sun was just about above the water; it looked beautiful, but then there was this darkness that came from nowhere, it started taking over everything. Every living thing fled from it, trying to get away from it. It swept over us." He paused. "I've never felt anything like it."

James wasn't exactly sure how to take the report, so he just nodded. "Hopefully, we can find a way out of here soon." He shook his head, "Don't tell anyone else."

Chris nodded, and concentrated on the woods around him.

"Hey, why haven't we seen any animals or anything?" asked Edward.

"I was wondering the same thing," said John.

"Maybe we're on one of those islands that the army uses to test bombs and stuff." Brian obviously didn't like his own idea. Experimentally, he tapped his fingertips on his wound and then winced.

"That'd be great," muttered Edward.

They continued walking.

"Can you hear that?" asked John. He stood in front of the line looking around.

"What?" asked Brian, suddenly concerned.

"Sounds like . . . I don't know."

Joshua walked past him. "Sounds like a canyon or a quarry up to the left."

John nodded. "Yeah, it does."

They followed Joshua to the source of the noise.

"What the heck?" They found themselves standing at the edge of a huge crater, the wind howling as it bounced off its walls.

"Can't even see the bottom," remarked James as he got down on all fours to take a closer look. It was true, the bottom of the hole was so deep that it was beyond the sun's reach.

"A bomb?" asked Brian.

John nodded. "Makes sense. Looks like we could be on government property after all."

"Restricted and forbidden government property," Chris added.

Joshua knelt down beside James. "They could be right, and if they are, who knows what we're being exposed to."

James seemed more concerned with the rock wall that stretched down into eternity. "No, I don't think this was a bomb." He ran his hand over the chipped rock. "Look, this was cut with tools."

"What?"

"I think you were right." He stood to his feet and looked at the huge crater. "Unless a meteor hit here, I'd say it is a quarry."

Joshua bent down to take a closer look. The rock did appear to be chipped away, maybe with an axe of some sort. He stroked the rock with his hand. "It's soft, easy to break."

"Well, we know someone's been here before."

Joshua studied the rock formation a bit harder. "Something's not right."

"What?"

"How wide would you say this is? Half a mile in diameter? At least?"

"Sure."

"This would be a pretty big task for the best machinery. Look at the walls, where the rock was cut. Usually, bulldozers and backhoes leave marks in the rock; you know, where the bucket's fingers scrape."

"You're right, there's nothing to indicate that this was made by any kind of machine." James looked towards Chris as he walked towards him.

"Strange . . . " Joshua stepped away from the hole, letting his eyes linger in its depths.

Chris patted James on the back. "We don't have much light left, we should get moving."

"Right."

They began walking again, getting deeper and deeper into the woods. Though unspoken, the quarry had left mixed emotions within them. And, once again, questions began to search for answers that were not yet attainable.

"I lost them!" John yelled in frustration. "They go through that stream over there, but I don't see where he came out."

James followed John's finger. "He could have followed the stream down for a while." He looked to Joshua. "What time is it?"

"I don't know, the stupid thing stopped working." He tapped the face of his watch.

"How 'bout you, Brian?"

"No, mine stopped too."

Curious, James surveyed everyone's wrists. "Does anyone have a watch that still works?"

They all shook their heads.

Chris asked the fearful question. "What time does everyone's watch read?"

"1:32," answered John.

"1:32," echoed Brian.

"1:33," said Edward.

Everyone else only nodded.

"What the heck does that mean?" asked Chris.

"It means that we aren't in Kansas anymore, Toto."

"Well, maybe the electrical storm had something to do with it," offered Brian.

"Or that face . . . " Chris was staring into nothingness.

James started walking again. "We aren't going to find Lance today. Let's get back to the beach before the sun sets."

As they followed their trail back to the beach, they talked among themselves, offering plausible answers to many of their questions, though not many of them were plausible.

"We were in the Bermuda Triangle when all this stuff started to happen." Everyone took the time to show Edward their feelings on that remark. "What? Have you got a better explanation? I mean, think about it, we could be in a different dimension or something. Or maybe we went back in time."

"Shut up," said Joshua.

"No, I'm serious. This isn't science fiction anymore, this could be a quantum physics thing. I mean, we know what happened with the Philadelphia experiment."

"Shut up, Edward!"

"Fine. I'm only throwing out suggestions . . . "

The truth of the matter was, no one wanted to even consider anything like that actually being true.

John suddenly stopped in his tracks, everyone behind him bumping in to each other. He held up his hand. "Wait."

James whispered, "What is it?"

John was staring intently at the path that lay before him. "This isn't the path we made."

"What? It has to be." Brian looked up into the sky; the sun was beginning to set.

"He's right." James knelt down and ran his fingers over the smashed grass and broken sticks. "This path was made by maybe one or two people, not six."

"It could be Lance."

"We followed Lance's prints into the stream," answered John.

"So there are people on the island, that's good news, right?" asked Edward, a little confused.

James and Joshua began searching their surroundings, but they couldn't see much through the dense jungle. "It's more than that. The tracks are just as fresh as ours." He looked into Edward's eyes. "Someone's following us."

"Okay," he turned away from James' intense eyes. "We'll be heading back to the beach right about now." He started walking back to the beach, almost jogging. Everyone else followed.

As the sun disappeared behind the jungle that peered over them, none could escape the feeling that the jungle was watching them, waiting. The temperature began to drop significantly, but it was still pretty warm.

"We should make a fire," remarked Brian. All six of them sat in a circle on the shore.

Edward looked amused by the comment. "Yeah, why don't you run and fetch us some wood."

James stuck his bare feet deeper into the still warm sand. "We'll get some wood tomorrow."

Chris was lying on his back, staring into the night sky. His head throbbed from where he had hit it with the rock, but he was able to still concentrate on the sky above. There was something that was bothering him, but he couldn't place it. And then it clicked. "Hey guys, do you recognize any of these stars?"

John laughed. "Last time I noticed, none of us were astronomers."

"Basic education, John. I don't see anything familiar up there."

James looked up to see what Chris was worried about.

"He's right. The stars look out of alignment," commented Joshua.

"What are you talking about?" asked Edward. Brian seconded the doubt.

Joshua pointed up into space. "See that star over there, the one that's brighter than the others."

"Okay . . . "

"That's supposed to be the North Star, Polaris."

"And you're going to tell me that it's not?" asked Edward.

"No, it is, except that it's also supposed to line up with the Big Dipper."

Chris continued. "The two stars at the end of the 'pot,' not the ones in the handle, are called 'pointer' stars, because the imaginary curve through them and out the top of the pot points to Polaris."

"So?"

"So, the Big Dipper is right there." He pointed. "And the North Star is all the way over there."

James asked, "Could it just be the season and location?"

Chris shook his head. "You can see the North Star all year round from the Northern Hemisphere." He paused. "But then, we're not exactly sure what our location is, are we?"

"You sure about that?" asked a skeptical John.

Chris smiled. "Oh yeah, I found it a good investment to study the stars. You wouldn't believe the way the chicks eat that stuff up. Makes for a better date, if ya' know what I mean."

"Let's run through this," said John. "We were what? Ten minutes in the air?"

"Sounds about right," said Brian.

Joshua caught on to John's line of thought. "142 mph . . . That's about 35 miles."

"So we should be no further out from Bermuda than 35 miles," deduced Edward.

"Well, then you factor in the water spout incident."

Edward shook his head, "But still, how much farther could that have taken us?"

Joshua smiled. "I think there are other questions that need to be answered first that may affect the one you just asked." He looked out into the ocean. "Like, where the heck is the wreckage from the plane? And how did we all end up together, unhurt, on this island?"

"It's almost like we were transported here or something." Edward was staring at the sand his feet were buried in.

"Seems that way . . . " They all sat in silence.

James spoke up, "Tomorrow we'll walk around the island, see if we can't find anything from the plane. If you can manage, I'd suggest getting some sleep."

"Do you think we should set a watch?" asked John.

They all looked into the jungle and shivered. They could feel that something was very wrong in there.

"I'll stay up first," said Chris.

"You know," started Brian. "Maybe Edward wasn't so off in his suggestion earlier. I mean think about it, we were lost in the Bermuda Triangle, we saw that face, and we ended up in a place where the sky is even different. Maybe we are in a parallel universe or something."

Joshua lay down in the sand. "Get some sleep, Brian. It'll do your head good." But what he didn't tell anyone, what no one told each other, was that the suggestion really did scare them.

:::: *Day Two*

James sat in the sand, facing the ocean, and watched the sun rise into the sky. His thoughts were distant, alive back in New York with Kirsten and Jessica. As he watched the beauty of creation unfold before him, the pain in his physical body disappeared and was replaced by a sharper pain- the realization that he may never see his wife and daughter again. A tear slipped down his cheek, and he began to pray.

Joshua's eyes flickered open as he awoke. Sitting up and looking around him, he noticed James sitting down by the water with his head in his lap. Joshua stood to his feet and made his way down to his friend.

The sound of the crashing waves covered the approach of his friend, so he was startled at the sudden impact of a hand striking his back. James looked up to see Joshua standing over him.

"What are you doing?" asked Joshua.

"Praying."

The answer took Joshua back a few steps. "Praying?"

James shook his head.

"I never knew you as one to pray."

James looked up into his friend's eyes. "I've changed since the Gulf."

"I can tell."

"It's a good change."

Joshua sat down next to James and they both watched the sunrise. "So what happened?"

"I found Christ, or He found me." James expected a laugh of unbelief from Joshua but was surprised when it didn't come.

"I dated a Christian once. Well, she called herself a Christian. I'm not quite sure she was." His gaze was locked on the huge ball of fire and the waves that rolled beneath it. "She took me to her church a few times, took me to some parties with her friends. I liked her a lot. We slept together a few times. I think it bothered me more than it bothered her, actually."

James turned his head to face Joshua.

"I didn't get it. We would go to her church and listen to the pastor preach against fornication, and then I would get back to her apartment and she was taking off her clothes before the front door was even closed. Of course that didn't bother me, but I started to wonder why it didn't bother her, and then *that* bothered me. She wanted me to convert to Christianity, but I didn't see anything different in her that I would be converting into." He paused. "Her friends were different. They walked the talk. Their religion, or faith, or whatever, was real to them. I picked up the looks they shot at my girl while she wasn't looking . . . I knew I was dating a hypocrite. It bothered me more than I ever could have imagined, being with someone who was just putting on the faces, saying the right things, but was really just a liar. I thought that either God wasn't real and that all these people were stupid or what her friends had was what was real, and she was just playing the fool." He looked over at James and met his eyes. "That was two years ago. I gave up on her and her religion, but I've been observing you, and I can't ignore the change in your life. You're a different person, James."

James shook his head. "He's real. I woke up one day, sick of who I had become and wondering if there was more to life. I dismissed the evidence for years, believing in evolution and atheism instead. I knew that both were illogical, but I pleaded ignorance. Finally, one day, I decided that I wanted the truth- whatever it was."

Joshua nodded. "Truth is so obscure in these times and falsity so established, that unless one loves the truth, he cannot know it."

A surprised smile spread James' lips. "Blaise Pascal."

He nodded. "I think I'm ready for the truth, James. I knew I didn't want what that woman had, but even though she claimed to have the same thing as you, I can see that wasn't the case. I want what you have."

"And what is it that I have?" asked James.

"Peace."

"Knowing you are a child of the creator and sustainer of all things, definitely gives you peace."

"I'd imagine so."

Before anything else could be said, Edward walked up beside them. "Hey, you guys know where Brian went?"

James looked confused. "What do you mean?" He looked over the beach and saw that everyone but Brian was present.

"His footprints go off in that direction." He pointed down the coast.

James and Joshua both got to their feet and started heading towards the tracks. "What the heck is he thinking?"

Chris joined them. "Should we go after him?"

John had already started following the prints. "Of course we go after him."

Again, it was John who walked ahead. It was what he was trained to do. Edward walked behind him, then Chris, James, and Joshua. They had followed the set of footprints for half an hour and, as far as they could see, the prints continued to stretch to the horizon.

"So, what about the people you killed?" Joshua asked James.

"That's a bit harder to get over. I mean, the reality of life is that people die. I felt guilty about the people I killed in the war, but death is total in every generation. Everyone dies, it's just a matter of when and how. Once I became a Christian, actually, it was a while after I became a Christian, I realized that people's souls aren't subject to other people."

Joshua looked up from his steps. “What do you mean?”

“I mean, you can’t go to hell because of another person. That wouldn’t be fair at all.”

“So, in other words, you believe that you weren’t responsible for sending those people you killed to hell.”

“Right. Every person has an opportunity before they die to accept the truth. So in the end, they are without excuse. That’s what the Bible says.”

“But what about the families . . . ”

James squinted into the sunlight. “That’s when it gets really hard to be human.”

John stopped and kneeled down. The neat footprints in the sand were no longer one step in front of the next but indicated that the person had started to move back and forth and sideways. “He saw something over there.” John stood back up and looked into the direction of the tree line. “He was walking forward, turned to look behind him, started back peddling, turned and sprinted.”

Everyone weighed the evidence and agreed. The footprints were now a good four feet apart from each other, indicating that he had, indeed, started running.

“I don’t get it.” They stood on the beach, the wind blowing their hair and clothes, staring into the woods. Brian’s footprints suddenly took a 90° turn straight into the jungle.

Chris whined. “Man, you gotta’ be kiddin’ me. I don’t want to go in there again.”

John shot him a look. “How old are you?”

“Shut up, John. It don’t matter how old I am! You think whatever’s in those woods cares about how old I am?” He started to walk towards the trees, muttering under his breath, “Probably eat me or something.”

Right before they entered the cover of the jungle, Joshua had a thought and looked up into the bright sky. “No sign of air traffic either.”

“What, you mean like contrails?” asked Edward.

“Yeah.”

“You know, some people believe that contrails affect global warming.”

“Yeah, I’d buy that. They turn into clouds which reflect sunlight, and they probably trap radiation from the earth’s surface . . . It’d have to affect the climate somehow.” They were walking through the woods now.

Edward continued to talk- it helped take his mind off the present. “Some people say that they’re spraying chemicals up there. That people have even died from the stuff those things are spitting out. The more adamant people even ascribe it to a government agenda, secret tests and stuff."

Even James couldn't hide his amusement.

"I think you've seen one to many X-Files episodes, Agent Mulder."

Edward smiled.

Unlike the previous day, the jungle was full of life. Monkeys swung from tree branch to tree branch, tropical birds flew through the sky, and the sound of a million insects filled the air.

John stepped over a log as he paid careful attention to the wildlife around him. "Isn't it kind of odd that there's so much life in here today, and yesterday we thought we were the only living things on the island?"

"Maybe we're on a different island today," laughed James.

"Or maybe we're not on an island," added Chris.

"Makes you wonder, doesn't it?" Joshua's statement carried a more serious tone.

"I guess we can rule out the atomic, radioactive island theory." Edward smiled.

"One possibility down, a million more to go."

The tropical climate dampened their clothes with sweat and humidity, causing them to cling to their bodies, so it wasn't long before the shirts came off and were tied loosely around their waists. It was amusing to see the difference the years had made. James was in perfect shape, his profession and hobby the reason for that. Joshua, being a Navy SEAL, was even bigger. He could bench press 440 pounds, and it was obvious. Chris was in shape but without the build. He weighed only 183 pounds, compared to James' 195 and Joshua's 225. Edward's body revealed signs of what it once was, but depression and stress seemed to be eating him away physically. Though his stomach was used to sit ups, his ribs were now visible on his back. John was in good shape for his age but nothing more.

Sunlight poured through the canopy and stroked the jungle's floor and all that lived within. With the birds and animals bringing life to the island, it actually was an incredibly beautiful place.

The jungle was thick, John having to walk through vines and under branches in order to stay with Brian's tracks. "Pretty unbelievable, isn't it?"

"What's that John?" asked Edward. He was nearly exhausted from the hike, and he secretly wondered how much longer they'd be walking. Too much further and he might be willing to leave Brian in the woods. The years past taunted him even now, his body weak and tired. His thinning hair barely prevented his scalp from being burned, and he silently cursed his body and his three wives for making him this way.

"That a week ago I was just living a normal life. You know, going to work, driving my car, hugging my girl, kissing my girl . . . "

"No further please." He held up his hand.

"One week ago. Now I'm so far from what used to be normal that the old normal seems so abnormal that I can't even imagine myself being there again."

Chris rubbed his head. "Yeah . . . "

John pushed a branch out of his way. "I don't even know where I am! Let alone how I'm going to get back!" He let go of the branch and it whipped back into Chris' face.

"Ouch! Would you watch it?" He rubbed his face.

James, Joshua, and even Edward stifled a laugh.

James listened to their conversation, but soon became bored with it and found himself thinking of his own wife again. He couldn't imagine what she was thinking or going through right now. Or what she *would* be going through- James didn't know if he was supposed to be back today or tomorrow. But he knew that she wasn't going to be happy to discover him not on the plane, and that thought almost made him sick. He then thought of his brother, Steve- the only reason he left his family in the first place. There were still questions that Lance would have to answer to bring clarity to the whole situation with him, but at least he was still alive- if Lance was telling the truth, that is. The only thing that James was concerned with now was getting back to Kirsten, and he suddenly realized that the uncertainty they both felt about his short trip turned out to be pretty accurate after all.

"So, James, you have any theories on who wrote the ransom note?" asked Chris.

Joshua's eyebrows went up, curious to hear James' response.

But James only shook his head. "I have no idea."

"Could be that he was lying," said Joshua.

"Could be," responded James as he looked into the distance, through the endless labyrinth of trees.

"It's kind of scary when you think about it," said Chris.

"Why's that?" Joshua wanted to know.

James knew the answer, he'd gone over it in his own head a few times already, but just to hear Chris say it sent chills up his spine.

"Because whoever wrote it wanted James in Bermuda. If Lance and his people didn't write it, then it means someone else wanted James down here."

Joshua looked away in silence, contemplating the scenario.

John and Edward had gotten a bit farther than the rest of the group, so when James, Joshua, and Chris found them standing still, looking ahead at something, they strained to see what the spectacle could be.

As they walked up beside their two transfixed friends, one of them whispered, "Forget the X-Files, we're talking Twilight Zone . . . "

James brought his eyes around to face whatever it was that provoked the statement of awe from Edward, and what he saw sent electricity racing through his nervous system. Edward softly hummed the Twilight Zone theme song in the background, only amplifying the electrical storm within his neurological process and sending hair on the back of his neck standing straight up.

An open field lay spanning the near distance, the jungle around it too afraid to touch it with growth. The grass was waist high, and it was waving back and forth with the wind's every stroke. But what the wind did not move, could not move, was the geometric shape that seemed to entertain only the sky. The pattern was indistinguishable from ground level, but all knew exactly what they were looking at. Whether they believed before that moment mattered little now. In the place they found themselves, with the recent string of events, it could be nothing else. For once, anything else would seem too far-fetched, unrealistic. The fact that that was true proclaimed to each of them just how far away they were from the reality they thought they once knew.

They stood in silence, waiting for nothing, looking for nothing, and expecting less. Their sense of reality, all expectation, had just been decapitated. They realized that what they had come to casually call 'reality' was dead, non-existent in this place.

The wind blew, the grass swayed, but all sets of eyes remained unmoved, as if the longer they stared, the more things would make sense. Whether it was the image that enslaved their emotion or the strange feeling that lay thick in the air, no one could say, but both were definitely present.

James cracked his lips in an attempt to speak, but he would need to try a second time. "Can you feel that?"

Joshua wasn't sure if James had whispered out of amazement, or fear of being heard. "Feels like someone watching us . . . Staring us right in the eyes."

They began to take a few steps backwards.

Until John pointed into the crop circle. "Brian's tracks go right through the center of it."

There was hesitation before anyone suggested what they knew must be asked. "Do we go in after him?"

Chris' eyes parted from the pattern and, for some unknown reason, rested on John's bare back. A harsh story of survival, of fear, and of pain, was scribbled into his skin by the North Vietnamese Army. And as Chris read it, he realized that if the situation they were in scared the person who had already been through hell, then he had every reason, himself, to be afraid. "Let's go." He forced his feet in front of him and entered the field, stepping on the smashed-down grass.

It didn't take long for John to notice the grass they were walking on. He never missed much that could be seen with the eye- the very reason he walked ahead of the team both here and in Vietnam. "Look at this." He kneeled down, concentrating on the ground.

"You think this could have been made by those guys and their walking planks?" asked Edward.

They had all seen the special on television, the secret of crop circles revealed to be a bunch of bored men walking on wooden planks in the middle of the night, never to be caught by the CIA, NSA, FBI, NASA, the police, or any other investigative unit in the world. The looks Edward received would have been looks he would have received a week ago if he had suggested that they were looking at a UFO-made crop circle. But not now, now the normal was replaced by the supernatural, and anything not supernatural was no longer normal. What difference a couple of days could make in one's view of reality.

"Walking planks . . . right." John ran his fingers through the grass. "This grass is braided in threes." More silence.

"Let's keep walking," said Joshua. "I don't like being in the open like this." His eyes traced the tree line that surrounded them, and once he thought he saw something running through the edge of the jungle. The strange feeling that kept bringing chills to his body wouldn't subside either.

"Yeah, I think that's a good idea," said James as he continued forward, eyes locked in the jungle where he too thought he saw something.

They walked through the geometric shape that was only distinguishable from the air, but was impossible to miss from the ground, and they grew closer and closer to the jungle it separated. Clouds were beginning to form in the warm sky, and the wind was picking up noticeably. It seemed as if another storm was coming for them. The idea did not appeal to any of them, though the cool breeze felt good against their sweaty bodies.

This time it wasn't just John who noticed. Everyone stopped dead in their tracks and, for a second, just stared at what lay on the ground ahead of them, not sure how to react. Though they didn't know what the crop circle looked like from above, they could tell that the design tapered off into some kind of head, and it was what lay in the center of the head that had captured their horrified attention.

It was Brian. He was lying, covered with braided grass, unconscious and naked.

EIGHT
My name is Brian

Profanity escaped through surprised lips, the scenario continuing to prove everything about itself to be wrong.

Did they have the courage go forward? To approach the unknown and all its trepidation? Or did they dare retreat and leave behind a friend? Neither prospect appealed. A few seconds slipped by unnoticed as hesitation bound them all with indecisive fear. No one wanted to walk forward; yet walking backwards was almost equally horrifying. So it wasn't surprising that those who walked closer to Brian were those who were the closest to him. And those who took a step back were Joshua, Chris, and Edward.

John recklessly tore through the knotted grass, which entangled Brian, with his fingers. "He's freezing cold!"

"Is he alive?" asked James already expecting the worst.

"Yeah." He finished tearing through the grass and was now trying to shake him awake. "He's breathing, but I can't believe how cold he is."

James, John, and now Edward kneeled around Brian; Chris and Joshua delaying. They searched his body, attempting to find any type of wound that would prove to be the reason for his unconsciousness, but none was to be found, only the long cut on his head from the crash. The only thing that seemed abnormal, besides him being without clothes, unconscious, and lying in a crop circle, was the pale tone of his skin and the low temperature it took.

"We're not alone . . . " Chris' voice betrayed his feelings as he looked around.

"Yeah, I got that much already," said John, looking up from his friend.

Brian's eyes suddenly snapped open.

"He's awake!" Edward grabbed him, attempting to lift him to his feet, but Brian unexpectedly grabbed him by the throat and threw him to the side.

The fact that Edward slid through the grass for a good thirty feet caused everyone to take a few steps back.

"What . . . " John stared in unbelief as Brian quickly got to his feet. Whether he should turn and run or stay and plead with his old friend was a matter of debate that was quickly sentenced. He took a few more steps backwards, bumping into Chris and knocking them both onto their backs.

"My name is Brian."

The simple statement struck everyone weird. It almost sounded as if Brian was trying to convince himself or remind himself of who he was. There was also something about Brian's eyes that struck James as odd. They didn't look like Brian's eyes, but before he could place his thought on reason, Brian blinked and whatever it was was erased, along with his identity crisis.

"Did you see that?" whispered Joshua over James' shoulder.

Before James could respond, Brian looked at him and asked, "What's going on?"

James and Joshua exchanged a curious glance as Brian visibly struggled to understand his current situation.

"Do you think he was abducted?" asked Edward.

John laughed to himself. "I don't even know what that means. You talking Martians and flying saucer stuff?"

"Are you kidding me? You've got a naked guy in a crop circle, what else could it be?"

"It could be anything." He paused, taking in his surroundings. "Just like we could be anywhere."

They were almost back to the beach, the jungle passing them by unnoticed. There was no longer an awareness of beauty or awe from nature- there were other things on the mind. Things like Brian, who was walking naked behind them whistling a song. Brian's sudden and surprising show of strength had morphed into a paranoid fear, but more recently that had even changed into what could be mistaken for nothing less than happiness. This guaranteed a close eye being kept on him by all. Brian didn't seem like Brian as of late, and every once in a while he would fit a chorus into his whistling melody. "My name is . . . Brian! My name is . . . Brian!" That this behavior troubled everyone was an understatement. They all knew Brian well enough to know that Brian was no longer 'Brian,' no matter what he was saying.

Their conversation tickled James' ears and orchestrated his own thoughts. What was going on? How did all this happen? Why? Trying to find his place in the center of the present proved only more frustrating and disheartening. He began to whisper prayers to the only One who knew what was going on. The fact that, no matter where he was or what was going on, the Person he prayed to was the same, helped him enough to lift his head.

The sound of Joshua's voice cut through his thoughts and prayers. "You hear them talking back there?" Edward and John were walking farther back, Brian even farther.

"Alien abduction?"

"Yeah . . . So are they crazy or could they be on to something?"

James looked back over his shoulder to see his friends. "I can't say that I believe in aliens."

"Really? Even with the stuff we've seen through the years? The little stories that slip through the 'classified' channels?"

"I admit there's something going on, there's too much evidence to ignore it. But as far as it being little green men from Mars, I don't think so. I think there's a deception taking place and that it's evil, but not extra-terrestrial. If you want to talk about demons and spiritual forces, then I'm more prone to lend a listening ear, but as far as all this stuff being strictly physical . . . No way."

Fixed in thought, Joshua pondered the spoken words. "All the reports we have of flying saucers and stuff do seem to defy all of our natural laws. The speed at which they travel and the turns they make at that same speed, all without creating a sonic boom . . . "

"Seems more like they're extra-dimensional, huh?"

Joshua obviously didn't take that question lightly. "James, if all this supernatural stuff is extra-dimensional, and we seem to be right in the middle of it, could we . . . " He trailed off to gather his thoughts. "Instead of demons, or whatever you want to think it is, visiting *us* . . . Is it possible that, here and now, *we* are the visitors?"

The look in James' eye betrayed his reaction despite his efforts to mask it. For the first time in a very long time, James was terrified.

Sand crabs flopped around in the surf until they tunneled themselves into the wet sand, air bubbles escaping the small holes. A few seagulls cawed as their eyes searched for signs of the very same crabs that had escaped the swooping passes of the predators by going south into the earth. There was life to be found on the tropical beach, but the seagulls might as well have been pigeons huddling into the corner of an overpass, and the crabs passing cars beneath; to the men who sat on the beach, all that seemed to be alluring before had become insignificant now.

The afternoon was hot, and with no breeze to offer any temporal relief, turning to the cool ocean waters was all that seemed to bring any sort of positive. With nothing to do, James, Chris, Joshua, John, Edward, and Brian sat on the hot sand- each in his own process of thought.

Even though James had replayed the events of the past few days over and over in his mind, they did little other then drive him to despair now. The longer and harder he thought, the more unpleasant his situation became. So many questions . . . Yet, even now, in the midst of the mystery, he was beginning to find himself lost in the present- losing sight of the whole picture. He concluded that it was probably a good thing. To spend the next week trying to find an answer to where he was, why he was, how he was, and when he was- it would accomplish nothing. Instead, he would concentrate on those things that would keep him alive, like food and water. As time continued to unfold and reveal her will, James found himself less concerned with what was going on and more concerned with the pain within his own body. The same went for everyone. They were hungry, they were tired, and they were all confused and scared. Those were the issues that took center stage within, the questions of where and when they were had been temporarily set aside for the time being.

However, despite being more concerned with resting and recovery, the one thing that did not escape anyone's attention was Brian. He was acting bizarre to say the least. James presently watched him skip through the water like a little girl, empty hands moving about as if they were holding a small plastic shovel and bucket. He had John and Edward's shirts tied around his waist, but he seemed too happy to even care about the loss of his clothes or even how he lost them.

"He's beginning to scare me." John's voice interrupted the private conference that was getting no where fast within James' reasonable mind.

"Me too."

"I know that looks like Brian, but it isn't."

At first James laughed at the statement, but then the remark triggered something within his cognitive mind, and he suddenly remembered the pages he had turned on the airplane and in his hotel room- the book that sat on his shelf back in New York, the book he never remembered getting in the first place. The writer of the angelology book had written about demon possession and gave some documented accounts to show its validity within the boundaries of reality. Some of those accounts were characterized by muteness, blindness, convulsions, self-destruction, insanity, superhuman strength, and/or occult powers. The documented accounts were both biblically based and historically based. And because of what James witnessed before him now, he wasn't so sure that Brian wasn't abducted- just not by an alien.

John's face looked painfully red due to the abnormal amount of time spent exposed to the sun's harsh power, but his eyes glowed with acute awareness, numb to the physical pain, focused on everything around him. His lips were dry and his voice hoarse. "James . . . "

James knew what he was going to say so he was nodding his consent even before John asked.

"We need water. Food would be nice too."

Joshua was lying on his back about thirty yards away with his shirt over his face and sand on his chest, a precaution against the sun's rays. James knew he wasn't sleeping but racing through the same thoughts that everyone was. Figuring that Joshua could use some sport to ease his heavy mind, James told John to take Joshua. "We'll stay here and keep an eye on Brian. Be back before the sun starts setting." He then urged John to be cautious. "Remember, something's here, and it was following us yesterday."

John nodded and stood to his feet. "How could I forget?" As he walked towards Joshua, he watched Brian splashing around in the water, behaving as if he had lost his mind. "You better keep a good eye on him."

A cool breeze swept the tropical sands and pulled at Chris' clothes. The sound of the waves crashing, the feel of the warm sand beneath him, and even the sun's heat all conspired together to present him with a false reality, for as he lay half asleep, he thought of himself as being in Bermuda, outside the hotel. When the wind let go of his clothes and the sun's heat was no longer relieved, discomfort demanded that his consciousness come to attention- and so it did. The first revelation that manifested itself was actually based on memory- the darkness and the cold sweeping over everything. This memory served to alert Chris to his situation and erase all beliefs of a relaxing nap. As his brain caught up with itself, he remembered the most recent events up to the time he had lain down and closed his eyes. Now he came to attention, no idea how long the time had been between the shutting and opening of his eyes.

Sunlight caused him to retreat back to shut eyes and sleep began to pull him back into a more pleasant world. He was willing to be led, the present nightmare fading into a non-existent state as sleep numbed his mind and senses.

This time something woke him up. He opened his eyes and quickly attempted to discover what it was that caused him to come out of the sleep he was enjoying. James seemed to be asleep a short distance away, and Edward was waist deep in the ocean. Chris sat up, confused. Something woke him up. Then he realized that he hadn't seen Brian.

"Nice nap?"

The voice scared Chris enough to make him jump. Turning to face the one who spoke, he found himself looking up at Brian. Brian's body was blocking the sun, which hid his features in a silhouette. "Yeah." He turned his back to Brian and sat facing the ocean. Brian's shadow stretched down across the sand in front of Chris, and Chris was wondering what Brian was doing standing over him.

Then he noticed the shadow- that it was wearing clothes. He spun around to see Brian, and, sure enough, he was wearing a pair of jeans and a white t-shirt. "Where'd you get those clothes?" asked Chris more than a little suspicious.

Brian smiled. "Over there." He pointed down the beach.

Chris shook his head and stood to his feet. "What?" And then he noticed the pistol that was tucked into the front of Brian's new jeans.

"I found all of our gear; it must have washed up in the surf." There was something about his disposition that was troubling.

Chris looked around and noticed James getting to his feet. Edward also just reached dry sand. Both noticed Brian, and they both began to make their way over to them. The lone fact that their coming comforted Chris told him that something wasn't right with his present circumstance, and he took a step back from Brian.

Brian noticed. "What's wrong, Chris?"

Chris shook his head. "You tell me, Brian."

"Right, my name is Brian."

"I know." Chris blinked a few times, as if each time would bring more clarity to the scenario. He found it troubling that he couldn't determine if it was Brian who said that or not. No one else was around, but it didn't sound like Brian's voice.

He spoke again. "I said, 'my name is Brian.'"

It was not Brian's voice.

Tripping over his feet, Chris fell to the ground, frantically trying to escape the person before him.

"Your name is Chris Roberts, and we don't need you here." The voice that was coming from Brian, but couldn't be his own, was cursing Chris even while Brian pulled the pistol from his jeans and brought it up, the barrel bearing down on Chris.

Chris barely had time to gasp before the trigger was pulled and the shot pierced the island's sky. If it hadn't been for James' speed that enabled him to reach Brian just as he fired, the bullet would have killed Chris, but instead it buried itself harmlessly into the sand.

James and Brian fell hard into the sand, the hit delivered comparable to an NFL highlight. The pistol flew from Brian's grip and the duffle bag that was slung over his shoulder, unnoticed before, slipped off.

"What are you doing?" screamed James, getting himself into a sitting position on top of Brian.

"Get off me!" The voice that escaped from Brian seemed too deep for any man, a sound expected from some B horror movie. He punched James in the chest, and James flew off him and into the sand.

Brian stood to his feet, pausing only to lift the duffle bag which he then swung into Edward's face as he ran to attack him. Edward's feet went straight into the air and he landed on his head.

Pointing at James, Brian screamed, "You! We need you!" He then pointed at Edward. "But you! We don't need you!" He threw his gaze onto Chris who was running for the pistol. "We don't need you either." Brian stretched his hand out and right before Chris reached the pistol, he was elevated off the ground and thrown away from it.

Brian then began walking towards Chris, his intent crystal clear.

"Brian! Stop it!" James pleaded with him, though he knew it wasn't really him he was pleading with.

Brian simply looked back at James. "My business is not with you, Christian. It is only with those whom I do not have use for." He returned his attention back to Chris.

Edward wasn't sure what was going on, but he knew that whoever reached the pistol first would have control, so he went for it.

James, noticing Edward's intention, charged at Brian, hoping to draw his attention away from Edward's attempt at reaching the weapon. Kicking up sand in his wake, he tried at another tackle, but Brian turned at the last second and side-stepped the attack leaving James to recover by coming out of a tuck-and-roll and back onto his feet.

"Why do you test me, Christian? Leave me, before I take your life as well."

Now that Brian was facing James, his back was turned to Chris, and Chris didn't waste the opportunity. He took off running down the beach, putting as much space as he could between him and whatever wanted to kill him.

James answered the threat with surprising confidence. "You can't touch me."

Whatever was inside of Brian laughed out loud, its voice echoing against the tree line. "Foolish Christian, do you not know where you are?"

Edward picked the gun up and aimed it at Brian. "Brian! Stop this, now!"

Eyes sweeping to Edward, Brian smirked. "Edward . . . I require only one soul today, but if it be not Chris Robert's, then it will be yours."

The hand that held the gun steady was forced open, and Edward watched as the weapon flew from his hand and through the air into Brian's waiting hand.

Chris had managed to establish a significant amount of distance in his escape, but not enough. Brian aimed the pistol at his back and pulled the trigger. He chuckled while watching Chris manage a few more steps before collapsing into the sand.

"No!" James charged Brian once again, only this time he led with his feet and kicked him in the chest. Brian fell backward into the sand, visibly shocked.

Edward tried to help but was kicked for getting too close to Brian. He flew a good ten feet through the air before sliding through the sand and realizing a sharp pain in his chest.

"You have no power over me!" said James through clenched teeth as he rolled around in attempts to wrestle the gun away. But the scuffle was dismissed with ease.

Brian grabbed him by the shoulders, completely stopping him from moving. The strength exhibited was superhuman, and James' natural muscles, even though straining to the point of bursting, veins pressing hard against his skin, could do nothing against the grip.

"Poor, James. So confused, so ignorant . . . If only you knew where you were, then maybe you'd begin to understand." He transferred both hands to James' neck.

Though Brian's hands were only placed on his neck, James still couldn't seem to move the rest of his body, as if he were bound by some invisible force. Brian squeezed tighter, and he now began to see black spots creeping into the corners of his vision, warning him of a near fateful end. James couldn't grasp the reality of it all. Every day he lived seemed to race through his mind's eye and then, at some point within the movie, all of this started. It was poorly scripted, a change so drastic that the viewer would be lost in the stupidity of the plot. It made no sense. He was almost sure that he would wake up and find his wife holding him once again, wiping the sweat from his face and rubbing his tense back. He would thank her, kiss her, and thank God that it was all a dream. But as the darkness spread and his consciousness began to flicker, he knew that even this was too weird to be a dream. It was a perverted sort of reality, but it was reality. There would be no beautiful face to wake up to, no eyes to get lost in, no touch to melt to. *If* he ever awoke again in this life, he had no clue as to what he would possibly find. Nor did he want to know. He knew where he was going, that heaven's doors were opened to him, and that was a thought more appealing than waking up again on this beach.

Whatever was inside of Brian could be detected through the eyes- a glazed over, sadistic impression not to be missed. It glared up at James as it crushed his neck, a satisfied expression being painted over the face that did not belong to it. No longer horrified by the supernatural presence that was taking his life, James surrendered his struggle, ready to enter heaven. At least until a voice so acid deliberately escaped Brian's body.

"It's truly a pity that you won't be around to witness what's in store for your lovely family back in New York . . . "

The statement might has well have been a knife stuck straight into his heart, killing him and yet ushering back the desire to live like a tidal wave. Utter despair and an image of his wife on their wedding day flashed into his mind, and just as darkness swallowed the picture and the whole of his vision, he whispered, "Oh God."

NINE
Contact

Food would be a bit harder to find than water, but no ill complaints resulted. The jungle stretched before them, a snapshot of beauty. Never before had their eyes witnessed such utter splendor. It was an atmosphere stolen from fantasy, a white unicorn soon to run through the sunlight that poured through the canopy far above. Many jungles had Joshua traveled throughout the world, but none compared to what he saw before him now. Mist danced around their feet as they walked through a slight clearing, the tall trees spread out some. The light that shone through the trees came down in beams, spotlighting the ground on which they walked. A few tropical birds, displaying their many colors, flew by overhead, startled at their arrival. They disappeared into the near thickness-parts of the jungle that light did not reach. Somewhere in that direction was a waterfall, the sound of it playing soothingly in the air.

Joshua stepped through the small stream that snaked across the ground in front of them, not caring that his brown boots had just finished drying.

John followed, captivated by the serene air that seemed to hang over everything. He half expected to hear a little melody being played by one of those jewelry boxes, the ballerina spinning gracefully on her one foot. Enchanted was the ground they traveled, striking and passive.

"Strange, isn't it?" asked Joshua.

John answered half-heartedly, still taken by his surroundings. "What's that?"

"This place. It's almost like every time we enter the woods, we enter a different kind of world. I mean, first it was someone following us, then it was a crop circle, and now it's the most beautiful fairy tale I've ever seen."

"Makes you wonder, doesn't it?"

"There's not much happening that doesn't."

They carried make shift spears- long sticks with sharp rocks from a river bed wedged at the point. Continuing to walk deeper into the jungle, they searched for signs of animal life, hoping that they might be able to catch something edible.

"We might be able to find some fish near the waterfall," said John.

"Your fishing that good?" He turned to follow the sound of the falling water.

"It's been a while," he admitted. "But give me a fish and something to throw at it . . . "

They walked outside of the sunlight's reach, continuing on through the darkness towards the sound of rushing water.

"It's been a little while since I've seen James," began John. "Maybe ten years by now." His eyes swayed from the beauty around him for just a second as they looked into years past. "He used to call me 'Uncle John.'" He laughed. "When Steve became an agent, he started to move a lot, you know, wherever they would send him. It hasn't really been the same since."

Joshua smacked his neck, squashing a bug as he wondered where John was going with this.

"I remember I was at a party for Steve right before James left for the Gulf. I don't think I've seen him since." He paused for a second, his mind recalling old memories. "Man, seems like yesterday."

Joshua looked over at him. "I met him in the Gulf. We ended up fighting along side each other, saved each other's lives."

"Aren't you a SEAL?"

"I was. I retired from that a few months ago."

"You like it?"

"Being retired or the service?"

"Being retired."

"Nah, can't get used to it. At first it was nice, but once it became longer than a vacation . . . "

John asked, "Have you kept in touch with James since the war?"

"Yeah, off and on. Mostly through mail though. I think Chris actually sees him more than the rest of us."

"Chris was a Marine in the Gulf, right?"

"Yeah, same platoon as James. They even went through boot camp together."

It was obvious that John was thinking a lot about the next question, a question he was determined to ask. Joshua got the feeling that this was where the whole conversation had been heading from the beginning.

"So does he seem a bit different to you now? I mean, from what he was before?"

"Before the Gulf? I'm not sure. Like I said, I didn't know him before the war. But he's changed since the war. " Joshua laughed. "Oh, yeah. He's hardly the same person I knew before."

"Think it was his marriage?"

Shaking his head as he answered, he said, "No, not really. I mean, I'm sure that played some part in it, but I think it's his Christianity."

John shot him a look of unbelief. "His what?"

"I think the change in his life is actually due to him finding God."

John's face betrayed his surprise and bewilderment. "He's one of those now?"

"That's what he told me."

John pondered this for a while. "I can't believe it. The James I knew would not even go near a Bible."

"I'll tell you what, all jokes aside, I'm jealous."

"Of what?"

"Of whatever it is that he has. My whole life I've tried building an image for myself. I've had everything there is to have. The girls, the money, the fast cars, the muscles, the kills, being the best at everything I've ever done . . . But, like James said, I just wake up in the morning feeling empty. For some reason I still haven't found what I'm looking for. But James found it."

John chuckled to himself. "James said all that? That he woke up empty and God filled him with all he ever wanted?"

"He didn't have to. I saw it in his eyes."

"Bull."

"That's what I always thought. But, come on, James is changed, you have to admit that."

He shook his head. "Yeah, now he seems soft, out of touch with reality. Who cares if he thinks he found God, if he needed that crutch to get him through life then he wasn't all that strong to begin with."

"If God's a crutch to help you through this life, it's a crutch I'll take."

A look of disgust washed John's face. "God . . . " He laughed. "God, God, God. You wonder what He was thinking when He made this place." He used his hands to gesture at the surroundings. "Or when He sent me to Vietnam and killed my fiancé while I was away. Or why He made such a crappy world where nothing works and everything sucks. Tell me, Joshua, what was God thinking? And what does James think about that?" He spit on the ground, a sign of his disgust. "Man, I wonder why Steve never told me. Little James a Christian . . . "

Obviously there were some grudges and hard feelings towards the Higher Power for allowing certain events to pass. Joshua knew that, whether James was right or wrong, John was too hurt to see either way, his view twisted with bias. "I'll tell you what, John, James was never soft. He was a machine, built by the Marines. He knew no weakness. I mean, I watched him fight right next to me and he fought like you couldn't imagine. He was ruthless, didn't matter who he killed, because he enjoyed the killing. He was one of those guys that just seemed to go into a zone when the fighting started. So, I'd have to disagree with you on the issue of him being soft and weak. In fact, if I were to ascribe an image to the opposite of those things for a class I was teaching, the picture on the board would be of James Streen."

"But you agree that's what he's become?"

"Not at all. How can you call someone like him weak? For someone who was once a blood thirsty predator killing his enemy for mere pleasure to become a loving husband and father, a believer in a Higher Being . . . " He trailed off, suddenly realizing something else. "Have you heard one swear from his mouth the entire time he's been here? No drinking, no women, no nothing. The man is not the same, and for you to ascribe that kind of change to a weakness he has is ignorant, or self deceptive."

John reacted with a daring look. "What are you trying to say?"

"Maybe there's some truth to all the stuff James believes, and maybe you're starting to see that truth, but you don't like it, so you try to psychologize his situation ascribing it to some weakness within his personality . . . "

"Shut up." John picked up his pace and walked past Joshua. Before he disappeared behind a group of bushes he looked back over his shoulder, a layer of poison on his tongue. "Are you a Christian too?"

Joshua stood there thinking about the question for a few seconds. For some reason, the words of the question seemed to linger in the air around his head, waiting for an answer. *Are you a Christian too?* The question demanded an answer, an answer Joshua knew to be of great importance, but an answer he was not ready to give. "John!" He called after him, annoyed that he now had to chase him. Walking through the jungle, eyes fixed ahead trying to see John, he didn't see the fallen branch that stretched across his path. He tripped and fell onto his stomach, now really aggravated and building up some harsh feelings towards John- the words being muttered from his lips expressing them. And then he laughed. A Navy SEAL tripping over a branch in the jungle . . . Had anyone been around to witness it, he would have been really hot, but seeing that no one saw him, he only laughed at himself. As he got to his feet and brushed himself off he heard a distinguished, "Pssst" come from somewhere ahead. It was a noise that turned him back into a soldier. Like the sound of a trumpet signaling an army to attack, he immediately took off sprinting through the thick plant life, hands moving fast to spread a way through the vines and branches. When he could finally see John up ahead, he immediately stopped running. John's attention was centered on something ahead of him, something that Joshua couldn't see from his own location. But whatever it was that captured John's attention, it required a certain degree of care, thus the reason for John's hand signaling Joshua to be still and quiet. Joshua watched as John got ready to throw his spear.

He walked softly towards John until his eyes captured what had created the whole situation. Leaning lazily against a tree about thirty yards away from John was a gorilla. It was eating a piece of fruit, not a care in the world. It hadn't detected John's presence, and John was going to try for the kill. Joshua wasn't too sure whether that would be an act of courage or an act of stupidity. Through the years Joshua had come to realize that there was a very thin line separating the two. Nothing about his situation looked good, but he was bound by circumstance. If John didn't manage to kill the gorilla, which Joshua was sure would be the case, then they were in big trouble, but there was no way to stop John from trying without alerting the gorilla to their presence. Joshua could only watch powerless as John prepared to launch the spear at the gorilla. He got himself ready to run.

Snap.

The gorilla looked up from its eating, eyes frantically moving back and forth searching for danger. Its small ears were attentive, the brow ridges set in a raised position creating a wide-eyed expression of fear.

John knew if he was going to try to take this thing down that he had to do it now, before it spotted him. He cocked his arm.

The 360 pound gorilla suddenly stood to its full 5'9" and spread its arms revealing an 8½' arm span. There was no doubt that the gorilla could crush John's skull to powder if he was found.

Delaying his attack, John hesitated, hoping that his eyes would not meet the animal's.

But they did.

The black mammal fell forward onto the back of its knuckles and charged John's position.

"Oh no." John was about to turn and run, but fear and shock had gripped his feet to the ground. He merely watched as the huge mammal crashed its way through the jungle, running straight for him.

Joshua waited for the gorilla to get closer before he attacked with his spear, a very risky plan but none other came so quick to mind. The animal was almost in range, and he silently cursed John's stupidity.

Snap.

Why that particular sound transcended the noise the gorilla made as it recklessly plowed through everything in its way, was not clear. The only thing that was clear was that something else was nearby. The sound of a broken branch coming from John's right, the gorilla's left, was so significant that it captured the attention of every living thing within hearing distance. The gorilla stopped dead in its tracks, turning its head quickly to the side, suddenly more concerned with whatever else was among them.

John and Joshua turned their attention to that general direction as well. The jungle seemed to hold its breath for a split second, waiting for the new life form to reveal itself.

Snap. Snap. Snap.

It was getting closer, whatever it was. Though John and Joshua stood ignorant of what was coming, the scared gorilla did not. It managed only a few steps away from the unseen before its fear was manifested.

An explosion of broken branches and flying leaves rocked the stillness and ended the quiet tension, the suspense being justifiably answered. The gorilla had only enough time to let out a cry of hopeless horror before its head was detached from its body and sent flying through the air with a sickening sound.

It was too dark to be certain, too quick to be sure, but whatever burst through the foliage and engulfed the 360 pound gorilla was not an animal. It was a man. The attack was so fast that neither John nor Joshua was able to see anything other than the gorilla disappear out of sight, its head rolling to a stop at John's feet. But now, though little sun seeped onto its body, it was unmistakable what stood before them. They could only watch in terror and awe as a shadowy figure about 9' tall stood over its prey.

Joshua ripped his eyes off the predator and shot them over to John, but John was transfixed with what he was seeing, too afraid to even breathe. They didn't dare move.

The huge figure tilted its head back as if it were savoring the pleasure of the kill. Before gathering its headless victim, it searched its surroundings. Finally satisfied, it bent over, grabbed the gorilla, and tossed it over its shoulder with the careless effort of a toddler carrying her rag doll. It walked out of sight.

It seemed like an hour passed by before either moved from the positions that so graciously hid them from certain death. John kneeled to examine the gorilla's head. "It came clean off," he muttered.

Joshua walked up behind him, his eyes lingering in the direction the 9' man had disappeared in. "What was that?" he whispered.

John could only laugh. "I have no idea." His laugher trailed into cursing, thinking of every foul thing to say of the place they were trapped in.

"The sun's going to start setting in a couple of hours." John noticed that his hands were shaking.

"We need to at least get some water."

Joshua nodded, still not convinced that the thing was really gone. He wanted to get out of the dark part of the jungle and back into the light. "We can get it at that stream we got the stones from. That was fresh water."

John stood. "Let's get out of here." As they made their way quickly and quietly back to the spots in the jungle where light stroked its life, they couldn't help but to keep looking behind them. They knew for certain now that their survival depended not only on them getting off the island, but staying alive long enough to just find out how.

❧❧❧

Joshua and John had filled themselves with water to the point where they could feel it sloshing around in their stomachs as they ran. How would they even begin to tell the others what they had witnessed? How would the news be taken? Would it be just another oddity to be tossed onto the pile of strange events that seemed to originate from the very soil of this bizarre place? Or would it be something more significant than the crop circle, the night sky, the quarry, the stopped watches, the face in the clouds . . . The least the news would do would be to add one more reason for getting off the island as soon as possible. John had seen a lot in the wet jungles of Vietnam, he had encountered impossible situations, and he had learned to survive. But this was different. Joshua too had made a profession of killing ruthless people, terrorists, enemy soldiers, etc . . . There was little that fazed him anymore; he had gone through most of what there was to go through. However, as he followed John out of the jungle and onto the hot sands, he admitted to himself that whatever lived on this island was something that he did not want to meet under any circumstance whatsoever, because he was scared of what he didn't understand, and he couldn't understand how a 9' tall man could take a 3601b gorilla's head off with a mere stroke of his hand.

It took Joshua and John a little while to find everyone, but as they reached the surf and the clear ocean waters, they were able to spot them a bit further down shore. Even at their distance, they immediately could tell that something was wrong. They took off sprinting down the wet sand, the surf splashing up and soaking them. When they finally reached their friends, confused and out of breath, they discovered Brian lying in the sand unmoving, Edward and James tending to Chris' back. They also noticed something else-an open duffel bag full of equipment.

James looked up from Chris' bloody back, something in his eyes communicating a recent catastrophe. "I need a drink." His words were lazy, stoic.

Joshua answered, eyes trying to put together what could have happened. "There's a stream close to the tree line . . . " He pulled his eyes off Chris and introduced them to James. "What happened?"

James sighed, leaning back on his knees. "Brian attacked Chris."

"How?" He didn't understand the bloody wound.

Edward held up the pistol.

"Where'd that come from?" asked John.

Looking defeated and sounding hopeless, James said, "There's more." He waved in the direction of the duffel bag. "That's my bag that I brought on the plane with me."

"Where'd you find it?" asked Joshua as he ran and slid next to the bag, anxious to learn of its contents.

"I didn't. He did." He nodded at Brian who appeared to be out cold.

"He shot Chris?" John seemed more surprised than confused.

"Yeah. He almost killed James too," said Edward. "He was talking crazy. Said that they needed James and that he required a soul to take and all kinds of crazy junk."

"'They'?" asked Joshua.

Edward only shrugged. "You got me, man."

"So what happened?" John was looking Brian over, but there seemed to be no injury inflicted.

Edward shrugged. "He started talking about something happening to James' family and then James said, 'Oh God.' As soon as he said that, Brian fell unconscious on top of James."

Joshua registered the conversation into his mind and turned it over a few times, but most of his attention was on the contents of the duffel bag. He pulled out a sub machine gun and inserted a clip. "Is he going to be okay?"

"Chris? He'll be fine, I don't think the bullet hit anything major. He'll be in pain until we can get it out, but he'll live." James turned his attention to Edward. "How are you?"

Edward touched his chest. "Bruised rib, I don't think it's cracked."

Joshua stood to his feet. "If you want something to drink, we should probably go now, before it gets too dark."

James and Edward both nodded. "John, would you mind staying with Chris and Brian?"

"No, but hurry back will ya'? No sight seeing."

Joshua quickly assembled an assault rifle before throwing it to John.

As Edward got to his feet and walked to Joshua, who would be leading them to the water, he patted John on the back as he passed by. "If Brian wakes up, hold on to that as tight as you can."

The look Edward gave him raised a few questions, but Edward just kept walking. "Yeah, like I said, hurry back." He then swept his eyes over to Joshua and got his attention. *Are you going to tell them?* Joshua understood the look and nodded. Then they all walked away, towards the trees.

"We'll be back soon," called James over his shoulder.

"You better be," muttered John as he sat down next to Chris and trained his rifle on Brian. "You better be . . . "

The walk, like many of the walks taken, was made in silence, each holding up in their own place of mind, pulling a chair up to the table of reason and trying to negotiate logic. The most recent events left everyone speechless. What could they say? Perhaps they were too afraid to hear their own words describe their nightmare. Maybe they were getting far enough with logic that they realized settling with ignorance might be a better deal than winning understanding. The understanding that they were seeking would possibly drive them to utter despair.

Joshua led them through the woods, doing his best to keep the branches he was moving from snapping back into James' face, which had happened twice already. He hadn't told them yet of the incident. He wasn't sure how. As he recited what he would say, he realized that he had, in fact, little to say.

The sound of running water trickled over James' ear drums and alerted him to its presence. "It even sounds like it tastes good." His throat was dry and his tongue swollen between cracked lips.

Edward laughed, about to change the subject. "You know, I sort of thought this whole thing would be a vacation."

James stepped over a fallen tree as he answered. "Yeah, well, not much has gone the way it was planned, has it?"

Joshua looked at his friend with sincere eyes. "I'm sorry about your brother, James."

James shrugged. "I'm sorry that I drug you guys into this mess."

"Well, like you said, it wasn't planned to go this way." Edward smiled; it was one of those forced smiles. "Unless you left out a few major details."

They approached the small stream that snaked through the labyrinth of tropical trees. James and Edward wasted no time in getting the cool fresh water down their throat. They lay, stomachs flat, on the ground and submerged their whole heads beneath the water, swallowing as much as their mouths could hold at a time.

A sigh of satisfaction escaped James' lips as he rolled onto his back, hands placed on his stomach, hair soaking wet. Edward followed suite.

Joshua let them lay there for a few minutes, resting satisfied and refreshed, before he would bring even more bad news to their already weary, spent minds. "James, about the food . . . "

"Yeah, we'll have to find something." He watched a few birds fly by overhead.

"We found a gorilla."

"A gorilla? Here?"

Joshua only waved at them, signaling them to follow him. As he led them in the direction where the thing had attacked, he stole a glance at the sun and hoped it would stay up just a little bit longer.

"Where we going?" asked Edward.

"I want to show you something." He walked, machine gun ready, eyes searching the woods.

When Joshua entered the darker parts of the jungle, James and Ed were a little hesitant to follow.

"Do we have to go in there?" The sun had begun its descent.

Joshua didn't answer but just walked onward. Five minutes later he was standing exactly where John had stood just a couple of hours before. He kicked the gorilla's head over to his two confused friends.

"I believed you; you didn't have to bring us all the way . . . "

Joshua looked them in the eye as he cut James off and started talking over him. "John was standing right where I am now; I was standing a little further over there. The gorilla sat at that tree over there. John was about to throw a spear at the gorilla when it spotted him and charged him." He paused. "But before the gorilla could reach him, something exploded from the jungle and just . . . " He searched for a word that would help describe the picture, but none came to mind, he only nodded towards the detached head, its eyes set back in the skull staring wide in horror.

"What was it?" asked James.

"It was dark . . . "

James noticed something on the ground and he wandered over to where the attack must have occurred. He walked carefully, not wanting to disturb the footprints left behind by predator and prey. He muttered, "Looks like the gorilla didn't even have time to respond to the ambush . . . "

"He was so fast," his words contained a sense of awe that did not go unnoticed. Neither did the pronoun he used.

"*He?*" asked James.

Hesitation stunned his tongue for a second, but there was no denying what he saw. "Whatever it was that killed the gorilla, it was a man."

"What did he have, a sword?" asked Edward, studying the head.

"He didn't have any weapons, only his hands."

"What?" James turned, looking up from the scuffled ground.

"There's more. This guy . . . was really tall."

His voice serious and somewhat afraid, James inquired, "How tall?"

Joshua shrugged. "Nine feet, give or take."

"Nine feet?" Edward was a bit skeptical.

But the news was taken a bit differently by James who was searching the jungle's floor once more.

And then he saw it.

"Oh my God . . . " It wasn't a vain use of His name, but a cry for help. James dropped to his knees, captivated and horrified by the footprint that was imbedded in the ground before him.

"What is it?" asked Joshua.

A frightened, glazed over look in James' eyes accompanied his words. "This footprint has six toes." And for the first time, James had an idea of what was going on in this place. And now, more than ever before, he wanted to wake up.

TEN
A VISITATION

Driving home was difficult, perhaps the most difficult thing in her life. She had waited at the airport for three hours, not knowing what to do. She had gotten a babysitter so that she and James could have the night to themselves, expecting him to walk off the plane he was supposed to be on and into her arms. When that proved not to be the case, the world she knew and stood on suddenly dropped out from beneath her and left her plunging into a bottomless pit of spiraling chaos. First came the skip of a heartbeat- panic, then the loss of breath accompanied by an exploding feeling in her chest. After that came a fit of paranoid insanity revealed through a pair of frantic eyes. When her fear was finally confirmed and it was an established fact that James was surely not there, her knees began to shake and the tears then began to flow. Standing alone in the midst of airport crowds, everything spinning around her, her sudden disorientation began to make her dizzy.

She didn't have the presence of mind to signal her intent to change lanes, and she cut someone off, receiving the blast of a horn in return. She didn't even notice. Her hands were shaking so much that she had to hold onto the steering wheel with all her strength, her knuckles white. All she could think of was, *why didn't he call?* After that, her mind lost itself in all the endless possibilities of 'what could have happened.' Of course it was nature for the worst possibilities to appear before the mind's eye first, the less devastating possibilities remaining unseen behind the dark shadows of fear.

Ten minutes later she pulled the station wagon into the driveway. Turning the key in the ignition so that the car shut off, she sat there, motionless, staring out the windshield at the white garage doors that stood closed in front of her. James' BMW sat next to her; she tried not to notice it. Trapped in a world where thoughts and feelings dictated body control, it was obvious the significance of her situation, for it took her a few minutes before she even realized she was still sitting in the car. She opened the door, got out, shut it, and ran to the front door of her house. As she fumbled with her keys, trying to locate the right one through swollen watery eyes, she leaned on the door.

It pushed open.

Kirsten took a step back, heart suddenly racing. Could James have come home early to surprise her? She had dropped Jessica off before going to the airport, so it was possible. She quickly scrutinized the door. There seemed to be no sign of forcible entry. *But why hadn't he called since that one day?* She peered through the crack between the door and the doorframe and could see down the hallway into her house. She saw someone at the end of the hallway, in the kitchen. He had his back to her. Then he turned and walked past the hallway.

Kirsten pushed the door open a little more, straining to see who was in her kitchen. Was it James?

She stepped inside the house.

Walking quietly and cautiously down the hallway, making careful effort not to disturb the pictures that hung on the walls, she could hear a man's voice.

And it wasn't James' voice.

She began to back-peddle, reversing her direction. But then the front door slammed shut.

The man in the kitchen suddenly appeared at the end of the hallway, alerted by the loud noise. He looked to see what had caused it and found Kirsten standing in front of the door.

Kirsten let out a gasp as she met eyes with the man that was in her house- the same man that she had seen the other night.

Steven Streen.

She turned and threw herself into the door, wrestling with the doorknob, but the door would not open. She turned her head, to prepare for whatever was to come, but there was no one there.

The policemen smiled both a grateful and sympathetic smile as they accepted the glasses of iced tea made and handed to them by Mrs. Streen, their friend James' wife.

"Thank you, Mrs. Streen."

She just nodded.

Amidst those who were searching her house for clues as to who could have been in her house were George and Fred, two of James' good friends and partners. George approached her and laid a hand on her shoulder, nudging her slightly into another room. "Kirsten, you said that the door was open when you got home?"

She nodded. "Yeah."

"And you're sure you locked it before you left?"

"Absolutely."

"Why?"

She gave him a blank stare.

"I mean, was there anything significant that happened that makes you remember locking the door?"

"Yeah, I locked it with James' keys."

He put his hands on his hips and looked to the side.

"What?" she asked.

"There's no sign whatsoever of anyone being in your house."

"I know there was someone in here," a tear rolled down her cheek as she fought to control her emotion. "I saw him walk past the hallway. I started to sneak up to the kitchen to see who it was, but when I heard him talking, I knew it wasn't James."

"You heard him talking?"

"Yes."

"To himself?"

"I don't know . . . I guess." Her frustration tainted her tone of voice.

"What was he saying?"

"I don't know!" She settled down a little bit, recanting her first reaction. "I'm not sure, something about a message."

George scratched his eyebrow. "A message . . . Now, you didn't recognize the guy?"

She hesitated. She hadn't told them who it was, or who it at least looked a whole heck of a lot like, but she didn't want to lie either. "No. He looked like someone, but it couldn't have been him."

The curiosity that appeared on George's face was the only reason she wanted to avoid this detail. "Who did it look like?"

She paused, looking out the windows in her house, not wanting to see his eyes when she answered. "It looked like James' brother."

"Steve? The one he went to go find in Bermuda?"

Kirsten nodded, still not able to meet his eyes, and brought her hand up to her mouth as more tears rolled down her face.

George sighed as Fred walked into the room. He leaned on the doorway, making it clear that he was going to interrupt them.

"Hey Kirsten, what happened up in Jessica's room?"

"Uh, last week, during the storm, a tree broke the window. James covered it with plastic until he could get it replaced." She looked up to the ceiling, as if that would prevent the tears from rolling out from her overfilled eyelids. "He was planning on doing that tomorrow."

George walked close to her and put an arm around her shoulder. For a split second he was not the police chief, he was a friend, and his words were sincere. "It's okay. It's all going to be okay . . . "

She wiped her eyes.

"I didn't mean that." Fred's voice brought back a question thought to have been answered.

Kirsten looked confused. "What do you mean?"

"I'm talking about Jessica's bed."

She straitened her posture, bringing George's arm up with it. "What about her bed?"

Now it was Fred's turn to look confused. "Well, it's present condition. . . "

Kirsten shook her head. "What? I made it this morning."

The look that flashed over Fred's face gave away something that he was suddenly trying to hide. Without another word, he turned and left the room.

But his quick retreat was not clever enough, and Kirsten ran after him. "Fred! Fred!" She followed him up the stairs and down the hall, bumping into officers wearing latex gloves and dusting for finger prints. When she came rushing into her daughter's room, she immediately brought her hand up to cover her wide mouth.

Fred wasn't sure what to do, so he grabbed her hand.

Kirsten looked in horror at her daughter's bed, which was cut open, the bed's insides poured out and onto the floor. She squeezed Fred's hand tighter. Her voice was shaky and weak and, hidden behind a wall of fear, was almost inaudible. "What does that mean?"

Fred moved her out of the room as the investigators began taking pictures. As they walked back down the stairs, George was making his way up.

"What is it?" He noticed that something was obviously wrong.

Fred only communicated with his eyes that he should see for himself.

George ran past them and to James' daughter's bedroom.

"You didn't see where the guy went?" asked Fred.

"No. I turned around and there was no one there. I didn't search the house, I just called George. He told me to leave the house and to go over to a neighbor's until he got here."

Fred's eyes searched the walls within his friend's house. He saw the bookshelf, he saw the pictures . . . "Kirsten, James is okay. Wherever he is, I'm sure he's okay." He paused. "And I'm sure he's thinking of you."

As strange as it felt, her lips spread into a smile.

Fred wiped the tears from her eyes. "James loves you so much." He smiled. "We're all sick of hearing about you, because then we have to go home to our own wives. I have never heard him say one negative thing about you, and he *never* stops talking about you."

Her smile faded and she leaned against the wall. "Then where is he?" She slid down the wall and sat on the floor, arms pulling her knees into her pregnant body.

Fred's eyes began to grow damp, and he left the room.

No one pretended that everything was all right. All knew James too well to pretend. No matter what, if everything was okay, they all knew that James would have found a way to call his wife at least to let her know what was going on, if not every day to simply hear her voice.

George walked down to the bottom of the steps scratching his forehead. "Kirsten, do you mind if we search your bedroom?"

She could only manage to shake her head, and George headed back up the stairs.

The phone rang and a police officer answered it. "Yeah, hold on." He covered up the mouth piece and leaned around the corner. "It's for you, Mrs. Streen." He handed her the phone,

"Hello?" It was Beth Bristow, the woman who was supposed to be watching Jessica for the night. Kirsten blurted out, "Is everything okay?" After she learned that everything was fine she asked, "Would it be okay to let her stay there for a little while longer?" The Bristow's were great people, people they knew from their church. Kirsten knew that she could depend on them for any help she might need. "Thank you so much." She hit the off button and set the phone on the floor next to her.

Just then George came walking back down the stairs, this time he seemed to have something in his hand that captured his attention. "Kirsten," his voice sounded troubled. "Do you know what this is?" He handed her an envelope.

She reluctantly took it from his hands and opened it up, not bothering to notice who it was sent from. She pulled out a letter and opened it up.

> IF YOU WANT TO SAVE STEVEN'S LIFE
> THEN SEND $500,000 TO THIS ADDRESS BY
> 4PM JULY 20TH . . . IF YOU FAIL TO DO SO
> THEN YOU FAIL YOUR BROTHER. IF ANY
> AUTHORITIES ARE INVOLVED, YOUR
> BROTHER WILL BE KILLED WITHOUT HESITATION.

Her arm fell limp to her side, the letter fluttering from her fingertips. Fear, dread, betrayal, and understanding all flooded through the gates of comprehension too quickly to be categorized and compartmentalized. The tears could not be withheld and this time they were finally accompanied by a sorrowful sob.

George bent over and retrieved the letter, looking around at his men. He knew there was little he could do. If James went to resolve a ransom situation on his own, then who knows what could have gone wrong. He knelt down in front of Kirsten and placed his hands on her knees. “Kirsten, I’ll do everything I can do to find out what’s going on. I promise you, we’ll find James.”

She looked up at him through wet eyes. “Thank you.”

“Do you need a place to stay tonight?”

Kirsten looked around, fingers covering her mouth. “I . . . ” Images of the other night quickly flashed in her head and influenced her decision. “Maybe.”

“You can come back with me. We have a guest room we would be more than happy to have you stay the night in.”

Kirsten nodded, and George helped her to her feet.

“Go get whatever you need.”

She made her way up into her room.

Once she had disappeared up the stairs, George called over one of the officers and handed him the note. “I want you to take this to the lab. I want to know who wrote it. Was it a he or a she, were they right handed or left, how old, and how they hold their stinkin’ pen.”

The officer nodded and ran out the front door and into the night.

Fred walked over. “What is it?”

“I don’t know. There’s something about that letter that seems weird.”

“Like what?”

“I’ve never seen writing like that before, at least not by hand.”

“Typed?”

He shook his head. “There’s no indentation on the paper.”

“Could be a photocopy.”

“I don’t think so. There were no shadows. But we’ll wait and see what the analysis is.”

Fred sighed. “You gonna’ take her back to your place?”

He nodded. “Yeah, maybe Brenda can help her out a little.”

Fred looked down the hall and at the pictures that hung on the wall. “I wonder why someone would want to kidnap his brother.”

“We’ll find out soon enough. Do me a favor, talk to your buddy in the Bureau and see if he can’t find anything out for us.”

“I will.” He shook his head. “I hope he’s okay.”

At that moment Kirsten came down the stairs with a small bag. As she walked past George and Fred she said, “I just checked his gun safe. He took almost everything.” Then she stopped and turned to face them. “And the guys he asked to go with him, war buddies. Do you think he maybe forgot to mention something to me?" She turned and walked outside to George's car.

Fred watched as she crossed the lawn. "Man, that just doesn't seem fair, does it?"

"Which end?"

"She has the most loving husband ever, and he can't even apologize and make up. It would tear him apart if he saw her mad at him like this."

"She's not mad. She's scared and confused. Deep down, she knows that James was only trying to protect her."

"Just doesn't seem right."

"You're a cop, how much of what you see is?"

❧❧❧

The talk was light, George not really sure of what to say, and Kirsten not wanting to say much of anything. They sat at a red light, the light mixing with the rest of the street lights and painting a kaleidoscope of colors. The red hue from the traffic light shone down onto the windshield of the black Explorer. The reflections reminded Kirsten of the blood that she had seen drip from her television, and she was relieved when the light turned green. As George applied pressure to the gas, his cell phone began to ring, breaking the awkward silence.

"Hello?"

"*Hey Chief.*"

"What have you got?"

"*Well, the information you wanted about the note . . .* "

"Yeah."

"*Uh, I'm not sure how to say this, Sir, but, whatever wrote it, it doesn't seem to have been a human hand.*"

"What do you mean?"

"*Well, we pretty much knew that right away. The writing was too perfect; no human could write that letter free-handed. It's like drawing a perfect circle free-handed . . .* "

"That's been done before, hasn't it?"

"*Sure, but that was one circle. We're talking about that degree of perfection with every stroke in this letter. It's unheard of.*"

"So, you're thinking machine?"

"*That's what we assumed, but all the tests we ran on the paper came out negative for that as well. It wasn't typed . . .* "

"No indentations."

"*Right. It wasn't typed and then photocopied, and it doesn't seem to have come out of a printer either. We've ruled out all kinds of stamps as well.*

We checked for prints too, but the only prints on it are yours, James,' and Kirsten's. So if someone did write it free-handed, they wore a glove. And if someone did print it out, they fed the paper into the printer wearing a glove."

"So what are you saying?"

"*I have no idea what made this letter.*" There was a pause. "*There's something else too.*"

"What?"

"*We checked the location of the drop off.*"

"Yeah?"

"*It doesn't exist.*"

"What do you mean it doesn't exist?"

"*Go figure, Chief. Doesn't make much sense, does it?*"

"No, it sure doesn't." He looked over at Kirsten who obviously had heard the whole conversation and was just staring out the passenger window, praying. "Do you feel like working late tonight?"

"*You want me to start digging in Bermuda?*"

"Yeah,"

"*You want me to take a flight?*"

"No, use the telephone. Find out where he stayed . . . "

Kirsten cut him off. "The Southampton Princess hotel."

"Did you hear that?" asked George.

"*Yeah, got it.*"

"Pack your bags though, just in case."

"*All right, Sir. I'll talk to you first thing in the morning. You tell that pretty lady that her husband is no fool, and that we'll find him.*"

He hung up the phone and looked at her. Knowing that she had overheard the request, he said to her, "You don't need to be told. You know that better than anyone else."

As they drove beneath the night sky and streetlights, though unmentioned, they both were thinking the same troubled thought. *What was going on?*

They drove beneath an underpass, and Kirsten's tired eyes followed a man walking down the sidewalk towards on-coming traffic. She would have dismissed him upon first seeing him, except that he seemed to be staring right at her. As they drove past him, he turned his head, following her with his eyes. He moved his mouth, and, as if he were sitting next to her, Kirsten heard the words his mouth formed. "I have a message for your son."

She jumped and quickly looked over to George who was concentrating on his driving, still captured within his own thoughts. He obviously didn't hear the voice. Turning her head to look behind them, all she saw was an empty road outlined by two vacant sidewalks. And though the man was gone, his words were left to echo in her head, *I have a message for your son.* Kirsten's hands were embracing her pregnant stomach, as if she were trying to protect her unborn. Once she became aware of this reaction, fear ripped through her soul like a bolt of lightening, striking her heart.

ELEVEN
HUNTED

A new sound resonates within the humid air- the sound of machine gun fire. A short burst over the radio signals trouble as the soldier on the other end screams for support. His voice is cut off and the transmission abruptly ends. James looks to his radio man.

"Where are they?" he screams.

The radio man looks confused. "He didn't say!"

A nearby explosion sends the whole team diving to the ground. The sounds of battle are getting closer.

"James!" John bursts through some bushes, running straight at them. "We need to move, now!" He slides onto the ground, next to James.

"What's going on?" asks James as another explosion attempts to drown out his voice.

"They're all dead! We gotta' go!" Even as he speaks, NVA soldiers can be seen running towards their position.

"Let's go!" James gets to his feet and helps up another, who suddenly goes limp in his arms, half of his face missing. James drops him to the ground.

They all begin to run through the jungle, shooting aimlessly over their shoulders at the NVA. Three of the men that are running in front of James suddenly disappear, falling beneath the jungle's floor. Their screams are cut short as the sharp bamboo puncture their bodies. James attempts to stop running and slides to a halt just inches from the hole. He dares to look over its edge and sees two of his friends lying dead, perforated by the many punji sticks that rise from the ground, their tips razor sharp, now colored with American blood. One of his friends is still alive, trying to scream, the bamboo through his throat making it difficult. He turns his head away from the gore in time to see five NVC soldiers bearing down on him.

He pulls the trigger and the M-16 jerks violently against his shoulder. Three of the NVC are torn apart by the bullets and drop to the ground. The other two charge with bayonets that are fixed onto their AK-47s. James screams as they gouge his body over and over again. He sees his own blood splashing into the air with each retracting blade. Finally they seem content with their work, and they are finished with him. They roll him over the side and into the pit. James watches as the sharp bamboo rushes up fast to greet him.

With a yell, James snapped into a sitting position. The cool night air blew against his wet skin and helped to awaken his senses. He gasped for air, allowing time for his body to understand the difference between dream and reality yet again.

"The war?"

James looked over to see Edward lying on his side, leaning on his elbow in the sand beside him, hands folded. The moonlight glowed off his figure. "Yeah." He didn't elaborate. He ran his hand through his hair, wishing that it was Kirsten's hand and not his own.

"I still get them too." He lay carefully onto his back.

The sound of the waves crashing and the moon lighting the cloudless sky presented sort of a placid atmosphere. James took it in as he recovered from yet another Vietnam nightmare. He asked, "Can't sleep?"

Tenderly touching his rib, he shook his head. "Only in spurts. Every movement wakes me up."

James looked up into the night sky and at the moon. He wondered if it was the same moon that hung over Kirsten's sky. A twinkle caught his eye, and he noticed the moonlight reflecting off his wedding ring. After studying the ring on his finger and all that it stood for, he slipped it off and held it tightly in his hands.

"They'll be fine, James. He was just trying to scare you, is all." Edward was referring to the words Brian had spoken earlier, words that were still haunting James' emotions.

James nodded before steering his eyes to Brian, who was still unconscious. "I know. The Lord is watching over them. Satan can't touch them."

Edward asked, "Do you believe in Satan?"

James lay back down, staring at the moon. "I believe he's real, if that's what you mean."

"Do you think he's here, now?"

"On this island?"

"Yeah."

James thought about it for a second. "I wouldn't think so. I can see thinking that. It wouldn't be hard to imagine this being his home, but that would be silly."

Edward's voice sounded unconvinced. "Why would that be silly?"

James smiled to himself. "Maybe this is his vacation home." It came off a little more sarcastic than he had intended and Ed's response was defensive.

"Have you got a better explanation?"

James knew he couldn't engage Edward in a theological discussion about spiritual forces and expect to make any sense to him, so he decided to let it go. "I'm working on one."

Edward closed his eyes. "Well, let me know when it's complete." He fell asleep, leaving James alone with the thoughts of his family and the most recent events.

The explanation he was working on had its roots all the way back into the book of Genesis. All the way back to the beginning of time. Six fingers and six toes, nine feet tall . . . The Bible spoke of similar people in the Old Testament- Genesis, Numbers, Deuteronomy, Joshua, Second Samuel, and First Chronicles. Mighty men of renown they were called. The angelology book that James had begun to read also spoke of these 'giants' in relation to demons. Admittedly, the theology of this particular area seemed somewhat far-fetched to him, but now he wasn't so sure. As fatigue grasped his mind, he found it hard to differentiate between his logical mind and his imagination. Fallen angels and giants, the Bermuda Triangle and quantum physics, Vietnam . . . It all sloshed together, making one specific train of thought impossible. He dismissed the whole thing and decided to rather think of his wife. A thought more appealing anyway. Drifting into sleep, eyes closing out the bright moon, the sound of the ocean growing fainter, he slipped his wedding ring back onto his finger and wondered why, after all these years, John had suddenly appeared in his dreams.

:::: *Day Three*

Suppose a dream could answer a question all else could not, could the dream be trusted? And if so, what did it mean? Strange things, dreams . . . Very strange indeed. There were times when James filled his mind to overflowing with facts, details, and theories and, upon awaking in the morning, somehow awoke with a clear picture of it all. Perhaps it was his brain working overtime . . . or perhaps not. Whatever the case, a similar experience greeted him this morning.

"Okay, hang in there with me." He was talking to Chris, John, Joshua, and Edward. Brian was still out cold. The sun had just begun its climb into the sky, peeking above the ocean's rolling blankets. "I know this is going to sound strange to you. Believe me; it sounds strange to me too."

They waited with anticipation.

"Now, regardless of whether you believe the Bible or not, the Bible does make mention of giants that have six fingers and toes."

John rolled his eyes. "Come on, James, give us a break."

"Hold on, just hear me out. Now, there are all kinds of different theories about this, from the ludicrous to the even more ludicrous, but they make sense within the light of Scripture so this is where I want you to bear with me." He paused, trying to gather his thoughts. "One of those theories is that fallen angels mated with women and these giants were the offspring. This happening in the time of Noah, they would be destroyed in the flood. However, the Bible does speak of them after the flood as well."

"You think we're in some kind of multi universe? Where the events of our time never transcended this time?" asked Edward as he tried to suppress the shooting pain that just ran up his side.

Joshua shook his head. "You mean, the Bermuda Triangle swallowed us up and spit us out in an Old Testament world?"

"I'm not saying we're back in time or anything like that, I'm merely comparing our present situation with that of Noah's," answered James. "The two seem very similar."

"Whoa!" John leaned back into the sand. "That's a huge mouthful of crap to swallow at one sitting."

Chris shook his head. "So we find Noah, have him build us a boat . . . a small boat ya' know. It doesn't have to be an ark or anything . . . " His wound did little to effect his normal personality traits.

James sighed. His words sounded ridiculous even to himself. "Okay then, Joshua, you make a case out of this." James knew Joshua had a logical mind and would just recite the facts. He needed to hear them come from somebody else for a change.

"Fine." Joshua set his eyes on the rising sun as he quickly formed a rough draft in his brain. "We are flying through a tropical storm in the Bermuda Triangle, we get lost. We see a face from hell in the clouds, and then we fly into a waterspout. Presumably the next day, we wake up to find ourselves on a beach, no sign of any wreckage. Just us . . . alive. We go into the woods, we see a crop circle, a quarry, and learn that we are also being followed. The place is evil, there's no doubt about that, you can feel it in the air. At night time we discover that the sky is a little different than it should be, and we later learn that all of our watches stopped working at the same time, again, presumably when we entered the waterspout . . . "

"Or arrived here," threw in James.

"Objection!" cried John. "You're leading the witness."

Joshua complied. "Or when we arrived here. Brian disappears, we find him in the crop circle. He is . . . different. Perhaps possessed. He exhibits signs of something taking control over him, supernatural strength, a voice not his own . . . He refers to James as 'Christian,' and he tries to kill Chris. At the mention of God, it seems that whatever is inside of Brian flees, leaving Brian in a coma or something. Next we learn of there being giants here with six toes, and it's a strange matter that the Bible talks of such men."

There was a long silence, everyone deep in their own thoughts, trying to figure out what all those facts meant.

Chris broke the silence. "You know the stories. The Philadelphia Experiment, using a magnetic field to turn a ship invisible, actually transporting it to Norfolk, Virginia . . . The stories the men have told, about where they went . . . "

"That stuff's a bunch of crap," complained John.

"Is it? Then you have all the stories about the Bermuda Triangle. Stories that are very similar to the Philadelphia Experiment. Planes and boats disappearing to who knows where."

John was becoming agitated with the direction the conversation was heading. "Look, I'd be a naïve fool to try and pretend that this place was just another one of Bermuda's islands. But why the explanation has to be time travel, multiple universes, or Bible fiction is even more preposterous."

"Well then what's your impression of the crop circle? Where'd that come from?" asked Chris.

"There have been crop circles made all over the world, what does that have to do with where we are? It's been a long time, but I don't recall David and Goliath fighting in a crop circle."

"I was just wondering if you were willing to attribute the circle to UFO's, is all," explained Chris.

John shook his head. "Does it matter?"

"It might," stated James. It was obvious that John wanted to keep his mind as far from the supernatural as possible. He had a worldview established, and a supernatural reality would destroy it. He would stick to his truth and experience as long as he could, even if it was beginning to sound illogical.

John looked at James with disgust. "So where does your God fit in to all this quantum physics, UFO stuff?"

James wondered where this sudden hostility had come from as he shook his head and answered honestly. "I don't know."

"Well, maybe you should find out."

"It's obvious that none of us really know anything about quantum physics," said Joshua. "Except for common knowledge about photons and black holes, all we have is an impression. And the impression that I get, as I look around this place, is that perhaps something in that world of science is pretty close to the mark."

"You think we're in a different universe?" John's voice was sarcastic.

"I think we're in a world a lot different than our own. Whether that be an island somewhere in the Atlantic or a land from the days of Noah, I have no idea. I think it's safe to say that none of us has any idea. To get bent out of shape about it is ridiculous, John. You want to play the skeptic while the rest of us search for anything that'll fit the missing space, go right ahead. But quit the sarcasm, I don't much appreciate it."

John smiled. "Sorry, didn't mean to hurt your feelings."

"John!" James snapped and took him by surprise. "Relax." It felt awkward, rebuking 'uncle John.'

John stood to his feet, but before he walked away he said, "You want to know where we are? We're in hell. None of us survived the storm." He turned and walked down the beach, hands in his pockets.

After a few moments of silence, Edward asked, "Are we?"

"No, of course not." James sifted sand through his fingers. He was about to add another thought when a shadow swept over him. Startled, he quickly looked up to see what was bearing down on him.

"We have to get off this island." Brian stood, shaking with fear, eyes lost in a far-out gaze set somewhere in the unseen.

James and Edward hopped to their feet immediately. "Are you okay?"

Brian only looked at them as he spoke, his words coming slow. "I know what happens here. I saw it."

"Do you remember what happened to you?"

His eyes told all. "I'll never forget." Then he looked into the woods. "They'll be coming for us soon."

Joshua got to his feet. "Who?"

Brian's gaze was fixed a hundred yards away now, on the tree line, and he brought his arm up slowly and pointed in that direction. "Them."

Curious and a bit troubled, they all turned their head to see what Brain was talking about.

"Whoa!" Chris jumped to his feet. "What the heck is that?"

Something moved behind the trees, hidden underneath shadow.

"What is it, Brian?" asked James taking a step closer to both Brian and the woods.

"It's them."

Joshua caught a glimpse of something as the morning light stroked its body. “Those are men.” He sounded surprised by his discovery. He strained to see more and was rewarded by his efforts. “They’re carrying swords . . . ”

“They’re hunting us.” Brian suddenly didn’t seem concerned with his own words, divorced from the reality that should be introducing fear.

“I see them,” said James. And indeed he did. They moved carefully through the trees, watching them, stalking them. “Who are they?” he whispered.

“Who?” He shook his head. “I’d be more concerned with *what.*”

Joshua cut in, a little frustrated with Brian’s sudden stoic philosophical approach at answering questions. “What do they want?”

His answer made everyone take a few steps back. “Our souls.”

James picked up an assault rifle and threw the bag over his shoulder before taking off down the beach. After witnessing some of the power that resonated in this place, he had no intention of meeting anyone that lived in it-especially when they wanted to kill him already.

Joshua grabbed the other rifle, leaving Edward with the sniper rifle and Chris with the sub machine gun. Brian picked up the pistol, though he was confused as to where it came from. They all ran as fast as their legs would take them and with what little energy they had.

James bolted past John who was still walking down the beach with his hands in his pockets. He turned just enough to make sure John heard him. “Run, John!”

John watched, bewildered as James took off down the beach, kicking up sand in his wake. Then Joshua ran past him screaming the same thing, “Come on, John! Run!” After Edward and Chris ran by him, almost knocking him over, he turned to see what the matter was and was terrified to see Brian running at him waving a pistol. He started running, assuming it was Brian they were all running from. But Brian passed him too. “Run!”

“What’s going on?” he screamed. Turning his head in the direction they had all come from, he noticed the group of men running through the woods, near the tree line. He could see the swords gleaming in the early light, and he cursed as he back-peddled and turned to follow after his friends. “Wait!”

They ran like they had never run before. James was leading, but Joshua and Chris were gaining on him. Chris looked back over his shoulder and could barely make out the dark figures still tracking them from inside the woods. If they broke the cover of the woods, then they could easily be put down with the guns, but there seemed to be no sign of them doing so.

“Any ideas?” yelled Joshua as he caught up to James. Running was the only quick solution, but one with no end. Because they had no destination, running in circles may have been just as effective.

Before James could answer, a strange sound blasted in the air, and like everything else in this place, he knew it could not be a good thing. Then, suddenly, the response to the sound came. Breaking the horizon's sandy plains was another group of men, and though they were too far away to count, James guessed they were numbered around twenty-five. "Oh, great!" He broke left and ran straight towards the woods. The worst plan was no plan, and James knew they were in deep on this one.

Edward's chest was on fire, each step threatening to snap his rib and puncture his lung. He didn't know how much longer he could keep it up, and when he saw James change direction and run for the woods, he cursed. He cursed the vanity of running away from people with swords when he held a rifle, and he cursed his old age for robbing him of the fitness he once knew. He was wondering what in the world James was thinking, and then he saw the twenty-five other men running down the beach at him wielding swords and spears, waving them crazily about their heads. He cursed again and without hesitation changed his direction to follow James and the others into the woods.

James knew it would be close. As his legs carried him closer to the jungle, the men that were running within the tree line were attempting to cut off their path, to beat them to their point of entry. Not sure whether they would get their fast enough, James cocked his rifle, preparing for battle.

They weren't fast enough.

The men with swords moved through the jungle like fish though water. They countered the obstacles as if they were running track and jumping hurdles. Jumping over bushes and vines, ducking under branches, and side-stepping trees all without slowing down half a step, they effortlessly beat James to his point of entry.

Not trusting his eyes, knowing that the jungle was hiding the enemy he could not see, and knowing that they were waiting for him, James broke right, avoiding entering the beautiful wildlife and ran along side of it.

Joshua knew what James was trying, but its success rate was in serious question. He was trying to draw the men out of the woods. Since they were equipped with only swords and spears, they would have to come in close to use them. If they broke the cover of the trees, and were to step out onto the sand, then they would be no match for the assault rifles. However, the longer they ran along the jungle's edge, still on the beach, the closer the other twenty-five men came.

Edward couldn't do it anymore. His legs went numb, and he stumbled to the ground, trying to breathe. As he sat there on the beach, he watched his friends continue to run away from him, not noticing his fall. Then he noticed something else- a man, skin darkened by a life under the sun, muscular, wearing only a loin cloth, and holding a spear. He exploded from the woods and jumped high into the air, bringing his arm back to launch the crude weapon at Edward. Edward brought the sniper rifle up, no time to aim, and fired from his hip. The blast rocked the island's early morning sky, sending birds fleeing from the tree tops. The man landed in a heap five feet from Edward, his body spitting out blood.

The blast stopped both James and Joshua dead in their tracks. They turned, not knowing what to expect and saw Edward laying in the sand, a man dead at his feet. After taking in Edward's situation and his obvious inability to continue running, they took off back in his direction, intent on defending him. They knew the natives would take advantage of the injured; it was the rule-especially in a place like this.

John was taking up the rear, no weapon in his possession. His side started to cramp, but adrenaline pushed him through the pain. Suddenly, one of the stalkers dove out from behind a tree and ran after John, sword raised in his hand. He closed the distance with remarkable speed, supernatural speed, and just as he reached John and prepared to remove his head, he let out a yell. Startled, John turned just in time to throw himself to the ground, the blade of the sword passing just inches above his head. He got back to his feet and found himself staring at a man who clearly wanted nothing other then to rip out his heart. "Hi."

James reached Edward, Joshua still trailing, just as two of the dark men decided to exit the cover of the woods. Getting to one knee, he aimed down the barrel of the assault rifle and squeezed the trigger twice. Both men fell dead to the ground. James then struggled to help Edward to his feet. "Come on, you have to try!"

Edward's face grimaced with pain as James wrapped his arm around his waist and picked him off the ground. Another of the natives came running onto the beach, ready to throw a spear. Joshua shot him through the head.

"Come on! Help me!" yelled James.

Joshua ran to the other side of Edward and helped lift him into the air. Quickly taking in his surroundings, Joshua noticed that John was having a problem a bit further down the beach. And as he spotted two more men making their way towards John's back, he knew John's problem was about to get a lot worse. "James!"

James looked over to Joshua, sweat rolling down his face.

"John!" Joshua pointed down the beach.

James' heart picked up in pace as he watched his friend trying to avoid being cut in half. "Chris!"

Chris didn't need to be told, he saw what was going on, and he sprinted down the beach to help John, his wound starting to bleed again. Brian followed.

"There's still three more around here somewhere," said Joshua to James.

"Keep your eyes open!" was the reply. The twenty-five other men were getting very close, and James knew that if there was any chance at losing them in the woods, they'd have to start moving in that direction now.

Joshua got out from under Edward's weight and handed him over to James. "I'll be right back." He ran into the woods.

"Joshua!" James called after him, but it was no use.

John ducked as the sword passed over his head, and then he charged, head first at the man, hitting him before he could finish his follow-through. Both men were sent into the sand, and John punched the face of his attacker until it disappeared in blood. But the man was strong and ignored the blows being delivered to his face. Instead, he concentrated on reaching the sword that was just out of his reach. He stretched out, his fingers touching the handle.

John didn't let up with his blows, and he was now covered in blood himself.

Despite the blows, the man grabbed the sword and thrust its handle into John's head, knocking him backwards. As John lay there, disoriented in the sand, the man stood to his feet and walked over to him. The white of his eyes was all that could be seen, the rest covered with a mask of red that was dripping down his bare chest. And then a short burst of machine gun fire sounded, and the man was thrown backwards into the sand. This time he would not be getting up again.

Chris fired the sub-machine gun at the two men who had tried to sneak up on John, hitting one in the back but missing the other. Brian chased the other through the woods until he had a clear shot. Holding the pistol out in front of him with two hands, he squeezed the trigger and watched the fleeing man fall to the jungle's floor.

Joshua walked quietly through the brush, feet careful to make no noise. His eyes searched the jungle for signs of the remaining three men, but they were good at hiding. He walked, rifle against his shoulder, finger on the trigger. There was no movement, no noises coming from the jungle. But he knew that if he was going to be attacked, they would have to come out of hiding to do so. So he waited.

The twenty-five others were only fifty yards away now, and they did not appear to be happy.

"Go! Go! Go!" screamed Chris as he, Brian, and John made their way back to James and Edward.

James signaled for them to enter the woods and run past him- they did. Edward threw John the sniper rifle as he passed.

Still holding up Edward, James turned and walked backwards into the woods, firing the assault rifle from his hip at the small army that was bearing down on them. Three dropped and were trampled by the rest. Then two more fell. James handed the rifle to Edward and threw him over his shoulder before running after the others.

Joshua watched as his friends tore through the woods, attempting to get as deep into the jungle as possible as fast as possible. He waited and watched until the three men stepped out of their hiding places and followed after James, Chris, Brian, Edward, and Joshua. It was amazing, the way in which they hid themselves. They had only been ten yards in front of Joshua, yet Joshua was about to walk right past them, not witnessing any sign of them being there at all. But they didn't see him either, and he aimed the rifle at their backs and put them down one shot after the other. Just as he finished the last one off, the remaining twenty men poured into the jungle, hot on the trail of his friends. He hid behind a tree and picked off four more before he was out of ammo.

It didn't matter what was in front of them, they ran straight through it. Sticks, thorns, vines, it didn't matter. Adrenaline pumped through their veins and overrode their pain receptors, though they would certainly feel it later on . . . if they lived that long. The jungle was alive with life today, but as the five men recklessly plowed though it, all its life scurried away to escape.

James struggled with each step, and Edward cursed in pain. Every once in a while one of the natives would get too close and Edward would shoot them, or at them. It wasn't the easiest of exercises, shooting a rifle at a moving target while being draped over someone's shoulder. Concentrating on aiming wasn't his first priority either. With his mid-section over James' shoulder, he was absorbing a lot of tough blows. Every time James would jump over something, Ed would get a little air between himself and James' shoulder, but that small distance was closed roughly whenever James' feet landed back on the ground. Head pounding, the constant whip lash threatened to knock him out. His stomach was both sore and upset, his muscles being hammered by James' shoulder making him want to cry and puke. But the number one attention getter was the tremendous pain in his side from an injured rib that felt as if someone was twisting a red-hot knife in him. So, with his attention mostly occupied within his own physical hell, he wasn't too concerned with the fact that he was putting more bullets in the trees that surrounded them rather than in the natives who were chasing them.

"What the heck!" Frustration, confusion, and pain surrounded Chris' outburst. They broke through into a clearing and found themselves standing at the edge of the quarry.

John turned in time to see James struggle into the clearing to meet them. "We have a problem."

James took note of the situation and then looked behind him. They were still coming; he could see them moving through the trees. "Where's Joshua?"

Gasping for air, Brian answered, "I don't know."

"What do we do, James?" Anxiousness resounded in John's voice. They couldn't skirt the quarry, it was too huge, and they couldn't go back into the woods without running into their pursuers.

"There are only twenty of them, right?"

Chris answered between breaths. "That's all that might have been chasing us, but who knows . . . " His thought was cut off by an explosion of brush as a native ran into the clearing just feet in front of them. Brian dropped to one knee and brought up his pistol, only squeezing the trigger twice before the native was on top of him. But that was enough. He threw the lifeless body behind him where it slid off the side of the quarry and into oblivion.

All eyes were now on the woods that were just ten yards in front of them, expecting more foes to burst through at any second. With their backs to the bottomless pit, they would have to put down any attackers as soon as they broke the cover of the jungle. That meant that every shot had to be accurate. A miss could be all the time a native needed to launch a spear or sword or to run into them, sending them all into the depths of the island forever. James set Edward down a little rougher than Ed would have liked, and he let him know so as he handed the rifle back to him.

The first man to enter the clearing took three bullets to the chest and fell at John's feet. The next two came at the same time, one dropping even before he could escape the woods, the other actually managing to throw his spear despite being mangled with bullets. The spear flew harmlessly overhead of John, but the native, with incredible determination, refused to die short of him. He stumbled onward, the barrage of firepower at close range not doing much for his physical appearance. He made it through the ten yards of hot lead and finally fell into John, and his momentum threatened to throw them both over the side of the quarry. Using the native's momentum against him, John grabbed him and turned, attempting to guide him past and into the quarry himself. The native flew over the edge but grabbed John's hand just before disappearing. Now the native's momentum had worked against John rather than for him as he began to slide towards the hole.

"John!" Edward screamed and crawled over to him, grabbing his legs and preventing him from sliding any further towards eternity. Then the bloody native did something unheard of. He started climbing up John's arm.

"Shoot him!" yelled John, who started to feel himself sliding again.

James and Chris didn't dare take their attention off the jungle in front of them. As much as they wanted to help, they knew another attack could kill them all. But Brian only seemed to be in a daze, eyes set into nothingness.

"Brian! Help them!" James pleaded with him.

But Brian didn't respond.

Edward was beginning to slide now as well, the native pulling them towards the hole as he climbed up. "Somebody, do something! I can't hold on much longer!" The native now had a hand on John's neck and was reaching for his shoulders, which were now hanging over the abyss.

Chris got to his feet and ran over to Brian, never taking his vision or aim off the jungle. He put out his hand. "Give me the gun, Brian."

No response.

Chris stole a quick glance at Brian and noticed that his eyes were closed. He reached for the pistol and ripped it out of Brian's hand and threw it across the ground to John. It stopped against John's body, but by his thigh.

"It's by your leg!" yelled Edward.

"Can you reach it?" asked John, the native's hands now on his shoulders.

"Not without letting go of you!" Which he was almost ready to do anyway, fatigue and pain now beginning to take over.

By now, John's face was buried in the native's bloody chest. "Well, don't do that." He was hitting the native in the kidney with one hand while trying to reach for the pistol with the other. His finger brushed its handle. "Almost. . ."

Just when James had decided to take the chance and help John and Ed, three more natives burst through the woods.

When John heard the gunfire, he knew that reaching the pistol was his only chance. He got another finger on it and began to slide it towards him. He grabbed it just as the native reached over his head and grabbed his belt, pulling him even closer to the hole. John brought up the pistol and fired it into the native's stomach. The native let go for a second and began falling into the hole but caught a handful of John's hair on his way down. John let out a yell, wincing in pain, the native holding on for his life, dangling over a very long drop.

James and Chris finished the third native off just in time to see the outcome of John's predicament.

John had the pistol aimed right between the native's eyes, but the native's face, what was left of it, looked indifferent. John peered into his eyes and saw nothing looking back at him. The eyes were lifeless, black like a shark's. It was almost as if the man had no soul, no spirit. John pulled the trigger and the force that was dragging him to hell was broken. Edward helped get him completely back onto the ground.

"Are you okay?" asked James, eyes still trying to detect more attackers.

John rolled onto his back, letting the emotion brought on by near death pass. "I'm great."

Chris' eyes searched back and forth into the trees, but all was still and quiet. Everyone held their breath, waiting. "They're hiding . . . " He whispered.

James couldn't believe what it had taken to put down the few natives. They were definitely not normal people. He whispered to no one in particular, "Who are these people?"

Brian responded, "They're the people that live here."

His eyes reacting to the sound of Brian's voice, James found Brian standing like a rock, his eyes fixed on something distant. "Brian," James wanted to know if Brian was conscious of the last few minutes. "Where's your pistol?"

He squeezed the hand that had been holding it, and, for the first time, his eyes broke away from whatever it was they were attached to. His facial expression communicated his feeling as he struggled to understand how the gun could be in his hand one second and gone the next. "I . . . I don't know."

John rolled over onto his side and looked at his old friend. Something was definitely wrong with him. Changing the subject, he asked, "How long do we sit here?" His eyes joined everyone else's in searching the woods that stretched out before them, waiting for a sign of the enemy.

"I don't know," stated James. They sat motionless; the only sound to be heard was their own heavy breathing.

"How many are left?" asked Ed.

Brian counted five dead on the ground in front of them and two that had gone into the quarry. "There were twenty-five, right?"

"Coming at us on the beach," answered Chris

James said, "I got at least five."

"Then whatever Joshua got."

"I think I hit two," added Edward.

Five minutes passed by. "We can't stay here like this, what if they went to get help?" asked John.

James knew he was right. "Okay." He reached into the duffel bag that was hanging from his shoulders and took out another clip. After loading the rifle, he stood, gun trained on the woods in front of him. Slowly moving towards the woods, he called back over his shoulder. "I'll cover you and make sure they don't follow. You guys skirt around the hole."

"And go where?"

He looked up beyond the trees and could barely make out higher ground. "Meet me at the top of the waterfall."

John nodded in return as he helped Edward to his feet. "Come on, Ed." They began to walk cautiously around the bottomless hole, careful not to take their eyes off its edge or the jungle that surrounded them.

He watched two of the men talking to each other. Though they were too far away from Joshua to be heard, it was obvious that they were frustrated and confused. Then one started yelling at the other.

In English.

It was broken and distorted, but it was English. But before this phenomenon had a chance to penetrate Joshua's stunned mind, one of the two men suddenly lashed out with a spear and ran the other through, laughing as he watched his comrade struggle to hang on to life. And then Joshua watched in horrible amazement as the wounded man pulled the spear from his body and swung it at the other, cutting open his face. Both men screamed out in pain as they began to beat each other with their bare hands- until one of them was able to find a rock.

Joshua stumbled backwards away from his hiding spot, leaving the protection of the large ferns. With wide eyes fixed on the carnage, he didn't notice what was standing behind him until he bumped into it. He spun around, ready to attack. Towering over him was ten feet of horrendous wickedness. Its body sculpted from rock, eyes dark and gleaming, hideously ugly . . . It was holding a sword that was close to 7' long, and Joshua didn't need to count its fingers to understand his situation. The giant stood, looking at him through lazy eyes, waiting for him to run. And run he did.

James listened to the jungle's music. It was a deception, how soothing it was. It was as if the jungle tried to convince him that the past ten minutes had not happened, that it was all a dream. He watched the leaves flutter whenever a breeze swept through. It was calm, normal- or so it seemed. His vision followed a lizard that ran up a nearby tree, its eyes rolling around in their sockets looking for its prey. Birds began to settle back into their tree of choice, and the tropical habitat seemed to return to its natural self. That meant one of two things. One: the enemy was no longer present, or two: they were very patient. James began to wonder about the natives. Swords, spears, and loin cloths . . . certainly didn't seem 21st Century.

A noise rebuked James' mind for wandering off in distant thought and brought him around to face a shaking branch. It was too difficult to see through the ferns that crowded the jungle's floor in that direction so he began to move slowly towards the shaking branch.

Joshua threw himself into a wall of vines, hoping his momentum would carry him through the nature-made wall. He came up from a tuck and roll just in time to duck under the huge blade of the giant's sword. Though the sword missed him, it did not miss a nearby tree, and the sword cut through it like it was paper. Joshua continued to run, not knowing how he was going to lose death as it bore down on him, swinging crazily with the fires of hell.

There was nothing there. James stood, tired of the game. He had a gun, they had swords. *Bring it on.* But nothing came. He only found himself standing, alone, in the middle of a jungle, and as he looked up into the sky, past the towering trees, he suddenly felt really, really small.

And then he heard another noise. It came suddenly and out of nowhere, a noise that sounded like a hundred whispering voices. It started out low, its volume barely audible. But it seemed to be getting louder. And then James realized that it wasn't getting louder, it was getting closer. What he could only describe as a gust of wind seemed to accompany the voices, and he could see it moving through the dense jungle, bending the trees and blowing loose foliage out of its way. It no longer sounded as speaking voices though, but screaming voices . . . terrible haunted voices. And as it got even closer, the gust of wind began to appear as if it had some sort of physical property to it, because, though transparent, James could see it coming straight at him, almost like a cloud of water. All he could do was throw up his hands to cover his face as the screaming force blasted past him. The gust caught his pants and hair and pulled at them, leaves and other debris swirling around him. Frantic eyes searched the treetops, and nervous hands shook as they gripped the assault rifle. As if bullets would help him against such a foe, he brought the rifle up to his shoulder, still looking for whatever it was that had just swept past him. But it was gone. For now.

"James!" Joshua's voice cut through the dripping suspense.

James swung around in the direction he heard the voice, startled and eyes racing all around him, trying to locate Joshua.

"Run!"

"Where are you?" yelled James.

"Just run!"

James' feet began to move, dragging his body along with them. Then he saw Joshua burst into his line of sight from around a row of trees. "Joshua!"

Joshua ran towards him, but it was clear that he wasn't intent on slowing down. "Run, James!" He was through pleading, and now he sounded frustrated at his friend's unwillingness to comply.

Just before James turned to follow, he saw the giant crashing through the woods, violently swinging the sword at small trees and vines and anything in its path. As if it was cutting a trail though tall grass with a machete, it easily cleared a way through the thick jungle, a wake of splintering wood and flying leaves filling the air.

It was one of those moments in time where what you saw short-circuited your brain and made you numb. James stood, not able to move a muscle, not able to comprehend what he was seeing, not able to understand the seven foot long sword. Not able to understand the most bizarre of all his dreams. The giant brought the sword back, a terrible expression of hateful satisfaction on its face, and began to swing the instrument that would cut James in half like he was a stick of butter.

But the wonder faded just enough for his arms to begin working, and he brought the machine gun up, his thumb switching the rifle to auto-fire. The giant was only four feet away when he pulled the trigger and held it down. The giant screamed and fell onto the ground, sliding into James' legs and sending him flying through the air.

Joshua was already there when he landed. "Come on!" He was grabbing him under the arm, dragging him away from the fallen giant.

James allowed himself to be drug away, but he couldn't take his wide eyes off the giant that was already getting back to its feet.

There seemed to be no sign of the natives. John was leading Edward, Brian, and Chris through the woods. It was scary how fast everything came back to him, he thought. The jungle, the running, the shooting and killing . . . He felt as if he were back in the jungles of Vietnam, only now they weren't running from VC or the NVA but from giants and men with swords wearing loin cloths. Not to mention the other weird stuff that seemed to roll over this place like the tides on its beach. *Does the Bible really talk about this stuff? Was there really a time that knew this place?* His thoughts rebuked all he wanted to believe, but he had to admit to himself that something spiritual was taking place here.

A voice cut into his thoughts and brought his senses back to his physical surroundings.

"I think we're getting close." Brian could hear the sound of rushing water somewhere in the distance.

Though there seemed to be no viable threat at the moment, Chris would not be taken off guard if that proved only a deception. He followed John and Brian with eyes locked on the surrounding areas, trying to ignore the burning pain in his back. Every shaking branch, every falling leaf, every scatter of an animal set his reflexes on fire, and he had to exert self-control to not shoot everything that moved.

Edward was struggling. He wasn't so sure about his rib now; it felt like it could be cracked after all, the pain making it hard for him to even breathe. As he fought his way forward, a sudden thought buzzed in his brain. Like a shot of electricity, it jolted his perception while it taunted him with mockery, yet the voice was remorseful at the same time. It simply said, "You're not going to make it."

A large outcropping of rock stretched across their path, forcing them to either climb over it or go around it. Deciding against climbing over, they skirted around the rock wall and slid down a dirt hill until they were faced with a staggering scene of both beauty and dire news. It was beautiful, a forest of bamboo as far as the eye could see, the early morning sun showing itself, through the mist that was rising from the ground, and streaming through the midst of the tall plants.

The bad news was that the bamboo was rooted in thick mud- that being evident without even getting close. If they were going to continue on their present course, they would have to travel through tight bamboo and thick mud. Neither was appealing.

"What now?" asked Chris.

John turned around and looked at the hill they had just slid down and then looked at the endless bamboo that was before them. "Let's keep going. I think we're almost there."

There was no time for complaint or disagreement; they knew they had to keep moving- that their lives depended on it. Besides, John was a professional point man, and they trusted his instinct. They knew if anyone was qualified for the position, it would be someone who led a team through the Mekong in the dead of night or the Ho Chi Min Trail in a thunder storm. Even if John's decision did take them knee deep in mud, they trusted his experience.

"Let's . . . " Chris didn't even care what he was going to say, the thought was as irrelevant as any other thought separated from what he just witnessed, and that was John stopping dead in his tracks and quickly bringing the assault rifle up to his shoulder. He searched the trees, looked through the floating mist, and waited for a reason to shoot at something.

"What is it?" asked Edward, fear lining his words.

"Shhh. . .," whispered John. He swung around to face the other way.

Two minutes passed by and nothing presented itself, so they continued onward, into the thick mud and cluttered bamboo.

As soon as the last person entered into the mud and discovered what everyone else had already learned (that quick travel would be impossible through two feet of wet dirt), there was a loud noise that sounded from the right, somewhere from within the bamboo.

This time everyone brought their guns up and aimed them towards the sound.

Brian pumped the shot gun James had given him out of his bag before running off into the woods. He brushed the trigger with his index finger, ready to fire. But again, nothing resulted, and they all relaxed.

Just as Brian took his left hand off the pump and dropped the shotgun to his side, a huge figure erupted from the bamboo beside him, shattering it like it was glass. Brian had little time to react, his left hand just grasping the pump when the huge sword pierced him through.

The giant threw its head back and let out a gratifying yell, lifting Brian into the air on his sword.

Brian's wide eyes couldn't believe what had happened, but before he was able to understand it, the giant pulled the sword out from him, swung it around in his hand, and brought it back down in a swinging arc with such speed, no one knew what had even happened. Until Brian's upper torso fell backwards and into the mud.

John screamed, rage bringing the veins in his neck to surface. He and Chris both emptied their weapons into the giant's chest, and it fell over with a splash and then disappeared beneath the mud.

They couldn't grasp it, couldn't accept it. It had happened too fast. The shock prevented them from moving. Years of friendship ended in only a few seconds . . . how were they supposed to cope with that?

"Come on!" Chris was the first to begin moving, probably because he was the least attached to Brian. He urged them to keep moving, but they wouldn't move. They just stood there staring at Brian's broken body, trying to understand the suddenness of his death.

Then the mud began to separate and the giant began to struggle at its surface.

"Let's go!" yelled Chris. "Do you want to be standing here looking at two dead friends?" He pulled them towards the thickness of the bamboo.

Without a word, they reluctantly gave in and began to run with Chris, away from the muddy sword that just broke the surface of the mud.

Upon reaching dry ground again, they allowed their adrenaline and their emotion to push them even harder through the island's cursed trees.

And then the ground gave way beneath their feet, and they fell into darkness.

"I hope they're okay." James' voice was worried. They were standing beside the waterfall. It poured over the edge and into the still water one hundred feet below. The view from the edge of the waterfall was hindered by the jungle's canopy but still a sight to see.

Joshua didn't know how to answer, because they could very well be dead- all of them. He looked around, contemplating their situation. The waterfall was beautiful, as was to be expected in a tropical climate, but the beauty aspect failed to suck any awe out of them. "I'm starving," said Joshua.

James looked at him and laughed, suddenly thinking it odd that he had. He wondered if it was a sound this sky had ever heard before.

"Edward could be slowing them up," offered Joshua.

James sunk to his knees. "I brought them here, Joshua. If anything happens to them . . . "

"It wouldn't be your fault."

"Logically, but not emotionally."

"You said it yourself, death is total in every generation, it's just a matter of how and when."

"I know. I know God has the final say, that whatever He allows is allowed for a reason, but I still don't know if I could handle losing one of them here- in this place."

Joshua knelt down beside him, making sure his voice could be heard over the waterfall. "James, as soon as the waterspout sucked up the plane, you were no longer responsible for anything that was to happen. You are in the same situation as we are, and it's just as much our fault as it is yours. This was not part of the plan any of us had designed, especially you."

James suddenly thought about his brother. "Something's been bothering me."

"Only one thing? I just ran away from about forty things that are bothering me."

James dismissed the light comment. "If Lance was really telling the truth about not knowing anything about a ransom, and that he was told to keep my brother on an island, whoever wrote the ransom had a reason for writing it.

It's that reason that bothers me. It's the only thing I can't figure out. What was the reason behind the letter?"

Joshua looked into his friend's eyes. "I've been thinking about that too . . . And the only thing that I keep coming back to is that, whatever the reason, it got us here."

"That's not a pleasant thought."

"Not at all." He stood back to his feet and, for the first time since standing up there, he noticed a clearing down to his right. He looked harder. "Huh, that's interesting." He pointed down towards what had captured his attention. "That must be the crop circle we found Brian in yesterday."

James stood back to his feet, his muscles sore and aching, and when his eyes found the sight, his heart skipped a beat.

"Strange design, isn't it?" asked Joshua, not noticing James' reaction to it.

James stood, motionless, observing the crop circle from the higher ground. It was a design that he had seen before . . . many times before. In the worst of all his nightmares, that image had played a huge part. Only now he wasn't dreaming. His nightmare was now a reality.

Before he could utter a word to Joshua, an arrow pierced the air that separated them. They turned to face their hunters, but they found only rocks and brush, no sign of anyone.

Another arrow streaked by, this one taking a bit of skin off Joshua's face.

"We're in the open," whispered James. The nearest protection was behind where the arrows seemed to be coming from. They were trapped, the waterfall at their backs.

Two more arrows were released from somewhere in the woods, one of them burying into James' shoulder. He cried out in surprise.

"We can't stay here!" Joshua yelled as he pulled the arrow from James' shoulder.

James knew what their only option was, and so did Joshua. "On three."

"One."

"Two."

"Three!"

They jumped over the edge, disappearing within the sheer power of falling water as arrows filled the air.

TWELVE
PUZZLING PIECES

It's different this time. As bullets pierce the air and tear through trees and bodies in explosions of splinters and flesh, something is out of place.

Though fear grips every part of his being, James realizes something as he mows down two more VC. The knowledge is difficult to explain, and there is no time to sort through it now. He dives behind a tree, avoiding the grenade that is thrown his way. It explodes and rocks the ground he's lying on, bringing with it another flash of knowledge. He looks scared . . . worried. And then that fact reaches deep enough to establish a root. He holds on to it, knowing that the answer is alive within this connection. But the connection is undefined, and he doesn't know what is connected.

He sees himself struggle on his stomach, crawling to a friend. Placing a hand over the wound only causes more blood to flow. He's desperate and doubtful- it's written on his face.

Another flash. This one bringing some light that will remain. Realization begins to break through the smoke and despair of a day gone terribly wrong. He watches still, waiting to see what will happen to himself.

Another hold. His consciousness begins to scale the steep wall.

He's running now, trying to catch up with the others who are suddenly way ahead of him. But an explosion sends him flying through the air.

He twitches as a result, and another hand-hold is found.

Enough self-awareness grabs a hold of his mind to know that he is dreaming, yet not enough to wake him up. He can only watch himself as if he were watching a movie, though everything he feels on the big screen, he also feels from where he is watching.

Another Vietnam dream- at least this time he knows it's a dream. With the realization comes a degree of control, and he's able to influence the script just enough to stay alive in his nightmare. He shoots more Vietnamese as a result, enemy soldiers suddenly very inaccurate in their aim.

"Another Vietnam nightmare." The voice slices through the jungle's atmosphere and transcends every sound of battle. It's a voice detached from the chaos war brings.

James watches himself look around, trying to detect the source of the words.

"I think I've seen this one before." The voice is bored, and the jungle is suddenly rolled up like a scroll and discarded, as if it were only an image projected against a green-screen.

James is left standing in a completely white room, its edges unidentifiable. In fact, as he observes his new surroundings, he realizes there are none. He's no longer observing himself as a spectator now, but from first-person, and he begins to walk towards a wall. But as he walks, the wall remains at the same distance. Then he realizes that there is no wall- there is no anything. Only a bright void.

"Too many reruns on that station. Why don't we dial up a new series?" A man emerges through the brightness and walks in front of James. Immediately, James knows that this person is crafty, untrustworthy. He carries himself with such confidence that the world must be his. The thin smile that spreads his lips . . . arrogant. Yet he's a genius.

"Who are you?" James hears his own voice for the first time.

He shrugs. "Who do you want me to be?" He smiles again, waving his hand with casualty. "I have so many names."

An enemy in a nightmare is usually identified as such right away with no prior knowledge within the boundaries of the dream. More than not, it is commonly something feared in reality transferred into the dream-world, but the fact that James does not know who this person is, troubles him enough so that he moves restless in his sleep- the physical result of what is happening within his imagination.

"Oh, I forgot to welcome you!" He laughs. "Oh my, where are my manners? Please forgive me, sometimes I'm such a horrible host." He speaks friendly, but perhaps a bit more sarcastic. "You see, I'm so busy that sometimes it just slips my memory." He continues waving his hands, entertaining more of himself it would seem. "I mean, I have to be here then I have to be there . . . Oh my, it never does end, does it?"

James slowly steps backwards, but again, no distance is gained.

"Excuse me? Are you uncomfortable? I mean, it would just be a sin if my guest was to be uncomfortable, now wouldn't it?" He looks up into the brightness, a hand on his chin. "Hmm . . . How would this do?" He stretches forth his hand and James is immediately knocked backwards and into a red sofa. "That should suit your fancy quiet well, I should suppose." His voice changes with the look in his eye as he adds, "Besides, you should probably be sitting for the next show."

"What next show?"

The man walks over to James, the dream not allowing the details of his clothing, hair, or skin- only his gender, eyes, lips, voice, and mass. He places both hands on the arms of the couch and leans down so that he is eye level with James. He whispers icily, "Do you know who I am, James Streen?"

Searching for the answer he is sure he knows, his attention is grabbed by the flames that are dancing in the man's eyes.

Another smile. "They say the eyes are the windows to the soul . . . " He leans even closer, his nose touching James,' whispering even softer. "So tell me, Christian, what is it that you see?" Before James can answer, the man spins away from him and waves his arms at the void.

Another scene. This one is not of the wet jungles in Vietnam but of a street in New York.

His street.

"Familiar?" the man asks.

James leans forward on the couch.

"You see!" he yells. "The suspense! It works every time! Did you know that you can put anything in front of a person as long as it's wrapped with suspense? It's great!" He is now walking around, excited about the topic at hand. "Through suspense, I can gain an access into the mind." He taps his head. "Because when something is suspenseful, it captures the attention. But the attention is so concentrated on circumstance that it misses the subliminal stuff, the conversations and the words that promote my ideas." He laughs again.

The image that surrounds them begins to move, as if James were on one of those theme park rides traveling down the street- heading towards his house. The words that had escaped Brian's mouth the day before race through his mind and anger begins to pulse through his body. *It's truly a pity that you won't be around to witness what's in store for your lovely family back in New York . . .*

Laughter echoes off the houses that line the street, but the few people who are out don't seem to hear it. Nor do they see James and the man who is now crying with laughter. "Do you see what I mean?" he bellows. "Look at you!"

Taking his eyes off his surroundings, James stabs them at the demon, devil, or whoever he is. Everything within him demands that he get off the couch and stop the man before his house is reached, but he can't move. He is now sitting on the red sofa outside of his door, his BMW to the left in his driveway. The door swings open and they move through it.

Anger is still present; the desire to rip the man apart still strong, but a new emotion grabs his being as the hallway passes them by, the kitchen coming closer. Fear races chaotically through his body, confused and aimless. Sweat begins to drip off his chin and splash onto the tile floor.

The man sits beside James, entertained by the virtual reality he is creating. Leaning over he whispers, "Do you think God is going to protect your family from me when you're gone?"

James attempts to turn his head away from the kitchen, away from whatever it is that he is going to see, but his head is unmoving, his eyes unable to even blink.

"Let me fill you in on a little something, James. You're going to die here." He shakes his head. "So what? You die, go to your pitiful, boring heaven, yada . . . yada . . . ya . . . But, before you die here, I want you to know something." His lips touch James' ear as he whispers, "Your wife . . . will be mine. Your daughter . . . will be mine." His pleasure passes into disdain. "You fool."

They enter the kitchen, and there is screaming. Tiny drops of blood are on all of the cabinets, even more on the floor.

The screaming grows louder.

The counter blocks the image of what is happening, but James does not need to see in order to understand. The sounds of a struggle fill the room, his wife's voice at its limit. The reflection in an adjacent window reflects a man, Kirsten's body not visible beneath the window frame. His entire being screams out, what he is witnessing enough to change his life forever.

"You are so weak. Look at yourself, about to explode with hate and anger. All because of your stupid whore. We haven't even got to your daughter yet . . . "

The kitchen passes by and they begin to climb stairs.

"Isn't this so much better than those stupid Vietnam reruns?"

Every vein in James' body presses against the surface of his skin, and a few drops of blood leak from exploded capillaries. His body is soaked with sweat, the blood pressure in his head making his cranium feel like it will detonate.

The bathroom door swings open, and James cannot breathe.

"After God takes both of her parents, she will begin to hate Him. She will begin to hate herself." He smiles. "And she'll believe all the lies I put in her head."

The water in the bathtub is red with blood, the fragile wrist dangling over its side still leaking onto the floor.

Something happens and James' tongue is loosed. "You're a liar." His words come out rough.

The man smiles, blushing a bit it seems, and takes a bow. "The father of." He returns standing straight and chuckles. "So you know who I am now?"

He takes his eyes off his daughter and places them into the man's. "I know who you are, Lucifer."

"Lucifer?" He laughs. "Tell me, James, do you have enough faith in your God to believe that He loves you?"

"Yes."

"Then you are a fool."

"We'll see who's the fool."

More laughter. "Is that a threat?"

James' words escape sealed lips. "That's a fact."

The creature sighs as the bathroom vanishes and is replaced by a stone room- dank and dark. "Damn Christian . . . " He gets up to his feet and begins walking away from James. "I *am* going to kill you. And I *am* going to have your wife and daughter . . . " He looks back into the face of a man who doesn't know what to believe. "And, oh yes, most importantly, I will also have your son." Then he smiles. "Sweet dreams." He disappears through the stone wall.

As James sits, no longer on a red couch but on a stone slab, his eyes stuck on the spot of the wall the demon disappeared through, he realizes something that frightens him.

He realizes that he is awake.

Confusion tangles his ability to discern between dream and reality once again, and he wonders how long he has been awake. His heart pounding violently against his rib cage, he drops his gaze to his body. He sees the sweat. He sees the blood. And the horrible question haunts his mind, *was that a dream?*

"Where are we?" Joshua's voice bounced off the stone walls that surround them on all sides.

James traced his hand over the stone, his fingers falling between the cracks that separated what appeared to be cut rock. "I don't know." He was trying to find a way out, feeling for anything that would indicate some kind of door. His arm throbbed, but the arrow had not sunk too deep. The wound wasn't even worthy of being compared to other battle scars he had racked up in both the Marines and the police force. Of course, infection had a way of changing things.

Joshua stumbled towards James, hands stretched out ahead of him, protecting him from obstacles hidden by the darkness. "How long have you been conscious?"

"I don't know." The shroud of darkness made any concept of time impossible.

"How's your arm?"

A sudden burn raced up his arm just as he answered, "It's fine. I think it pretty much stopped bleeding."

Joshua's attention was now concentrated on a dim light, barely visible across the cool floor. He began to feel his way towards the corner of the room, where the light seemed to be the strongest. "Where do you think this is coming from?"

James turned his head towards Joshua's voice. "I don't hear anything."

"No, this light. Can you see it?"

James began to feel his way towards Joshua's voice, and, sure enough, his eyes were able to detect a slight ray of light barely caressing the dark ground. "That wasn't there before." He kneeled down, bumping into Joshua who was already in a lower position.

"A cave?"

James peered through the crack, his eyes hardly picking up the light. "Maybe . . . " He stopped in mid sentence when the light bounced and changed form. "Did you see that?" he asked.

"A candle." Joshua's voice was uncertain. Not uncertain in his answer, but uncertain as to what his answer meant.

"It must be another room." Turning, he sat on the ground and leaned his back against the wall. It was cold to his bare skin. He had no idea where his shirt was, just that it was no longer tied across his waist. "It's impossible to tell how long we've been in here."

Joshua mimicked James by turning and sitting next to him. "We're not dead from starvation or dehydration . . . "

They both sat, waiting for something to happen. Anything to happen.

Haunted by his most recent dream, and the fact that he wasn't sure if it were a dream or not, James leaned his head back against the wall and lifted his eyes towards the ceiling. "Jesus . . . help us."

They sat in silence for a few minutes before Joshua asked a question. "James, how do I get what it is that you have?"

James turned his head until his friend's features were barely recognizable. "You confess with your lips and believe in your heart that Jesus Christ is Lord."

He thought about it for a few seconds. "I remember enough of what the pastor would say every Sunday to know what it is I'm to believe. That Jesus Christ died for my sins."

"Do you believe that?"

Another pause. "I realize that if He didn't, I'm in big trouble. I know there's a God and that I have sin and that if no one took care of my problem, then I'm in big trouble."

"He took care of all your problems, Joshua. He's just waiting for you to apply the solution."

"Okay."

James smiled before leading his friend in the sinner's prayer, and, in the darkness of a cold stone room, possible death awaiting them just beyond its walls, no clue as to where they were or how they got there, a prayer was uttered . . . and a soul was saved.

And the angels in heaven rejoiced.

Though their circumstance gave no reason for joy, there was, nonetheless, joy present. For the past half hour, a friendship established under the cruelest and most testing of environments was elevated to a new plane. Now, not only was their friendship linked by a common goal of survival, but they now shared the same destiny- their friendship eternal. And despite all reason to despair, James, instead, was overjoyed. In the grand scheme of things, being able to lead one of his best friends to Christ was worth everything that had happened so far. And he wouldn't trade it if he could. If the recent, most bizarre and terrifying events were the human cost for a friend's salvation, then it was a cheap price to pay in relation to the eternity that was thus assured. The ultimate price was already paid with perfect blood dripping from a Roman cross, and anything that it took to bring someone to that realization would be much appreciated in forever.

After the glorious half hour passed by, a friend's future secured, rejoicing in the Savior's grace, and sweet fellowship, their attention was brought back to the stone that surrounded them. Like being dropped from bliss and landing hard in a swamp, a sudden noise rang out and demanded a sense of awareness be renewed within their present physical practicality.

"What was that?" James' voice was tangled with excitement and suspense.

Joshua turned to look into the small stream of light that managed to escape the smallest of cracks between two of the stones. But the crack was way too miniscule to allow one's vision passage into the next room- if indeed it was another room. "It sounded like it came from the other side."

After a few minutes went by, Joshua gave up and returned to his prior position. "James . . . " His voice made it clear that he was about to change the more recent subjects. "The crop circle . . . what's going on? I saw the look on your face. You've seen it before, haven't you?"

"Yes," James surrendered.

Joshua asked, "Where?"

If there had been an ample amount of light in the room, Joshua wouldn't have been able to miss the hesitant look that accompanied the long pause. James struggled to clear his thoughts, to summarize his experience with the nightmares, and it was a good thirty seconds before he decided to start talking. Though not sure why, he felt that the story finally needed to be told, as if this place could explain it for him. "In a dream."

That was an answer that Joshua was clearly not expecting. "In a dream?" he asked surprised.

"Yeah. It's actually this re-occurring dream."

"Wait, let me get this straight. Your reaction to seeing the crop circle was because of a dream?" James only nodded, but Joshua didn't need to see that to begin to understand. "James, you think you might want to tell me about these dreams?"

After another long pause, he answered, "I've never told anyone."

"Why?" Even though he asked, Joshua was beginning to wonder if he really wanted to know.

"I dream of the war."

Joshua let out an audible sigh of relief. "Oh, James, that's normal. I have nightmares about the war." He laughed. "I thought you were gonna' tell me this super-freaky nightmare that was gonna' give me goose bumps and sleepless nights."

"The Vietnam war."

This confused Joshua. "Your dreams are about Vietnam?"

"It's more like my dreams are *from* Vietnam."

"Stories Steve told you?"

"Steve never talked about the war."

"Maybe you saw *Platoon* one too many times."

"Never saw it."

They sat in silence for a little while.

Joshua reached out into the darkness and rested a hand on James' shoulder. "These dreams, they bother you that much?"

James chuckled under his breath. "I wake up sweating and screaming. It's not like a normal nightmare . . . it's more like a memory."

"But you know that's not possible."

"I know. It's like I got stuck with someone else's nightmares."

"Vietnam nightmares . . . that is weird."

James sighed. "There's more."

Suddenly knowing the freaky stuff was gonna' start now, Joshua cautiously answered, "Okay."

"There's this presence in the air, like an evil spirit or something. I never see it, but I feel it. I don't expect you to understand how this could be so terrifying. I mean, to be able to describe the *feeling* . . . You could have a nightmare that makes you scream at the top of your lungs, but in your dream it's just you sitting in an empty room. Now when you go to work the next day and tell people about your dream, they smile and say something like, 'Sounds scary.' But they don't know how it could possibly be scary, sitting in an empty room. But that's because you can't describe to them the presence of evil you felt while sitting there. The *feeling* of it."

Now came the goose bumps, and Joshua rubbed his arms. "Okay, I get it."

James was staring into the darkness, putting to words images that he never imagined he would try to remember on his own. "Sometimes the dream plays out long enough, before I wake up, and I see the image."

"The image in the crop circle?"

"Yeah. The jungle thins out a bit, in fact, it seems more like a forest now that I think about it. There's a pretty good distance between the trees, and the ground is covered with only grass, low grass, as if it's been cut. It's like a scene straight from *Apocalypse Now*. I can tell some kind of ritual had taken place, some kind of evil sacrifice." He paused. "There are . . . crosses."

"Crosses?" Joshua's voice whispered in the darkness.

After a moment's silence, James answered. "Yeah. They're all crucified. To trees, to the ground . . . "

Now it was Joshua's turn to pause. "I saw something similar in Caqueta, near the Amazon. We were hunting down a drug ring that fled north from Peru. They were sneaking the stuff into California from Mexico. The CIA was able to track their movements back to Peru. And because the money that came from these specific sales was being funneled into terrorist organizations, some responsible for embassy bombings, we were sent in. Somehow, they knew we were coming and they packed up and fled into the jungles. When we finally tracked them down, it appeared something else had gotten to them first." He paused, allowing his thoughts to morph together. "I remember walking through the grass . . . It was red with blood. But the area . . . Man, the air in that place, the way it hung over everything, you could *feel* the evil, and you knew that whatever happened there- it was something unimaginable. No crop circle though."

James swallowed. "There's a figure, constructed out of branches and vines, set up like an icon. It resembles the shape of a dragon. Same design of the crop circle. And the impression I get every time I see it, is that it's a signature marking the work, as if it were an art piece. And then, sometimes, I actually see a crop circle. It's a weird part of the dream, like it's unconnected from the rest- just a random image of a crop circle, but it's the exact same one that's here."

"If the image is a signature, then maybe the same author is behind this place and your dreams."

Chills raced through James' body as he contemplated Joshua's words. "That's not a pleasant thought."

"No. It sure isn't."

The air in the room suddenly seemed cold, and the two men were trying to stay warm by bringing their knees into their chest and rubbing their arms.

James spoke, his voice less troubled and more reflective now, "Edward asked me if this was the Devil's home."

"Yeah?"

James laughed. "I told him it was a stupid idea."

Joshua swallowed the lump in his throat. "I did overhear that conversation."

Images of the demonic figure laughing about Kirsten and Jessica faded into James' mind's eye. "I might recant."

They sat in silence, another piece of the puzzle poking around their minds but not falling into place. There was more than what they had to put together, but they were suddenly too tired and scared to care anymore.

James' voice broke through a more recent veil of fatigue. "If whatever was responsible for the designs here is responsible for the designs in my dreams," he moved his finger back and forth as if it helped explain his situation. "Then maybe there's a way to get from here to New York."

Joshua shook his head. "When's the last time you saw a six fingered giant strolling through your neighborhood?"

Allowing a smile, he answered, "No, I guess you're right. Not too much from here making the round trip to the real world."

"It does seem as though we're in a spiritual place, almost a different realm."

James shook his head in agreement. "The realm Noah knew."

Just then there was a sound and a sudden burst of light that exploded from above them, and as they looked up, they were blinded.

~~~

Not able to see anything other than the bright light that just contrasted the dark room, James and Joshua could only guess as to what was going on until their pupils adjusted to the sudden difference. They could tell that they were outside, the feel of soft ground under their feet, along with the sounds of snapping twigs and brushing plants. There were a few people that were pulling them along towards a destination unknown. Though the people were not speaking, they could be heard breathing hard as they quickly shoved them along.

James squeezed his eyes closed, attempting to relieve the pain, and when he opened them again, he could see a little bit better.
~~~

“Where we going?” asked Joshua before a hand was roughly placed over his mouth demanding him to be silent.

The more James’ sight returned, the clearer his situation became. He counted seven men around him, a few making sure he kept up, the others leading . . . watching for something. The fact that they weren’t talking and had stopped Joshua from talking revealed their intent of trying to move from one place to another without being detected.

Now able to see almost perfectly again, James noticed the features and clothing of those who were herding him off. They were dressed and looked exactly like the men who had attacked them earlier, but there was something obviously different about these particular men. Their demeanor was drastically dissimilar, expressing caution, concern, and care. Their touch was not cruel as if they considered James and Joshua to be prisoners, but their prodding and pulling told of a high degree of urgency. It was clear that they were not safe, their association with James and Joshua appearing to be the very reason for the presence of danger they were quickly walking through.

James knew that these people were not enemies.

Joshua was also able to see now and when he turned to look behind him, to see what it was that they were fleeing from, he saw only a couple of large rocks, a small tunnel in the midst of them. And then he saw something else further back, running through the trees waving a sword. “Oh no . . . ”

One of the men closest to him turned to discover the reason for his remark and responded to the sight by pushing Joshua in the back so hard that he almost fell over. The man ran past him, pointing over his shoulder, signaling the others. They all abandoned their brisk walk and broke out into a sprint. James and Joshua followed, the giant closing fast.

Sweat stinging his eyes, James tried desperately to wipe it away, blurring the bouncing scene before him for a mere second. He wasn’t sure how much more running he could do, his legs numb beneath him.

The man running closest to him must have noticed. He turned and whispered, “It’s just around the bend.” He pointed in the direction he spoke of.

James’ feet slowed, his body suddenly unresponsive, his mind paralyzed. Though broken and distorted, the words the man had spoken were English. He stood motionless, attempting to make sense of yet another thing that contained none, until Joshua ran into his back and pulled him along, snapping him out of it. They both ran, able now to hear the giant’s heavy breathing coming from behind.

THIRTEEN

AGAINST HOPE

Kirsten opened her eyes, bringing to realization another day.

She wished she hadn't. She wished she could spend more time ignorant towards her state of affairs, numb to the pain until all was made well. And yet, she sat up and swung her feet onto the floor with an urgency she never before had. There was work to do. There were things to find out. And even though sleeping in ignorance was more appealing, it would serve her husband none and thus would be counter-productive to her own self interest.

She took a few seconds to gather in her strange surroundings, the previous night rushing through her short term memory. As she got to her feet and crossed the room, she stopped only to grab a hooded sweatshirt- black, zipper down, large . . . James' favorite one. Passing by the bathroom, she pulled the sweatshirt over her t-shirt and zipped it, throwing only a casual look towards the open bathroom and into the mirror. Looking that bad in the morning should be illegal, she thought. But she could hardly bring herself to care. Instead, she was drawn straight to the voices she heard coming from the kitchen at the end of the hallway.

It was a scene wrapped with chaos and hectic confusion. Phone held up to an ear in one hand and a bagel spread with cream cheese in the other, George was attempting to eat breakfast while hunting for clues and information over the phone. But whoever was on the other line mustn't have been too good with the English language- this the reason for George's frustration and repeated questions. He seemed to be the kind of guy that would find it impossible to rub his belly and scratch his head at the same time. His hand that held the bagel moved about, its action accented by his dramatic tone, the bagel itself yet to reach his mouth. It was obvious that this bothered him.

Fred walked by, face buried in a stack of papers he was holding and completely didn't notice Kirsten standing in the doorway. Without looking, he reached down onto the table and picked up a cup of coffee, bringing it to his lips, never diverting his eyes from the words on the material he was reading.

Brenda, George's wife, was busy making scrambled eggs at the stove. She was actually the first to notice Kirsten's presence. "Oh, Kirsten!" She made the short journey across the kitchen floor and embraced Kirsten.

"Good morning," managed Kirsten.

Fred and George finally acknowledged her presence with a nod of their head, but nothing more. They were all business.

"Okay, thank you." George hung up the phone, finally took a big bite of his bagel, and dialed another number.

"Here, you have a seat, Dear." Brenda gently urged Kirsten into the chair she had withdrawn from beneath the kitchen table. She then returned to the eggs that were frying on the stove.

Kirsten sat and watched, feeling helpless. It was as if the room was spinning all around her, her emotion and feeling of helplessness that exclamatory. The sound of frying eggs, the rustling of paper, George's voice, the tick of the clock that was nailed above the refrigerator, the occasional passing car, her own heart beat, were all amplified to a deafening degree, mixing together to create a perfect soundtrack for her confused, worried, and fearful state.

But another voice broke through the chaos, a comforting voice, a voice that gave peace, strength, and hope. A voice that empowered her to ask the question she needed to have answered. And though she felt as if a question at that time would interrupt the steady flow of progress, she asked anyway. She needed to know.

"Have you found anything out?" Her voice was barely audible, cautious, fearing both the response and the answer the response could bring. The fact that George and Fred barely even acknowledged her made her feel inferior and in the way, so she wasn't sure how they would take an interruption. But more than that, she was quite aware that they had figured something out, and that something could be bad.

Fred's eyes lifted from the papers in his hands, peeking above the rims of his glasses. George turned his head, phone still held to one ear. They both looked at her, and the look was not hard to read. They were in business mode, and they did not want to be interrupted. As if Kirsten just asked James a question while he was watching the Bills game, the response she got was the same. *My brain is targeted on one thing . . . one. Anything added is a distraction affecting my ability to concentrate on the target.* She cowered inside, despair clutching her heart as she felt not only helpless but in the way. There was no sympathy in the room, and it was sympathy she needed the most.

And then it snapped. The tension suddenly disappeared after both George and Fred were rebuked by their own ignorant response. George abruptly looked outside himself and saw Kirsten, on the brink of tears, just wanting to know anything about her husband. And the sympathy came. He hung up the phone, cutting off the voice that was still talking on the other line, and Fred dropped the stack of papers onto the table, taking off his glasses.

Sighing, George set down his bagel and leaned forward onto his elbows. The way he rubbed his forehead told Kirsten that whatever it was they found out was not particularly good news.

So she held her breath and tried to drown out the exploding heart beat that was blaring within the tiny confines of her cranium.

"We did find something out," he began. "A couple of days ago there was an incident at the hotel James was staying at."

"An incident?" her shaky voice uttered.

Another sigh. "Apparently there was a shooting."

Fred interrupted, "Actually, more like a firefight."

George nodded. "Authorities say two people were killed. It's quite a scene they described."

Kirsten obviously began grasping for anything, even straws, desperate for hope. "Are they sure he was staying at that hotel?"

Fred held up a paper. "They faxed us the bill and the credit card info he used to pay for it."

"The authorities described a fast getaway by those involved, fleeing the scene before they could arrive. Witnesses say that one man was being carried and forced into the cab. They found the cab driver, and one of my men was able to interrogate him."

"Over the phone?"

"No, he flew down early this morning. He's actually doing some digging down there right now. Anyway, the taxi driver said they were being chased by a couple of cars, a lot of bullets exchanged both ways. Said there was quite a large amount of damage and casualties left in the wake of the chase." He waved his hands, signaling that he was fast forwarding the story to get to the point. "They escaped unhurt. He said they had him drop them off in a field by the ocean. Evidently they were going to fly to an island or something."

Fred held up some more papers. "An American did rent a seaplane. Actually, he bought it. That in and of itself raises a bunch of questions."

Kirsten shook her head as if all the new information would fall into place.

"That's where our trail ends. With all the information gathered from witnesses, the authorities, and the taxi driver, it appears that your brother-in-law got mixed up with something big. Now, our government is denying that Steve had any IRS business down there, but I think they might just be covering for themselves. We're still looking into that."

The phone rang.

George answered, “Yeah? That’s what I thought. Okay, keep looking.” He hung up the phone and immediately dialed another number. “Yeah, it’s George, I want to know what the weather was like four days ago in Bermuda, particularly over the ocean near Southampton. Call me back when you find out.” He hung up the phone again.

“What is it?” asked Fred.

“He found the taxi driver who drove James from the airport to the hotel. James told him that he was there looking for his brother, asking questions about the cartels and drug trafficking. The driver gave him a contact. That contact is now dead.”

“What?”

“It gets more interesting. He ran into James the day after, and he says James claimed to have had the meeting with the contact, even though the contact had already been killed.”

Fred leaned forward. “Can we get the IDs of the two people killed at the hotel and forward them to the Feds? If this does involve a cartel . . . ”

George cut him off. “It’s already being worked out. But there’s something else.” He looked into Kirsten’s eyes. “Apparently the weather wasn’t so good when they took off for the island, and people are telling me that it only got worse. The taxi driver was the last to see the plane, so I have people looking into that as well.”

Kirsten asked, “You think that maybe they crashed?”

George shrugged. “There’s a possibility, but there’s also the possibility that they reached the island and are still there. The problem is, no one knows what island they were going to.”

“Except the guy they took with them, probably to lead them to his brother. If we can ID the two bodies and connect them with a group, we can go hunting for someone else who may know what island they were keeping Steve on.”

George covered his face with his hands and whispered, “This doesn’t make any sense.”

They both knew that it was practically useless, attempting to go about this in any normal way. The evidence already collected was too bizarre to lead to any plausible answer. On some levels, all seemed normal, natural- a cartel dealing with a nosy IRS agent snooping around in the wrong places. Of course, they both knew that was a guess, a conjecture imagined. However, the other pieces of evidence, like the note not written by humanity and the non-existent drop off location, threw a whole new spin on everything they thought they could come to assume. In the end, they had to admit that nothing made sense.

ஃஃஃ

The images, memories really, teased her desire and taunted her fear. Her husband's touch- the way his fingers traced her face at night, how they glided through her hair, secured her own hand . . . The smiles and the look in his eyes . . . seductive, teasing, cute, happy, proud, humored, joyful, appreciative, and caring, they all were looking straight at her, begging her to respond in a reality she had no control over.

His life.

Their life . . .

Was it reasonable to hope? As she waited on the front steps of George's house for him to take her back home, she thought about that question. James was either dead or he wasn't, hoping would not change that fact. Of course she wanted him to be alive, so therein was the hope- the wanting. Yet there was more, she was sure. She remembered that it was written about Abraham that he "hoped against hope." He was hoping in the promise of God, that he would be granted a son, despite all else that seemed to make it impossible. But Kirsten had received no such promise concerning her husband. She didn't want this wishful hope, she wanted the hope that all believers have in Christ, that Abraham had in God's promise- an expectant hope wrapped in faith.

Faith . . .

She looked up into the afternoon sky, the puffy clouds outlined with the sun's rays. Taking the second, she contemplated the vastness of the sky, the universe, of reality. Then she reminded herself of Who it was that was sustaining it all. She knew, intellectually, that she could never complain about anything Her Savior saw fit to allow, but she had to admit that her emotion detested the very idea of living the rest of her earthly life without James.

Faith.

The Holy Spirit must have been acting as the Comforter again, she thought, because the text of Hebrews chapter eleven raced through her mind, verses she never thought were memorized.

You are not the only one to ever enter a trial. Every trial has a purpose and an end, it's faith that believes it no matter what. Trust Me, Kirsten. I've already died for you and empowered you through My grace. Do you think I'd stop now? I know what you need before you even ask. Trust Me, My dear child.

The words were not audible, but the difference would have been the same. Had George not opened the door behind her, she would have started to walk down the driveway, praying for that faith. But now she'd have to pray silently as George drove her home. Before she opened the passenger side door, George already in the process of shutting his and turning the ignition, she prayed out loud, “Lord, thank You for James, for making him my husband, and if he’s not with You right now, I beg that You would be with him wherever He is, and please let us find him.”

“Thank you, George.”

“Please, it’s the least I can do. If you need anything, I mean anything, you call, okay?”

She forced a smile and nodded. She walked to her door and watched him back out of the driveway. She waved as he drove away. He beeped twice.

Then she turned around and saw the front door.

It was open . . .

Again.

FOURTEEN
REVELATIONS

English- that's what the voices were speaking. That was the newest piece of bewilderment strewn across a street already cluttered with absurdities. The language was rough, uneducated, and, at times, not even recognizable, but it was English.

Chris leaned forward in the darkness and whispered into John's ear. "It's English." His voice betrayed his confusion.

"Yeah . . . It sounds like some form of Old English or something. It's broken though, like a child's."

Edward asked, "So what does that mean?"

No one knew.

But Chris took a shot at it anyway. "Well, if they're speaking English, then England would have to be a reality here too. At least in some respect."

"Unless, in this world, we just hear them in English. You know, in our own tongue." Edward's answer did not amuse John.

"Did you ever stop to think that just maybe, they speak English because they live on a British island?"

Shaking his head, Chris surrendered. "Who knows?"

The only thing they knew was that they didn't know anything at all- that was the only truth they were sure they owned. As they sat in the darkness and listened to the voices, they fought against the fear that held their hearts with confusion. They didn't know where they were, how they got there, or who the men were that were speaking English, but they did know that they were in danger.

And that Brian was dead.

That fact alone was enough to slap their sense of reality 180°. Death was even natural, coping with it, life. Everything else that was going on, the things witnessed, were not natural at all, and trying to cope with all those things combined completely stripped them of all sense of reality. There wasn't much more they could take before losing their rational minds, and the more time spent in this place, the more strange things defied all they knew about reality and slowly chipped away at their sanity.

Suddenly, they realized that the voices they were hearing were growing louder, getting closer.

"They're coming back," John whispered. No one knew whether that was good news or their last news. How any news could be good, no one was sure, yet they were still alive after being captured. The imagination could create an infinite list of ideas as to why they were kept alive, but not many of them were appealing.

They waited.

Suddenly there was light as a door was opened and two men were pushed into the room. Then the door closed and darkness returned.

"Who's there?" asked Edward, ready to defend himself.

"Ed?" It was James' voice.

"James?"

James laughed. "Thank God you're okay. Is everyone here?"

Chris responded, John responded, and Steve responded.

"Where's Brian?" He knew before he even asked, the bad news emanating off his friends like the smell of sweat.

"He didn't make it."

The sentence hung in the air for a long while, emotion struggling to grip a slippery reality, a painfully sad reality.

Joshua laid a hand on James' shoulder.

"I've been thinking," began Chris. "If we are in the past, transported here by some kind of electromagnetic charge produced from the storm in the triangle, how are we ever going to get back?"

It had been half an hour since the news of Brian's death was introduced to James and, in that time, he had a rough time making sense of anything. Even simple thoughts were complicated by his inability to cope with his friend's death. But, despite all that, a realization suddenly exploded in his mind and answered a question that had haunted him since awaking on the beaches of this evil place. The thought prompted him to straighten up, a new twinge of desire beginning to burn within his weary body. "No."

Everyone looked at him, confused by the strict disagreement to a theory he himself had previously supposed.

"We're not in the past."

"Why do you say that?" asked Edward, curious.

James stood to his feet, amazed that he hadn't thought of it before, that he hadn't been convicted of it before. "If there is such a thing as time travel, then there can be no reality." Though he was moved by his new found discovery, he was still far wearier, so his demeanor had hardly changed.

John looked up at James under heavy eyelids. "Explain."

"If reality, this reality, can be made non-existent by someone going back and changing the past, how realistic is it? All that we know about our own existence would be in question if there was a possibility that tomorrow we may have never existed at all. If someone goes back in time and changes something that, in effect, changes the circumstances around our births so that we were never born, is this reality that we are experiencing right here and now reality, or is it merely an illusion? If we went from existing to never existing then were we ever part of reality?" He answered his own question, "Not from the perspective of the changed world, because there would be no knowledge of a reality being changed."

John shook his head. "So time travel can't be possible because it would have the possibility to erase reality?"

"It just opens the door to all kinds of absurdities. Every time someone would go back, everything that happened from that point on would have never happened, including that person being born. So ultimately, you have someone existing that was never born changing the future that never happened."

"This just sort of hit you?" asked Joshua, slightly amused.

James looked down at him. "Well, I just had this thought that if God was sovereign, then time travel would be impossible. It would mean that God would be conducting things and then erasing all that He had orchestrated, starting over again. Like realizing He made a mistake and going back to change it. But that's not the case. God doesn't change, He's immutable."

Sighing, John chuckled. "I was with you on your first point, but because God doesn't exist, I'd have to disagree with your second."

James smiled a patient smile. "How can you hate somebody that doesn't exist?"

John retaliated, "I don't hate . . . " And then he trailed off, knowing it was worthless. Everyone knew he hated God, including himself.

"So, God would never permit someone changing the things He predestined to happen . . . "

Joshua's sentence came unexpected. Predestination was something James hadn't been confronted with for years after becoming a Christian, and Joshua threw it out in casual sentence just a day after- if it was, in fact, the next day. James still wasn't sure if it was the same day or the next week. "Right, God isn't up there complaining every time a person changes His script. If that were so, then man would have more control than God, and if that were the case, we would be god-status, and He'd be subject to our decisions. It's absurd, God isn't subject or dependant on anything, thus the reason He is God."

"But what if God predestined time travel in some circumstances?" asked Chris.

James smiled, apparently the only one catching on to the fact that they were all having a presuppositional conversation about God. "Again, that would be God backtracking, erasing things that He already sovereignly allowed and predestined. For Him to do that would be for Him to have made an oversight the first time, and if that's the case, God isn't omniscient."

"Okay, so if we didn't travel back to a time where there were giants and men in loin cloths using bows and spears, then where the hell are we?" asked John.

Where the hell are we?

Chris and Edward turned to face him, fearing that he may have answered his own question.

Before anything more could be said, Joshua suddenly signaled everyone to be silent.

Someone was approaching the door.

They all held their breath, waiting for the curtains of time to be retracted and reveal the next act in their nightmare.

The door was removed from its position, and some light pierced through the darkness, until a figure stepped in front of it and walked into the crowded room, his silhouette the only thing visible. "Come." He stood in the doorway, waiting for them to obey.

James led them out, walking cautiously through the doorway and past the man. As he passed, he took a careful look at the man in the shadows beside him. He was about the same size as himself, his face serious but sincere. Scars traced his chest and shoulders, one reaching from his neck to just above his left eye. Animal skins covered his legs, reaching up to his torso. His bare feet looked as though they had never been protected by any type of shoe or sandal, the cold stone floor responsible for the callused skin on their bottoms. James didn't miss the smell of the man either, the smell of sweat and dust. And not able to be missed was the long knife tucked into a belt woven together with vines.

"This way." He led them down a corridor hewn from rock, candles burning from their anchors in the walls. It was cold and dank, obvious that they were underground. They continued walking until they came to a set of rock slabs used as steps. The guide led them up and over the rocks, a couple of them loose under careful feet. It took a few turns and a few more corridors before they found themselves facing a large door. The man opened it and motioned for them to enter in.

"Are we being invited *to* dinner or *for* dinner?" whispered Edward into John's ear.

"Shut up," was John's aggravated response- predictably.

They entered the room.

There were torches, supporting the movement of flame, lined down the room on both sides of the walls, a long table set in the middle of the same adjacent walls. Sitting beneath the shifting light, and partially hidden by the same, the long table was surrounded by dark faces- native faces. Some were old and seemed tired of the lives they led; others were younger and seemed to have at least a little more zeal in their existence.

Prodded by the native who directed them there, James approached one of the empty make-shift chairs that sat at one side of the table. Before sitting down, the torch-light fell over the table, and cautious eyes observed the setting of it, his stomach crying hallelujah in response. There was food, lots of food. Neither James nor the others could possibly care what kind of food cluttered the table, as long as it was pushed their way once they had been seated.

An old man sitting at the table's head nodded for them to sit. As they all took their seats and scooted their chairs closer to the table, they suddenly noticed, uncomfortably, that all the eyes in the room were focused intently on them alone. Curious eyes, cautious eyes . . . scrutinizing every move. It was obvious what they were thinking, looking for any evidence whatsoever that would provide an excuse to kill them. This would be one of the most uncomfortable meals ever eaten, but none could possibly care. They were too hungry to care.

And then he looked to the person who was sitting across from him for the first time. His heart missed a beat as his mind tripped over the sight.

Lance.

~~~

As soon as the introductions were made, James and the others were left alone to eat, though not despite close scrutiny from all else. The natives (if that's what they were) ate slowly, never taking their eyes from the six strangers. With food the only thing in his sight, James didn't even notice the questioning eyes, and between mouthfuls of food, he would mutter thanks to those responsible for supplying the meal. They merely nodded in return.

As Joshua noticed himself getting full, he also started to notice those who sat around him, and he quickly understood that, despite their hospitality, they had very little reason to trust them. He also noticed Lance, who seemed a bit uneasy himself. He could hardly wait to figure out what was going on.

Finally, after twenty minutes of non-stop eating and drinking began to wind down to a close, the old man at the end of the table spoke, anxious to settle the issues at hand. Previously introduced as Tahhowson (at least that's how it sounded), the man asked, "Where are you from?"

The sudden sound of his voice rebounded off the rock walls and inter-
~~~

rupted the sounds of their mannerless eating, informing them that the time had come to start giving answers. James pushed his plate away and wondered about the question, but before he could answer, John leaned forward onto the table and said, “The United States.”

The natives turned and looked at each other, speaking quietly among themselves.

“They’ve never heard of it,” whispered Joshua into James’ ear.

His statement was confirmed by Tahhowson’s reply. “We do not know this place. You are lying.”

Chris blurted out, sensing hostility beginning to burn among the natives, “No, we are not from here. We are from America.”

Lance shook his head. “It’s not going to work. They don’t know of any place other than this island. This is the whole of their reality, we’re aliens to them.”

Edward lunged across the table towards Lance. “Why don’t you shut up!”

James pushed him back against his chair as the natives struggled to understand the conflict between seeming comrades.

“Sorry,” said James.

A native to the left of Tahhowson leaned close to him and whispered something into his ear. James was able to hear it, and chills ran up his spine.

The man had suggested that they were spies.

“We’re not spies!” blurted Edward, who had obviously heard the suggestion himself.

“Then who are you?” yelled one of the men. He stood, passionate in his address. It was difficult to understand this man’s words, but the message was clear. “These men were sent from the gods to find us!”

That remark gained some followers, while Tahhowson waved his hand in calm fashion, attempting to settle down his people. “Then why were the tall ones trying to kill them?” he asked patiently.

“They had to have come from somewhere!”

The old man looked back towards James and his friends questioningly, waiting for an answer.

“Our plane crashed,” said Edward.

Lance shook his head.

“Plane?” asked Mahalalel, a native who had obviously seen much conflict in his thirty or so years. His body strong, his eyes alert, he reeked of a warrior’s scent. James liked him right away. He had fought beside people like Mahalalel before, people who knew where their loyalties lay and fought for a cause they believed, moral people, good people.

Joshua tried to interpret by making hand gestures. "Something that flies. We were in it, and then we crashed." He flew his hand into the table.

The man named Jared was the first to stand to his feet, though five others followed within the next second. They were all yelling something about the gods sending spies in cloud cars, or something similar. Whatever they were yelling about, James knew the situation was getting worse for them.

"Cloud cars?" whispered Joshua into James' ear.

James looked at him as the words grabbed a hold of his memory. And then he understood.

Both he and Joshua were aware of that term having been used in ancient records as referring to what were now commonly referred to as UFOs.

"I can't believe this," stated James in amazement as he watched the natives arguing among themselves. "They think we came from the gods in a cloud car, sent to deliver them to the gods . . . Just like the ancient myths . . . "

Joshua nodded, equally amazed.

"What are you talking about?" whispered Chris.

"Every ancient civilization, from Sumer, Egypt, to the Incas and Aztecs, to Rome, through the Dark Ages and into Hindu mythology, as well as Greek mythology, has recorded events concerning what they described as winged disks, cloud ships, flying boats, cloud cars, flying chariots, and so forth to describe what we would call a UFO."

Chris shook his head. "Wait, are you saying that you think they think we came from a UFO?"

"Well, to them it wouldn't be a UFO, to them it would be a vessel transporting us from the gods," he whispered back.

James whispered to himself, eyes gazing into nothing, "This is all ancient."

Lance leaned across the table, ignoring the arguing natives, and got James' attention. "There's some pretty strange things happening here. I don't know if any of you saw anything, but those ancient myths and legends might be something other than myth and legend."

James, John, Joshua, Chris, and Edward looked at Lance, studying him. He was no longer the cool henchman, if that's what he even was; now he was stuck in the same world as the rest of them, and he was just as confused and scared.

"We don't trust you," stated John.

Lance smiled. It wasn't the cocky smile he sported in Bermuda, it was a nervous smile. "Well, I suggest you start. For all our sakes."

Jared, the seeming ringleader of all their doubt, brought the strangers back into their conversation. "How do we know that you were not sent by the gods to find this place and turn us over to the tall ones?"

Joshua shook his head. "The tall ones already killed one of our friends. They would have killed us too, if you hadn't rescued us."

This resulted in more conversing between the natives.

James interrupted them. "Does this happen often? Cloud cars coming from the sky?"

They didn't seem to understand his question.

"Do the cloud cars come a lot?"

Mahalalel eyed him suspiciously. "Do you think us stupid?"

"I don't understand."

"They come every day, searching for us from the skies," he pointed towards the ceiling.

"Why?"

There was a pause. "Because we are pure blood." He took a knife out of his belt and, without hesitation, sliced the palm of his hand. He held it over the table and watched big drops of red blood splash onto the wooden surface. He continued, "Are you pure blood?"

"What is pure blood?"

Tahhowson asked, "How can you be alive and not know any of this?"

"Because we are not from here. We don't know how we got here, we just woke up in the sand."

"The gods rejected you?" He thought about this for a while. "If they rejected you then why send you with magic?" He motioned towards the corner of the room.

They all looked in the direction of his signal, and saw their weapons leaning against the wall.

Joshua tried to change the subject. "Tahhowson, the tall men are not pure blood?"

"No, not."

"What are they?"

"They come from the gods taking the women."

For the first time, Joshua noticed that there were no women present, and his mind went immediately back to the ancient stories and to the book of Genesis. "They take the women?"

He nodded.

"When did this start happening?"

Tahhowson looked confused, "Long times ago. Our fathers have kept record and passed on. When the flying circles first came, they did not know if they were bad. But then they came down to the ground and took our women. We tried to fight, but they killed us bad. Then our women had children that grew into the tall people. They started their own tribe and began hunting us down like animals, looking for our women to breed them."

Joshua was wondering if this was recorded history or mere oral tradition. "Has this been passed on through writings?" He made a hand gesture to help communicate.

Tahhowson responded, "Yes, our fathers draw the past so that we can learn, but we cannot read them. We look at the pictures to understand."

"Why can't you read them," asked Chris.

Mahalalel's trust for them was beginning to grow, whether he was aware of it or not, and he answered the question. "We cannot see what the words mean."

"It's in a different language?" asked Joshua, startled.

"Language?" He did not know the word.

John put his hand up to his mouth. "Their words were different?"

Tahhowson shook his head in agreement.

"Then how did you learn your words?"

"That is a question that we cannot find answering."

Mahalalel, despite Jared's disapproval, turned and whispered into Tahhowson's ear. As he was talking, his eyes kept sweeping over the strangers and he even gestured towards them a few times. Tahhowson was nodding in agreement to whatever it was he was saying.

Finally, Tahhowson stood up from the table, his old body still strong and unwavering. "You have answered not bad. You can go rest until then. We will get you later."

With that, Mahalalel stood, walked around the table and said to James, "Come."

James, Joshua, Chris, John, Ed, and Lance stood and followed him out of the room, down a corridor and into another room. Upon gathering in the larger room which was filled with beds and chairs and some food in wooden bowls, Mahalalel turned to leave. But before he left he asked James, "If not from cloud cars, then where did you come from really?"

"From beyond the water." At least he hoped, though that hope was losing credibility fast.

Mahalalel bowed. "I come back soon. Sleep." With that he turned and left, shutting the door behind him.

"Someone want to tell me what 'pure blood' is?" asked John, a little more than frustrated.

"Hold on, I think there's something else that we need to talk about first," said Joshua as he walked near to Lance.

Lance sighed before raising his hands. "What?"

Joshua grabbed him by the collar of his shirt, now torn and dirty, and lifted him to his feet. "You're going to tell us everything!"

He laughed. "Skin for skin, all a man has he will give for his life. Isn't that right, James?"

"That's Satan's theory," he replied, confused as to Lance's quote from the book of Job.

"Okay, I'll tell you about your brother. Just let go of me."

Joshua released him but not without giving him a shove, and Lance fell to the ground with a thud.

"You guys are taking this way too personal, I was only doing my job."

James couldn't believe Lance had the guts to make such a statement. "Yeah, well 'your job' is 'personally' affecting me. That makes it a personal matter."

"I already told you everything."

"No, on the seaplane, I asked if you told us everything, and you said 'not exactly.'"

Lance dropped his eyes to the stone floor he was sitting on. "Listen, I don't really know what's going on. I told you what I can understand, but you won't believe the rest."

Chris walked closer to Lance so that Lance could hear him clearly. Chris didn't like Lance at all, and he would love an excuse to kill him, but that would not come now. "You're just setting up the background for some wild story you're about to make up."

Lance was about to tell him to shut up but, his response being predicted and bringing a daring look to Chris' eyes, he decided to hold his tongue. "Your brother," he looked to James. "Got in trouble with us because of what he was trying to do."

"What was he trying to do?" asked James.

"He was tracing dirty money back to our business. If he connected all the dots, then he would have found a lot more than just dirty money, he would have uncovered an international conspiracy between two different governments."

"What are you talking about?"

"What I'm saying is, there's a lot of stuff going down, and the business is right in the center of it. We couldn't just sit around and let some punk destroy us."

"Okay, we've been through that part before. So you usually remove these people, but it was different in this case. Why?"

Lance shook his head. "I don't know. We never took anyone to the island before." He let his eyes take in his strange surroundings before continuing, as if perhaps they might complement or destroy his story. "One night, I saw my boss talking to some guy. It was at a distance, but I could tell they were talking about your brother. They were trying to figure out what to do about the IRS guy. I don't know why your brother was a different story than anyone else we've ever dealt with, maybe because of his position in the American government. In any case, I can't see my boss ever coming up with that idea on his own. I guess the other guy wanted your brother alive for something, maybe to get answers or an extra measure of leverage with the US. I don't know. All I know is that I've never seen the guy before."

James scratched his head. "So you think that this guy you saw talking to your boss wanted my brother taken to this 'island,' but for no reason you're aware of?"

"Basically."

"What do you mean, 'basically'?" asked Edward.

"Well, I don't know what their long term plan was, heck, I don't even know if your brother is still there." A slight glimpse of honesty traced his eyes for a second. "I honestly don't know much. I was never in that position to know things."

Joshua eyed him suspiciously, he believed him, but there was something Lance wasn't telling. "What is it that you don't want to tell us?"

It was obvious that Lance was uncomfortable now. He sighed in surrender before continuing. "I don't know, it was weird. I saw them talking in a parking lot . . . it was well lit. I turned my head for a second and when I turned back, my boss was walking towards me. The other guy was nowhere to be found. I mean, there's no way he could have gotten far enough away from the lights in the parking lot in that amount of time. I don't know, it was creepy."

"What did your boss say?"

"Are you kidding me? You never ask the boss anything."

Joshua got Lance's attention. "So where are we now?"

Lance laughed. "I have no idea! This place can't even be real on any other day of the week."

"Do you know what happened to you?" asked John.

"I woke up on the beach, saw you guys lying unconscious, and headed into the jungle, hoping to find my way to an air strip or some village with a jeep. I was a little surprised to find Indians instead. They took me to this place, and I've been here ever since."

"Did you see the giants?" James was curious as to how much bizarre stuff Lance had been exposed to.

"No, but they seem to be a real source of fear among the natives here."

"What have you told them?"

"Nothing. They don't know anything outside of their own experience, so nothing you tell them will make any sense to them, or they'll just match your words up to their own beliefs and make your words mean something they don't."

After Lance's speech was able to absorb some thought, John asked again, "So what does 'pure-blood' mean?"

Thoughts of Steve occupied most of James' mind and made John's question seem insignificant at that time. He closed his eyes, rehearsing his study while his mind's eye was fixed on his brother. "It's the mingling of men and gods. In Greek mythology, the writings of Sumeria, Persia, Egypt, South America, and most others, there are those stories of the gods mating with human females. The children born to those human women are people with extraordinary power, depending on which civilization you read from. Hercules is probably a good example from Greek mythology. But there's a theme that seems to connect them all: an intermingling between some extraterrestrial being and natural women producing supernatural offspring. Pure-blood, John, would refer to those people who were not polluted by the seed of the gods anywhere within their genealogy. Their blood-line is pure, is natural."

"But these are all hokey stories passed down around camp fires," said John.

"I know you don't believe in the Bible, but Genesis chapter six speaks of the same thing. Only the writer doesn't attribute the offspring to aliens or gods, but to angels. And it's interesting to note that the Bible says these people that were born out of these relations were giants. I've already told you this."

For the first time, John did not say anything.

"It says that God spared Noah and his family because they were pure in their generations, or their genealogy. Theologians have argued over this text forever, but I don't seem to have that luxury now. It seems pretty clear to me."

Lance chuckled. "What?" He looked around the room, trying to determine if he was the object of a joke. But no one else was laughing.

Edward stood up, his shadow being cast across the floor, reaching Lance's feet. "You didn't see the giants, you didn't see the crop circle, you didn't see Brian . . . " his words trailed off at the mention of his friend's name, and a tear slid down his face.

"The crop circle." James still sat, thinking of his brother.

Edward turned to face him. "Yeah?"

James' eyes lifted and searched for John's. When they met his, James leaned forward and drew a figure in the dirt with his finger. "John . . . "

As John watched James drawing some kind of design, he suddenly sat erect, senses on fire. "Where'd you see that?"

"The crop circle . . . "

"No, it's impossible."

"You've seen it before . . . in Vietnam, with Steve." It was a realization, not a question.

John looked up from the dragon-like design, a look of bewilderment on his face. "How do you know?"

"I've seen it in my dreams, in Vietnam."

"You what?" Edward and Chris leaned forward.

John dismissed the answer and continued to stare at the design, eyes watching a memory. "It was so bad . . . So evil. All those crosses . . . "

Another piece of the puzzle revealed, yet there was nowhere to fit it in.

Lance wasn't laughing this time. "What's going on?"

"So, wouldn't that mean that whatever was responsible for the designs in Nam is responsible for the ones here too?" asked Edward.

"It would be a logical deduction." He didn't mention that it was a deduction he had already made.

"Then there must be some connection between the two places. A way to get from here to there."

James stifled a bored laugh. "Yeah, if you're a spirit you can go anywhere you want, I suppose. In and out of dimensions, in and out of time . . . "

Edward didn't like the answer. "But we made that trip. We've gone from there to here."

James lifted his heavy eyes and nodded. "You're right."

Chris eyed James suspiciously. "How do you know all this stuff? About the legends and all that?"

"I don't know, just curiosity finding study, I guess. Stories I've heard, the cover-ups I've witnessed . . . " He looked over at Joshua before continuing. "Jimmy Carter's promise to reveal every piece of information that the country had on UFOs available to the public once he became president, and yet after becoming president he never mentioned a word about it . . . "

Joshua muttered, "Project Sign, in '47 and Grudge in '49."

"Bluebook, then Delta in '94," continued James.

"What are these 'projects'?" asked Chris.

"Government projects dedicated to the study of UFOs and abduction cases. Their findings were quite interesting. Terrifying, actually."

"Okay," John held up his hands. "This isn't the *X-Files* or *Close Encounters*. Can we all agree on that?"

"John, you're right, this isn't the *X-Files*. This is real." James got to his feet and walked to one of the beds that were positioned against the wall. He climbed on top of it, his body complaining about its hard surface.

"So you are sure that you want to reject the time travel theory?" asked Chris.

James closed his eyes, sleep inviting him to precious rest. "Yeah, it's illogical."

"And what here isn't, Mr. Spock?" asked John as he stood and also made his way to a bed.

Both James and Chris ignored John's comment, and Chris asked, "Alternate realities? A multi-verse?"

Right before sleep engulfed his brain, the words slipped from between his lips. "Those theories share the same problems. I'm thinking we're in a different dimension."

"Like dimension X?" The sarcasm in John's voice was not missed, but James had already fallen asleep.

Joshua sat silent, contemplating the different theories and decided that none made any sense. He then tried to simplify his situation by separating the facts from their theories. The Triangle, the sky, the giants, the natives and their stories, the crop circle, Brian . . . but there was nothing simple about any of that, and the human brain automatically started seeking explanations to that for which no explanation could be found. From what James had said, it sounded as if they were all trapped between the reality of the words recorded in Genesis chapter six . . . trapped within the days of Noah, right before the flood.

.:.:. *Another Day*

The door swung wide, a torch suddenly flickering light across the sleeping strangers. Mahalalel walked into the room, holding the torch above his head. He shook James until he awoke, and then proceeded to do the same with the rest.

They found themselves sitting at the same large table in the same room, only there was no food cluttering its surface this time. Surrounding them on all sides were the same men that had previously accompanied them during their first meeting.

"We've talked about your words," Tahhowson began. "We have hard time believing, but it could be right."

Mahalalel continued the thought. "It does not make sense that the tall men would want you dead if you were sent by the gods to find us. You say you came from the sky, but were not sent from the gods. Did you escape the gods and crash your flying disk?"

James rubbed his eyes, still feeling the effects of the last week or so. "We're not from the sky or from the gods, we're from across the water, a different land."

Mahalalel leaned over and whispered into Tahhowson's ear, "I told you!"

Tahhowson dismissed the excited remark and said, "There is nothing in the water, we have found nothing ever, only water."

Joshua asked, "How long have you traveled it?"

"Our people have searched for new land for days and days, but we have never found anything. But that does not mean you lie. We found your flying 'plane,' as you call it, we might have."

James attention was grabbed and smacked awake, and so was everyone else's. "What does it look like?"

"It does not look like the flying disks that come and take our women. It is broken and all over the sand."

"Can you take us to it?"

"No. It is not good where it has landed. That is their land, too dangerous. By the broken wood."

"Broken wood?" Joshua asked, having no idea what it could have meant.

"The sand is filled with broken wood, it has always been I think."

"A boat?" asked John, leaning onto the table.

Tahhowson nodded. "Yes, very old. We think that we built it and tried look for new land, but did not live through it."

"Could you show us where our plane is?" James figured the plane was in pieces, but if the skids were still intact, then just maybe . . .

For the first time during this session, Jared spoke. "That part of land is bad. Much evil lives there, the tall men and the gods themselves are in the air."

"I understand, but we have no choice."

"You will die."

The bluntness of the statement sent chills down the six foreigners' spines. They didn't need any convincing that the statement was of the highest probability.

Everyone sat in silence for a while, the mood turning somber, until finally Mahalalel spoke. "I will take you." The offer caused a protest among a few of the natives, but Mahalalel persisted.

After the room was quiet again, James expressed his thanks and prepared to leave, Tahhowson signaling that they could go. But as they stood, Joshua turned and asked Tahhowson, "How long have your people been living like this?" He waved his hand at the walls surrounding them.

Tired eyes, eyes that had experienced little more than a lifetime of pain and fear, answered his question before words were even formed. "We are not sure when the gods took notice of us, when they started taking the women; it seems from the pictures that it has always happened. But something sooner happened that seems to send my people into caves and hiding. But that is when our words changed, and we cannot learn the meanings of the records."

"What do the people from the sky want with you?"

"We are pure-blood, they want us dead. They want our women to give them more tall men and to raise more younger women for time to come still."

Joshua looked over at James. "The extinction of a people, selective breeding, producing hybrids . . . sound familiar?"

James shook his head. "Can the tall ones be killed?"

Jared spoke again, "Yes. But it is not an easy thing. We have fought them when they come looking for us, I have seen some fight for time without their own head."

"Where are they?" There was something in Chris' eyes that James had never seen before, so he wasn't sure how to interpret it. It wasn't just the adrenaline he was getting high on, but there seemed to be something deeper, as if he was beginning to care for these people. Or maybe he just wanted to kill a giant, James couldn't tell.

"They are in their big buildings. On the other side of the land, near your flying plane."

Mahalalel spoke to Tahhowson. "By your order, can I take some men to the plane with us all?"

Though reluctant, Tahhowson nodded his consent, and immediately four men stood from around the table, expressing their willingness to go. Among those standing was Jared.

Mahalalel stood and walked to the big doors at the end of the room. "You may go, we will come for you when the time is."

Joshua caught Edward's glance and followed it to the guns that were still leaning against the wall in the back corner. "Mahalalel, would you allow us to take our weapons, to get them prepared?"

It was decision time for the natives. Did they trust them? It took a few minutes to decide, but Tahhowson finally said yes. John and Edward went to retrieve them, and then they all walked back to the room, this time without a guide.

"This is crazy," whispered Lance.

Everyone ignored him.

"You can't possibly think the plane still works, what's the point in going there?"

Still no one acknowledged him. They only descended down the loose stairs.

"Look, the guy said we would die . . . " His voice trailed off as a face peeked around the corner ahead of them.

"Oh my . . . " Chris stopped walking.

Looking around the corner was a beautiful young woman, face innocent, eyes curious, but fear obvious. Yet, there was something else that marked her disposition. Hope. With much conjured courage, she took steps out into the hallway so that she was standing in front of them, facing them. She was beautiful, an angel's face. With a quiet, small voice, she asked, "Are you here to save us?"

The six men stood in awe, the question catching them completely off guard, but not knowing how to answer this precious fearful woman. Before an answer could be found, a man suddenly appeared running down the hallway towards them. He was yelling something that James couldn't understand, but his intent was clear. He grabbed the girl by her arms and shook her violently. "What are you doing! Get back with the others!" He then smacked her across the face, sending her stumbling backwards into the wall. He spun her around and pushed her back from where she had come, but not before her eyes fell back onto the six men who stood, unable to move. Her eyes, glazed over, screamed one thing, "Help us!"

After the native had pushed the woman down another hallway, he turned to face the foreigners, pulling out a sword. He began walking towards them, his eyes spitting fire. They all took a few steps back.

"Stop!" It was Jared's voice that boomed off the rock walls.

The man stopped in his tracks.

"Go back to your position."

The man, obviously wanting to do something else, bowed, and with a grunt, turned and walked back down the hall from which he came.

"Forgive him, he does not trust you, not with the women. You must understand, keeping them safe is the only thing that promises our future. The race of the pure-blood is dependent on them." With that he turned and walked away.

It was a few seconds before anyone moved or said anything, but Chris, as always, managed to look past the reality of the events. "I think I'm in love."

"Come on." They grabbed him, snapping him out of his dazed, lovestruck mood and drug him down the hallway.

III
Deliverance

FIFTEEN

Realities collide

It was fast approaching two hours now and with no sign of their traveling nearing an end. At first, the trek through the jungle was taken casually, the natives explaining more of their unfortunate way of life to the new strangers. It was a remarkable unit of time, unbelievable to any who did not witness it for themselves. Who would believe such a story, could believe such a story? Peter Pan seemed more believable than this, and yet it was real, terrifyingly real. The natives seemed to have no struggle grasping their habitat or the paranormal stability within it. A sure sign that they had never experienced anything else- this was their life, and they had naturally grown accustomed to it. This was normal to them.

It was fascinating, the degree of trust established so soon by the natives. Whereas one would expect the closest, most intense scrutiny on their part, instead, it took only the shortest amount of time to befriend them. And Joshua, for one, was having no trouble connecting the new friendship with an unmistakable look, of what could only be hope, resonating in the native's eyes. Hopeful expressions paired with the sort of question asked by the girl earlier in the day made for a very interesting circumstance. The imagination did not have to go too far out of bounds to apply plots similar to those read in numerous stories, stories about a group of people (from slaves to prisoners to citizens) who were expecting someone to deliver them. And if the stories could parallel this place, then the hopeful glimmer that was shining humbly in their eyes would be rooted in expectancy. The girl's question could not be ignored, the look in her eyes . . . She wanted to know if they were there to save them! To deliver them! What else could it be? The natives *were* expecting a savior. But why? What reason did they have to expect such deliverance? Did someone have a dream? A revelation? Whatever the case, the thought of James and company being their savior was quickly discarded as foolishness. So far, the natives were the ones proving to save *them.* In fact, as they had talked about the issue within the confines of their stone room, they realized that they were probably placing these natives in only more danger.

Mahalalel, without warning, suddenly dropped to his stomach. But even though no warning was issued, Jared and the four other natives were lying on the ground only a millisecond later. James and everyone else were left standing like the last guys to be picked for a team. It had happened so fast that for a second they were dumbfounded, their brains trying to catch up with the sudden turn of events. Once they were finally able to react, they simultaneously mimicked their guides by falling to the ground.

"I don't see anything," whispered Chris. He was looking around, through the trees, waiting for some sort of monster to materialize out of nowhere and engulf them. He tried to squeeze a level of comfort out of a tighter grip around the automatic weapon he held in his shaking hands. He wasn't quite sure what Jared had meant when he referred to the area of jungle they had recently entered as being 'the evil ground,' but he didn't need total understanding for it to entice his imagination.

With the first part of their journey being made practically carefree, Jared had turned around and abruptly put an end to that, introducing a new dispensation. He commanded that no sound be made, for they had entered onto the evil grounds of the gods and their princes. How this specific area could be far worse than the rest of this nightmare, Chris did not want to find out. But as he lay there, afraid to breathe, he began to believe that perhaps that was only wishful thinking.

James didn't see anything either, but he thought it wise to trust those who lived in an environment completely foreign to his own. He strained to see what caused the alarm, but he could only see uneventful jungle all around him. The sound of insects buzzed, and the calls of birds fluttered through the breeze along with the swaying branches- but that was it. But still he was not reassured. He flexed his index finger and rested it against the trigger, flicking the safety into the 'off' position. Feeling a tap on his leg, James looked back behind him to see John holding two fingers to his eyes and then pointing in a direction ahead of them.

John's face was set: stoic, concentrated. He was starting to become the soldier he once was. James never knew John as a soldier, and the sudden impassive look that glazed his eyes almost scared him. They were emotionless, cold . . . James recognized it as the expression of one trained and ready to survive . . . to kill. James felt a little of that finish beginning to seep over his own eyes, and he wondered if he should fight it. He followed John's finger to a general area but still saw nothing. Shaking his head, he began to turn back to John, but John unexpectedly grabbed his leg, keeping him from doing so.

John's voice was barely audible, his eyes still locked in the direction he had pointed. "Don't. Move."

Joshua watched, lying still on the ground beside Jared, as one of the natives slowly slid an arrow into his bow. The wind had picked up a little in the last half hour and dark clouds now littered the sky. Because of this, Joshua could not discern the difference between the sound of the wind blowing through the foliage and anything else. He pressed his lips into Jared's ear and whispered, "It's only the wind." It wasn't a statement, it was a question begging reassurance of what he hoped was only the wind.

Jared turned to look him in the eyes, and he whispered back, "No."

The blunt answer provoked Joshua to bring the assault rifle up to his shoulder and aim it into the woods, but Jared shook his head and grabbed the rifle, lowering it to the ground.

"No noise."

Lance wasn't used to this sort of suspense, not the suspense that hid danger behind countless trees under dark skies. Perhaps his cousin in Columbia was more familiar with this sort of stuff, but not Lance. Lance was used to dealing with danger under street lights and between buildings. Jungle warfare was as foreign to him as was celibacy. He struggled to stay still, to resist the urge to get up and run, to do something to break the tension. But where would he run to? He wished he had a gun, anything. And then he noticed one of the natives looking at him, staring at him. The native was not trying to mask his thoughts, his look a skeptical one. It was dead obvious that he had no trouble detecting Lance's fear, and his eyes stabbed at him, warning him to stay still and quiet.

The native with the bow began to draw back on the chord, aiming at something unseen. He held the arrow back, the muscles in his arms defined by the tension, and everyone held their breath, waiting for whatever was about to happen next.

And then he let go.

The arrow whistled through the air and disappeared.

No sooner had the arrow vanished into the green camouflage than Jared stood to his feet and began walking cautiously in the direction the arrow soared. He waved his hand at those still behind him, signaling for them to follow.

Joshua's confusion as to what just happened did not go unmatched, and he and James exchanged a mutual expression complete with raised eyebrows and shrugging shoulders. They all picked up their pace, curious to see what it was they seemed to be missing.

It was a hundred yards of dense jungle later that the natives stopped and kneeled down by something James couldn't see, a tree obscuring his line of vision. However, Edward evidently could see what it was they were looking at because he gasped, “Oh, my.”

The native that shot the arrow pulled it back out of his target- another native, one of the ‘sky people,’ as the ‘pure blood’ called them. The arrow had struck him in the heart and killed him immediately. Mahalalel seemed unimpressed by the phenomenal shot. His eyes were busy searching their surroundings so intensely that it appeared as if he was straining to see through the objects around them. “Take him.”

Obeying Mahalalel, one of the natives picked up the dead body and threw it over his shoulder.

“There will be more soon,” said Jared. “Let us keep moving.”

As they began to move again, John, James, Chris, Joshua, Edward, and even Lance had a hard time peeling their unbelieving eyes from the native who shot the single arrow through a hundred yards of dense jungle and killed a shadow.

It was late in the afternoon now, or perhaps even early evening. It was hard for Edward to tell. But the sinking sun began to stir disturbing thoughts about their return trip- if indeed there was to be a return trip. Edward guessed that not much was promised in this land. It would certainly be dark before they got back- to wherever it was they came from- and the thought of traveling the jungle in the dark was enough to enhance a heart rate. Looking forward to that was like looking forward to an appendectomy or worse. Worse was what Edward’s second wife experienced and later blamed on him. His body was sore, his ribs not letting him forget their painful presence. He was utterly exhausted, and the thought of much more walking made him want to cry. He stumbled over more of the jungle’s foliage-covered ground, attempting to do so quietly. He held his side and was now bent forward at the waist, the pain pulsing through his body with every beat of his heart.

James walked quietly up to Ed and put a hand on his back. “Are you okay?”

Ed gave his best attempt at a smile, which was really a miserable effort, and nodded.

“Hang in there.” James then walked past Lance and Chris and made his way to Joshua. “I didn’t imagine the island being this big.”

Joshua shrugged, “Maybe it’s not an island.”

It was clear that they were all tired, physically approaching their limit, but even more so was their mental state. And yet, in contrast, the natives hadn’t even begun sweating, and if it wasn’t for the narrow eyes scrutinizing everything around them and their body position ready to spring into action with the slightest sound, they could have been on a walk through the park on a day off work. It was implausibly astonishing.

"How'd the plane end up all the way over here, and we all ended up down there?" asked Joshua, shouldering his rifle as he stepped over a tree-trunk.

"I have no idea."

Chris quickened his pace until he was in between James and Joshua. "Hey, you know it's gonna' be getting dark soon."

Joshua was about to say something when Mahalalel turned and glared at them, holding a hand up to his mouth.

Joshua removed the rifle from his shoulder and concentrated, again, on his surroundings while Chris slowed his pace just enough to fall in step behind James. The rebuke from Mahalalel reminded them of the previous enemy they had failed to detect, and they repented.

The native that was carrying the dead 'sky person' on his shoulder broke away from the group and walked off to the left through some tall ferns and close to the edge of a huge hill that stretched down to a stream- though the stream and the bottom half of the hill were invisible, concealed under thick fog. He flipped the corpse off his shoulder and watched it tumble down the steep embankment until it entered through the ghostly fog's wide mouth and swallowed into the jungle-bed below. Hopefully some animal would find it before another 'sky person.' It was only after contentment passed through his emotions, that the native turned to rejoin the group.

It was only five minutes later when they finally reached the edge of the jungle, the beach just a few yards beyond. The natives crawled carefully towards the beach but stopped short of the bare sand. James and the other strangers had been watching them from a few yards behind until Jared looked back over his shoulder and signaled for them to join him.

James crawled quietly next to Jared, amazed at the native's level of caution. If this was the level of furtiveness required to go unnoticed in this world, it was a wonder that they had made it through the first two days alive.

"Look." Jared was pointing at something down the beach.

"I don't see anything," James said, frustrated.

Mahalalel crawled up next to James on his other side. "By the water."

James squinted, but could still see nothing.

"I see it," said John, who was looking over James' shoulder. "I think I see it."

"We need to inspect them," said Joshua.

Jared looked a little uneasy after that statement, and he exchanged an apprehensive look with the other natives.

Mahalalel turned and faced the strangers. “We wait until dark.” There was no qualm in his voice that requested someone else’s opinion.

“Are you kidding?” asked Chris.

Edward and Lance, though unvoiced, shared the same quick reaction.

Jared turned his attention away from them and away from the ocean and focused it on the tree-line that snaked away from them and stretched down the beach as far as the eye could see. “The gods put sky people in those woods. They only watch the water. If you go now, you will be dead before five steps.”

Edward collapsed against a tree, leaning his head back and looking up through the jungle’s canopy. The sun had already started its descent, and he could see the moon. “Great.”

It was a full moon. As if that came as a surprise. The moonlight reflected silver off the dark water and glowed off the cooling sand. The air was calm and uneventful. The wind had traveled across the ocean waters to God only knows where, the clouds going with it. It must have been five hours since they reached the beach, the natives taking turns keeping a look out, letting their stranger friends catch up on some much needed rest.

But now it was time to move, and everyone was wide awake.

Mahalalel made sure he had everyone’s attention, waiting to see their eyes glowing in the moonlight, before he started speaking. As he began speaking, he made a hand signal to the four natives armed with bows, and they quickly took off down the tree line, disappearing into the darkness. “We run fast. When we get there, stay low on the ground.”

“Where are they going?” asked Joshua, nodding in the direction of the four natives who had just left.

“They go to make sure any watchers see nothing.”

Then Jared got to his feet and jumped through the tree line and onto the sand, where he sprinted down the beach and out of sight. And without anymore delay, but plenty of apprehension, everyone else followed.

Jared made it to the skis first, jumping over and side-stepping huge pieces of broken wood that littered his path. He dove to the ground behind one of the skis and turned to watch everyone else follow his lead.

Once everyone was huddled together behind the skis, presumably undetected, James began to survey the area, looking for pieces of the plane. But though the moon was full and offered plenty of light, visibility was still difficult due to the amount of wreckage creating shadows across the beach.

John whispered into James’ ear, just loud enough to be heard over the ocean that was meeting the beach behind them. "There's the propeller." He pointed.

One of the propellers was buried half-way in the sand, its blades sticking straight into the sky and catching enough moonlight to reveal its peeling red paint. Just next to the propeller, they could also make out what looked like a piece of the windshield, reflecting the moon off shattered glass.

"What is all this?" Chris was referring to the wood. Even at night it was obvious the broken pieces had been there for a long time. They were mostly covered by the beach, and that which was exposed to view had also been exposed to the elements for a very long time.

"This is what we think the tall ones used to travel into the deep water a long time ago," said Mahalalel offhandedly. There was no wonder on his behalf concerning the broken ship, he merely wanted to do what they came to do and as quickly as possible.

Joshua was too curious. His concentration left the skis behind and followed the pieces of what did appear to be a ship. He quickly crawled away from the cover of the ski and dove behind a huge piece of wood that was sticking high out of the ground, much of it buried beneath the sand. As he ran his hand over it and examined it under a silver spotlight, his curiosity was quickly confirmed. There was no doubt that it was a ship. Joshua signaled for James to join him.

As James sprinted across the sand, he tripped over something and fell. Looking back to see what it was, he could only make out the edge of something barely piercing the surface of the beach. He stole a quick peek at the tree line before frantically attempting to uncover the object. Later on, he would not be able to give a reason for what drew him to the buried wood, but nonetheless, something about it captured his interest. After ten seconds of digging, it was established that the piece of wood was buried in the ground at almost a 30° angle. He turned and threw a handful of sand at Joshua, getting his attention. Once he had it, he motioned for Joshua to help him.

Jared and Mahalalel were both confused and frustrated by what Joshua and James were doing. "Get them in cover," whispered Jared to John, more than slightly annoyed. Mahalalel was keeping an anxiously steady gaze fixed on the tree line.

"Examine the skis, see if they're cracked or damaged, I'll see what they're doing." Then Chris ran away from Edward, John, and Lance and twenty yards later dove beside James and Joshua, who by now had uncovered six feet of what appeared to be a telephone pole. "What is it?" asked Chris, excitement burning in his moonlit eyes.

"Looks like a mast." Joshua answered without slowing down in his digging.

Chris surveyed the beach around him. "You think this is an old shipwreck?"

"Looks that way," muttered James.

"How do the skis look?" asked Joshua.

"I don't know, John and Ed are looking them over now."

"Go see what they think. If they think they'll float, then we'll drag them into the water and float them back."

"Okay," Chris ran off towards the skis.

"I wish it were day," said James. "It'd be a lot easier to find what we're looking for."

Joshua looked out into the ocean and could see rocks stretching out of the water, illuminated by the light of the moon bouncing off the waters around them. They were a good distance out and waves could barely be heard crashing against them. The waters seemed to turn treacherous after two hundred yards, suddenly filled with jagged rocks and boulders. "You think the ship hit those rocks out there?" asked Joshua.

James turned to see what rocks his friend was referring to. "Seems likely."

"Looks like an old ship, pirate ship maybe. 17th, 18th century . . . Hard to tell looking at the ruins in the dark."

As James continued to dig, shoveling sand out from between his legs, he said, "I wonder why the natives never excavated this."

"This is forbidden territory, the territory of the gods, remember?"

By now they had uncovered enough of the long object to wiggle it. "Well, it's obviously too small to be the main mast."

Joshua eyed him incredulously. "What are you talking about?"

"What?"

He smiled. "You don't know what you're talking about." He chuckled. "Main mast . . . yeah, right."

James returned the smile. "You're the Navy boy, you tell me what it is."

"I think I was a little too young to remember this model."

Taking a break from digging, James took a few seconds to think. "I believe that there were three masts: the main mast, the mizzen mast, and . . ."

Joshua shook his head and continued digging. "Okay Captain, why don't we just see if we can find a sail on this thing?"

"If the skis still float, then a sail would be a nice thing to have, wouldn't it?"

They continued digging.

"They look fine to me," said John. He ran his hand across the skis that once floated a Beaver DHC-2.

As Chris returned to them, he overheard John's analysis. "They want us to drag them to the water and float them back."

Edward's brow squashed in disagreement. "Back to where?"

Mahalalel answered, "The water is close to where we live. If you want to take it there," he looked around with eyes that were growing more and more paranoid with each passing second. "Please then do it now."

Edward nodded and took a deep breath, ready to endure the pain that would be accompanying his efforts at dragging the ski down the beach. "Ready?"

Taking one quick look over his shoulder and at the tree line, John responded, "Let's do this fast." He, Chris, Edward, and a reluctant Lance began pushing the ski down the beach like they were pushing a bobsled. Mahalalel and Jared began pushing the other one behind them.

Though there were only two natives on the one ski, their way of life was not as cozy as their four new friends, and they were used to such tasks. So it was not long before Mahalalel and Jared passed them and pushed the ski into the water.

Chris could only shake his head in disbelief as the two natives flew by them and splashed into the water ahead.

"I think I found it." James reached into the sand and around the wood, grabbing a handful of cloth.

"Is it really there?" asked Joshua in amazement.

"There's something here." James was on his knees reaching as far as he could down into the hole they had dug. The fabric seemed to be twisted around the pole and didn't want to come loose.

Suddenly Joshua started to feel tense, uneasy. He looked around, trying to find justification for his feelings, but there was nothing that he could see that would warrant panic. He watched Mahalalel and Jared slide the ski into the ocean, John, Chris, Edward, and Lance right behind with its twin. Everything seemed to be going smooth. But still, something seemed wrong. He didn't try to hide his apprehension as he whispered to James, "Just hurry up."

Joshua's voice seldom sounded that worried, and James stopped digging for a second. "What is it?"

But before Joshua could answer, there was a faint whistle in the air and then a loud *thud* as an arrow sunk itself deep into the wood they were desperately trying to dig out of the sand. Time disappeared for an instant while wide eyes went first to the arrow, which was still vibrating from the impact, and then to each other. How long they sat paralyzed, just staring at each other, they weren't sure. But eventually time became realized again, and surprise was swiftly replaced by resolution. Joshua got to his feet and began covering the forty-five yards separating him from everyone else. Intent on doing the same thing, James first reached down into the sand and grabbed a handful of the cloth, pulling with all his might. When the fabric tore, his potential energy suddenly went kinetic, and he landed on his back just as another arrow buried itself into the sand, barely missing his head.

Mahalalel and Jared were waist deep in the warm water, pushing the ski out in front of them, when they turned to see James and Joshua running down the beach towards them.

"Look," said Jared.

"Is something wrong?" asked Mahalalel, confused by the manner in which the two men were running. He began searching the littered beach for signs of the sky people, but it was too dark to tell if James and Joshua were just running clumsy and undisciplined, or if they had seen something that made them abandon all measure of stealth.

Mahalalel's question was quickly answered by a sea of arrows that suddenly began raining down on the beach. "Oh, no."

John, Chris, Edward, and Lance were only five feet from the water when three arrows bounced off the ski.

"What the heck was that?" asked Chris, standing up straight and looking around. Then he heard voices behind him and turned to see Joshua and James sprinting towards them, arrows striking the ground all around.

Jared and Mahalalel abandoned the ski and ran back onto the beach, aiming straight for the jungle. They passed their new friends, frantically waving their arms, signaling for them to follow. "Get to the woods!"

Hesitating, Chris and John looked at each other. They weren't so sure about leaving the ski behind, especially now that the other was floating freely in the ocean, a slave to whatever the currents willed. If the skis were their only hope out of this place, then there had to be ample reason for abandoning them. An arrow striking the sole of Chris' boot was enough reason for him, and he pulled it out and chased after the others. Despite the storm of arrows falling below a cloudless moonlit sky, John was still not ready to retreat. He tried to push the ski the rest of the five feet, but the front of the ski had buried itself into the wet sand. An arrow grazed his side, taking a few layers of skin off.

"Come on!"

John wasn't sure who had yelled it, but it didn't matter. Even if it was Lance, he had to admit that it was a good idea. Running as fast as his fatigued body would allow, he crossed his fingers and hoped that the falling arrows would not find a target.

It was amazing how dark it was . . . how utterly dark it was. After only a hundred feet behind the tree line, the jungle's canopy became so dense that it tolerated absolutely zero light seeping through its biological roof. With no light whatsoever, it was impossible to move quickly without running into a tree or some other invisible object. Mahalalel and Jared moved quicker than everyone else, being as accustomed to the environment as possible, but they were still moving remarkably slow. John and Joshua were not much worse, John having spent many a night in the dark jungles of Vietnam and Joshua with a list of night time missions executed in jungles all across the globe. Without such exaggerated experience, James, Chris, Edward, and Lance were walking with hands out in front of them, feeling for the person ahead, making sure they were staying with the group.

Jared turned and whispered over his shoulder to those struggling to stay behind him. "Stay together. No matter what happens, you must stay together."

"Where are we going?" Joshua could tell they were not taking the same route that had brought them there.

"We must go to a different place or they could find us and kill us all."

James called up from the back, not being able to hear more than incoherent whispering. "What did he say?"

Chris said, "I think he said that we aren't going back to the same place." And then he tripped over something and fell to the ground. James, Lance, and Edward all tripped over him, and Edward screamed when he landed. He landed on a rock and was sure that it broke his already fragile ribs.

Mahalalel stopped moving and stretched his hand out behind him to keep Jared from running into him. Jared did the same. "You must make no noise! If they find us, we will all die."

Through clenched teeth, Edward muttered, "Yeah, sorry about that." James helped him onto his feet and grabbed his hand, leading him through the pitch black jungle and all its obstacles- both natural and unnatural.

They began moving again.

"Hey, what about the other guys?" Joshua asked Jared. When no response came, Joshua began walking faster, outstretched arms attempting to locate his guide. But his hands only found empty air. "Jared!" He began to panic.

Then Jared's voice broke the tension. "I cannot say." But before he even finished his troubled thought, a scream pierced the night sky and seemed to shake the ground. It was a horrifying sound, the sound of excruciating pain . . . of death. It echoed off every cliff-side, every solitary rock; it bounced between trees and was amplified by every drop of water. It felt as if the whole earth was cringing from the agony.

"What was that?" asked Lance, not trying to hide the fear in his voice.

Jared could not be seen, but one did not have to see his face to know what it looked like. His voice was a strong blend of anger, remorse, and sorrow. "That was one of my friends." Then he was silent for a few seconds, gathering strength it seemed. "That is what we will all sound like if they catch us."

Once the chills subsided, and everyone was able to think again, they began to continue the train into the oblivion, the native's last screaming breath playing over and over again in their heads.

It seemed like forever. Their bodies screamed in protest and threatened to strike and override the brain's command. In actuality it had only been twenty minutes, but twenty minutes conscious of every passing second in complete blackness, knowing that death could come and sweep them in her arms at any given time, allowed for their concept of time to fade into one eternal cloud.

"How . . . how much longer?" asked John. Depending on the answer, he might decide to lay down on the jungle's floor, fall asleep, and hope that he never woke up again.

"Shhh!" Mahalalel stopped again.

"What is it?" asked Joshua.

"They are following us close."

James felt his way down the line until he was standing by Joshua. "Jared, is there a clearing around here?"

"Clearing?"

"A spot where there are few trees, where the moon could provide light."

"Yes. Why?"

"Take us there."

The first of the 'sky people' to enter the clearing was shot through the heart. And so was the next.

Joshua was lying on his stomach, resting the silenced sniper rifle on a fallen tree that was stretched horizontally on the ground in front of him. Lance, John, and Jared were lying on his left and Chris, James, Mahalalel, and Edward on his right. The clearing ended a hundred yards in front of them and with just enough moonlight, Joshua could see twenty yards into the trees through the scope. As soon as the natives stepped foot into the clearing, they were effortlessly shot and put down. But not lost was the awe inspired by the stealth they exhibited. If it were not for the rifle and high powered optical scope, Joshua knew that he and his friends would stand no chance. The way the natives were moving through the trees was impossible to describe. It was as if they were mere shadows gliding across the ground and finally settling against a tree. Also incredible was how they were managing to track them through the jungle in the dead of night.

"How are they tracking us?" asked Joshua.

Mahalalel seemed transfixed with the .308 Remington that was taking out a historically elusive enemy with such great ease. "The gods give them powers. They will find us soon if we stay here long. But your magic will give good time now."

"How long do we wait?"

"Soon we will go."

Edward was in extreme pain, his breathing torturous. He looked as if he were about to pass out.

James asked Mahalalel, "Will your people be able to help him?"

Taking a close look at Edward, Mahalalel answered, "They will do their best."

Something whistled overhead.

"What was that?" John was frantically searching for any sign of the enemy.

His question was answered by an arrow striking the tree they were all hiding behind.

"Where are they?" Joshua swung the rifle back and forth, the cross-hairs sweeping over dark jungle, but no natives.

"I don't see anything!" Another arrow sent John ducking for cover. The next arrow struck the tree an inch below the Remington.

"The scope is reflecting moonlight," stated James urgently.

Jared whispered, "In the trees."

"I know he's in the trees." But despite his searching them, he had still yet to locate him.

"No. In the trees." He pointed up to the sky.

Joshua didn't argue, but instead raised the rifle about two inches until the scope was staring at a shadow sitting aloft in a tree. But it wasn't until the shadow moved and an arrow streaked away from it that Joshua identified it as the assailant. He squeezed the trigger and watched the shadow fall to the ground. "Got him."

"Good. Now let's go." Mahalalel was on his feet and moving before his command was even complete.

Lance simply hated it. The whole thing, everything. They were in the dense jungle again so there was barely enough light to make out the guy in front, but at least this time he could see that. But that did little to raise his optimistic attitude. There was no way he could grasp even the steps he was taking now, or the breath that was giving him life. How could any of this be possible? How can it be real? Perhaps it wasn't, he thought. Perhaps, just maybe, it was all a dream. Maybe God was trying to tell him something and, like Ebenezer Scrooge, he would wake up in the morning a different man, a new man. He could live with that. In fact he began making hasty oaths, promising a change of life-style if God would make it all just go away. "I'll go to mass, confession, sell all I have, be a freakin' monk . . . "

James was walking right in front of Lance and heard his bargain. Chuckling, he turned to face Lance and asked, "You think that's what He wants?"

Lance looked confused for more than the first time today. "I thought that was what all you good Christians did to make the Guy upstairs happy."

"You ever read the New Testament?"

"No."

"Then how can you even begin to guess what the 'Guy upstairs' wants from you?"

Before an answer could be formulated in his tired mind, Edward fell to the ground behind him and landed against the back of his legs, dropping him to his knees. "Would you watch it?"

But Edward didn't respond.

James and John turned around and saw Edward lying on the ground, Lance trying to move him.

"He's not responding," said Lance.

"Carry him."

"What?"

John glared at him with icy eyes. "I said carry him."

A bit of that pride crept back and laced his words. "You carry him."

John smiled and a bit of light revealed his teeth. "You'll notice . . . " he looked around him to James and then behind him to Joshua and Chris, who were barely visible, still following Jared and Mahalalel. "That you're the only one not armed." He held the assault rifle up in the air, threatening him and making his point.

"He's your friend, not mine."

"Just pick him up!" yelled James. Then he added in a softer tone, "We'll take turns."

"Fine, whatever." Though it was said under his breath, it was loud enough for John to hear it.

"You know Lance, if you were to die here, do you think anyone would know?" Then John motioned for him to hurry up. "Come on, I don't think you want to get lost out here."

Lance threw Edward over his shoulder, not mindful of his injury, and walked past John who followed behind him.

Up ahead, Chris had noticed that John, James, and Edward fell behind, and he had Joshua and the two pure-blooded natives waiting for them to catch up.

"Thanks," said James as he walked past him while resting a reassuring hand on his shoulder.

"I figured you'd probably prefer staying with the guide."

"Oh yeah."

When Lance walked by with Edward slung limp over his shoulder, Chris quickly thrust two fingers to Ed's neck to feel for a pulse. Relieved that it was still strong, he walked in stride along side of John. "Do you think they're still following us?" he asked John.

Lance turned slightly to hear the answer.

"I don't know. I would think that they would have found us by now if they were."

Satisfied and slightly reassured with the answer, Lance returned his attention back to keeping James in sight. He also continued his unfinished confusing thoughts as to how he ended up in this place and how he could possibly get out of it.

The sound of running water now whispered through the trees and the air they filled.

"We are almost there." It was the first time Mahalalel spoke since hearing his friend screaming in painful woe.

Five minutes later they were standing on the edge of a cliff that stretched down thirty feet before meeting what looked like a lagoon in the silver moonlight. The lagoon was surrounded by caves on almost all sides, calm waters stroking their rocky formations.

"We jump." And then Jared did just that. He jumped off the side of the cliff and disappeared beneath the water below with a tiny splash. When he resurfaced, he was already swimming towards one of the caves.

"What about Edward?" asked James. "He's out cold."

Joshua took a step closer to the edge. "Me and Chris will get him as soon as he hits the water."

Not liking the idea, but knowing no other options were available right now, James nodded his consent. "Okay." Joshua and Chris jumped off, and James waited until they were positioned for the grab before he let Ed fall thirty feet through the air and into the dark water. He prayed Ed would land in a safe position and not on his neck or head.

Joshua and Chris dove beneath the surface of the water and reached out with both hands, grabbing Edward's pants just before he sunk out of reach and into the dark abyss.

James was more than relieved and thanked God when he saw Joshua and Chris start swimming with Edward, after Jared towards one of the caves.

James was about to jump, himself, when Lance asked him a question. "Hey, what's that?"

The curiosity in his voice seemed strange in that it was separated from the more recent attitudes acquired. Rather than a fear-filled suspenseful question, it sounded of wonder. James looked in the direction Lance was pointing and at first could see only the formless shadows that he knew to be one of the layers of jungle canopy. But then he noticed something breaking the surface of the top canopy and pointing into the cloudless night sky.

"A mountain?" asked John.

Mahalalel turned to see what they were talking about and quickly realized their inquiry. "That is where the sky people live."

"On a mountain?" asked Lance.

James took a cautious step forward, as if one foot closer to the object that was at least a mile away would bring significant clarity. "That's no mountain."

The moon hung in the sky right above the tall object and John kneeled to the ground and tilted his head down even lower to change his point of perspective. At that angle, the moon was directly behind the pointed object, creating a silhouette. And then there was no mistaking what it was. "Oh my God."

It often surprised James at how often people referred to God without even being aware of it, Him being a consistent part of their speech- in vain of course, but no one ever seemed to stop and wonder why or how that phrase was introduced to the human language if, in fact, no God ever existed. "What is it?"

"See for yourself."

Both James and Lance mimicked John's position, getting closer to the ground and looking up at the curious thing.

"No." Lance refused to believe the first thought that came through his head. "No. It's not . . . it can't be."

Slowly standing back up, mind blindsided by another quick left jab, James stood motionless. "Then what is it?"

"It's a mountain, just like John said." Lance was waving his hands and speaking fast, nervousness energizing him.

"That's a pretty geometric mountain, wouldn't you say?" John walked up beside James.

James turned to say something to Lance, but Lance wasn't there.

"Where'd . . . " Then his question was answered by a loud splash that echoed of the walls of rock below them.

Mahalalel didn't understand their amazement, nor could he. He knew nothing of the world that James and John lived in, and so neither could he make the startling connection between his and theirs. "Come, hurry." Then he jumped over the side, leaving James and John to stare up into the night sky at what could only be a huge pyramid.

Mahalalel had been waiting for them in the mouth of the cave and helped them out of the water once they arrived. "Come." He turned and led them deeper into the cave, deeper into darkness.

After a few minutes there was a strange sound and then a small flame that appeared dancing in the darkness. A second later, that same flame was successful in lighting a torch and providing a greater degree of visibility. Mahalalel held the torch out in front of him, shadows shifting off the rock walls around them. In the flickering glow, footprints could be seen in the sand, leading deeper into the cave. They were the footprints made by people wearing boots.

"Where are they?" asked James.

"Jared has them hiding. We go there."

They reached an area in the cave that was covered with about an inch of water and a rope hanging from somewhere above. Mahalalel made some sort of noise, a kind of signal it seemed, and Jared's voice suddenly interrupted the quiet sound of the burning torch and heavy breathing.

"I will help pull them up. Go cover our feet."

Mahalalel nodded and handed the torch to James before grabbing a tree branch covered with huge green leaves and running back in the direction of the lagoon.

"Where's he going?" John watched him run away while getting ready to climb the rope.

"To cover our tracks, I would guess." James held the rope, keeping it from swinging while John climbed up to where Jared had his hand outstretched. Once Jared helped John up into another section of the cave, James threw the torch up to Jared, and made the climb himself.

They sat huddled together in a small nature-made room. Three torches provided enough light to see comfortably and to provide some warmth to combat the chills that came with being soaking wet.

"Your head's bleeding again," Chris told James.

James touched his head and felt blood running down his fingertips and into his hand, but he knew the cut wasn't bleeding too bad, just that it was mixing with the water and making the blood thin and runny. As if he wanted to be reminded of the wounds he'd picked up, he also ran his hand over his arm where the arrow had pierced it. It throbbed like a huge needle was injected into it, but he was surprised that that was the extent of the pain- at least for now. "How's Edward?"

Joshua shook his head. "I don't know, James." He moved Edward slightly so that James could get a look at his side. "He's bruised pretty bad, I think it's definitely broken. Maybe some internal bleeding."

"Is everyone else okay?"

They all nodded affirmatively.

"So what was it?" Lance's eyes were almost daring them to give him the answer he already knew.

John sighed and rested his head back against the rock. "You know what you saw."

"Okay, then what does it mean?"

Joshua looked confused as did Chris. "What's he talking about?"

"A freakin' pyramid, Man." Lance laughed madly.

"What?" Chris sat up a little straighter. "You saw a pyramid?"

James nodded. "Yeah."

Chris leaned all the way forward now. "So what *does* that mean?"

All James wanted to do was close his eyes, to go to sleep. "Well, I think it would only confirm what we've already learned. All the ancient records or myths, whatever you want to call them, speak of men coming down from cloud cars and building cities overnight."

Jared looked confused. "You know of the records?"

With all the resolve he had, James continued to fight the temptation and need to let his eyelids drop. "Is that what yours say happened?"

"Yes. The gods sent down the tall ones and they began building . . . "

Joshua remembered the quarry. "The quarry . . . "

If fatigue hadn't consumed every cell in their bodies, then they could have spent hours talking about the pyramid and making connections to the giants and UFOs and fallen angels and all kinds of stuff, but their physical bodies simply could not withstand the effects caused by the events born to the last few days. But just when they were about to surrender to sleep and recovery, Mahalalel climbed into the room.

"It has begun to rain, so we are safe until morning. The rain will wash away our feet. We must rest now."

No one even dreamed of arguing or disagreeing. There hadn't been a more accepted order among them since someone yelled 'run.'

"Rain, huh? So the weather finally made up its mind." James closed his eyes, and everyone else began doing the same.

Joshua's eyes were barely open, but they were open enough to see something in James' pants. He was too tired to care, his mind losing grip on whatever it was. But then, for some reason, something struck him, and he sat up. "James."

James didn't even open his eyes; they felt as if they were welded shut. "What?"

"What is stuffed in your pants?"

"I ripped off part of the sail before I ran into the woods. I don't think it's big enough to help though. Not like we have the skis anyway."

Jared interrupted the conversation. "Perhaps it will float away from the evil land and come onto the ground near us. The water was moving in that way."

James yawned. "Yeah, if the tide was moving that way, then maybe we can still get it."

Joshua was wide awake now. "James . . . "

There was that tone again, and James painfully forced his eyes open, slightly annoyed. John, Lance, and Chris did the same.

"That's not a sail. It's a piece of a flag."

James looked down and pulled the fabric out from his pants and held it up in the light. Joshua was right. It was a flag.

James was sure his eyes were deceiving him- that fatigue had made him insane. But then John confirmed his hallucination.

"That's England's flag."

SIXTEEN
Theory Atlantis

:::: *New Day*

No nightmare came to prey upon a defenseless mind this time. Surprising, considering the circumstances. Of course, who would truly be able to tell the difference between a nightmare behind closed eyes and the reality of eyes open? But still, James thought it odd that the monsters of night had spared his imagination yet again. Perhaps dream-world just couldn't compete with the horrors of this place, and as horrible as the Vietnam dreams had been, any dream less than what he had been shown by the Devil, or whatever it was, would simply be a futile attempt to top what couldn't be topped. Maybe they knew.

They . . . James thought about that for a second. *For we do not wrestle against flesh and blood, but against principalities, against powers, against the rulers of the darkness of this age, against spiritual hosts of wickedness in the heavenly places* . . . Yes, he concluded- they.

The old and tattered fabric that was a piece of an English flag was experimentally massaged between his fingers. The flickering light from a hanging torch cast unpredictable shadows across the flag, teasing the eyes by revealing the English design only to shift and let darkness hide it the next moment. And though the flame created all sorts of shifting lights and shadows that swept across James' face, his eyes did not blink, but remained fixed on the mystery he held in his hands. How many more pieces were there to this puzzle? What else was there to discover- to either create or snatch hope away? Was there even an answer to the question, or was it to be an eternal search for the *proper* questions, and then only to find that those answers were useless in all practical purposes anyway? Perhaps the experience was just another level of life, or the reality of life. But then what was life? What was reality? Many say that one's own experience determines what reality is, but what if the experience isn't real? These walls that surround us and border us, creating an environment of containment . . . What if we could see through them and into the unseen, the unnatural? Is this what would be seen? Is this simply the world beyond the physical borders that blind us and desensitize us to what has been tagged 'paranormal'? And if so, what does one do to climb back over those walls? *Can* one go back? Would one want to go back? Certainly life could never be the same again, not with knowing what was taking place beneath the cloak of normalcy.

James finally blinked.

Normalcy . . . it was a deception, an illusion. Even without the reality of this place, the earth was wrapped within a blanket of ignorance. People had their houses, cars, jobs, televisions, DVD players, families, agendas, feelings and emotions, power, wealth, sex, drugs, games, looks, styles, churches, stadiums, boats, frequent flyer mileage, resorts, manicures, pedicures, and anything else that fills up those four letters- life. The human aspect and its struggle to lose itself in its idle surroundings . . . Not that all of those things are idle, but 'they' knew how to use them . . . how to hide behind them. Now, especially in America, things supernatural were laughed at, mocked at. If James were to escape and share his story, he would, no doubt, find himself not sympathy but a strait jacket. The human populace was dead and blind to anything they could not see with their eyes. But still . . . life goes on. It's not hard; in fact it's natural to become ignorant of those powers beyond the walls of our illusion. Humanity is so busy without being aware of the unseen . . . has always been. But now with the addiction to be entertained, and the things fed by those entertaining, those powers that pull the strings from some invisible realm have managed to convince the population that they don't exist. James thought back to the legends of the Greeks, mythology as it's now called. He thought of all the traditions passed down through different cultures . . . thought of the Bible and where he was now. And he wondered if the place in which he found himself would have been more believable back in a day when men were more likely to mind the spiritual instead of being so consumed with themselves and with stocks and stats and soaps and MTV.

He blinked again, this time becoming conscious of his thought process. He rubbed his dry eyes and sighed.

Did it even matter now? Was this searching and philosophizing even worth the time and energy? The basic truth, at its core, was that he was stuck in a place that was far beyond his experiential reach. That made the place strange, and strange, in this setting, was scary. He just needed to find out if there was a way, any way, to get back. Would life be different after realizing a place like this? He only hoped for a chance to find out. And as if the answer was to be found within the beaten flag, he stared at it, hands trying to squeeze a revelation out of its faded colors.

When no revelation came, he looked back at the others who were sleeping soundly and then, without protest, he joined them. But not before he felt a tear slide down his face and had a thought about his wife that shaped it.

It was raining hard, had been for quite a while now. The journey back to the pure-blooded natives' underground asylum was made through the early morning hours and the falling rain that distinguished them. The trek had gone without incident, with no sign of the sky people or giants. The only negatives were Edward, who was a burden, slowing down their progress significantly, and the driving rain that didn't feel so great in the colder hours of the day.

Thunder sounded and gently shook the ground. Chris opened his eyes and slowly sat up. Looking around, he quickly noticed his friends all sleeping around him covered in shadows. He looked around the cool room and observed that the torches had all burnt out. It hadn't been a dream after all. Fatigue and soreness massaged his body, and his brain told him that he needed more rest. With no protest, he began to lie back down. His eyes remained open for a while, gazing into the unseen, trying to unravel the mystery for the millionth time. Finally, his eyes became heavy and his brain surrendered wit to imagination. That's when he saw a shadow pass beneath the closed door that was across the room from him. Not sure if it was his imagination or if he actually did see a shadow, his mind began to fight the fatigue and his wits resurged to calculate the situation. The shadow moved. There was definitely someone on the other side of the door. More curious than concerned, Chris swung his sore feet over and onto the cold ground. The cold traveled up through his bare feet and all the way to his brain, waking him up enough to allow for some excitement. Quietly, he crossed the stone floor and approached the door, careful not to scare the person away. He reached out and grabbed the crude handle, but when he began to pull on it the door squeaked and the shadow disappeared with the pitter-patter sound of bare feet running across stone. Chris quickly pulled the door open and could just see a pair of legs run around the corner and up the stairs. He ran into the hallway and rounded the corner just in time to see the person reach the top of the stairs.

"Wait!"

The sound of his voice startled the person, and the person froze. Like a child caught with their hand in the cookie jar, the person slowly turned their head to look back down at the one who had called out. And it was with wide, anxious eyes that the person found Chris standing beneath her.

Her. Chris was paralyzed. It was her again, the girl he had seen the day before, the same girl who asked if he was here to save her. Her beauty struck

Chris like a two ton steel beam, and he would have passed out if he hadn't remembered to breathe at the very last second. Surprisingly, she looked much different than the men; she had a much lighter tone to her skin and a softer face. If it wasn't for her dress and her rough image, Chris thought that she might actually be someone from earth. Her eyes radiated with life, every emotion being broadcasted like high beams from a set of headlights. Her hair was long and blonde, falling straight onto her shoulders before separating down her chest and back. Their eyes met for an awkward second, yet a second that was aware of itself on both ends. Before she turned and hurried off out of sight, she almost smiled. Chris would have chased her, but he didn't want to meet any of her native boyfriends again. And besides that, he wasn't even sure if he *could* move. He felt stupid, like he was in second grade again, but with no one around to see his paralysis, he didn't care what he looked like. Like he just got a wink from the prom queen, he realized that it may have been in high school when he last felt this way. After a deep breath, he finally began walking back to the room as a smile tugged at the corners of his lips.

After entering back into the room and closing the door, he turned to see Joshua sitting up in his bed staring at him.

"What was that all about?"

As Chris shrugged, he couldn't stop the grin that came induced by the girl that looked like a Greek goddess to him.

Joshua eyed him suspiciously before getting to his feet and stretching.

Chris walked back over to his bed and climbed up onto its hard surface. He lay on his back, hands folded under his head, and stared through the ceiling and into his mind's eye. And, miraculously, all the evil in this place was lost to him, replaced by the beauty of an angel.

Joshua didn't miss the look on Chris' face as he walked past him, and he thought it strange that Chris was still smiling. An alarm sounded in his subconscious.

"You okay?" asked Joshua.

Although aggravated about opening his eyes and having the image erased, he still managed a wiry smile. "Oh yeah."

"Brian said he was okay too. You understand my concern."

Chris laughed. "Oh man . . . I may be possessed, but not by some evil spirit."

Joshua didn't even try to understand, he simply left Chris alone to his imagination and turned his attention to the guns that were leaning against the far wall. The sniper rifle fitted with a silencer, two assault rifles, the submachine gun, and the pistol all seemed silly now. How does one battle the supernatural with natural weapons? Joshua checked the remaining ammo and was not surprised to find that they were almost out.

"How low are we?" James was awake and sitting on the bed watching Joshua.

"Maybe enough for one more encounter like we had before. Nothing else."

"I don't know about you, but my sword fighting skills are a little rusty."

Joshua ignored the comment and left the guns, walking closer to James. "What's going on with that thing?" He pointed to the tattered flag.

James looked at it before answering. "What do you mean?"

"I know what it looks like, but if that is what it is then . . . what does it mean to us?"

"I think it means there's a way to and from this place. And so far all evidence leads to that way being somewhere out in the ocean."

"You really think this is an island?"

James shrugged. "Maybe we're just on some island that no one has set foot on in two hundred years."

Joshua didn't buy it, mostly because he knew James didn't believe it himself. So he ignored the suggestion. "I've been thinking, Mahalalel said that their language suddenly changed at some point. Changed into English . . . And isn't it strange that an English ship washed up on these shores a long time ago? Maybe around the same time the language started to change?"

With a slight edge of surprise in his voice, James admitted, "Yeah. I didn't even think about that." He looked back down at the flag. "I guess it makes sense. I mean, it doesn't make any sense, but what a coincidence that would be, huh?"

John's voice added to the conversation. "I've been thinking about that too, and there's something else."

Joshua and James looked over to see John lying on his side, his elbow on the bed and his hand holding up his head. "What?"

"Did all this strange stuff start with the ship or did the ship merely enter the same nightmare we did?"

James looked confused. "You mean what if the ship introduced the stuff to the island?"

Shaking his head in protest, Joshua argued, "The natives said that all that stuff with the gods and the giants was recorded before the language change."

An evil grin materialized on John's face. "And yet the language *did* change."

James nodded. “He’s got a point. How did a few English sailors change a population’s language? And we’re not talking about normal citizens either.”

John’s smile faded. “Interesting, isn’t it?”

Lance was up now and walking around, stretching his legs. He wondered when the natives were going to come and get them for breakfast or lunch or whatever it was now. That’s the way it seemed to work, anyway. “I don’t understand your fascination with the flag.”

John raised his eyebrows. “You don’t?”

“Big deal, a ship was shipwrecked here a long time ago . . . so what?”

James answered patiently. “So now we know that there is a way to and from this place.”

Lance shook his head. “How do you figure? The natives told us that no one who has ever set out into the ocean has ever returned. Obviously there’s a way to get here, because we’re here. How you conclude that there is a way back from that is what I don’t understand.”

Everyone looked at each other for a few seconds, realizing Lance’s point.

“Go back to sleep, Lance,” answered Joshua.

Lance raised his hands. “Hey, I don’t want to be the guy to kill hope, but come on, we’ve got pyramids out there.”

“Pyramids, crop circles, the Bermuda Triangle, demons, giants . . . What are we, inside *The World’s Biggest Mysteries* or something?” John laughed sardonically. “This is ridiculous.”

Joshua changed the subject by stating to everyone, “We should check the beach for the skis. Hopefully they washed up again.”

“You think our luck has changed?” asked John sarcastically.

“We’d be stupid not to look.” Then Joshua picked up one of the assault rifles and loaded it.

“Where you going?” asked Chris, awake from his daydreaming.

“To find Jared. We need to find those skis.” Then he walked out the door and disappeared around the corner before anyone could chase after him.

John walked over to Edward and checked his pulse. “His breathing is getting weaker.”

James walked back to his bed and knelt beside it. He folded his hands and began to pray. Lance, Chris, and even John didn’t think it was such a bad idea.

Joshua wandered around the stone corridors for nearly four minutes before bumping into another person. If Joshua was still unsure about his theory concerning the native’s hopes of salvation and them being the instruments to be used, his doubts were now completely gone. At first Joshua was a little concerned about walking around the corridors unguided and uninvited, but that turned out to be a concern unwarranted. The native that he ran into was about six foot six and nearly two hundred and fifty-five pounds of nothing other than muscle. Perceivably, Joshua's heart skipped a beat when he rounded the corner and his six foot frame bumped into six extra inches of towering rock. But instead of the native's reaction being hostile or defensive, it was friendly and warm. In fact, after a few moments, Joshua couldn't help but to think that the guy was kissing up to him. The massive native introduced himself as Lud while engulfing Joshua in a back breaking embrace. Unlike the other natives that Joshua had met, Lud's English seemed a lot cruder and harder to understand, almost as if he was babbling. And then he noticed that Lud had only half of his tongue. His physical features now catching Joshua's attention, he quickly noticed the high-definition scars that were raked over his whole body. He was missing two fingers from his left hand, and his right fingers looked as if they had been crushed to powder at one point. Whatever this guy had been through, Joshua did not want to know. Yet, regardless of the obvious torture the man had endured, his face was not marked by hardship and bitterness. Where one would expect cold, stoic eyes, his brown eyes still had a softness to them. Joshua was pleasantly surprised to find that Lud was only too happy to assist him in finding Jared.

An hour later, Jared was leading them to the beach beneath a sort of sky that people board up their windows, pack their bags, and hurry out of state to avoid.

"So who's the guy?" Chris had to yell just to be heard over the wind.

Joshua turned to see who he was talking about and smiled when he saw Lud. "That's my new friend!" he yelled back.

"That's 'your new friend'?" He laughed. "Are you serious?" A huge wall of wind hit them like a blitzing defensive line, and they were all pushed sideways a few steps. The noise of the wind was incredible as was the force it was moving through the trees around them. Twigs, leaves, and dirt were pelting them with stinging force, creating small scratches and red bumps.

"I bumped into him when I was looking for Jared!" Joshua shielded his eyes from a gust of wind that had picked up some dirt for the ride.

"And friends ever since, huh?" His chuckling was drowned by the weather. "Love at first sight!"

Joshua gave him a hard shove. "Watch it! I'll tell him to rip your head off!"

Looking back over his shoulder at the huge native, Chris commented, "He is a big boy!" Then Lud caught his eye and gave him a huge toothy grin.

Chris gave him a fake smile with a head nod in return while muttering a few things under his breath. This only made Lud's smile bigger and the adjective's in Chris' mind concerning that growing grin were beginning to disturb him, like maybe he heard Chris' mumblings. Chris timidly gave his 'ah ha just kidding' smile and turned back around. "Nice Lud."

Mahalalel was not with them this time, only Jared, Lud, and another un-introduced native who resembled more of Jared's 180 pound frame rather than Lud's massive size. The three natives walked onto the wet sand and headed straight for the rough water. James, Joshua, Chris, John, and Lance followed.

"With the waters this rough, it'd be hard to tell how far the skis would have drifted before being deposited back on the beach or being carried out to sea." John was squinting down the shoreline, peering through the driving rain and into the cloudy horizon.

"We'll soon find out!" yelled Joshua. They continued down the beach, one eye on the violent waves searching for the seaplane's ski, and another on the swaying trees and what might be behind them.

James shouldered the rifle and looked out into the ocean; they had been following the three natives for a half an hour through the soggy sand and the lashing rain. The entire time, James' eyes had not departed from the distant horizon that hung over the white caps miles and miles away. In fact, the only people that seemed indifferent towards the direction over and beyond the sea were the three natives, who were only searching the beach in front of them for any sign of the skis while taking casual glances at the tree line that stood 150 yards away. And James knew that it was because, as far as they were concerned, there was nothing to see in that direction, only endless water. But none of the strangers could help but to wonder if earth was just over the horizon and barely out of sight. Any sign of a ship or a plane was secretly hoped for, but not expected.

Their walk down the beach lasted another ten minutes before Jared called out, "There is something ahead!"

James and Joshua instinctively un-shouldered their rifles and ran after the natives, Lance, Chris, and John following right behind them. It was too far away to see exactly what it was, but it seemed to assume the same shape as one of the skis, and a minute later, out of breath and gasping for air, James and Joshua were leaning on it and thanking God.

Thunder exploded from the heavens and lightening struck into the ocean, and, as if on cue, hail began to mix with the rain.

"Come on, let's get this back!" yelled James over the sound of hail bouncing off the ski.

"Do you want to take it into the water?" asked Lance.

Jared answered, "Yes! I think we should get away from here!"

John quickly looked around, startled by his answer, looking for signs of giants. "Why?"

"We are too close to the ground of the gods! This is a sign of their coming!" He held out his hands and looked up into the falling rain just as thunder shook the sky and a bolt of lightening ripped it in half.

"You could have told us that before we left," muttered Chris, not wasting any time and beginning to push the ski towards the water.

Pushing the ski through the water turned out to be infinitely harder than it sounded. The violent surf did not stop pounding them, trying to throw them back onto shore. Under different circumstances the objective may have been fun, but swallowing more than enough salt water and being relentlessly beaten by the fiberglass ski made it anything but. The lightening didn't raise any smiles either.

"Wait!" John was pointing at something from up on the ski, but nobody seemed to notice him. He had to scream three more times, competing with the deafening roar of the ocean, before they heard him. "There's something in the surf!"

Joshua looked in the direction John was pointing and, at first, could see nothing other than the foamy waves. But then a dark object was tossed out of the water. It was caught by the same wave that passed it and then it was spiked back into the water. Since Joshua was closest to it, he left the side of the ski just as a huge wave picked it up and tossed it over his head. He dove beneath the water to avoid a concussion. Once under the water, he decided to swim towards the object beneath the surface, opting to fight the undertow and rip tide rather than the crashing waves. After pulling himself along the bottom as long as his lungs would allow, he emerged out of the water only to be greeted by a wave that found a lot of itself in his mouth. Joshua doubled over and puked. After recovering, he noticed the dark object only five feet in front of him, but he still couldn't tell what it was. He reached out for it just as the tide retracted and took the object closer out to sea. Joshua waited for another wave to come and push it closer to him- there was no way he was going out any further into these waters. His wave came and the dark object flew past him towards the beach. This time he was able to get a pretty good look at it, and it seemed to be about four feet long . . . with a strap. Whatever it was, it was heavy. It wasn't floating on the surface but sinking as soon as the violent tide released it. If it weren't for the fierce waves, the object would be fixed in the sand at his feet. He fought against the waters and waded out to get between the object and the endless sea behind him. When the tide retracted, he fought against it, feeling the sand around his feet being pulled towards the depths. Leaning forward, with water striking him at the waist attempting to knock him over and pull him into an undertow, Joshua got ready to catch the thing as it rushed straight back at him. The impact was not anything like Joshua expected or was ready for. Whatever it was, it was heavy, and it knocked him backwards into the arms of the tide. If it weren't for his feet being buried in the sand, he would have been going wherever the ocean took him. But his feet were anchored and he grabbed the object, which he immediately recognized as a canvas bag, and waited for the water to release him. When it did, he stood back up and wrestled his feet out of the sand, throwing the bag over his shoulder.

"What is it?" asked Chris excitedly.

Joshua, now tired from wrestling the ocean, rejoined his friends in escorting the ski back to a more suitable area in which to build something that would help them leave this place. "I don't know! I haven't had the time to check!"

"Wait a minute!" Chris leaned forward to get a better look at the bag that was slung over Joshua's shoulder. "That's my bag!"

"What?"

"It is! That's my bag! It was on the plane!"

"Are you sure?" James yelled.

Chris attempted to wipe the water away from his eyes just long enough to get a clear view. "Yeah, I'm sure!"

"What's in it? It weighs a ton!" Joshua could barely see anyone on the other side of the ski, the rain falling so heavily that it was like a white curtain.

Everyone strained to hear Chris' answer over the roaring ocean and booming skies.

Chris smiled despite the lightening that seemed to be getting closer. They were all expecting to feel a shock travel through their bodies at any second. "Guns!"

"Ammo?" asked James.

"Oh yeah!"

It was significantly dark now, though the dense cloud coverage had a lot to do with it. The rain had not let up, and the wind began to blow as if it was making a wish and the trees were candles. The sound of the wind howled as it blew into the cave that led to the natives' secret home. Tired and hungry, the eight men went straight for the dining hall. Though they were soaking wet, they didn't care. They wanted food. Besides, the strangers had nothing to change into anyway.

"I'll be right back, I'm going to check on Edward." James turned from the doors that Jared had just swung open and began walking away from the smell of roasting meat. The aroma almost lifted him off his feet and carried him right into the room, just like in the cartoons, but he owed it to Edward to at least make sure he was doing okay before satisfying his hunger. He walked down a corridor, the sound of his wet boots squishing on the stone floor. He came to the end of the corridor where it joined another hallway that went to the left and to the right making a 'T.' James scratched his wet head in confusion. He could have sworn that the hallway led to steps and not another corridor. He turned back around to look down the hallway he had come through, but only lit torches were there to see. He shrugged and decided to go left. The hallway looked identical to the one he had just come from with no doors on either side. He walked to the end. Now he came to a set of stairs, but they stretched upward instead of down. He turned around and went back the way he came, passing the corridor he started out in on his right. This time he came upon a crude wooden door on his left, but he knew it wasn't the room they were staying in so he kept going. As he neared the end of this corridor, he could tell that it bent to the right. He was almost to the bend when he heard a voice come from behind.

"We need you."

He spun around, slightly startled at the sudden noise, but there was no one behind him. He stood there, motionless, eyes searching the stone walls around him. Though he found UFOs and giants with six fingers to be weird, talking walls would be something entirely new.

"I need you."

This time the voice seemed to echo off the wall from around the bend. The voice seemed familiar to him, yet somewhat eerie.

"Where are you?" he asked as he approached the bend.

"I'm here," came the reply. And again, this time it seemed to come from behind him, back where he was before.

He spun around again, only to see nothing. "Stop playing games with me. Come out and show yourself." He began to get a strange feeling in his stomach and the hairs on his neck were standing up. His bold challenge was supported by a soft bundle of nerves that probably resembled a frying egg at the moment.

"Would you like all the power in the world to be yours?"

"What?"

The voice seemed to be swirling around his head now.

"Think of the world in this troubled hour. It needs a savior, a ruler. It needs you. I need you."

James took the rifle off his shoulder and held it tightly in his hands. "You want me to help you?"

"Yessss . . . " As if the answer slipped off the tongue of a serpent.

"Then come out and let me see you."

"If that's what you wish."

Immediately, footsteps could be heard coming from around the corner and getting closer. James held the rifle pointed in the air, but with his finger on the trigger. He didn't want to startle the native, but he also had a strange feeling that what was coming around the corner just might not be a native.

He was right. What did walk around the corner almost gave him a heart attack.

It was his brother, Steve.

"Hello, James." He said, smiling.

James took a step back, his senses blazing. "What are you doing here?"

Steve looked surprised. "Aren't you happy to see me?"

"I haven't decided yet."

"James, it's me." He stretched out his hands.

"I haven't decided that yet, either."

"Come on, James. I've been waiting for you."

"Waiting for me? From where?"

Steve looked around. "From here, of course."

James' eyes did not hide their skepticism. "How'd you get here?"

"James, so many questions . . . so many wrong questions."

"*Wrong* questions? Then what is it you'd have me ask?"

"Did you not hear my proposal?"

"You want me to save you?"

"Not just me, James, the whole world."

"What the heck are you talking about?"

"It doesn't matter. Just answer my question. Do you want more power than you could ever imagine? To save the planet and to bring peace to it?"

A twisted smile spread on James' face. "Oh, and I suppose you have the power to grant that to me?"

Steve nodded. "Yesssss . . . "

James thought he saw something in Steve's eyes, something similar to what he had seen in Brian's before. "If you have the power, then why don't you do it yourself? You don't make sense. How could you have power to give someone all the power imaginable and yet be powerless to use the power yourself?"

Steve smiled a sardonic smile that made James shudder. "James, answer the question."

"It sounds to me like you're describing the Messiah."

"I am."

"You're asking me if I want to be the Messiah?"

"Do you?"

"I think the position is taken."

Steve smiled, this time a patient smile. "You don't know what you're passing up."

"Who are you?"

Steve disappeared, evaporated into thin air, and another familiar voice sounded from behind him in the same instant.

"James, save us."

James knew the voice before he even turned around, and his heart wanted to explode as a surge of emotions electrocuted it.

It was Kirsten.

The sight of her almost dropped him to his knees. He wanted to run to her, to embrace her and kiss her, but he knew that it was a dark deception, that it wasn't her. "Why don't you show me who you really are?"

Kirsten smiled a strange and distorted smile that didn't belong to her. "I'm afraid that wouldn't be possible, Sweetheart. You see, I need you." She walked close to him and put her hands on his shoulders.

"What do you mean?" His voice was shaking, his emotions stirred by her touch.

She looked at him as she always had, so loving, so caring. She leaned up close so that her lips were touching his ear. She whispered, "Because if I show you who I really am, I'm afraid you might die." Then she playfully kissed his ear

James stepped back, snapping out of the fantasy and recognizing what was going on.

"Come on, James. I miss you." She began to slide one of the straps to her dress down off her shoulder.

The initial emotions passed as reason got a hold of them, and James suddenly became filled with rage. "Don't you dare!" he yelled.

"Don't what?" she asked, sliding off the other strap.

He raised the rifle and pointed it at her. "Stop it!"

"Are you going to shoot me, Baby?"

As he turned to run away through the bend in the corridor, he said through gritted teeth, "Get away from me." He didn't look back, but he could hear her voice echo off the walls after him.

"Okay, James, if you will not save us, then maybe our son will."

James stopped dead in his tracks. "What did you say?"

But there was no answer.

He walked back around the corner, dreading what he might see, but saw nothing. She was gone. "What do you mean?" he yelled. But the only answer that came was from his own voice rebounding off the walls around him. After a minute or so, James went back to searching for Edward, even more confused and emotionally disturbed than before. His lips barely spread to allow the prayers through.

❧❧❧

It was ten minutes that seemed like forever, but James finally found the room and Edward still in it.

"Where is everyone?" Edward's question was voiced before James even had time to notice that he was awake. His voice was weak, and it was obvious that there was incredible pain with each breath. He struggled to sit up, his face wincing in pain.

"You're awake!" James hurried to his side.

"Yeah, unfortunately."

"We were worried."

"I hope I wasn't too much of a problem. I know I had to have held up the getaway process quite a bit."

"Yeah well, your big butt was a nice shield from all the arrows."

Edward laughed and then regretted doing so. "I think I definitely broke them."

"I think so too." James helped Edward to get his feet onto the ground. "Are you hungry?"

"Yeah, I'm hungry." Then he rubbed his head, trying to gather his senses. "So what'd I miss?"

"We fought the sky people off with the .308, and Jared and Mahalalel led us to a cave where we spent the night. Early this morning we came back here. Then we went looking for the skis, hoping that they washed up on shore."

"Any luck?"

James laughed. "Luck? No, nothing happening here is lucky. But we did find one of the skis, thank God. We brought it back, and we'll start building a boat to get us out of here soon."

"Good. If you don't mind, I'd like to get back home."

A sudden twinge of sympathy shone from James' eyes. "I really thought we were going to lose you."

Edward nodded. "I don't think I'm quite out of the woods yet."

"None of us are." Then he offered to help Ed towards the door.

Finally noticing that James was soaking wet, he asked, "You look comfortable."

"It's like a hurricane out there."

"Wonderful."

"Shall we eat?"

"Let's." As they struggled to the door, Edward stepped out of his self-conscious world and the pain that drew attention to it, and noticed that James seemed different than normal. He wasn't quite sure what it was, but something in his eyes broadcasted an emotion not there before. "Are you okay?"

James was caught off guard by the question. "What? Oh, yeah, I'm fine. Just some strange stuff going on." It was one of those answers that weren't entirely true, but to get into the discussion the truth would have brought was incredibly undesirable at the moment. He was okay in one sense, and he would be okay in all others, so he justified his answer.

Edward had one arm around James' shoulders, and James had one of his own around Ed's waist, careful not to touch his ribs. "So was it a ship?"

Now in the hall and sure they were heading in the right direction, he smiled. "Yeah, it was a ship."

Edward detected something in his voice that seemed to be baiting him. "What is it?"

"Well, how can one put this?" He paused for affect. "It appears to be an English ship."

"A what?"

"You heard me right. I found a flag wrapped around a piece of wood."

Edward looked at James incredulously. "What does that mean?"

James felt as if he were dragging Edward and a quick look at his dragging feet confirmed his theory. "Well, that's the million dollar question. These people speak English and that wasn't always the case. Odd that an English ship crashed here at some point."

"Maybe the same point."

"Yeah. But the thing that doesn't make sense is that the language would have been changed by the English men that were on board."

Despite the pain that was coursing through his body, Edward was thinking clearly and deductively. "The natives said that the gods were coming for their women before the language changed. That means that all this bizarre stuff was already going on when the ship arrived."

James nodded. "That's what we're thinking."

"You're right, that doesn't make sense. How could English sailors find enough influence to change their language, let alone just stay alive?"

They came to the stairs, and James had to exert great effort to help Edward up them without hurting him. Once at the top, both men were ready to sit down for a while.

After they began walking again, Edward said, "It's all so bizarre. How does this place connect itself? What does one strange thing have to do with the other? The ship, the natives, the giants, the crop circle, the quarry . . . "

James cut him off. "Well, I believe I can answer that one."

"The quarry?"

"Yeah. We got a glimpse of where these 'sky people' dwell. Seems they used the rock for their buildings."

"How big are the buildings? That quarry was so huge you couldn't see its bottom."

As they reached the doors that led to the dining hall and James reached out to open them, he said, "They're pyramids."

Edward was taken aback by the statement. "What?"

James urged him forward with some added push on his back. "Again, you heard me right, but come on, let's eat. We'll talk about this later."

Breathing, awake, and somewhat able, Edward entered the relieved welcome of those whose hearts were heavy with concern for his well being and life. If the truth be told, hardly anyone truly believed Edward would make it out of unconsciousness, so watching him walk through the doors with James was a miracle that no one denied. A few emotional minutes passed before everyone returned to their meal, in which time hunger pains dimmed in light of a friend come back to life.

The meal was delicious; the fact of Edward's physical existence still among them an added flavor. What sat before them was some sort of meat, but it was not revealed what kind and no one cared to ask. There were about ten natives sitting with them at the long table- Mahalalel, Jared, and Lud among them. Light conversation was only admissible because of the common knowledge that as soon as the meal was digested they would be right back trying to find a way out of this place. Those questions could afford to wait until they had at least finished their meal. Every once in a while, a native would peek his head into the dining hall to get a look at the strangers, but only to be ordered to leave by Jared. This helped confirm the sincerity of the girl's question. And at one point in the meal, even that girl had stuck her head into the doorway. Chris' reaction to this particular intrusion was suspiciously noted by the natives that surrounded him, and laughed at by his friends.

Edward had to eat with great effort, it hurt him to swallow as well as to breathe, but he was more hungry than he was in pain. He seemed distant, as if his mind was wrestling with something, and no one noticed that he hadn't taken his gazing eyes off the food that was in front of him even once.

An hour later they were lying on the stone beds in their provided room, full and momentarily satisfied. Mahalalel had offered to show them the entirety of the hideaway the pure-blooded called home, but James and all else could only think of one thing, and that was sleep. The meal had hit the spot, and they could feel themselves growing lethargic, so with great politeness, James had asked if it would be okay if they just returned back to the room.

Though the beds were uncomfortable, none of them entirely used to sleeping on a slab of rock, they had no trouble falling asleep. In fact, they had to lie on their sides and prop their heads up so that they wouldn't fall asleep. Sleep would have to wait a little while longer. There were things to discuss now.

"So tomorrow we start building?" John asked it as a question, though his voice left little room for disagreement.

James yawned. "Yeah. We're going to need to come up with a plan. Any ideas as to how we should build this thing?"

James, Joshua, John, Chris, and (at times) Lance spent the next half hour discussing and debating different technical ideas as to how the boat should be built. They were so into their thoughts and ideas that it took that half hour for them to notice that Edward had not said a word since dinner.

"Hey, Ed, you okay?" asked James.

Edward didn't even acknowledge the question or the one who asked it.

"Yo! Edward!" Lance yelled.

This time Edward blinked and his mind returned to the room. "What?"

James asked, "Are you all right?"

Edward simply nodded.

"You have any ideas?"

Edward hadn't heard a single word of their conversation and mistook the context of the question. "Not really." He paused, a look of frustration on his face. "Are you sure it was a pyramid you saw?"

Everyone exchanged glances wondering where Edward had been for the last half hour.

"Yeah, pretty sure." Curiosity grabbed James' attention, wondering what Edward was thinking.

"Weird stuff, man." Lance rolled onto his back and shut his eyes.

Suddenly, Edward looked up from the ground he was staring at and his eyes refocused onto the people in the room. "Yeah, especially since we don't even know who built the pyramids in Egypt let alone who could have built them here."

"Maybe the same people," Joshua muttered.

"Have you ever studied the pyramids before? I mean, the Great Pyramid of Giza, which is one of the Seven Wonders, is probably the largest building ever made. It weighs almost six million tons. We're talking 2,300,000 limestone blocks at two and a half tons each. And, oh yeah, there's only a

.02 inch gap between the stones for cement. Precision? Those specifications exceed the tolerances allowed for the tiles of the space shuttle. It's also aligned to true north better than the Paris observatory. Its four sides are aligned to the four points of the compass with only a one-twelfth degree of variation, and that could well be from gradual movement of the earth's axis. The edges of the pyramid are straight to less than half an inch along its perimeter, and, on top of that, it hasn't even settled an inch. Tolerances like these aren't even matched with all the technology we have today."

Everyone stared at him, blank expressions all around.

Edward shrugged and then winced, remembering his physical infirmities. "I'm only saying that no one knows what they were built for. Their creators had to have had a purpose. I mean, calculations that precise together with that size and mass . . . The amount of work would be tremendous. There had to be purpose behind it. And I'm just wondering if the purpose might be the same here."

Joshua was the first one able to speak. "That's what you've been thinking about all this time?"

Edward shook his head. "No."

Everyone leaned forward, not knowing what to expect next.

"Well, this might sound a little crazy to you, but all these things have been tied together before."

"What things?" John asked.

"UFOs, pyramids, the Bermuda Triangle . . . "

James sighed. "You're not going to go New Age on us are you?"

"Just listen. My son wrote a research paper for his literature class his senior year of high school. He chose to do it on Plato's *Critias* and *Timaeus* with special attention to the dialogue between Solon, the Greek statesman, and the Egyptian priest."

"It's been a while since I've been reading my Plato," replied Chris with just a hint of sarcasm.

"Atlantis."

Chris' eyebrows raised. "Oh." Then he lay back on the bed and chuckled before closing his eyes.

Edward shrugged. "Yeah, that's what I've always thought too. But I helped him do a lot of research on the subject, and I just can't stop thinking that maybe it's pertinent to our situation."

Lance sat back up. "Why?"

"According to Plato, Atlantis was an island continent between the Caribbean and north Africa that was destroyed by catastrophic events."

Lance shook his head in disagreement. "Historians believe that if Plato's account was based on truth then it was linked to a catastrophic earthquake and flood caused by a volcanic eruption on the island of Santorini that wiped out the Minoan civilization on Crete."

Edward stifled a yawn before responding. "I know. Just listen. Many people have believed that, number one, Atlantis was real and, number two, that it's now buried beneath the ocean floor in the Bermuda Triangle."

"I thought many were speculating it to be buried under ice in Antarctica," stated James.

"Some people do, but many others believe that it's in the Triangle."

"Yeah, tell him why," commanded Lance.

"Things that have been found. Temple ruins, remains of a highway, coal, gold, and iron . . . "

"That stuff is hardly fact. When you researched, did you use anything other than some nut's web page?"

"True, it's all debatable. But there is the pyramid. Even Newsweek reported that."

"Again, a possible geographical anomaly. I mean, these people think that Atlantis was run on some kind of power crystals or something. They think these crystals are now at the bottom of the Atlantic and that they're responsible for causing all kinds of strange electromagnetic waves and stuff. And by 'stuff' I mean, time warps, access to parallel universes, black holes, you name it."

Edward yawned again and looked as if he was going to fall asleep in the middle of his lesson. "Look, all I'm saying is that we're lost somewhere in the Bermuda Triangle, and there's a pyramid on our island."

John spoke from within a shadow in a corner of the room where the light from the torch failed to reach. "But why do all those things support Atlantis? The hundreds of planes and ships that have disappeared prove Atlantis? What about AUTEC?"

Chris opened his eyes but did not make any extra effort to move. "What's AUTEC?"

Joshua answered for John. "Atlantic Undersea Test and Evaluation Center. It's in the Bahamas, on the island of Andros, I believe."

John nodded his approval while Chris asked what that had to do with tea in China or cheerleaders in sports.

Lance stood to his feet, the flaming torch hanging above his head lighting up his face. "Some people think that it's an underground Area 51, mostly stupid people from the states."

"UFO sightings in the Bermuda Triangle, UFO sightings in New Mexico . . . " Edward carefully lay down onto the rock bed. "There always seems to be some kind of top secret government test facility nearby. Is it all a hoax? Well, we've been here for how many days? You tell me."

Joshua scratched his unshaven face that had grown enough to be called a beard. "Wasn't Atlantis supposed to be a utopia? Advanced civilization, paradise on earth? Look around, man."

Edward didn't answer for a while and everyone thought that he had fallen asleep, but then his lips spread and began to move. "Where have all the boats gone? Where have all the planes gone? Where have all the people gone? Where have all the boats gone? Where have all the boats gone . . . "

Now Chris opened his eyes and sat up, Edward's melody making everyone suspicious.

He continued, "Oh boy, where have they all gone?" He paused again. "It's been suggested that the Bermuda Triangle is a gateway to another place. Maybe Atlantis, maybe not. Maybe another dimension, maybe not. Who can really say? But you can't seriously deny that it is a gateway to *somewhere,* because we went straight into a big mean face and now here we are. But where is here? Here is where . . . "

James looked at Joshua. "What's he doing?"

"I was just going to ask you."

Now there was a smile on Edward's face, but his eyes were still closed. "What if the Bermuda Triangle didn't have anything to do with Atlantis or gateways . . . What if the Bermuda Triangle was just a supernatural habitation of the 'gods,' these spiritual forces and their giants. What if this place we're in right now is what's responsible for all the bizarre things taking place in the Atlantic." His smile grew bigger. "What a discovery we would've made, huh?" He laughed out loud. "But it is a doorway, whether something from here controls it or not . . . I bet if we looked around we'd find the *Patriot,* the *Wasp,* the *USS Cyclops, Proteus, Nereus, Anita, Milton Iatrides* . . . And the planes, so many planes." He opened his eyes. "Did you know that they say over a thousand ships and planes have disappeared in the Bermuda Triangle?" He closed his eyes again.

James called him. "Edward?"

"Yes, James?"

"You learned all this from helping your son with his research paper?"

"Yes."

Lance sat back down on his bed. "I'm telling you, he probably got all this information off the internet, it's full of all kinds of crap like that. Psychics channeling spirits from Atlantis, people who were from Atlantis in their previous life, the crystals, the advanced language found on artifacts at the bottom of the Triangle that connect to the Great Pyramid in Egypt . . . I live in Bermuda, I've heard all the stories. They're all nonsense."

Everyone expected a response from Edward but all they got was the sound of his snoring.

"And now he's asleep, great. Unbelievable." Lance lay back down.

"You people are free to believe whatever you want, but I'm going to go to sleep and when I wake up, I'll be in my bed with some hot girl who no doubt kept me up all night drinking and partying, got me to take a trip that went bad which is where this crazy messed up dream came from. So see you all never again."

No one had paid any attention to him; they were all far too busy trying to figure out what had just happened.

There was a look of concern in Chris' eyes as he looked around the room, trying to get a feel for how everyone else was feeling about their situation. "I hate to be the class idiot, but what if we did find one of the ships that went missing?"

Joshua held up the English flag. "Seems we already did."

John was staring out into space, concentrating on his mind's eye. "The Triangle only got its name in the 60's, but things have been recorded happening since the 16th century. Aside from the Atlantis stuff, what if this was a quantum experience?"

"Like the Philadelphia Experiment?" asked Chris.

"Yeah. I mean, I saw on one of those unsolved mystery shows with a story about this girl who was flying a plane over Turk Island. The ground staff saw her circling aimlessly in the sky and tried to raise her on the radio but couldn't. But they could hear her conversation with her passenger over the radio. She was saying something like 'I can't understand this, this should be Turk Island, but there's nothing there. This island looks uninhabited.' She circled a few more times before flying away and never being seen again."

"Some story." Chris noticed that James was still staring at Edward. "James?"

James didn't answer but now everyone was staring at him, wondering what he was thinking.

"James, what is it?" asked Joshua.

James took his eyes off Edward and moved them around the different faces in the room. "Edward doesn't have a son."

:::: *Another New Day*

They were all eating the breakfast the natives had prepared for them. The meal was being eaten in the same room with basically the same people. Jared, Mahalalel, and Lud were there. There were a few other unfamiliar faces, and James couldn't help wondering how many natives lived in this underground labyrinth of caves. The food was satisfying and they were all grateful to have it, but their appreciation was lost in the confusion the night before had brought.

Edward acted as if nothing had happened, as if he had been asleep and missed the entire conversation he started and orchestrated. This made everyone else a bit uneasy. James had even more on his mind. With his little experience in the hallway just before finding Edward awake, he had a lot to occupy his mind with. Even the discovery of Chris' guns did little to cheer them up.

Mahalalel noticed their downcast appearance and asked, "Is all well?"

But before anyone could lie and ask when they could build the stinking boat so they could just get out of there, the big doors burst open with a loud crash and a bloody native stumbled in.

The native was barely alive, yet there was an intense fire raging in his eyes. He was covered with blood, most of it dry and crusted, but a few wounds were still spitting fresh blood. His face was bruised and swollen, his eyes barely visible. A few of his ribs seemed to be exposed on his left side as well. All the energy he had left seemed to be just keeping him from falling over. He leaned heavily into the wall.

"Shem!" Jared stood to his feet and ran across the room.

James could barely recognize the man, but he was able to tell that it was one of the natives that had been with them that night in the jungle- one of those whom Jared was sure had been tortured to death.

Jared looked more furious than anything else. "What have they done to you?" He ran up close but did not touch him.

Shem lifted his chin with great effort and, with an amazing force of will, raised his blazing eyes to meet Jared's. "They're coming."

Then he collapsed onto the floor.

SEVENTEEN

RETURN

Days seemed indistinguishable. They melted together in flashes of blurred events distorted by unbalanced emotions. Yet they continued to come, trudging through an ocean of spilled tears and stepping over pieces of shattered hope. The question why was exhausted, now irrelevant to a broken heart. With whatever resolve she could muster, Kirsten continued to live. I can do all things through Christ who strengthens me . . . Though the words rang true in her mind, she couldn't help but detect a slight edge of bitterness now coating her spirituality. She hated that, saw it as a sign of weakness, of failing the test. But she knew what James would tell her if he could. God loved men who wrestled with Him, who came before Him honestly. Fellowship was not broken by those men, but rather refined in the end. Now, Kirsten had to attempt to bring her charge against God, seeking something from Him, rather than to just shut Him out and continue the journey into loathsome bitterness and resentment. She needed faith, and she needed strength. If not answers, she needed comfort.

Kirsten reached over and hit the alarm button, putting an immediate stop to the loud buzz noise that was piercing her patience like a scalpel. She rolled back onto her back and stared at the ceiling, trying to keep any thought from finding residence in her mind. All she wanted was five minutes of peace, five minutes of feeling relaxed and rested. She hadn't taken the time to notice the numbers on the clock, but she could tell from the light that was coming through the window that it was almost afternoon. The night before she thought she heard voices in her room, and she had trouble falling asleep. After praying for nearly an hour, the voices stopped and she fell asleep shortly after. Yet despite the strange things that had been happening in her house the last week, she was too upset to be scared. Fear was not making any profit off this prey. The weird events washed over her like water over stone, too much emotion already packed in to allow room for fear.

The five minutes passed and she could no longer fight off the waves of attacking thought. They came storming through the barricades like a flood and were in control of the territory almost immediately. The strongest of the thoughts was a new one, yet the one she feared the most, the one she hoped she would never have to yield to. Against her will, she began to think of what the rest of her life was going to be like without her husband.

Jessica came running into the bathroom just as Kirsten finished dressing. "Mommy! The men who are looking for Daddy are here!"

Kirsten wrapped a towel around her head and followed her daughter to the front door.

"Hi, Kirsten." George walked past her and made his way into the kitchen.

"Hi." Fred followed.

"Did you find my daddy?" asked Jessica, hope burning in her eyes.

George forced a smile as he pulled a chair out from under the table. "No, Dear, not yet. But don't you worry; we're going to find him." He tried not to be affected by the frown that extinguished the fire in her eyes.

Kirsten finished closing the door and joined them. "So what is it that you've found that made you drive over here instead of just picking up the phone?"

Fred motioned for her to have a seat, which she did. "Our guy in Bermuda called us yesterday."

George picked up the rest of the story. "You know that the IRS has been denying that Steve had any official business down there. Well, apparently, that story has changed."

Kirsten sat up a little straighter. "What do you mean?"

"It seems that we weren't the only ones looking for him. Turns out, the CIA has been looking for him too. We aren't sure why, but it's an announcement loud and clear that Steve was there in the middle of something big. His mission, official or unofficial, seems to have been planned by our government."

"You said, '*weren't* the only ones looking for him.' Did they find him?"

Fred cleared his throat before speaking. "The CIA took some photos via satellite- photos of the Bermuda islands. Turns out, they found exactly what they were looking for. A few hours later a SEAL team was transported to one of the deserted islands."

The phone rang.

Kirsten ignored it and pleaded with Fred to continue. "Go on."

Fred looked over at the phone that was hanging on the wall. "You're not going to answer that?"

"Just tell me what happened."

"Okay." He tried to ignore the ringing as he began his report again. "Evidently, Steve was sent to Bermuda not only by the IRS, but by the CIA as well. From what we understand, it was supposed to be an easy job- in and out. We're not sure what went wrong."

The answering machine beeped and the voice that was now being recorded by it sent chills through Kirsten's body.

"*Kirsten, it's Steve.*" There was a long pause.

George and Fred exchanged a knowing look before studying Kirsten's response. They thought she would run to the phone but were more than surprised at her reaction.

She couldn't move. Was it really Steve? Or was it another trick? Was it the real person she knew, or was it the intruder she had shot at before?

"*I heard about James. I'm going to do everything that I can to make sure he is found . . . I hope that you are hanging in there. My little brother will do whatever it takes to get back to his family. I'll try calling again later.*" There was a beep and then silence.

"The SEALs found Steve and brought him back to the states. He's at the pentagon." George looked for some kind of positive reaction but found none.

"So the IRS and CIA have major concerns in Bermuda, and James found himself right in the middle of them."

"That's definitely the way it seems."

"And I'm guessing that the CIA found no evidence of a plane or plane crash on this island that, no doubt, James' prisoner was taking him to?"

Head sinking a bit, George looked across the table to a woman who had just been handed a new life. A life consisting of giving birth to a child that would never know its father and another that would someday forget who he was. It didn't seem fair. "No, there was no sign of James ever making it to the island."

Kirsten nodded and wiped a tear from her eye as she stood up. "Well, we all did what we could, didn't we? I mean, we can't find someone who isn't in a position to be found." Then her single tear was duplicated until her face was wet and she could no longer hold them back. Fred embraced her, and she buried her face into his shoulder, shaking uncontrollably in his tight grip.

"Look, this doesn't mean that we've lost him." George's voice over the phone sounded slightly different than when in person. "The weather was terrible; they could have gotten lost or made an emergency landing on one of the other islands."

Kirsten was no longer fooling herself. She was no longer hoping that James was still alive but rather hoping that she would have the strength to live life without him. "It's been how long?"

George sighed. "If the plane crashed . . . He could be stuck on one of the deserted islands. With no way of contacting anyone and no way of making it back to mainland, he would be just like Robinson Crusoe, waiting to be rescued."

"From what I recall, Robinson Crusoe waited a pretty long time."

"Well, times are different. I have a friend at the CIA who is taking every opportunity he gets to take satellite images of the area. The Coast Guard is patrolling the area nearby, and our guy in Bermuda is on the trail. If he's still alive, we're going to find him."

After a pause, Kirsten asked, "George, do you really think he's still alive?"

Silence.

"Neither do I. Thank you for everything." She hung up the phone. She wanted to cry, but no tears came. She wanted to scream, but she couldn't raise her voice. She was about to collapse into James' chair when the phone rang again. She answered it.

"It's Steve." His voice sounded tired.

"Hi, Steve." It came out shaky. She felt horrible that she was not happy for him, that she didn't care that he was alive. Had James been here with her, she would have been exuberant, but James was not there and that meant that there was no good news to be heard. She hoped that Steve understood.

"If I understand this right, James went to Bermuda looking for me?"

"Yes. He took Edward, John, Brian, and some other guys too." She heard Steve swear under his breath.

"The people here are telling me that things got ugly down there."

Kirsten told him everything she knew. "They were hoping that they could find one of these guys and have him lead them to you. But it looks like they never made it to where they were going."

"If they were heading to the island I was being held on, then no, they never made it."

"What is going on down there? The CIA? What were you doing?"

After a short pause, Steve answered, "I can't talk about that over the phone."

"So will I see you anytime soon?"

Ignoring her question, he continued with more of his own. "James' chief, his name is Fletcher or something?"

"Yeah, George."

"Do you have a number?"

"Yeah, why?"

"You said he has a man down there, right?"

"Yeah."

"Well, I imagine I could be of great help to him."

"You're going back?"

"I wouldn't be able to live with myself if I didn't. My little brother left everything he loves to find me, I don't even have anything I love."

"Will the CIA let you?"

"Unless they're monitoring this call, they won't know."

EIGHTEEN

ADAPTATION

Questions were forgotten. It was no longer the same. No longer did the unexplainable vex their simple minds and torture their understanding. Their futures could not spare any more time spent in confusion and utter helplessness. Fear was gone, and so was everything that had been invited by it.

James Streen checked his automatic weapon one more time. The way he was feeling was by no means new to him, though it had been a while since a situation like this had involved him. Unlike the last ten plus years spent in SWAT, his present situation related more to his experience as a Marine. And it was a Marine that he had become again. His mind was clear, void of the nightmares it once had the luxury to entertain, void of all the strange events it had failed to process. It was now in cruise control, the result of years spent training. He looked down the barrel of his automatic rifle and into the thick jungle that stood before him. To his left were the friends he brought with him to this awful place and to the right were those who called this place home. They all lay flat on their stomachs, still and unmoving. Up ahead and in the trees were more natives armed with bows and arrows.

Thunder exploded overhead as another bolt of lightening ripped through the sky. The wind was howling through the trees, testing their strength.

They continued to wait. Uncomfortable in the puddles that were almost completely submerging them, they never moved their eyes away from the jungle before them, knowing that the scout could run up at any moment. There was a tension that seemed to squeeze everything, the men, the trees, the air. It was the feeling common to those who knew they were about to die, who were about to engage in battle.

"So tell me about heaven, will you?" Joshua allowed his eyes to stray from their target and over to James who was lying beside him.

The question seemed to be lost within James' head, bouncing off locked doors and dead ends within his psyche. The man that James had always feared becoming, the man he had left behind in the Marines, undeveloped and immature, was trying his hardest to be born. James was letting him.

Joshua noticed the stoic look and set face that he had only seen on James' face once before. "James?"

He blinked, water falling from his eyelashes, but nothing more. His mind was in a different place, a place prepared for war.

Reaching over, Joshua grabbed a hold of James' arm and shook him. "James."

This time James turned his head in Joshua's direction, the locked doors in his mind suddenly swinging open. "What?"

"It's been a while, hasn't it?"

"Feels like yesterday."

A moment of silence. "I asked you about heaven."

James wiped the water from his eyes before speaking about the place he was sure he would soon be experiencing. A smile tugged at the corner of his mouth as he began sharing verses from the book of Revelation. It was a strange thing- the peace that was felt in times like these. He would be leaving his wife and children behind, never to see them on this planet again, a thought that usually crushed his heart, and a thought that had pushed him to survive these past days. But now, with death staring him in the face, he didn't notice those details, but only the open gates of heaven and eternal joy. Peace. Strange, but a reality.

Another hour passed by. Still nobody had moved. Doubt began to set in, fear that perhaps Shem had been mistaken, hallucinating in his pain. It was impossible to know for sure. He couldn't be asked, because he had already died from his wounds.

John was growing more and more annoyed at the whole situation. This wasn't his war; this was none of his business. Why should he die for these people? He just wanted to get out of this place. Seeing James and Joshua praying only made him angrier, bringing back memories of his fiancé and expecting the same ill treatment now. He mocked the idea of a loving God. Either God was evil or He wasn't in control- that was the deduction John had come to. Swearing under his breath, he squeezed the rifle tighter. But it didn't make him feel any better.

Chris was staring at Lance. Lance's whole body was now covered with water, except his head, which he was holding up and resting against the stock of the assault rifle. He looked scared, broken. For some reason, Chris started to feel sorry for him, started to sympathize. If Lance was to die, he'd get only what he deserved, but that logic just didn't seem to justify itself anymore within Chris' conscience. Maybe because Lance had become one of them. It wasn't the same as in Bermuda; he was no longer their enemy. Now he was an ally, fighting a common enemy and just hoping to survive. Chris hoped he would. The imagination couldn't produce an accurate portrayal of what the upcoming battle would be like, Chris not knowing what to expect from an army of giants. He rolled over onto his back, sub-machine gun across his chest, and rested his head in the mud. He closed his eyes and started to pray. For the first time in his life, he started to pray.

The natives that surrounded them numbered about sixty. There was no way to tell how many sky-people would be coming, but Mahalalel seemed to think they would send a number matching their swollen pride. They were hoping to be underestimated. It was really the only chance they had at surviving.

A new noise suddenly made its way through the torrents of falling water, thunder, and howling wind. One would certainly have missed it, if not expecting it. It was the sound of feet running through the puddles and mud. Jared stood to his feet, trying to see through the walls of water that were falling from the dark sky.

"They come! They come!" The native suddenly became visible as he exploded through the rain and ran straight past his positioned comrades.

Jared whistled, getting his attention. "Here. Come here." The pure-blooded native squatted and looked in the direction of Jared's voice, but it was obvious that he still couldn't see him. Jared stepped out from behind the layer of trees he had been behind. "Here." The native saw him and ran to him, eager to deliver his report.

"They are many, but not so many. We were right."

"The tall ones?"

"Twenty or so."

Jared looked away from the scout, contemplating their strategy. Twenty of the giants would be extremely difficult to put down, but when considering they could have sent hundreds, it was definitely an arrogant miscalculation. Or was it? "How many of the men?"

"A hundred."

"How long?"

Before the scout could answer, the ground began to shake.

James looked from Jared and the scout to the ground around him, wondering what was going on. The puddles began to vibrate with ripples that soon turned to small waves. Even through the severe storm, the advancing army of supernatural soldiers could be felt.

Lance looked away from the sights on the rifle and over to the natives. They seemed calm, intent. He turned to see the Americans. They didn't look scared, but a little anxious. Lance was definitely out of place. He thought about running. These men had all been trained to fight, had experienced war. Not him. He was scared. A firm hand grasped his shaking arm.

"Just stay ahead of them. Conserve your ammo. Don't get close." Chris released his arm and raised the sub-machine gun, aiming it through the rain and into the unseen beyond.

"Here they come!" yelled Jared, gripping his sword.

"There must be hundreds of them," Joshua yelled over the weather.

Just then, a group of giants broke through the rain and fog and entered sight. They were huge. They stood still, scrutinizing their surroundings.

Why'd they stop? James removed the safety from the rifle.

The giants that could be seen seemed to be picking up on their presence somehow. Moving back and forth, they studied the trees and the ground.

"They know." Joshua whispered but was sure James couldn't hear him over the rain and wind. Then he noticed the tracks in the mud. He grabbed James' shoulder and pointed.

At first, James didn't know what Joshua was excited about, but then he saw it too. The scout's tracks. They stopped and turned back the way he had come, leading to where he was presently hiding. James knew it was only a matter of time before the giants noticed.

Wind blasted through the trees and wisped the giant's long wet hair around its face. Its eyes pierced through the wet strands, searching for signs of its prey, wary of a trap. Then it saw the footprints. Its eyes widened as it raised the six foot long sword. Then its head snapped in the direction of the hiding natives.

The natives that were positioned above in the trees were waiting for the remaining sky-people to come within range of their bows. As suspected, the giants walked out in front, their dominant presence not to be hindered by the speed of ordinary sized men. It was another aspect of their pride the pure-blooded were counting on. They pulled back on their bows, aiming the arrows at the hundred men below. Preferring to wait until a closer proximity was reached was no longer an option. The giants below had begun to make a fuss about something. They had been found. The wind would affect the accuracy of long range shots, but there was no longer any choice. The giants needed to be distracted and lured back the way they had come- now. The natives up in the trees fired at the sky-people below.

Arrows whistled from the tree tops, their sound hidden by thunder and powerful winds. They struck the unsuspecting sky-people, dropping a handful of them to the watery ground right away. The targets had been those in the back so no one noticed their fall. More arrows were released. More sky-people fell. Again, unnoticed.

Below, the giants were ignorant of those being killed behind them, but they were no longer ignorant of the pure-blooded natives they were hunting.

Joshua set the cross-hairs of the scope over the face of one of the giants. He tapped the trigger with his finger, waiting for an excuse to pull it. "Come on." The giants were supposed to be turned around for the attack. They were running out of time.

Jared looked in horror as the giants walked closer to his position, following the scout's tracks. It wasn't going to work. They were all going to die.

One of the natives in the trees noticed the giants below walking straight for his comrades. From his bird's eye perspective, he could see exactly how the situation was unfolding and how it would ultimately end. If he didn't do something right now. He pulled back on the chord and aimed at a body that was closer to the giants rather than in the back where they had been focusing. He shot the arrow, and it struck the soldier in the thigh. The result was exactly what the archer had hoped for. The sky-person clutched his thigh in surprised confusion, screaming out in pain and alerting the small army of their being attacked.

The giants turned towards the cry and saw arrows streaming down from the sky, picking off their small army, one-by-one, with accurate precision. They raised their swords and ran towards the trees that were housing the archers. Their war cries were as disturbing as their image.

Joshua sighed in relief as he watched the giants turn and run away. He was sure Jared did too. Now they waited for the signal to attack.

It came. Jared stood and began running quietly towards the giants, and everyone else followed. The giants didn't know what happened. Striking trees with their swords, some of them actually falling over with added force from the wind, their backs were turned to the charging pure-blooded natives. The natives went for the back of the legs, attempting to disable them rather than taking the time to kill them. Time was the issue of importance. Surprise only worked in the first few moments of the battle, and if they wanted to capitalize on their small advantage of surprise, they would have to render inoperable as many of the enemy as possible as quickly as possible.

Cries of pain and anguish rose through the tropical storm and competed with the thunder. The pure-bloods were screaming and yelling now, fighting for their own existence as a people. The element of surprise took out a few giants, but not many more. Since then, the remaining ones had turned and started to fight back. The archers had been spotted by now, and they were taking arrows in return. Half had already fallen to their deaths. The battle had begun. But it may have been over before it started.

It was hard to watch. Joshua tried not to notice the magnified view of the natives being cut apart by the insane savagery the giants were fighting with, but it was impossible. He had to watch and watch closely, waiting for an open shot. One came as a giant swung its huge sword at a pure-blooded native and removed his head. The native's body dropped beneath the scope and the crosshairs were over the giant's head. Joshua squeezed the trigger. The giant blinked and stumbled backwards, confused. It brought a hand up to its head and wiped away blood. The giant didn't understand. Jared and some others finished it off. Joshua brought his sights over another giant.

James circled the battle through the woods, intent on sneaking up from the side rather than running straight in. He needed to conserve as much ammo as he could, and so he needed the element of surprise. The rain still fell and thunder still shook the sky, but the sound of the battle transcended all of that. As he ran through the trees and vines, the wind trying to knock him over, he couldn't help but to think of what would happen if they lost this battle. What would happen to the natives? What would happen to his friends? His legs moved faster. Content that he was parallel with where he wanted to be, he began making his way back towards the battle. His mind was clear, he was relaxed. He was ready.

Lance hadn't moved. Even when everyone around him had gotten up and took off running, either towards the huge beasts or into the woods, he remained frozen to the ground, unable to move. Joshua was still next to him about ten yards away, and that was comfort enough to convince him to stay. And then Joshua got up and ran into the woods as well. Lance closed his eyes, trying to wake himself up from the worst nightmare he ever had, but the sounds of screaming and clashing swords did not fade into the sounds of chirping birds in the morning or the crashing Bermuda waves. He gripped the rifle tighter, knowing that if he was going to survive, he might have to get up at some point.

John and Chris walked together through the woods, firing at the sky-people from a safe distance. If they were going to be attacked, the sky-people would have to enter the thick woods towards them. Chris mowed down two of the men with the sub-machine gun, its force propelling them to the ground. But there seemed to be so many.

Joshua climbed a tree about sixty yards away from the fighting and got comfortable after making sure he had a clear line of vision to the battle. He fired one shot at a time, watching the evil army fall short one person at a time. But he knew he would run out of ammo well before the army was finished, and he knew his shots were doing little to help the natives who were being massacred by the giants. But the giants didn't seem to mind bullets, they merely shrugged them off and continued to fight. Joshua figured he had killed about twelve of the sky-people so far, a small dent in a hundred man army. It looked as though seven giants were down, a huge accomplishment for ordinary men, but still a long way to go. He continued to aim at the more ordinary enemy.

Jared jumped to the side as the huge blade ripped through the air he had just been standing in. Before the giant could pull its sword out of the mud, Jared counter-attacked by swinging his own sword, waist high, at the giant's right leg. The giant reached out and grabbed his arm, halting his swing. It pulled Jared across its body and flung him into a three foot deep puddle. As Jared recovered, the giant retrieved its sword out of the mud. Its eyes were void, lifeless, like a shark's, and yet they seemed to pierce the very soul. The nine foot giant stretched its arms over its head, thrusting its sword into the air, releasing a blood-thirsty cry of barbaric passion. Jared took the opportunity and threw a small dagger at the giant's vulnerable chest.

The dagger stuck. The battle cry was abruptly ended. The giant ripped the dagger out of its chest and threw it to the side. It then began walking swiftly towards Jared, intent on not wasting anymore time with this prey. It was annoyed.

Jared looked around for help, but there was not a single one of his comrades that wasn't in the process of fighting for his own life. He was on his own. The giant seemed to walk in slow motion, everything around him slowing down. Even the trees seemed to be bending at a slower speed. Saliva dripped from the giant's mouth, its evil grin revealing teeth that had known human flesh before. The dramatic perception snapped, and then everything seemed to happen so fast. Jared spun, avoiding the thrust of the giant sword, and swung his own, dragging it across the giant's chest. The giant didn't seem to notice and was bringing its sword around again. This time Jared threw himself to the jungle's floor and between the giant's legs, hitting both with his sword as he passed between. Before Jared could come out of his tuck-and-roll, the nine foot monster turned, with lightening speed, and brought the sword down from above its head. Jared only had time to move his head, which saved his life, but not his left ear. He screamed in agony, clutching the side of his head. The giant wasted no time wallowing in satisfaction this time. It lifted its leg and began to bring it down, right on Jared's head. Jared closed his eyes, his last thoughts being of his people.

A loud crackling noise exploded through the rain, and the giant toppled over onto its side, its eyes wide with surprise. Its massive bare chest was covered in holes spitting blood. Jared opened his eyes and was amazed to see the giant writhing around in the mud, the puddles turning red around it. A whistle caught Jared's attention, and he turned to see James standing at the edge of some trees. The magic stick he held in his hands was smoking. James nodded before disappearing back into the woods. Jared got up. He picked up the giant's sword and, with great effort, ended the giant's confusion and pain.

Guerrilla warfare was not something the Marines had especially taught James, but it was not hard to pick up. As he jumped over a fallen tree and ducked under a web of vines, he couldn't deny the discouragement that was seeping into his mind. It had taken way more ammo to put down that giant than he could afford. There had to be another way. He ran to a nearby tree where he could just see the fighting through the rain. Occasionally the white sheets of water would splatter red. He worked fast. Unhooking the strap from the automatic rifle, he tossed it around the tree, tying it off. He then stuck the barrel of the gun into the strap and twisted the rifle end-over-end until it was twisted tightly against the tree. It was a practical bipod, steadying the weapon for more effective accuracy. James looked down the site and squeezed the trigger, a sky-person running past him suddenly catching the short burst of fire and flying through the air. He aimed at another.

John stepped into a puddle that was more like a small lake and fell into it with a belly-flop. The sky-people were too involved with hand-to-hand combat to pay any mind to the few men sneaking around the perimeter of the battle, shooting them with their magic sticks, even if it was putting a huge dent into their numbers. Few had turned to combat these white strangers, but the pure-bloods only used the distraction to cut them down. But when they saw John fall and his magic stick fly from his hands, five of the sky-people responded immediately. One ran after the gun, while the others ran to John, who was struggling to make his way out of the deep water.

Chris ran by a wounded native and struck a charging enemy in the head with the butt of his machine gun, sending the man's feet right out from under him. The wounded native finished him off. Chris kept running. He fired from his hip, sending sky-people to the ground, trying not to hit his own comrades. It was confusing, a huge mess of people sword fighting in close proximity in a blinding rain storm. Chris only could hope that his bullets were finding their intended targets. His clip ran dry. He pulled it out and reached into his pants, pulling out another. Before he could slam it in an enemy soldier jumped onto his back, slicing at his throat with a knife. Chris immediately dropped his chin to his chest, stopping the knife's movement. Reaching up and grabbing the sky-man, he pulled him over his head and threw him to the ground. The soldier was back on his feet charging before Chris had a chance to check his injury. The charging soldier led with a scream and a punch aimed for Chris' head, but Chris knocked the fist to the side with his left hand while side-stepping the attack and bringing his right arm up, striking the attacker across the chest, clothes-lining him. Two other soldiers appeared through the rain, waving swords red with blood. Chris slammed the clip in place, but an arrow suddenly pierced his arm, forcing him to drop the gun. He winced in pain, grabbing the arrow and pulling it out with a yell. The first attacker received the same arrow in the face, but the other was able to get a full hit into Chris' side. Chris doubled over from the pain. The sky-person had hit him with the handle of the sword and was now bringing the blade down to finish the job. The only thing Chris could do was throw himself at the soldier, hoping the soldier wasn't fast enough to adjust his swing. He wasn't. The sword passed behind him, the handle striking him in the back rather than the blade. They both fell into the mud.

Joshua found John in his sites and worked fast to take out the sky-people that were closing in on him. He had gotten them all but one when one of the soldiers picked up John's rifle and pulled the trigger. The inexperienced soldier did not hold the butt of the rifle tight against his shoulder, and his wrist snapped from the intense reaction. Bullets sprayed the sky, the ground, a few pure-blooded natives, and some of his own people before the rifle fell to the ground. Joshua was about to finish the man when an arrow whistled by his head, taking a layer of skin off his cheek. They spotted him. He swung the optical lens around, sweeping it back and forth over the jungle's floor, but he couldn't see where the arrow had been fired from. Another one. This one stuck in the tree right above his head. He had to get down.

The fighting had only been going on for five minutes, but Lance could have sworn an hour had passed. He still sat there, clutching the weapon against his chest, listening to the horror that was unfolding just twenty yards away from him. He wanted to run. He tried, but his feet didn't obey the command. A pure-blooded native flew over his head and landed behind him, rolling across the ground in a twisted heap. Lance swallowed, fear gripping his heart. *Breathe.* He pressed himself harder into the ground, as if that would hide him. Suddenly, the rain that had been stinging his flesh for the last couple hours stopped. But it was still raining. Through sobs of terror, Lance forced himself to look up. Towering above him was ten feet of nightmarish fantasy. The eyes looked straight through him. Its muscles flexed. It was so tall that Lance almost couldn't make out its face in the rain. He lost control of his bowels. *Move!* The giant took a step closer. *Move!* He couldn't. *Shoot it!* His hands fumbled with the weapon until it bounced away from them. All he could do was turn his back as a massive hand grabbed him and lifted him straight into the air.

Mahalalel looked up, straining to lift his head out of the puddle. The world blurred, darkness enclosing on his vision. He couldn't tell where he was bleeding from, the rain that was falling made it impossible to tell. Maybe from all over. He didn't feel any pain, but he knew he was in trouble. He watched as the battle unfolded around him. Friends, family . . . he helplessly watched them being cut down. It all looked so chaotic. Blurs of movement through the pouring rain, splashing mud, flying arrows, cries of pain . . . He felt helpless, his people were becoming extinct and there was nothing he was doing about it. He tried to move, but his body didn't respond. His strength was draining away, his head felt heavy. Three sky-people and a giant fell dead. At least he would die proud. His people, the pure-blooded natives that the gods hadn't been able to enslave and destroy, were fighting like true warriors. If it weren't for the supernatural mingling between gods and men, they would have actually won their independence and stamped out the evil from their home. But there they stood- swinging swords that were so long they prevented any attacker from getting close. The arrows didn't seem to faze them. It was actually a miracle that ten were lying dead or wounded. But there were fifteen still wreaking havoc among his people.

His vision faded, and his head dropped beneath the water.

Jared and Lud, along with another native, thrust their swords into the back of a giant that had been preoccupied with tossing someone around. It was too absorbed in sick gratification to notice the three pure-bloods rushing from behind. It dropped the man and arched its back in pain, trying desperately to remove the cause of it. Jared and Lud were thrown off before they could retract their swords, but their other comrade was able to hang on for more of the ride. He managed to get his arms around the giant's neck, holding on for his life. It grabbed him, but he kicked down onto the swords that were sticking into its back, and it released its grip, howling in pain. The native dropped to the ground from the massive shoulders, pulling out two of the three swords on his way down. He tossed one to Jared.

Lance was sure his body was broken. The monster had whipped him around like a rag doll, bouncing him off the ground and nearby trees. He felt like jelly. If it weren't for Jared, Lud, and the other native, he would already be dead. He watched as the giant, one sword still stuck in its back, charged the three men. Lance turned away as the native he didn't know was smacked with the giant's backhand. The native's neck broke immediately. The rifle. Lance could see it. A new determination began to kindle within his body, and he began to crawl. Would he reach it in time? Jared and Lud had no time. He forced himself to his feet and began running, stumbling towards the rifle. Feeling his balance leave and his feet fall out from under him, he used the last of his strength to dive towards the gun. He slid through mud and water, the slickness carrying him past the rifle. He turned around and tried crawling back to it. The pain came. It felt like electricity shocking and stunning him. He couldn't move. He saw Jared raise his sword, intent on ending his life in a suicidal charge of rage against a greater enemy that was killing his people. Lance reached for the assault rifle, stretching his fingers. His middle finger stroked the strap. He inched himself a little closer, gritting his teeth.

Jared charged, sword raised over his head in both hands, releasing a bone chilling cry. The giant smirked, paying no more mind to the blood that was flowing down its back.

Almost. Through tears, Lance grabbed the strap and pulled the rifle to him, catching it in his arms, sitting up, and aiming it at the giant all in one quick, painful motion. He squeezed the trigger.

The giant's body convulsed and twitched, the rain around it turning red. Jared made use of the moment and finished his suicidal attack.

Lance collapsed onto his back. The sounds of battle, the clanging of swords and occasional gunfire, became distant, and soon silent. He realized he was passing out and couldn't help but to wonder if he'd ever open his eyes again. *What was James saying about heaven?* He knew he wasn't going to find out.

Ignoring the pain, Joshua continued to run, firing the automatic pistol at whoever got too close. The arrow had missed his heart and lungs, but was still doing some damage as long as it was in there. It had been ten minutes now, and the battle was finally showing signs of slowing down. But Joshua was on the run, he didn't have time to analyze the progress of the battle. There were at least three of those 'sky-people' chasing him. The Remington had run out of ammo, and he had no time to reload. He had slung it over his shoulder, pulled out his pistol and started running. He didn't want to run too far away from the battle. Once he killed the soldiers chasing him, he wanted to be able to find his way back to James and the others as quickly as possible. He wanted to make a move, to turn and shoot, but they had bows and arrows, and, even though they were running full speed, they were dangerously accurate. If he stopped, he'd be an easy target. He fired a shot over his shoulder.

Thunder exploded in the sky, shaking the ground. The rain did not let up. James was with John and Chris- they were shooting at a giant that was chasing a few of the remaining pure-blooded natives.

Bodies littered the wet soil, most of the puddles red with blood. There weren't even two hundred bodies participating in the fight, but the close proximity in which the fighting occurred left bodies on top of bodies.

Empty shells were spit from the automatic, falling to the ground and steaming from the cool rainwater. Joshua joined them. They noticed the arrow sticking out of his chest. He reloaded the Remington and concentrated on the enemy soldiers that were running away. None could escape. They needed all the time they could get. He set the cross-hairs over bare backs.

A few giants remained. They were injured and dying, but they would not lay down and admit defeat. The twenty remaining pure-bloods were down to fourteen by the time the last giant was in the mud. It was over.

Jared leaned heavily against a tree, his eyes filled with emotion. He had not expected to live, and now, the sight before him made him wish that he hadn't. His friends, his brothers, were no longer with him. Twenty minutes ago they had all been there, by his side. Now . . . gone. His whole life was spent with these people, and the rest of it would be spent without them. He felt sick, bile rising in his throat. He'd lost plenty of brothers over the years, but not like this. He counted thirteen of his people still alive. Thirteen. Forty-six of them were strewn about the jungle's floor, some piled on top of others, some too dismembered to tell who they even were. Body parts floated in the deep puddles, impossible to tell whether friend or foe. It was a gory mess. The rain tried hard to clean it up, but there was too much blood and it only made it more graphic.

Mahalelel staggered up behind Jared and rested a compassionate hand on his shoulder. "My friend . . . "

Jared turned and embraced Mahalalel, not noticing his near fatal wounds. His tears were hidden by the rain splashing his face. After a moment of silence, he managed to speak, separating himself from Mahalalel. "What do we do?" Then Mahalalel's wounds became obvious. His right shoulder was open and washed clean by the rain, revealing a portion of white bone. His stomach was sliced deep, and he had an arrow sticking out of his side. Jared's expression changed as he noticed these things.

Mahalalel ignored the response and looked through the rain and to the white strangers. They were attending to one of their own. "They won it. Without their magic sticks, we all had died."

"Yes. But it is no end. The gods will tell. They come back. They kill all."

Heavy eyes, not knowing whether to hope or despair, met Jared's. "Do you believe?"

Jared dropped his gaze to the ground, focusing on the water splashing off it. "I cannot know."

"Then we all will die."

❧❧❧

"What now?" Joshua couldn't bring himself to ignore the jungle around him, waiting for another arrow to scream through the air again. His chest burned like someone lit it on fire and tried to put it out with whisky. Removing the arrow had been no picnic.

"They come back." Lud's pronunciation was terribly hard to understand, but there was no mistaking his words.

John looked over the corpses. "I'm not staying around for that."

"They need us," answered Chris, trying to stop the bleeding from his neck. Fortunately, the knife did not enter the jugular. Stitches would certainly help, but he would live. If the bleeding stopped.

"For what? So that we can die with them?"

"So what do you have in mind?" asked James.

John shrugged in disgust. "I'll swim if I have to."

"And you think your chances are better swimming?"

John took a few steps closer to James and pushed him in the chest. "What do you want from me, huh? You want me to fight another war that I don't belong in? You want me to look up to heaven and beg God for mercy?" His voice was attracting the attention of the survivors. "Is that what you want, James? You want me to find your brother? You want me to save these people? You want me to forget what happened to Jennifer? You want me to pretend that God loves me? What is it you want from me?"

James grabbed John by the shoulder, pushing him backwards until he hit a tree. "I want you to grow up! You want to blame God for everything that's gone wrong in your life? Fine. Now what? Where does that leave you? God's against you, so what good will ever come out of your life? Why don't you just kill yourself? Oh no, that would be exactly what God would hope for isn't it? So you spend the rest of your life fighting the very one that gives you breath!" He released his hold on John. "That sounds like the life to me, man." James turned his back and started to walk away.

"What do you know, James?" John screamed as he ran and pushed James from behind. "Huh? What the heck do you know? You have your wife! You have a kid! You have a freakin' family, man! What do you know?"

Knocking his arms away, James pushed back. "It's not what I know, it's *who* I know! Now I'm gonna' tell you something, John. And you listen real good, because I don't know if you'll ever hear it again. God loves you!"

"Then why'd he take Jennifer from me?"

"For goodness sake, John, that was thirty years ago!"

"And my whole life has gone to hell since then!"

"Why?"

"Because, I can't let her go . . . " He dropped to his knees. "Why?"

James knelt in front of him, brushing his wet hair out of his face. "That's the question that has ruined your life. And it's the wrong question to ask. You've been fighting against the very One who wants to heal you, to give you a new fresh start. He's been holding out His arms to you, and you just knock them away and curse His name. You want to know what pain is? Try God putting on this filth," he pulled at his skin. "And coming to earth. God was born in an animal's feeding trough. God! Thirty years later, John, He was beaten beyond human recognition by hands that He created. They mocked Him and taunted Him, tempting Him to bring down legions of angels to stop the insanity! They spit in His bloody face! Us! Humanity! Spit in the face of God! Then we nailed Him to a cross and gambled over His clothes. You want to know what pain is, John? How about God being tortured so that you could be healed by Him, so that you could be with Him forever! Pain? He did all that for you and so much more, and it was for nothing, because you won't accept it! All He did for you, and you spit in His face. Guess what? Every man dies! It's life, a part of sin. But God gave Himself to die so that you didn't have to." He thrust a finger into John's chest. "Do you understand what I'm saying, John? Jennifer was going to die anyway! You just hate that she died before you could get married and spend your life with her! But why trade that hurt in for eternal damnation when you can turn it into healing and eternal life?" James got back to his feet and walked away, looking up into the sky, feeling the rain fall on his face. He prayed. He heard John begin to cry.

Chris was moved by the scene, conviction racing through his soul. But he didn't think now was the time to talk about it. "What do you want to do?" His neck hurt, his arm throbbed, and the bullet wound in his back from Brian still hurt pretty bad too.

James looked over at Joshua, hoping to see a look that would communicate what he was thinking. "Let's talk to Mahalalel."

They left Lance propped up against a tree and walked towards Mahalalel and Jared, stepping over dead bodies in the process.

"Mahalalel, what do you want to do now?" James asked.

Hurt and hopelessness coated his painful answer. "There is nothing to do now." He waved his hands over the carnage, fresh blood flowing from his stomach as he removed his arm from applying pressure to it.

"Will they come back?"

"Oh, yes. With much more. They will not be proud again."

"Then they'll find your home."

Lightening flashed. "The gods told them, I imagine."

"Are there more of you? More pure-bloods?"

"Yes, there are many places underground like we have."

"How many men?"

"Not enough. When they come, we will be helpless to stopping them."

James traded glances with Joshua again, hoping to see something in his eyes.

Chris came between his thoughts. "This may sound stupid, I don't quite believe it myself, but there's a girl down there who I am willing to fight for."

The look that crossed James' face betrayed his initial reaction to the statement.

Chris held up his hands. "I know it sounds crazy. But whatever I feel for that woman . . . "

"A woman you've never spoken a word to." Joshua cut him off, almost laughing.

"Well, yes, in fact, I have said a word to her, but that's not the point. The point is that I've never felt this way before. And I don't want to lose it."

"Whatever. So you'll fight?"

"Yeah, I'll fight."

Before James walked away, he patted Chris on the shoulder. "You may want to find out if she's married."

Joshua caught up with James. "So what do you have in mind?"

"A Bible story."

"A Bible story?"

He nodded. "God tells the Israelites to take the land He has given them. They'll have to fight for it, but God promises it to them. They send spies into the land to scout it out. They find that the land is full of giants. They bring back a negative report- they can't defeat the giants. Two men, Joshua and Caleb, stand against the negative report and promise they can take the land. But the people lose trust in God. There is land, even today, that God promised them was theirs if they'd only go and take it. Land they have still yet to go into."

"You think we can go into the land and take it?"

"There's another story, in the book of First Samuel. Jonathan and his armor-bearer are positioned at a Philistine garrison. They're thinking about over-throwing it themselves. Jonathan says, 'Come, let us go over to the garrison of these uncircumcised; it may be that the Lord will work for us. For nothing restrains the Lord from saving by many or by few.' And God gave them a sign, and they defeated the garrison by themselves."

"Do we need a sign?"

"You're His child now, He's given you His Spirit; what's He saying to you?"

"Like a conviction, you mean?"

"Yeah."

"He's saying that these people need our help."

"That's what I'm getting too."

The environment didn't seem so mysterious anymore- perhaps because things now demanded their more immediate attention. They were in combat. It didn't matter where or why, it only mattered that they were. Whether or not they noticed, themselves, they had adapted to the setting. Now, they were just like the natives, only concerned with surviving. Weird and strange things would no longer leave them puzzled. They had just fought twenty-five giants. The adaptation was complete. They were soldiers again, and soldiers fought. Police investigated, and the FBI traced down conspiracies, but soldiers didn't have the luxury of asking questions. It was kill or be killed, the most primitive and basic philosophy. It was all that was on their minds. Crop circles, dreams, stars, giants, demons . . . the answers could be searched for later. If they survived.

A half an hour later, they had come up with another plan. Once the rain stopped, they began burning the bodies.

NINETEEN
A BROTHER'S BURDEN

Lying open on the neatly made bed was a suitcase, empty. Its contents were across the room being scrutinized by careful eyes and meticulous hands. The rain clouds outside the hotel window either expounded on the situation or added to it. The day was dark, both in the physical and metaphysical sense. What had to be done hung over the whole island, even if there was only one person who knew what would happen. Steve Streen finished inserting the bullets into the clip and now slid the clip into the handle of the pistol, hearing it click in place. He cocked it and set the safety. He stood up, sliding the gun into the back of his pants, beneath his belt. Then he picked up the other pistol he had already inspected, an automatic just the same, and tucked that beside the other. He grabbed a light coat and put it on, confident that the back hung low enough to cover the concealed pistols. Walking back to the bed, he picked up the two Uzis and threw them into a gym bag. He zipped it up. Standing, he noticed his reflection in the mirror across the room. Slowly, he walked to the mirror, studying the face that was staring back at him.

He had called George Fletcher and had been given the whole report. It didn't make any sense to him. The whole business of a ransom note was ridiculous. Nobody in this business kidnapped people. But the facts just got weirder from there. The address being bogus, what they were saying about not knowing what could have written it . . . Steve would have never believed any of that, or connected his previous business in Bermuda with it, but the report of the chase and the shooting had merit. James had gotten into the middle of something trying to find him, and now he was missing. So Steve would find his brother, just as his brother had set out to find him.

He turned away from the mirror and walked out the door, gym bag in hand. He thought once more about contacting the guy Fletcher had snooping around down here, but he doubted the guy would endorse what he was about to do, let alone join him. He walked into the elevator and hit the button for the lobby. There was a *ding* noise, as the doors closed, and soft cheesy music to accompany his descent. Three minutes later he was in a cab heading for Hamilton.

The beautiful scenery of Bermuda had no affect on Steve, he didn't notice it. He would have had the same reaction to a Serbian forest or a city slum. The cab pulled up beside a club, and Steve told the driver to wait for him. He got out of the cab, taking his gym bag with him.

The front door swung open, the people inside not bothering to look up from their conversations and drinks. That was their mistake. Steve dropped the gym bag at his feet and reached into the back of his pants, pulling out the two automatic pistols. When the bartender noticed, it was too late. Steve shot him in the chest. Another man sitting to his right reached under the table. Steve shot him without hesitating. There were seven others in the club. Steve ignored the ones who tried to hide under the tables and shot the others. Standing still, observing the room, Steve put the pistols back into his pants. He then bent over and picked up the gym bag, making his way towards a door covered with hanging beads. As he unzipped the gym bag, he wondered if James would approve of his methods. He wondered what his Christian brother would think of this. He didn't care. Uzis in hand, he kicked the door open and spun to the side of the doorway, his back against it. Shots were fired from inside the room, screaming through the doorway. Steve kicked the door back shut and walked to the other side. He waited for about five seconds before positioning himself right in front of the door. After making sure his shadow didn't stretch underneath the door, he fired the machine guns through it, splinters of wood flying throughout the room. He heard a scream come from behind the door and stopped shooting. He opened the door and walked though.

"What is the meaning of this?" A large man with white hair was grasping his left shoulder. He was bleeding from both legs as well.

Steve had hoped he wouldn't kill him. He knew it was a risk, but he was too angry to care.

"Do you remember me?"

His voice sent chills through the fat man. His voice came out shaky. "The police will be here any second."

Steve shot him in the foot, and he screamed. "You didn't answer my question."

Through curses the man yelled at him, "No! I've never seen your stupid face before in my life!"

Steve stepped closer.

The man recognized him. His eyes told as much. "Oh, my . . . "

"Where is he?"

The man was confused. "How-"

Steve cut him off by shooting him in the other foot. "You didn't answer my question."

The man screamed in agony. "Who?"

"My brother."

"Your brother?"

"Did I stutter?" He raised the Uzi.

"No! No!" He pleaded by holding up his hands. "I'll tell you, I'll tell you!"

"I'm listening."

"I don't know." He realized that was the wrong answer and started speaking fast to explain himself. "I mean, we were just watching him! He contacted us! He set us up, but we countered! They shot some of my men, and took one with them! No one has seen them since!"

"Where's Alexanders?"

The man's face paled. "Are you serious?"

"Are you trying to avoid the question?" He began to raise the gun again.

"No! But listen to me. They'll kill you before you even get close. Besides, nobody knows where your brother went."

"I do. And so does Alexanders."

"Are you going to kill me?"

"Thinkin' about it."

"You're in the United States government!"

"Yeah, I might lose my job. Tell me where he is."

"If I tell you, promise not to kill me."

"Fine. Tell me."

"He has a meeting with the consul general."

"An interesting conversation I bet that is." He turned and walked out of the club, stopping only to pick up the gym bag and replace the Uzis. Much to his surprise, the cab driver had remained. Steve got back in and told him where to go. Hearing the gunfire and now where he was to take his passenger to next, the cab driver looked more than hesitant to comply. But an automatic pistol being pointed at his head was a great motivator.

They were going to visit Mr. Alexanders, member of the House of Assembly.

The cab pulled up next to the curb and Steve got out. Before he could even shut the door, the cab driver gunned the accelerator and took off down the street, breaking the speed limit. Steve stood and watched, thinking. He looked up to the Sessions House, knowing it was where Alexanders would retreat to after his meeting. He suddenly had second thoughts about his plan. He was smarter than this. He hadn't survived all those years in Nam by making passionate, rash decisions. He had to lay aside his emotion and think. Emotion would get him killed before he could save his brother. Think. He studied what he could see of the City Hall building. The weathervane depicted the 17th century flagship, *Sea Venture,* the ship that brought the first colonists in 1609.

Dark rain clouds drifted overhead. He began to study City Hall Square. It was bounded by Victoria Street, Church Street, Washington Lane, and Wesley Street. Office buildings fronted the square. Business men decorated the lawns of these buildings, wearing their jackets and ties with Bermuda shorts and knee-hi socks. Steve always thought it was a little weird- jackets, ties, shorts, and those ridiculous socks. While it was true that most men his age wore hi socks, he realized he must have been captured, in some degree, by the new culture. He killed that pointless thought. Though he wasn't sure which buildings were which, he knew he was staring at insurance, management, reinsurance, and service companies.

Steve set the gym bag down at his feet and leaned against a tree, studying the City Hall building, waiting for Alexanders to come out. Steve would intercept him on the way to the Sessions House. He only hoped that the old guy at the club was too scared for his own life to contact Alexanders. No doubt, Alexanders would have him killed for talking, just as he probably had the guy killed who was supposed to help James.

Twenty minutes later he saw Alexanders walk down the sidewalk towards the Sessions House. Steve moved quickly. He picked up the gym bag and began jogging towards his target. He came up behind him.

"Excuse me, Mr. Alexanders?"

He turned his head, looking back over his large shoulders, but did not stop walking. "What?"

Steve took a second to observe the man who was at the center of the conspiracy he was originally sent to help unravel. He weighed around 250 pounds, black hair slicked back with a gel of some kind, and looked to be a little out of shape. He liked his strong drink and his expensive food. A man of his level didn't have to lift his hand to do a thing, he merely pointed and his dirty work was carried out. A coward hiding behind a presupposed power.

Not now though.

"Would you mind coming with me?"

Alexanders shot him an impatient look. "Get lost, pal."

Steve stepped closer, pulling one of the pistols out of his pants and sticking it into Alexanders' back. "I'm not asking you, I'm telling you."

Alexanders stopped walking. "Are you crazy? Do you know where you are?"

"Oh, yeah. So, considering my determination, you might think of taking me seriously."

"What do you want?" He was arrogant, more annoyed than scared.

"We'll get to that. Right now I want you to get on the next bus. Don't do anything stupid, or I'll kill you."

They stood in silence until a bus came. Just in time, too. People were starting to notice them. They got off at Front Street, right by the Bank of Bermuda, and walked between the bank and the Royal Bermuda Yacht Club and into a secluded Point Pleasant Park.

Steve directed him to a bench. He sat down.

"Now, what the he . . . "

"Shut up. I'm the one with the gun, so I'll be asking the questions."

Alexanders' eyes raged, but he didn't say another word.

"My name is Steve Streen."

It took a few moments but recognition finally struck.

"You're the IRS agent."

"That's right. The one you had sent to your little island."

"Don't think we don't know what's going on. We're well aware of your being here on behalf of the CIA as well."

"Is that a confession?"

He smiled. "You could spend the next five years digging and not find a thing. It's bigger than you and your CIA."

"You think of yourself too highly. Interpol is onto you and so is the Caribbean Financial Action Task Force."

Alexanders laughed. "Ants in a world of giants."

"You don't think the CIA knows enough? Why else would they send a SEAL team after me?"

"It doesn't matter. The traces of this thing go way beyond me."

"To the consulate general? Or perhaps straight to Britain itself. Canada?"

"Theories, aimless shots in the dark. You have nothing."

"And yet you had me kidnapped."

"That was our mistake, I can see now. We should have just killed you."

Steve shook his head. "Now there's something that I've been dying to figure out. Why exactly didn't you kill me? The people you're doing business with kill people like me all the time."

Bored of the conversation, Alexanders asked, "What is it you want, Mr. Streen? Revenge? You come back to cap the main man?"

"I came back to find my brother."

"Ah, yes. Your brother . . . James, is it?"

"Where is he?"

A cruise ship drifted past in the harbor just fifty yards away.

"I don't know."

Steve punched him in the face. "You better find out quick."

Alexanders spit blood. "I would think that your agencies back in the states would have told you what they learned. And that you'd realize you're wasting your time with me. By the way, I don't think those agencies know you're here, do they? No doubt you've been debriefed along with the soldiers that rescued you. I'm to believe that they let you waltz straight back here on your own?"

Steve ignored him. "We both know where they were headed."

"No doubt."

"So where?"

He laughed. "You really think that I'd give you the location to our secret island?"

"The SEALS have already been there."

"True. And when was that? Long after your brother went missing. Tell me, did they find your brother or the airplane they took on the island?"

"You're going to help me find him."

"My dear friend, he is shark food."

Steve hit him again, cursing his arrogance. He took out a pistol and a silencer from his pocket. He began screwing it on.

"Are you going to kill me?"

Steve looked at him with eyes that stabbed ice cycles. "No, I'm just going to shoot you a few times."

Ignoring the threat, Alexanders laughed again. "Listen to yourself. Resorting to frustration and rage . . . If there is a conspiracy, it's hardly developed enough for anyone to reveal it, and you've come looking for your brother whose plane crashed in the ocean. Looks like you lose in every way, Mr. Streen."

"Did you send a ransom note to my brother?"

"What?"

"That's the only reason my brother came down here. Somebody sent him a ransom note."

"You're mistaken. We don't do that sort of thing."

"Well someone did."

"Mr. Streen, we are not in the business of kidnapping . . . "

"Then why'd you kidnap me?" He was losing his patience.

"It's complicated."

"Tell me. I'm a smart boy."

"It wasn't my idea. It was someone else's."

"Whose?"

"Someone in a position much higher than my own."

"Why?"

He smiled. "I wish I knew. The fool almost cost us everything."

"This doesn't make sense."

"I know."

Steve rubbed his head, squinting. "Why?"

"It's the wrong question, Mr. Streen. Not that any question matters to you now."

He looked up at Alexanders. "Why are you telling me all this? You're not even putting up a fight."

"You have a gun pointed at me." He said that a little too loud.

"Keep your voice down."

"You don't actually think you'll make it off the island alive, do you?"

Steve started to feel nervous, his eyes darting through his surroundings. He had made a mistake. He hadn't thought through everything before acting. Had he analyzed the situation he would have realized it wasn't worth getting back involved with this junk.

The Royal Bermuda Yacht Club was adjacent to them. Someone was walking away from it and towards the park. It was a man and a woman. They were kissing each other and laughing. Steve saw what the woman's eyes were targeting- the waterside garden.

Then him.

At first he didn't think she noticed the pistol, but then she quickly moved the man's hand away from her and pointed at them. The man reacted by running back towards the Yacht Club, shouting for help.

"You see, it's only a matter of time . . . "

"You're right." He shot him in the head and then ran to the harbor, throwing himself over a railing and into the water just as a police officer started shouting for backup.

***

He would need an alibi. That meant he'd have to get to where the Agency left him- now. He couldn't take a ship back. Though that would be the easiest, it would take far too long. He needed to get on a plane, which meant he needed to get to the airport.

A half an hour earlier, he had prevented a rape behind a bar. The tourist had run off with her dignity, and Steve had run off with the rapist's clothes. He left the man tied up to a palm tree, naked. He wrote in black ink across his chest, "Hi, I tried to rape a girl, but somebody stopped me and tied me up."

Steve didn't feel an ounce of remorse for the man. He hated rape more than anything else. Flash backs from Vietnam would always make that so.

He got on the bus and sat down. He had left the gym bag in the water but still had his two pistols. He looked out the window, deep in thought. What if the guy in the club talked to someone else? They'd come looking for him. Or just report the incident to the Agency. Either way, Steve would be blamed for murdering a member of Bermuda's House of Assembly. Though the American government and agencies like Interpol would be more than pleased to hear that Alexanders was killed, politics and appearance would have Steve locked up or simply disappearing. Perhaps a heart-attack. But would the man have talked? Or would he have run for his life. He couldn't run- he had shot him in the legs and feet. He had to get out of Bermuda fast.

By the time Steve was sitting on the plane, ready for take off, he had ceased to care about his own well-being and began to spiral down into a saddened state for his brother. He had always been trained to survive and to never get caught. Vietnam was only the half of it. The secret ops he pulled in Cambodia and the surrounding countries were classified. No one knew about them. But as he watched the sunset from the window of the airplane, he thought it odd that it would end like this. His own government would soon be looking for him. He shook his head. He had made a mistake, broke the training, had let his emotion run the show. For what? There was nothing he could have hoped to come away with. James left in an airplane and didn't come back. The SEALs didn't find any sign of an airplane on the island he was rescued from, the island that James was probably headed for. *Probably.* What if their prisoner misled them? Told them the wrong island? But that would lead him straight to the beginning again, with nothing. Perhaps he could ask the Agency to . . . No. There was nothing else that could be done. If James was alive, he'd find a way back. If not, everyone had to assume he never made it to his destination once taking off in the plane.

The only plane that he could get on right now was headed to Miami. He would still have to get to Virginia. He noticed a man staring at him through dark sunglasses. The man must have thought the tint concealed his eyes, but it didn't. Steve's adrenaline started pumping. Something was wrong. They were onto him. He stood up and walked down the isle, towards the boarding ramp. The man got up and walked after him. Just as the last passenger boarded, Steve ran off the plane, ignoring the stewardess yelling that they couldn't wait for him to come back. The other man ran past her too.

Steve ran through the airport, searching for a bathroom that wouldn't be crowded. He found one. In order to board the plane, he had to ditch his pistols, so he would have to do this fast and without mistake.

The man came running through the door, a small pistol raised and ready to fire. Steve was standing off to the side of the door, waiting for him. The man must have thought he was heading for a window, because he didn't even look to his left or right. Steve was counting on this. As soon as he saw the gun hand, he reached out and grabbed it, twisting the wrist and using the pain to control the rest of the body. He spun the man into the wall and struck the man's elbow with his palm. The gun dropped to the floor. Steve hit the man in the nose with his forehead, breaking it. The man slid down the wall, unconscious. Searching the man's pockets, Steve found an ID. Interpol. Why was Interpol after him? It didn't make sense. A toilet flushed. Steve grabbed the ID and the gun and ran back out into the airport. He decided to take another plane. One to Philadelphia. One without someone following him.

By the time the Interpol agent woke up, Steve was nowhere to be found. Had he gotten on another plane? Or had he decided to go by boat? Or was he still here?

By the time all the airlines could be checked, it was too late. The flight to Philadelphia was only two hours. Steve was in a cab heading down Interstate 95 towards a train station when all the agents waiting for him at the airport in Miami were finally allowed to leave.

There was so much blood. The war was supposed to be over, most American soldiers back home by now. But Steve was not. Here he stood, in an isolated part of the Vietnam jungle, not far from the Ho Chi Minh Trail, dead, mutilated bodies at his feet. He looked around, suddenly feeling very strange. As if something was watching him. He held the M-16 tighter. Wind blew through the trees, but there were no sounds of wildlife. Something was out there. He hurried to a position more concealed and laid down. He held his breath. What was out there? The electricity that was coursing through his spine was new to him. He felt more like when he was a kid just after hearing a ghost story. The vibes were bizarre.

An hour passed, and birds began singing again. He got to his feet and stretched, still feeling a little weird. He walked back through the carnage, wondering what had happened. And then he saw it.

Steve opened his eyes and immediately tried to assess his situation. The sound of the train's metal wheels running over the tracks sounded like gunshots. He sat up, sweating. He looked out the window, but it was too dark to see anything. Feeling the gun in his pocket, he began to relax.

The lights in the train were dimmed, allowing for people to sleep. Releasing the breath he was holding, Steve leaned back against the seat and looked to his left.

Two glowing red dots stared back at him. The train entered a clearing and moonlight briefly passed through the window, illuminating the figure that was beside him.

"What the . . . " His voice barely escaped his mouth. He stood up and pulled out the gun in one quick motion, spinning and aiming it at the figure. But the train entered the thicket of more woods and the moonlight evaporated, plunging the car into darkness.

His breath came weak, his hands shaking with fear. He couldn't believe what he had seen- what was sitting beside him.

Another clearing. More moonlight. There was nothing there.

TWENTY
Milton Iatrides

His hands were stretched out, forced down and open so that his palms were facing up. The spike sunk into his wrists, a stream of blood squirting from the puncture, spraying his outstretched arm and the splintered wood it was tied against. Lightening bolts raced up his arms and into his neck, the median nerve severed, shocking his nervous system. His hands contracted.

They moved his feet together. One spike would fasten them both to the wood. It took a few swings to drive the nail, the person swinging the hammer missing twice.

Chris screamed in agony as he was lifted into the air, pinned to the cross. He didn't think pain like this was tolerable, yet he wasn't passing out.

He couldn't breathe. He pushed up on the nail that was through his feet with a shout of anguish until the nail tore through the flesh and struck the tarsal bone where it could move no more. He exhaled. Then his arms and elbows popped out of joint, and his upper body jerked towards the ground. His chest was tight, his heart beating against its frame. He pushed up on the nail again, trying to take the pressure off his rib cage. It hurt so much.

Ten minutes later his thighs were burning, and he couldn't push up his weight anymore. Blood trickled down his arms, making it to the elbows before rolling to the underside of his arm and plunging to the ground far below. Blood oozed from the tear in his feet, putting a thin coating on the wood beneath him.

The agony . . . why? Why was this happening to him? He didn't remember how he got here.

He heard something to his right- somehow he had the presence of mind to admit the oddity in noticing any sound other than his own gasping for air. His attention divorced from all sense of outside awareness, due to his nervous system set aflame, he managed to look over anyway.

There was another cross. He couldn't tell what was on it. It looked like a skinned animal, flayed for its hide. The base of the cross was erect in a crimson puddle. Chris felt bile rising in his throat and he pushed up on the nail with all of his strength to let it out.

Then he noticed that there were thorns imbedded into the head of the beast. His senses bordering insanity, he fought to hold on to the last finger hold of self-awareness and wondered why someone would skin an animal, put thorns into its head, and nail it to a cross. The animal's mouth opened.

"Father, forgive them!"

The words were louder than thunder, more powerful than a strike of lightening. Chris' eyes went wide and, for a second, his mind was completely clear. It was no skinned animal hanging from the cross, but a man. Suddenly, Chris' own pain became insignificant. Now knowing what he was looking at, he took more careful notice of the man hanging beside him. He willed himself, against his nauseous stomach, to study the face of the man. It looked as if someone had ripped the beard out of his face and beat the thorns into his skull. The man's face was so disfigured with bruising and lashes that they must have beat him until they broke every knuckle in their hands. And then they must have skinned him before hanging him. His ribs were exposed, glistening white through the shredded flesh around them. Intestines seemed unrestrained and able to fall out . . . Then the man turned his head and looked at Chris. Two white eyes, both swollen, barely penetrating the bruised and bloody mess.

As their eyes met, Chris somehow understood.

The man asked through barely spread lips, "Why do you not accept this gift I have paid for with my own blood? Was the cost not great enough? Is this a cheap gift?" His voice was barely audible, pain, dehydration, and sorrow restricting it.

Tears dropped from Chris' eyes, his physical pain the only sensation keeping him hanging onto consciousness. "I'm sorry." His words barely escaped the wall of emotion his voice had to ram through. He wanted to turn away, to hide his shame, but the man's eyes captivated him.

"Do you believe?"

Chris swallowed with great effort. "I do."

For a second, Chris thought he saw the man's lips pull at the corners, spreading into a bloody smile. But he didn't appear to have lips anymore. And then he spoke three words- through bloody bubbles popping from what had to be his mouth. "I forgive you."

The words lifted Chris up off the spike through his feet and rushed through his lungs like fresh air. He never felt anything so refreshing . . . so alive. He thought he might tear free of the nails and drift upward into the clouds. But then the sensation passed. But only long enough for him to remember his pain, and he looked back to the man. But he had turned away from him.

"It is finished."

Chris woke up with such a start that he almost fell out of the tree. A bird screamed in surprise and took off in an agitated flutter.

"Shhh . . . " It was John's voice. "What's wrong with you?" he whispered.

Chris wiped tears from his eyes and leaned back against the tree, suddenly allowing his brain to interpret what had happened and where he was. He was about fifteen feet in the air, the trees surrounding him also full of pure-blooded natives. There were about three hundred of them gathered for the occasion.

The women had already been gathered together and hurried off to a secret location where they would remain hidden until the coming war was over. And, just in case no 'pure-blooded' male was to survive, three young males went with them. Three Adams. Chris had volunteered to go, typically.

Soon after burning the bodies, Jared had summoned all the 'tribes' together. An hour later, there was a small army of natives scattered throughout the jungle floor, rehearsing their mission.

It wasn't sure to work. In fact, the odds were stacked high against them. When the sky-people and their giants failed to return, the enemy would have to assume that they were killed. They would then assemble their whole army to finish the job left and avenge their dead. Seeing the rising smoke in the sky, they would head straight to the battle scene. While they made that journey across the land, the pure-blooded natives would slip past them and attack the enemy's own land. It was a brutal, savage plan- one of the oldest in the world. The genocide of a race. Every last one of the enemy would have to be annihilated. It was the only way to free the land from the curse. Not one person under the spell of the gods could be spared. Not a woman, for she may give birth to a devil. Not a man, for he may impregnate a woman with one. Not a child, for it may grow up to be one. The whole race of sky-people had to be destroyed to prevent the present horror from ever replaying. It was sick. But it was reality. In fact, the women would be the primary targets. If their ability to breed was taken, then the race would eventually die out. One woman giving birth could make all the effort worthless. Even if they destroyed the whole army of sky-people, they would have accomplished nothing if one giant was born and was able to reproduce. It was the only way.

Chris sighed, confident that his mind had caught back up with his circumstances, and then recalled his dream. He looked around for James, but he was barely visible in another tree ten feet away. Chris wanted to shout across to him, to hear what James would say about his dream. He needed answers. For some reason it felt like the most important thing in the world. But he knew there was no way he could have that conversation with James right now. Not without putting their whole mission, and thus existence, at stake. He gritted his teeth impatiently. What if he didn't get the chance to talk to James before the fighting started, and he was killed?

The answer came so clear it was as if someone shouted it. *You'll not see heaven.* He began to grow nervous, fearing the future. He'd never felt like this before. A cold sweat began breaking out on his forehead. "Oh God . . . "

"Do you believe?"

Chris swallowed with great effort. "I do."

For a second, Chris thought he saw the man's lips pull at the corners, spreading into a bloody smile. But he didn't appear to have lips anymore. But then he spoke three words- through bloody bubbles popping from what had to be his mouth. "I forgive you."

Chris shut his eyes, and his dream, James' conversation with John, and all the stuff he'd witnessed in this place fueled a prayer. When he opened his eyes, he knew he was different.

❧❧❧

The sunrise was hidden by intense clouds suffocating the sky. There was no wind, which seemed more than strange being that the clouds were moving so fast . . .

James could see a valley spread out below him some five hundred yards away. He looked around himself, using the morning light to explain what he couldn't figure out in the darkness of the previous night. He noticed immediately that the natives were all watching the valley, and he began to see a picture being painted across his logical mind. Apparently, the giants would be using the valley as their pathway. From here . . . he suddenly realized that he didn't know where *here* was. He turned around and observed the ground below him. He was in a tree, about twenty feet in the air. From his vantage point he could tell that the trees they were positioned in were on the top of a huge hill that overlooked much of the cliff they were on. The cliff then looked out over the jungle in all directions. The valley ran from left to right- or right to left, whatever. He didn't care to dwell on it. He looked up at the sky again. The clouds were moving so fast that it almost didn't seem real, like it was a video stuck on fast-forward. It didn't make sense. The air felt stagnant, humid, and had a certain thickness to it. It didn't move. James looked at the trees around him. The leaves weren't moving at all. Nothing was. Except the dark clouds shielding the sky. He felt his head tingle and then shuddered.

He looked to his right, observing the landscape below. There was a clearing off to the one side, just within eyesight. There were some cliffs nearby casting a mild shadow over the grass, and James wondered about the shadow. He couldn't find the sun anywhere, not even a trace of it. He looked around for more shadows, and he found one at the base of the tree he was in. But it was in a different direction. The shadow made from the cliffs over the clearing went from right to left. The shadow the tree was making was going from left to right. His head started tingling again. Something was wrong.

Joshua was studying the valley through the optical scope. There were no signs of activity. He hoped the natives knew what they were talking about. They had insisted that this was the way they'd come, but what if they were wrong? He rested the rifle on his lap. He was straddling a large branch, leaning his back against the tree- had been all night. The feeling in his legs escaped hours ago. He was dying to get out of the tree. The night before, he had asked Jared, as they were climbing, why they were going into the trees, and Jared had told him that the branches and leaves would hide them from the eyes of the gods. Now, seeing the whole scene before him, he finally understood. The ground below the trees was wide open. Because they were on one of the highest points on the island, someone looking up might have been able to spot them. But, being within the network of branches and leaves, it would be much more difficult for someone to discover them, while those in the trees had a clear view of the valley.

Joshua studied the jungle, wondering where the giants were.

The natives seemed restless, and that bothered John. He noticed that they kept looking back and forth from the valley to the sky. Sweat began to drip down his face, but he didn't notice. He thought of Edward being looked after by the native women and managed to smile. But as soon as the smile spread his lips, he shut it off and his face became hard again. Feelings of anger suddenly buzzed in his head, feelings induced from allowing himself to smile. And he suddenly realized that he *liked* being angry. The smile that crossed his face, had also defrauded it. He had reason to be angry, to be bitter, and, by God, he would be. A smile? How could he smile? But then his conscience called its first witness to the stand. *Why don't you want to smile? Is it because you hate the very idea of being happy? Are you so in love with hate that you enjoy its company?* The witness hesitated. *Say it! You love being hurt! You're trapped by it! You want to be angry!*

He shook his head, rattling the debate out of his mind. He just wanted to get out of the stupid tree.

❧❧❧

It was shortly after the rain had started when the valley suddenly filled with movement. What was moving was too far away to identify with the naked eye, but no one needed the extra clarification. There was no doubt as to what was coming through the valley. The pure-blooded natives began moving, running down the backside of the hill and down the cliff.

They moved fast, all three hundred of them- running down the cliff like a swarm. Trees flew by in blurs, branches tearing at flesh in flashes. No one cared. Adrenaline and purpose fueled their motivation. They were down the cliff and into the jungle in an instant. Joshua fell a few times, his legs not responding to his commands, and then feeling as if a million needles were stabbing him as the blood began to circulate again. He adjusted the automatic that came from Chris' bag to a more comfortable spot on his back before grasping the sniper rifle with two hands and gathering his feet underneath of him.

They didn't stop to take a break, and John cursed. He had barely made it down the cliff without his momentum sending him head-first into the rock, and now he was sweating profusely and trying to catch his breath. Thirty years ago he may have felt up to it, but not now. Now he only cursed his situation and everything about it.

The first twenty minutes went by quickly, nerves doing most of the work. In that time they had covered two miles. But adrenaline was wearing thin now- real thin. Exhaustion raked their bodies and clouded their minds. They wanted to stop, to rest. But they couldn't. They knew their survival was largely dependant on their ability to persevere right now.

The words of James' football coach sang clearly in his mind. *Mind over matter!* James often wanted to tell his coach to prove it, but, now, he was using that cliché himself, trying to convince his burning legs to take one more step. And one more. And one more.

They weren't up to this. Upon first arriving this would be no problem, but they had all lost weight and had little rest since. Not to mention all their wounds. They simply weren't up to par. They were physically drained. James prayed.

Twenty minutes later they came to a river and took, perhaps, the only rest they would get until this whole thing was finished. After that, they could rest as long as they liked, given they were still alive to have that option.

John was on his back, writhing around in the dirt, trying to catch his breath- a common sight at football practices after a series of sprints or ladders. He groaned, his eyes pinched shut.

Lance was lying next to him. He looked even worse than John. His face was pale, and he was vomiting. "I can't . . . " He would catch his breath. "I can't go on . . . " He would pant some more. "I . . . "

Chris and Joshua were sitting against some trees, breathing steadily through their mouths. They understood that the quickest way to regain a steady breathing pattern was to start one on your own. The heart had to settle down. Short raspy breaths wouldn't help. The heart needed deep steady breaths to get the oxygen it needed. Then the heart would slow down and the need for oxygen would decrease, thus catching your breath.

James was getting a drink from the river. He was drinking in gulps, ignoring the voice of his gym teacher in his head; *you're going to get cramps.* He had heard that was an old wives' tale anyway, didn't he? He continued drinking, splashing his face with the cool water in between gulps. After he was done, feeling like his stomach would burst, he rolled onto his back and stared up through the trees and into the sky. The clouds were moving so fast that it almost seemed as if he was moving. It felt like when he was stopped beside a Mack truck at a red light, and he could swear that his car was drifting backwards . . . The optical illusion was the same. James sat up and looked around him, suddenly feeling the birth-pangs of a headache and a bit nauseous. The natives around him were also lying down, catching their breath, although they didn't seem to be in such bad shape. In a matter of minutes they looked ready to go again. And they were.

Jared walked up to James. "Not much further. Over the river . . . "

James smiled, cutting him off. "And through the woods?"

Jared looked puzzled. "Of course, yes. When we cross the river over, we will break into group. We will move through land different, heading to same center."

"What's the center?"

"The temple."

It didn't take much of an imagination to paint a picture of what the temple might look like. Not after everything else they had seen in this place. James imagined some sort of Aztec design, but then thought better of it. Whatever it looked like, it had to be pretty big to be the center of the whole community. A god's temple for giants . . . It would be enormous. And that was just the rendezvous point. They had their work cut out for them. "How's Mahalalel?" he asked.

Jared shook his head. "He is badly hurt. He is with your friend now."

James nodded, his mind suddenly directed back to Edward. Before his mind could sink into the murky waters of guilt, Jared's voice interrupted him.

"We move now." He ran off and directed everyone to begin moving again.

By now, the army of giants would be a few miles from the site of the battle. There was no telling what they would do once they found the burning bodies. They would most likely continue to the refuge they had somehow found out about- probably through torturing the natives that went out with them to help look for the skis. But once they found it deserted? Then what? Would they come racing back? Or would they continue looking around? No one really knew. That gave them a short window of opportunity to work within the time they *were* sure of. The faster they moved, the longer that window would stay open. They swam across the river.

Once reaching the other side of the river, the small fatigued army rested again. The rain had raised the water level enough to make it dangerous, and a few would have been lost in its current if heroics by their companions didn't save them. Another rest was not favored but much needed. The power of the river had drained their last resurgence right back down to their previous, exhausted state.

The jungle around them was thick and dark. The sound of the river was strong enough to drown out the sound of the rainfall, but the rain couldn't be ignored. It seemed as if the jungle itself was beneath three inches of water. The sounds of insects were either absent or hidden by the more dominant sounds.

James watched with interest as Jared screamed orders to his people, competing with the sound of the river. Immediately, the natives got to their feet and organized themselves into groups. James didn't have a chance to count how many groups there were before they disappeared into the jungle. However, a group of ten stayed behind, and James figured this would be his group. He watched as Jared walked over to fill him in.

"These men go with you. You follow them." And then he turned and ran after a group that had broken off from the others and was heading towards the side of a huge hill covered with green life.

James noticed his surroundings and couldn't believe the view- the scope of it. The river was behind them but, evidently, it came from a waterfall he could see way off in the distance pouring over the side of a cliff that must be five hundred feet high. Mist danced high above the water, engulfing the falling torrents. In fact, there was mist everywhere. It was hugging the bottom of the trees and floating through their canopies too. It reminded him of a Hawaiian rain forest. And then he looked down at his feet and noticed mist circling them, as well. He reflexively picked up his feet. As he looked around himself and the others, he saw that the ground they were standing on was thick with mist when it hadn't been two minutes before. He had a weird feeling.

"You okay?" Joshua asked him.

"Yeah. Where'd all this come from?"

Joshua shrugged. “Probably coming off the river. The rain’s slowed down, temperature probably rose a little.”

“There was no mist when we crossed it.”

“I don’t know, James. If I was concerned with everything in this place, I wouldn’t be able to concentrate on walking.” He hit him on the back. “Let’s go.”

Chris, Lance, and John fell in behind. They followed the natives into the mist and disappeared through its open mouth, leaving the river behind as it began to spill over onto the grass.

They had quite an excursion, wading through a swamp, climbing the side of a cliff, hiking through a field of chest-high grass, and now walking through a creek bed. The entire expedition was breathtaking, and it was hard to believe that such beauty could really entertain such evil.

Lance held the shotgun ready, studying the tree line on both sides of him. They had taken the assault rifle away from him, deciding if he was to shoot, a shotgun would be more effective for him. He was scared. Something in these woods bothered him.

He wasn’t alone.

John kept muttering under his breath, “I don’t like this . . . I don’t like this one bit . . . ”

James could tell that Joshua wasn’t fond of it either. Traveling through the creek bed made them easy targets from the trees while their predator could easily stay out of view. Even the natives seemed to be expecting arrows to come flying from the trees at any second. They had their swords in hand, and their eyes were trying desperately to penetrate the tree line. Then, suddenly, they stopped dead in their tracks and dropped to their knees.

James stopped and signaled for the others to look around. They trained their guns on the jungle around them, searching for any sign of movement.

The flowing water trickled over half submerged rocks and played in the air like music. The rain had stopped and the insects could be heard contributing to the soundtrack. Joshua listened. Sweat began rolling down his face. His muscles were tight, his breathing more rapid but still controlled. His biceps were flexed under the weight of the sniper rifle he was holding steadily. He really didn’t like this.

The natives began moving forward, slowly- their eyes still searching for whatever had spooked them. James and his team began following, moving slowly through the shallow water. James was at the point, looking ahead and to the right and left. Joshua and Chris were walking back to back, Joshua facing the left side of the jungle, Chris the right. Lance was just trying to stay calm, his eyes darting all over the place while John followed up the rear, covering their six.

They had traveled like that for ten minutes. And then the natives led them out of the creek bed and back into the jungle.

"Do you hear that?" Joshua asked no one in particular.

"What is it?" John turned to face twelve o' clock, leaving the six to Lance for a second.

"Sounds like the ocean."

"Yeah, I hear it," said Chris.

"Where are they taking us?" asked Lance.

For a second everyone traded a hesitant glance before Joshua corrected him.

"You mean, *leading* us."

"Yeah, yeah, whatever." He brushed away a bug as fast as he could, anxious to get both hands back on the shotgun.

James said, "The creek we were following probably spills out into the ocean. There's gotta' be more creeks and rivers."

"You think they're leading us to another creek and we follow that one right into the 'gods' back yard?" asked Chris.

"They need fresh water too."

"We'll see." John turned back to six o' clock. "I've got a bad feeling about this."

Finally, they exited the woods and came to what looked like a lagoon. It was striking even under cloudy skies. Crystal clear water reflected the moving clouds perfectly as if it was a mirror. But that wasn't what anyone was looking at.

Everyone stopped.

"Tell me that isn't what I think it is." Chris began walking towards it.

One of the natives looked at him and warned him to be careful. At least that's how Chris interpreted it.

James and Joshua followed Chris while Lance and John kept their weapons facing the jungle, expecting some sort of trap.

There it stood, its broken hull buried in the sand. The lettering on her side was faded and peeling, but the paint was still darker where the letters had been so it was still legible. It read: *Milton Iatrides.*

"You've got to be kidding me." James threw the assault rifle over his shoulder and ran his hand across the rusted freighter, studying it.

"This is one of the ships that Edward mentioned, isn't it?" Joshua was looking for a way aboard.

"Sounds French," added Chris.

John turned, taking his eyes off the jungle for a second. "Hey, do we have time for this?"

They ignored him and the natives who seemed to be in agreement with John, and continued looking for a way on. The freighter was huge, but only about 5% of it was visible, the rest stretching down beneath the sand and water.

"The shore line must be receding." Chris walked into the water, raising the M-16, that had been recovered from the ocean just recently, above his head. When he came to the spot where he could reach up and grab the railing of the freighter, he pulled himself up and walked across the angled deck. The ship was almost completely buried in the sand. It was huge. Chris wondered if the ship was whole or if it had broken into pieces. It was hard to imagine a freighter being completely buried right at the shoreline. "Hey!" He called down to James. "Wouldn't this thing be full of water if it sunk and washed ashore?"

"Or it just ran aground." Joshua was climbing over the railing and onto the deck.

"That would mean people on board." James climbed up beside him.

Right before Chris entered the ship through a rusted door that broke off the hinges as he went to open it, he took a mental note of James and Joshua walking after him. He disappeared into the darkness of the ship.

"This thing is huge." Joshua studied what was left to see. He had boarded freighters like this more than once, eliminating terrorists.

James nodded and ran after Chris. It was almost too dark to see in the ship, and James, along with Chris and Joshua, ran into pipes frequently. They felt their way through the darkness for five or ten minutes. They walked down another set of stairs, their boots clanking on the metal.

"We must be about twenty feet below the beach by now." Chris sounded like he was in a trance, his mind brushing the possibilities the freighter and the old English ship created.

"What are you looking for?" Joshua's voice rebounded off the walls and seemed to hang in the stale air for a while.

"Anything that'll prove where this ship came from." Chris opened a door and walked through. He immediately tripped over something and fell to the ground. He reached out to see what it was and found himself grabbing the leg of a chair. "Careful."

Joshua walked past him and to a dresser or cabinet, he couldn't tell which. He swept his hand over the surface, running his hands over objects that once stood decorating it. He felt broken glass and then a glossy paper. A notebook, some objects he couldn't be sure of . . . "Kind of pointless without being able to see what we're looking at."

"Your eyes haven't adjusted yet?" asked James.

"Adjusted to what? You need some degree of light."

James walked up beside Joshua. "You're looking at a few odd decorative pieces, broken picture frames and pictures, a notebook, some coins . . . "

Joshua found the pictures with his hands and pulled them out from beneath the broken glass. He grabbed the notebook too. James took some of the coins.

"That should tell us enough." Between whatever was written in the notebook, the pictures, and the currency, they should be able to make a logical guess as to where the ship came from. "Let's go."

Chris asked, "Could we look for the logbook?"

"We don't have time now. If we live past today, we'll come back with torches. But we have to get moving now."

As they headed back up to the deck, Joshua asked, "If the ship sank, it would have sunk on an angle."

"Of course. Why?" Chris banged his shin into a pipe.

"If this ship sank, then nothing would have been left on the dressers or shelves, and I would think there'd be at least some water still in it."

James said, "So it drifted here, just like the English ship."

"Where'd the bodies go?" asked Chris.

"Freighters don't carry that many people. They could be anywhere. We'd need a lot more time and light to find them." Joshua stepped over the door that Chris had broken off and began climbing up the last few stairs to the deck.

"If they're still there," answered Chris.

"Well, if they're not . . . then they probably jumped overboard, rather drowning than starving. Or maybe the giants came and ate them . . . "

They all walked back into daylight, or what should have been daylight. It was significantly darker now than it was before they entered the ship.

"Uh, how long were we down there?" Chris was slipping the 16 off his shoulder.

"Man, this place just keeps getting stranger and stranger." Joshua looked over the contents in his hands as Chris and James noticed something very disturbing.

"Hey." Fear laced Chris' words. "Where's everyone else?"

James looked out over the sand.

Nothing.

"What's going on?" he whispered. He looked all around, but there were only trees and grass to see.

"Look." Chris pointed to the sand below them. "Footprints." They stretched into the jungle. Chris jumped over the railing, falling ten feet before hitting the sand. James followed.

"Or maybe our native friends took them."

Chris and James both turned from the tracks and looked back up to Joshua who was still standing on the deck of the freighter looking over the things in his hands.

"What are you talking about?" James asked.

But Chris noticed something in Joshua's voice. "Why would they do that? That would mean that they'd know about the ship, but they told us that. . ."

Joshua cut him off. "You better have a look at this." He jumped over the railing.

"What is it?" James couldn't figure out what would be more important than everyone else missing.

"Look at this." He handed over a picture. "The coins . . . US currency. They're pennies and dimes. None of them have a date over '68."

"What am I looking at?" asked James, confused. Chris looked over his shoulder.

"Oh my . . . " Chris grabbed the picture out of James' hands and held it close to his eyes. "It's not possible."

"What?" James didn't see what the fascination was. It was a picture of a family. It was a color photograph, so it couldn't be that old. The style of clothing on the parents seemed to indicate late sixties, early seventies. So what? "Yeah, looks like a French freighter ship that left the US around '70, probably Louisiana."

Chris shook his head. "That's not what we're talking about."

There was something in his voice that gave James goose bumps. "What?"

Chris handed the picture back to him. "You ever see that girl before?"

At first James didn't see it. But then he recognized her. He looked to Joshua and back to Chris. Disbelief and realization hit him at once. "They lied to us."

Joshua shrugged. "They certainly didn't give us the whole story."

"I'm not liking this." Chris subconsciously slipped his finger over the trigger of his M-16. The girl he was in love with was from the United States. Though she was the baby in the picture, there was no questioning the similarities between her and her mother.

Joshua was trying to put it together himself. "They couldn't fathom that we came from somewhere from out there." He pointed back over the lagoon. "And yet, they knew about her, knew about this ship . . . I wonder how many other ships are around here."

"I thought she looked different than the rest of them," muttered Chris.

"Maybe that's why the native guy didn't want her talking to us." Joshua suddenly looked to James.

James knew what he was thinking and immediately knew why his initial response was disturbing. "Maybe the salvation she was talking about wasn't for the race of 'pure-blooded' natives . . . but for herself. And perhaps others like her. Like us."

They stood in silence for a few minutes, the weight of possibilities pressing them down, squashing their brains.

Finally, they snapped out of it. They weren't sure what was going on, what would happen to John and Lance, why the natives had lied . . . but they intended to find out.

"Let's get moving."

They headed off in the direction of the footprints.

TWENTY-ONE
SECRETS AND LIES

James' theory, concerning where the natives were leading them, gained legitimacy when they lost the footprints at another creek.

"Looks like you were right. This creek probably goes straight into their city," said Joshua.

James knelt down at the water and dipped his hand beneath its surface, studying his contorted reflection. He was surprised at the face staring back at him. It almost had a full beard, looked tired, weak, and the eyes looked cold, distant. But he knew it was his own face. He felt exactly the way he looked, the ripples only making the picture complete with chaos. "It doesn't make sense. What could have happened that made John and Lance just take off with them?"

Chris knelt beside James, also catching a glimpse of himself in the water. "Look, I know that I don't know John all that well, but you have to admit he's been acting strange."

"You think they left us there?"

Chris looked around. "They did."

Joshua walked past them and through the creek. "He's right, they did leave us. The only thing that may soften that reality is why."

"Well, it's not like some bad guys were coming and they quickly hid in the woods. Come on, they continued on without us. We've been following their tracks for twenty minutes. They left and didn't look back." Chris stood and walked after Joshua, leaving James to sit and think about it.

After a few more seconds of staring at himself in the water, James stood and walked after Chris and Joshua. They walked through the stream against its current. The water was only two feet deep at places, so it was relatively easy travel. "That girl . . . " He was beside Chris now, watching his feet as he carefully placed them around the larger, more awkwardly shaped rocks.

"What about her?" asked Chris, cutting him off.

"If she was a baby in the photo . . . " A thought struck him. "Joshua, is there a date on the back?"

"No. But there's a page in the notebook that's dated 1971."

"So she'd be thirty-two or thirty-three by now, assuming the picture was taken in the same year."

"Do you think there are others?" Joshua asked as he studied the landscape before him.

"I don't know . . . "

Chris cut him off again. "I think there are."

James could tell from Chris' tone of voice that he had a scenario painted out in his head. "Why do you think they didn't tell us?"

"The same reason we didn't see them, the same reason they didn't want us to see them."

"Which is?"

Chris shrugged. "I don't know, man."

Joshua slowed down enough so that he was closer to James. "He's got a point."

"I understand that, but why would they be keeping people prisoner? What need would that fulfill? And why didn't they treat us the same?"

A small cabin sat fixed among cut grass, just alongside the creek. It looked like a replica of some old pilgrim construction, set up on display in a historical park. But this was not a historical park. The house was configured with intersecting logs, even had a chimney poking out of a slanted roof. The trees surrounding it blocked all light from revealing more detail, and the darkness that kept it shrouded created an eerie manner about it.

"What is that?" Joshua's whispering voice carried with it the sense of shocked confusion they all felt buzzing in their heads.

James didn't answer, but only crawled through the water, back hunched, rifle trained, towards the creek bank. Chris and Joshua followed form.

They walked through the grass, towards the cabin. James gave them a series of hand motions signaling them to secure the perimeter of the house. They acknowledged with a slight head nod and each took a different side of the cabin, skirting it, looking and listening for signs of activity from within.

Joshua reached a door and stopped immediately. Two feet were protruding from the doorway, the door broken off its top hinges and hanging at an angle. He waited for James and Chris to finish their sweep and converge on his location before entering. One quick look confirmed that there was no immediate danger.

"Looks like our 'pure-blooded' friends were here all right." Joshua let the rifle hang relaxed at his side.

There were five natives strewn about the house, their blood decorating the walls and floors of their home. It wasn't difficult to tell that they had been killed with swords. Four men and a woman.

"Wait. Look at this." James was kneeling over one of the bloody corpses. Reaching out, he rolled the dead native onto his chest, revealing a large hole in the center of his back.

"He's one of ours." Chris recognized him.

James nodded.

"That's a shotgun wound," stated Joshua. "Lance . . . "

James stood up and looked around the cabin. It was divided into four rooms, one with a large bed. There was blood all over the bed, which was made up of animal skins over straw, and leading out to where the bodies now lay. "Looks like there was a little party going on in here."

"The natives enter the doorway, sneak into the cabin, and take the three men and girl by surprise. They drag them to here . . . " Chris looked around. "And Lance shoots one of the natives in the back right there." He was pointing to a spot on the floor where blood was splashed rather than streaked.

"And then what happened to Lance? If he turned on them, why didn't they kill him?" pondered James.

Joshua offered a suggestion. "Maybe they made a run for it."

They stepped back outside, searching for signs of a foot chase. They didn't find one.

James looked up to the dark sky, and a few raindrops splashed against his face. "Let's keep moving."

They came upon five more cabins repeating the same story. The 'sky-people' who had lived there had been killed, taken totally by surprise. But still no signs of Lance or John.

Chris looked up from the blood and took notice of the cabin's architecture. "What, we go from a noahic culture to a 17th century wilderness one?"

James walked out of the house. "Yeah, it's got me confused too. I didn't expect to find the jungle sharing both log cabins and pyramids."

Joshua began walking down the creek again, heading towards a stream of smoke that was barely visible on the horizon. As he turned back to see if James and Chris were following, he saw a small boy walking out of the jungle dragging a dead monkey by a leg. He quickly raised his rifle, lining the sights up to the boy's forehead, at the same time alerting Chris and James to the boy's presence. They both dropped to their knees and swung their weapons up and around.

"Jeez, Joshua, it's only a boy." Chris dropped the 16 to his side and stood back to his feet.

"I don't like it," stated Joshua through tight lips.

James stood up too. "We can't kill him."

Joshua blinked a few times in disbelief. "Why not?"

" 'Cause he's just a boy."

"You heard what Jared said, we have to kill all of them."

Chris turned away from the boy and faced Joshua. "Jared? At this point we don't even know what Jared's up to. Who knows what we're in the middle of. Jared could be lying to us about this too."

The boy didn't stop walking. He continued to make his way to the cabin in a lazy fashion, his shoulders slumped and his steps short and purposeless. His eyes were cast down to the ground in a sort of tired gaze, and he never looked up or seamed to hear the discussion between the three strangers.

Joshua knew that Chris was right. How could he kill this boy based on Jared's word when Jared had been lying to them? He lowered his rifle just as he saw the boy's eyes drift up from the grass before him and slowly come to focus on Chris' back. There was something methodically evil about the way in which the boy's eyes slowly rose to Chris, yet without lifting his head. A smile seemed to spread on his lips. Joshua raised the rifle again just as a series of chills ran up his spine and the boy dropped the monkey and started running at Chris.

Chris registered enough information from Joshua's reaction to know what was happening. He turned around to see the boy flying towards him. Literally. The boy's mouth was open and an ear-piercing screech came somewhere from within it. Chris tried to jump out of the way, but the boy was too fast. All that Chris saw before him was a blur as the impact sent him reeling backwards and tumbling across the ground. When he opened his eyes, he couldn't believe the pain that the boy had caused. It felt as if he was hit by a middle linebacker. He stumbled back to his feet and noticed that he had rolled quite a distance. The boy was standing still, not sure what to do next. James and Joshua were both circling him with their weapons trained. The boy's hesitation was clear, his options were not. Would he decide to make a run for it? No. He charged the nearest person who shot him once in the head. The boy fell limp into the grass.

"Just a boy, huh?" Joshua lowered the smoking barrel.

"Who are these people?" asked Chris, quizzically.

"People that should have been destroyed by a flood." James took off running in mid-sentence, following the stream to whatever it would take them to next- hopefully John and Lance, but he doubted it.

Sweat dripped from their brows and splashed into the moving water. All three of them were bent low to the ground attempting to catch their missing breath. Above them hung a sky that was so dark, it looked as if it would start crying oil rather than water. Just under that, above the tree line, was the point of a structure misplaced in both time and geography. The huge pyramid stretched above the tranquil trees, its three corners converging into a needle-tip point.

Once they caught their breath, they headed into the woods that surrounded the mysterious structure. Using the trees for cover, they made their way to the final curtain and sank to their stomachs, evaluating the scenario.

The pyramid was gigantic, its base appearing to cover more than thirteen acres. There was no one in sight- dead or alive. A strange stillness seemed to emanate from the structure, yet not the same stillness that they had felt in the air all day, for there was a steady breeze blowing through the grass at the pyramid's base. It was the kind of stillness that you could imagine feeling in a ghost town fashioned by one of those old western scenes with the tumble weed rolling across the dirt road in small tornadoes of dust. Only there was no distant sound of the wind banging a saloon door against the wall.

Chris would be the first to make mention of the cliché. "It's too quiet."

"Shhh." James stopped breathing and tilted his head away from the pyramid so that his ear faced it. "Do you hear that?"

"Talking?" Joshua's voice was curious, nothing else.

"I think so." It seemed to be coming from the other side of the pyramid, though it didn't seem possible that they would be able to hear voices that far away. Unless they were rebounding off the pyramid somehow.

"No." Joshua's voice suddenly became more than curious. "It's yelling."

"Let's check it out."

Before anyone could think about protesting, Chris had already exited the cover of the woods and started for the base of the pyramid, his M-16 held tight against his shoulder, ready for any surprise. James and Joshua followed in like fashion.

It took them a little while to make it to one of the pyramid's three angles, but when they did their backs were immediately pushed back against the stone. Joshua was peeking around the corner, while James and Chris were scanning all other visible areas, waiting for someone to spot them.

"Clear." Joshua took off as fast as he could and Chris and James had trouble keeping up with him. It occurred to him as he was running, a figure wide open against a contrasting background, that perhaps they should have skirted around the structure through the jungle. But as he grew nearer to the next corner, he was glad they hadn't. The time would have been too great a cost to spend, and it didn't sound like Lance had that much time left.

All three of them rounded the corner with guns blazing.

The first native was struck and tossed to the ground so fast that none of the other natives comprehended what had happened. In their disorientation, five more were dropped. James was aware that the natives they were shooting could have been 'pure-blooded,' but in light of the previous events and the scene before him now, he could hardly bring himself to care. He shot two more.

By the time the natives figured out that they were being ambushed, it was too late. Not one of them had enough time to load an arrow or throw a spear. Those with swords stood even a lesser chance. It was over in seconds.

James ran over and slid to a stop next to John, who was lying on his back, staring into the sky. Checking his vitals reassured him that John was okay, but his eyes were still locked in some other place, and he was not responsive. James looked around, noticing Chris and Joshua bending over Lance, much the same way. James met their eyes and they shook their heads.

"He's dead." Joshua stood to his feet and walked over dead natives until he was beside James. "How's he?"

James sighed. "His vitals are good, but he's not responding." And then, as if on cue, John sat straight up with a shout that made everyone jump.

"No!" he screamed, his eyes darting all over the place, not able to rest on one single thing, but rather bouncing off one thing to another.

James put a hand on his shoulder. "John!"

His eyes began to focus for a second.

"It's okay. We're here." James let John come out of whatever it was he was in before asking him anything. It took about five minutes before John seemed coherent.

"What's going on?" He looked confused.

"Oh great," muttered Chris, turning his back to the pyramid and studying the tree line for the hundredth time in five minutes. They all thought the same thing.

James asked gently, "Do you know what happened?"

John looked into his eyes and then surveyed the ground around him that was littered with native bodies. And then he finally noticed the pyramid. "Oh no." There was a revelation of fear in his words, and the manner in which he stood only complimented those words. He looked over to Lance. "Is he dead?"

James nodded.

"We need to get off this island."

It wasn't exactly new news. "Why? What happened?"

Rubbing his head, John tried to awaken his senses. "Uh . . . They're using us. They made a deal with . . . " He seemed to get lost in his explanation.

"With who?" James was assuming the 'they' were the 'pure-blooded' natives.

"With the gods." Then John looked into James' eyes as if he had just realized his own words or recalled something horrible he had seen. "I don't know why . . . " He stumbled closer to the pyramid and collapsed to his knees when he came to a dead body. Rolling it over, all could see that it was one of the pure-blooded. John pointed to him as he talked. "He was talking to . . . " Then he looked towards the pyramid and searched the ground one more time. "He's gone. He was right here."

"He's lost it," whispered Chris to Joshua. "Just like Brian."

James needed to know more. "What were they talking about? What did they want with you?"

John shook his head. "I don't know. Something about a deal. Something about strangers being taken to the temple in exchange for something . . ."

"For what?"

"I don't know. Something for the pure-blooded . . . A secret between pure-bloods and sky-people."

"This doesn't make sense." Joshua walked up behind James and whispered into his ear. "What do you want to do?"

James turned to face him. "What would the 'gods' want with strangers?"

Joshua thought about it for a second, catching on to James' thought process. "You think that's why they were hiding the girl like that? Because they wanted her?"

"Maybe *need* her."

"So some of these pure-bloods offer a few strangers to the sky-people- in exchange for what?"

"Life? I don't know."

"But then why would they be killing all the sky-people they come across?"

James only shook his head in confusion. "I don't know. But I know I'm not going to like it."

Joshua repeated his original question. "So what do you want to do?"

A moan escaped one of the bodies, and everyone turned towards it.

"Maybe he has some answers." Joshua walked over to the dying native and flipped him over onto his back. It was one of the sky-people. He put the muzzle of the rifle against the man's forehead. "I'll send you to hell right now."

The native's eyes flashed with a certain fear.

"Tell me what you want with us."

"Will you let me alive?"

"I won't kill you if you tell me."

"He needs you." He spoke slowly, dying. "Some pure-bloods bring strangers, and he spares them."

"Where do the strangers come from?"

The native opened his eyes and looked into Joshua's. "The same place you come from."

"Why does he need them?"

"He needs the right one . . . to free us . . . "

"Free you from what?"

He was already dead.

Joshua looked back to James and Chris and they all exchanged a bewildered stare. "The plot thickens."

Then John walked past them. "I think we should really get out of here."

Just as they reached the creek bed, a group of natives exploded from the woods on the opposite side, waving swords above their heads and screaming. They ran down the bank and into the water like piranhas homing in on flesh. They were attempting to cover the forty yard width of the creek. They wouldn't be close to fast enough.

Joshua threw the sniper rifle over his shoulder and brought around the assault rifle, firing from his hip, spraying the charging natives with searing hot bullets. His bullets struck the water in front of the blood-thirsty natives, splashing them with near misses. But he only moved his wrist a fraction of an inch and his aim was corrected. A group of four twisted violently in reaction to the deadly hits piercing their bodies before falling lifeless into the shallow water.

James took more careful aim and was shooting at another group that was coming from farther down the creek. One after another, they dropped into the water and out of sight.

Chris was using the 16 to keep about thirty natives from leaving the cover of the woods. Splinters exploded into the air as the trees were shredded by the 5.56-mm bullets that were trying to find flesh. Chris let the empty clip fall into the water at his feet and he pulled another one out of his pocket. As he was doing that, three natives decided to make a run for the water. Chris watched them, hoping just a few others would follow. Joshua noticed the small party and yelled over his shoulder while firing, trying to alert Chris to their presence. Chris only nodded. Then, when they were in better range, he mechanically raised the automatic rife and squeezed off three shots. Three bodies fell, turning the water around them red until the current carried the blood, and their life, away.

"There's more up there!" yelled John who was gripping his rifle, but had still yet to fire it.

"I know." Chris turned to see how James and Joshua were doing with their other friends.

The creek was littered with about thirty floating bodies, turning the water a dark red for a good distance until it was diluted by more fresh water farther downstream. The bodies that weren't caught on the bottom or large rocks, drifted down stream with the current. James and Joshua reloaded their weapons.

"I've got about twenty up there in those trees," informed Chris. "But they don't look too eager to come down."

"Glad they don't have arrows. They're dug in pretty tight up there." James looked around for any more signs of enemy presence.

"They probably want us to come up after them," said Joshua.

A dead body drifted into Chris' leg, and he kicked it away. "What do you want to do about them?"

Before his question could be answered a cry broke through the silent hills up where the natives were positioned. They all dropped to their knees and raised their weapons, expecting to put down another charge. But it wasn't the sky-people charging them, but a group of ten pure-bloods attacking the sky-people from behind. The clashing of swords filled the stale air and echoed off the water, amplifying the sounds that had been foreign to earth for over a hundred years.

"Should we help them?" asked Chris.

"Which ones?" James looked at John for some kind of reaction but didn't get one.

The battle between the natives lasted about ten minutes, an occasional body tumbling down the hill and either being stopped by a tree or actually making it to the creek bed where it contributed more blood into the water. After that there was silence.

The sound of sloshing water broke the silent melody of the creek as the four strangers took a few steps backwards.

"Can you see anyone?" John asked, his voice reeking with fear.

"No." Joshua slung the assault rifle back over his shoulder and brought around the sniper rifle. He looked through the optical lens, sweeping its scope through the trees. The crosshairs dissected a figure still standing. It began walking down the hill, towards the creek. It was Jared.

"You have ten seconds to tell us what's going on."

Jared looked at Joshua questioningly. Then he transferred his puzzled gaze to James, who seemed to be expecting an answer too. "What do you mean?"

Joshua walked closer to Jared. He didn't care about the blood dripping off Jared's hand and splashing into the water, clouding it. He didn't care if Jared was about to pass out or die. He only wanted to know what was going on. "Why'd you lie to us?"

Jared's voice shook ever so slightly. "What do you mean?"

"I mean, why didn't you tell us about this girl?" He thrust the picture towards Jared until he saw realization flash in his eyes.

Now Jared began looking around. "Where are the others?"

"They're all dead. But not before one of them talked. So you better start talking."

"Please, we don't have much time."

"Then talk fast."

Jared sighed in defeat.

James used the break in his tension to add more clarity to the origin of the questions. "You led us to believe that no one else ever showed up here like we did. That there were no other boats. You almost killed us, proclaiming we were spies sent from the gods, remember?"

Joshua stepped forward again and waved the picture in the air. "We found another boat. And we hear this may happen often. Why would the 'gods' need us?"

"It's true," began Jared. "There have been others like you, but not all spoke your tongue. We think that our own speech changed by strangers like you who come a long time ago."

James remembered the English ship.

"Ever since then, the gods have wanted the strangers. They searched for them even more than our women."

"Why?" asked Joshua.

Jared shrugged. "I do not know." His gaze dropped down to the reddening water at his feet. "I hope to never know."

"What happened to the others like us?"

Jared hesitated. "You must understand that we were scared."

Chris spoke up from the rock he was sitting on. "You killed them?"

"We did not know what the gods wanted them for, but we knew that we could not let them have the strangers."

"Why save some?"

"After a while, we began to think that maybe we could make deal with the gods."

"So you traded them for what? Peace?"

Jared stifled an unpleasant laugh. "That's what they promised. They lied."

"What did they do with the strangers you gave them?" This was getting interesting, thought Joshua.

"I do not know. We never saw them again."

"Why keep the girl?"

"We thought that the gods may not want us to have them, that they could be dangerous to the gods." He paused. "And then the dreams started."

"Dreams?" asked James, more than curious.

"Of deliverance. Strangers coming to set us free."

Joshua held up his hands. "Okay, okay, but your men just took John and Lance to the sky-people."

Jared seemed remorseful. "I am sorry for that. There are some of us who have made secrets with the sky-people, believing that they will be spared if they offer strangers to them."

Joshua stood in silence for a while, thinking over things in his head, trying to categorize his thoughts. One look at James confirmed that he was too.

"So, let me get this straight," started James. "At some point in your history, strangers like us began showing up. You discovered that the gods wanted them, so you began killing them so that the gods couldn't have them. But then you thought that maybe if you delivered them to the gods, they would make a deal with you, letting you live in peace. When that turned out to be a lie, you figured that you would keep the strangers because maybe they were a threat to the gods, and then you started having dreams about strangers delivering you from the gods . . . But some of your people don't buy it, and they still seek to make a pact with the sky-people, delivering them strangers."

Jared nodded. "That is why the girl was kept secret from you. She was kept secret from most of my people as well. We thought if she had a child, that child would free us."

Chris got up off of his rock. "Have you tried?"

Jared wagged his head. "No, we have not. We raised her. She is like our child."

"Thank God," Chris muttered.

"So, to some of you, we're potential saviors, and to others, we're a mere bargaining chip?" James knew right away that Jared didn't understand so he reworded his question.

"Yes." He hesitated again. "We have never tried freeing ourselves like this. You are the best chance we will have ever." Then he turned and began walking down the creek.

Joshua checked his ammo before following. "Fat chance."

James whispered into Chris' ear, "Keep an eye on John." They headed off towards the temple.

TWENTY-TWO
Shadow of death

Little resistance had been met up to this point. Their journey to this strange civilization, in which they now found themselves subject, had been uneventful save a few sky-people attending to chores within the thick of the jungle. Those sky-people never learned of the danger that hunted them.

James now stared through the tree line, his mind paralyzed, his stomach sick. He had thought he had a basic understanding of what went on in this awful place but now realized that not even the most warped imagination could have come up with what he was now seeing. The wispy fog that lingered around the tree line danced gracefully up into the air, wrapping itself around the trees and creating a sort of transparent curtain separating the jungle from that which dwelt thereafter. But James recognized more than just a physical fog separating one side from the other. There was something else . . . something almost tangible. The fog merely represented a more sinister barrier separating two different worlds. As he reached out and thrust his hand into the fog, his senses caught on fire. The division was a supernatural one, the worlds it separated at odds. James pulled his hand back in and held it up to his face, studying it. Then he looked over at Joshua who had been watching the whole time.

"There's something different in the air here, even different than the rest of this awful place." Joshua closed his eyes, not wanting to witness the events on the other side of the fog, in the town they were positioned upon.

James whispered back, but he was talking more to himself than responding to Joshua. "There's no constraint." There was a sense of amazement in his tone.

Chris was lying next to James' other side. "Did you see Lance? What happened to him?"

"Now's not the time, Chris," responded James, a slight edge to his voice.

"Oh, I think now is exactly the time." He continued before James could protest again. “His body was charred. Burnt. But it looked like he burnt to death . . . on the inside. What could do that, James?”

“I don’t know, Chris.”

“There are strong powers at work here. Look at this,” he stretched his hand out towards the town, his fingers grazing through the fog. “Do you remember what I told you I saw when I woke up the first day?”

James looked into Chris’ eyes, suddenly seeing an open door. “Chris, there’s something you need to know.”

Chris managed a smile, perceiving James’ line of thought. “I already know.” And his eyes told James just that.

A pleasant smile graced James’ ruddy face, his eyes burning with eager questions.

“I’ve been watching you. I’ve been listening to your conversations with Joshua and John . . . This place,” He looked around him. “There’s no denying the spiritual, the supernatural. I’ve just seen too much to be ignorant any longer. I think of all the things I lived for, and now, being faced with the strong possibility that I may never leave this place, I realize that there had to have been more.”

James rested a hand on Chris’ shoulder. “Do you have any idea how long I’ve been praying for you?”

Chris blushed and turned away, smiling.

“I only wish you weren’t so stubborn. Maybe if there was another way you would’ve accepted Him, you wouldn’t have drug me to this place.” He smiled and questioningly raised an eyebrow. “So this is what it took for you to come to the end of yourself, huh?”

Laughing in return, Chris nodded. “Yeah, I guess so.” Then he became serious. “You know, I don’t want to sound selfish, but it’s worth it. For me.”

“It’s worth whatever it costs, Chris. And, hey, we don’t have to fear this stuff, because the Bible says ‘Greater is He that is in you, than he that is in the world.’”

Chris nodded. “I don’t understand where we’re at, James, or what’s going on, but I do understand that God placed me here and saved me here.” His smile came back and stretched from ear to ear. “And I think I found the girl I want to marry here too.”

James didn’t know how to respond so he just returned the smile and slapped him on the back. Chris then asked in all confidence, “Lock and load?”

James drug his head back around to face a civilization void of any kind of law- moral or physical. “Oh yeah.”

They sat there for a few more minutes, enduring the sight before them. The town was made up of cabins and huts, a long street dividing it into two sides. There were no trees near the houses, only cut grass and rocks- grass and rocks that were stained with blood. When they first came to the town, up from the creek, Jared made them stop and watch before eliminating it like the others. After watching a woman throw a screaming baby against a large rock, and swing it, by its feet, into the ground until it became silent and limp, the Americans understood what words could never convey- the absolute potential of evil. It was a wonder that the sky-people were even in existence, given that their pastime seemed to be rape and murder. It was chaos, utter chaos. Women were fighting over lovers who were laughing and cheering them on, there was a group of men chasing an injured dog, throwing spears at it and then each other, young boys were raping women out in the open and gathering amused audiences . . . Every vile thing that could be imagined was surpassed by the sight before them.

"Look." Joshua was shocked. "There's no hate."

"It's sport to them." James let his gaze rest on Jared, wondering how long they would have to stay hidden and be forced to watch.

Jared responded to James' gaze. "Now you know the difference." And then he got to his feet and disappeared through the fog.

Joshua grabbed James' shoulder before James could leap after Jared. "If we're going to stand any chance against the giants, then we're going to have to preserve our ammo. I think we should maybe try using a sword while surprise is on our side."

James nodded. "You're right." Then he made sure Chris understood. "Are you ready for this, John?" John hadn't moved or even blinked since reaching the tree line. He seemed to be in a comatose state.

He didn't answer.

Joshua put both the sniper rifle and assault rifle over his shoulders and grabbed the shotgun out of John's hands. "Let's get this over with." Then he followed after Jared, leaving John behind.

The first people they came to were on the outskirts of the town, behind the farthest cabin. Three men and a woman. The woman's screams weren't gaining the attention that the other abominations were and nobody was around to see Jared cut the three men down and save the woman. But instead of thanks and gratitude, the woman got to her feet, pulling a knife out of the ground, and charged him. A few seconds later, she fell to the ground, joining her three assaulters.

"Split up!" ordered James. "We'll be more effective if we spread out."

Joshua and Chris nodded before running to the nearest huts.

The sky-people were all demon-possessed, James was sure. The 'gods' that they worshiped, the aliens that came in cloud cars, were demons, enemies of the cross bent on destroying humanity. The strength they exhibited was supernatural and as James watched a child throw a full grown man through the wall of a hut, the words he had read in his angelology book came flooding into his mind. It seemed like so long ago, almost a lifetime ago, that he was sitting on the plane next to the old lady reading things that just had no grip on his personal experience. Now, he realized that the same grip might just kill him. He shot a native and picked up his sword.

Joshua had only limited practice with a machete, and even that had been much more than a while ago. He was nervous, his free hand always ready to retreat to the more modern and effective weapons that were on his back. And yet, he had cleared out three huts with the strange sword. He was impressed with himself, but the constant realization that he didn't really know what he was doing kept it from turning into a dangerous arrogance. He ducked under a crazy swing and quickly thrust his sword up before the native could finish his attack swing and recover for a defensive maneuver. The native didn't scream. He dropped his sword to the ground and simply stared into Joshua's eyes. The eyes were hard and dark as coal, no life, nothing genuine, not even pain. And yet the eyes seemed to taunt Joshua, as if they were smiling at him. Joshua pulled the sword out of him and he dropped to his knees. When he looked back up to Joshua, his eyes were no longer dark, but glowing green- and this time, he was smiling. Joshua swung again.

Everything had started out exactly as it had in every village and town thus far, until a sudden turn of events had them running from a suddenly organized townsfolk and taking refuge in a cabin. It was odd. Every native in the town, no matter where they were, all turned their attention to the four strangers at the same exact moment. It was like something out of an old zombie movie. As they left their sport behind, they closed in on a new prey.

"Push!" Joshua screamed as he dug his shoulder into the wooden door. The sky-people were trying to get in.

James, Chris, Jared, and Joshua were trapped in a house, finding an army of evil encircling them. John was still in the woods, again afraid to move on and fight with them. They could have used his help now.

The door banged open an inch, a beam of daylight slicing across the dirty floor.

Chris spun his back into the door and used his feet, but they kept sliding out from under him in the dirt. "They're going to get in!" There were over a hundred of them, all pounding against the house.

James waited until another organized ram opened the door a crack before sticking the barrel of the assault rifle between the door and its frame. Hot shells bounced off the ceiling and landed on flesh, causing Chris, Joshua, and Jared to grit their teeth in pain. The stream of bullets killed the force trying to open the door and James brought the barrel up just as the door slammed shut again. But then more sky-people took up the task.

"We need to save the ammo!" yelled Joshua, pushing so hard the veins in his neck looked as if they were going to explode.

"We're not going to need it if we don't live to use it!" yelled back James.

Then, suddenly, there was a new noise. A thumping banging noise.

"They are using swords and axes," stated Jared, stoically.

Confirming his statement, the blade of an axe broke through the door, showering splinters and just missing Chris' head. "We can't hold them!" Chris took his back off the door and swung around, using his hands again. The blade was pulled out of the door, and he wasn't going to sit there and wait for it to go through his back.

"Wait!" James yelled. "Do you hear that?" He was looking up at the roof.

"You may have missed that we're a little preoccupied!" Joshua shot back, his strength fading quickly. "If you'd be interested in helping . . . "

James ignored the retaliation and began walking away from the door, into the center of the cabin. His voice came out as a whisper, the revelation too dramatic to shatter with loud words. "They're on the roof."

Chris wanted to curse but instead pushed harder against the door, dodging another blow from the axe.

Small amounts of dirt were beginning to fall from the roof now. There was definitely someone up there. Though the cabin itself was constructed with logs, the roof was only made up of sticks and straw, not making it impossible for someone to get through.

And then it opened in a shower of broken sticks and flying straw as a native plummeted through the opening and into the cabin, landing on his side. James charged with his sword raised and struck the native down before he could gather his senses. But the native that came down after him landed on his feet. James turned just in time to duck under the lethal arc of a blade. Brining his sword up and attempting to strike the native, before he could recover from his miss, proved futile. The native swung his sword back around and blocked James' blow with ease. He opened his mouth and screamed, his eyes on fire. James faked a blow with the sword, getting the native to react to his right hand while he delivered a punch with his left. The native fell to the ground and should have been knocked out, but he was standing up again almost immediately. "Great." James began backpedaling. The native thrust his sword straight at James' heart, but James side-stepped to his right and turned, bringing his sword down on top of the native's, sparks shooting into the air. James spun away from the native's sword and brought his left elbow up and around, striking the native in the back of the head. The native stumbled forward but didn't fall. He turned to face James again, determination and impatience distorting his face. *Perhaps there is a little hate here,* thought James.

Despite the deafening roars coming from the mass of evil attempting to crush down the door and the piercing clanging of swords echoing off the walls, Joshua was able to distinguish more footsteps on the roof.

James brought his sword up above his head to block the downward attack of the native and then, as fast as he could, swung downward to block another immediate attack. His arms were burning, and he was getting slower. The native across from him only seemed to be getting faster. He lowered his blade and began to reach for the shotgun. That's when three more sky-people crashed to the ground around him.

The room disappeared in clouds of dirt and dust, and James couldn't see anything. He forgot the shotgun, fearing he might shoot his friends, and gripped both hands on the sword, holding it out in front of him- waiting for what he imagined would be a terrible feel of steel cutting through him. Then shots rang out and pierced the dusty air.

Everything was still, silent.

The pressure against the door ceased and the cries of the sky-people from beyond it had died. After what seemed like forever, the dust cleared and settled onto the ground, revealing four dead natives, bleeding profusely from gunshot wounds. James stood among them, staring at the smoking sub machine gun in Chris' hand.

Everything was slow, cautious, as if their reaction would bring death howling through the door if it was too sudden or loud. Their wide, anxious eyes all met with questions and then looked for answers by nervously sweeping up to the ceiling.

Chris swallowed the lump in his throat. "I have a bad feeling about this."

They backed away from the door, dropping their swords and retrieving the more familiar metal, slipping fingers over triggers.

The expression on Jared's face revealed confusion, but before he could confirm his appearance with words, it changed. His eyes suddenly abandoned the cloak of caution and darted all over the room and up to the ceiling. Because he smelled something.

Joshua knew exactly what Jared was thinking and he ran to try the door. It wouldn't open. "It's not opening!"

"What do you mean? It opens in!" yelled James, finally moving from the place he stood.

"I know that, James!"

Chris tried to help by pulling on the door. "He's right, it won't budge!"

"How's that possible?" James joined them, pulling with all his might.

"They must have hammered a piece of wood to the door and across the side," commented Chris, trying to peek through a crack in the wall and confirm his theory.

"Then what's keeping us from pushing it open?"

"Maybe they wedged something up underneath the doorknob." Joshua stepped away from the door and began searching the house, looking for another way out.

"That door didn't have a doorknob." stated Chris. "And I didn't hear any hammering."

James looked up, everything else around him freezing. "Do you smell that?"

"Smoke." Joshua began searching faster. "They're going to burn us alive." And, as if on cue, flames began licking their way through the holes in the roof.

Jared ran past Joshua to the far room. There was a window there, but something was wedged against it. "We are trapped."

The sparks were spreading the fire through the straw, and soon the entire ceiling was engulfed in a raging blaze. The temperature intensified unimaginably fast.

"We have no choice!" shouted James.

Joshua coughed, as smoke crawled through his lungs, and nodded his consent. He pumped the shotgun and aimed it at the door.

Just as their fingers began applying pressure to the triggers, and they were about to use most of their ammo to blow apart the door, it swung open.

The torrents of black smoke that poured out through the doorway made it impossible to confirm more than a vague figure of a person separating the smoke and flames from the outside air behind him. But James didn't wait for a formal greeting. Rushing the door, he stumbled out into the grass, coughing and vomiting.

Joshua had barely begun to rub his stinging eyes when he felt strong hands grab him under his arms and lift him off the ground. Whoever had grabbed him was dragging him away from the burning cabin. Though his vision was marred with blurriness, he was able to see the distinct shapes of bodies scattered on the ground in every direction. He also noticed James, Chris, and

Jared being carried away with him. He also noticed John walking freely among them.

James could hear Jared speaking with the other groups of pure-blooded natives behind him. Thank God they had showed up when they did. Though James' attention was centered on what was before him, enough of his attention recorded the words spoken behind him. The natives were confused as to why Jared had stayed in the cabin so long, almost to the point of death. Jared responded by telling them that the sky-people had them trapped in there. "How?" they asked. Jared told them about the door being nailed closed. They simply responded by stating, "There was nothing over the door."

The ground was littered with dead bodies, the cabin burning in the background, pouring black smoke and hot flames into the sky. Not one member of the community was left alive. Even the infants were not spared.

James stood, silent, in the midst of the madness. His eyes rested over the carnage, trying desperately to understand it all. Nothing he had seen in Iraq was like this. This was evil in its purest form, converting people to non-human slaves, programmed for pointless acts of cruelty. But still, it was hard for James to see them as the wicked irredeemable people they were. Nothing he had ever experienced had dealt with this sort of race- irredeemable characters from an ancient tribe in the Old Testament. The present dispensation, the age of grace under the New Covenant, seemed a far cry from the days of swift judgment and justice. What lay before him now was a scene from one of the Old Testament books, God's commandment to destroy an entire people. James would have to admit that the thought raised more questions than answers. *But in God's sovereignty, in His very essence, He is just and merciful, righteous and vengeful. He is the Lord God and He does all things according to the pleasure of His will. That man would find some problem with that is insignificant. What is man that He is mindful of him? How could man protest the Most High? His ways are not our ways, His thoughts are not our thoughts. The wisdom of man is foolishness to Him . . . He does as He sees fit, and how can man foresee what is and should be?* All these thoughts flooded into James' mind as he continued to survey the town. He thought of the people that had been enemies of God with hardened hearts- people like Pharaoh. These sky-people were all crazy, worshipers of Satan and lovers of his lies. They were produced from unnatural means, means that many have theorized landed those fallen angels in a greater judgment than the ones who simply rebelled. The words in the angelology book pulled on the rope, dragging a kicking human understanding closer to the line of surrender. Then James remembered the flood, the reason God had to destroy the earth, and understanding then began to triumph in the tug-of-war. The days of Noah . . .

A hand resting on his shoulder interrupted his thoughts.

"We should get moving." Joshua took note of James' posture. "How are you?"

After a few seconds passed by, James shrugged. "I'm praying that this is just a bad dream."

"I think we're well beyond that possibility, James." He pulled on his arm. "Come on, we're going to the temple."

The temple looked like something out of Aztec history, its shape resembling the basic design of the pyramids, in that it was shaped as a triangle, but without the fine edges. The bricks used to make this mammoth of a building were arranged in such a way that one could climb up its side as if they were steps. Its peak was invisible, hidden in the low-lying clouds. About a hundred yards away from it, on all four corners, was a pyramid that stretched upward, but still beneath the shadow of the temple. It was a design James recognized. From the air it would look like a huge square with diamonds at its corners. It resembled the icon he saw in his dreams.

"There are two giants standing guard at the temple entrance. A few patrols of sky-people making rounds . . . The rest seem like worshipers." Joshua dropped the scope from his eye and his eyes refocused.

"What are they worshipping?" asked James.

"Can't tell. They're all gathered together in some kind of courtyard laid out at the temple's entrance."

"What about the pyramids?"

Joshua shook his head. "I didn't see anyone."

Jared responded, "There is much more. I do not understand."

"Well, maybe they're all inside. Or maybe they sent more soldiers after you than we thought."

Jared didn't respond, but turned and walked to his men.

The temple was obviously the center of the community, the pyramids and the villages spreading away from it in all directions. The jungle ended two hundred yards from the four pyramids, tiny paths leading to the villages, but there were still trees scattered all over the temple's base and around the pyramids. The dark clouds weren't moving so fast now and they were casually rolling by overhead. With that change came the return of the wind which was now breezing consistently through the trees. Tiny rain drops fell from the sky, but it seemed as though it were only a matter of time before the sky released its full load onto the people beneath.

"It's starting to get late," Chris observed.

"That's not going to be good for us." This coming from the detached voice of John who suddenly had less to say.

A sideways look was the only response Joshua had. He didn't want to be here in the dark, didn't even want to know what happened here when it got dark. "Thanks for sharing your genius with us."

Everyone was tired and well beyond their mental and physical limits. This made them all sensitive and moody, especially towards John, who seemed to have decided that fighting with them was no longer his thing.

Jared walked back over and explained that they were going to wait until more groups of natives showed up before raiding the temple and surrounding pyramids. "They should be here with us soon," he had said.

Looking out across the grass and through the trees, James observed those walking about and attending to different things. Though his eyesight wasn't good enough to tell what exactly everyone was doing, he was able to tell that the behavior was much different here than in the village they had just come from. There seemed to be at least some kind of order established in this place. James turned over on his back and stared up through the jungle's natural roof, tiny raindrops splattering against his face. The sun would begin to set soon and now that he was still, his muscles relaxing for the first time since crossing the river hours ago, he began to realize just how tired he really was. He closed his eyes, his mind drifting through clouds of confusion and uncertainty, searching for that still small voice he knew was there. Somewhere.

When James opened his eyes again, he found himself staring up to at least a hundred natives. Not knowing which natives were surrounding him, he quickly got to his feet, reaching for his weapon.

"James!"

It was Joshua's voice. He quickly walked from behind the natives. "We need to go now."

James recovered his awareness, allowing it to catch up with his circumstances, and took note of the sky. The sun had begun its descent. It was going to be dark very soon.

Once he was sure James had recovered from the detached effect his nap left him in, Joshua began again. "We need to go right now. Jared just talked to a scout that was sent to monitor the giants' movements. They'll be here in an hour."

James was wide awake now. He picked up the assault rife and the stolen sword and brushed past Joshua. "Where's Chris and John?"

"Chris is praying over there," he nodded in a direction off to his left.

It was a pleasantly strange thing to hear, that Chris was praying. James smiled, though it didn't make the journey to his face.

"John's missing."

James stopped dead in his tracks. "What do you mean?"

Joshua shrugged, "I mean, he's gone. No one knows where he went."

Time didn't afford the emotions that wanted to surface, and James continued walking. "Where's Jared?"

"He should be here any second. He went to scout through the surrounding woods. As soon as he gets back, we're on our way to the temple."

James turned to face his friend. "What's the plan?"

"Most of us are going straight into the temple, some are staying behind and making sure no sky-people can alert the giants before they get here. Then some are clearing out the pyramids."

James nodded that he understood. He also understood that Joshua was wound really tight. He wasn't so confident in the mission. "You think we have a chance?"

"Hey, with God all things are possible, right? I remember that much from church, but I don't know what we're going to find in that place."

Chills ran up James' spine as he thought about it, Mahalalel's words coming back to memory. *They use the women . . .*

Just then Jared appeared through the trees. He only nodded once before everyone turned and followed him out of the jungle and into the more open ground surrounding the temple and its pyramids.

James made sure his rifle was loaded and that the safety was on before throwing it over his shoulder. As he ran, he gripped the handle of the sword until his knuckles turned white. Chris ran up next to him, Joshua right behind. Their feet moved in unison to the natives' pace which was leading them to the very heart that generated all the evil in this bizarre place. And then James took note of the sun as it dipped below the tree line and thunder banged through the sky.

TWENTY-THREE
Hope lost

Sounds that were normally too insignificant to notice now seemed piercingly loud, each noise breaking through the callused walls building around her heart. As soon as headway was made and the walls seemed to be making progress a sound would pierce through, and reality would destroy the attempt at stoic conversion. She couldn't do it. She couldn't ignore the pain. Sitting in James' chair, it no longer felt comfortable, no longer felt secure. Now it felt cold and hard- the way she wanted to feel. But the tears that were rolling down her cheeks convinced her it was a futile effort. As she sat there, staring out the window, eyes not focusing on anything physical, she was conscious of the stillness. It was so quiet, she could almost feel it. There was the tick of the second hand coming from the clock hanging over the television. The refrigerator in the kitchen was humming again. There was the occasional traffic outside, the faint voices of people talking. The birds weren't singing, but they could be heard. Neighbor's pets . . . Her own daughter's hamster running endlessly in its wheel. The house would settle creating creaking noises that seemed to complement the stillness. The wind stroked through a neighbor's wind chimes, also brushing branches against the siding of her house. So still, so peaceful. Yet she was far from being at peace.

She leaned her head back and closed her eyes, the fingers on her left hand running through her daughter's hair. Kirsten could feel her breathing against her large stomach and chest. The sound of a vehicle accelerating caught her attention, but it braked almost immediately, and there was the sound of something plastic being slammed. Then the vehicle accelerated again. The mailman, he must have missed something his first time around. She opened her eyes and let them fall to her sleeping daughter. She had cried herself to sleep. Kirsten could no longer act like James was coming home, not after so long. Jessica caught on.

The sun was wearing its red glow now, readying for its dip beneath the horizon. Kirsten's imagination played with the strange events of the past few days, and she remembered that the front door was unlocked. But she was not in a state to care, and she soon joined her daughter, falling asleep as the pale sound of a squirrel running across the power lines and then jumping onto a weak branch faded out and her unconscious imagination faded in.

Her eyes flickered in response to the dream, but did not open. However, for a fraction of a second, her subconscious recorded another sound as it gained just enough awareness. Deep within her mind, she heard the shower running from the bathroom. Or perhaps it was just part of her dream. And just like that it was lost, drowned out by yet another dream of her husband.

Jessica stirred and Kirsten's eyes opened. She yawned and looked up at the clock, but the room was dark, and she couldn't see it.

"I'm hungry," Jessica complained sleepily.

"Okay." Kirsten moved her off her lap, and Jess walked over to the couch where she collapsed and fell asleep again. Kirsten's brain told her body to stand up, but the only thing she got in response was a sense of numbness. She leaned back against the chair, waiting for the circulation to begin in her legs.

A shadow glided across the wall behind the TV.

Kirsten sat up straight, her heart pounding in her chest. She immediately remembered deciding not to lock the door. She ignored the thousands of needles jabbing her legs and slowly turned around to see what had passed by the hallway.

He was leaning against the doorway.

Kirsten would have screamed if she hadn't already prepared herself for another terrifying sight.

"Nice nap?" The man's voice was tired and strained.

Kirsten didn't answer, but her hands began shaking.

"You okay? I hope you don't mind, but I took a shower."

Still Kirsten's eyes seemed to pierce the soul of the man standing in her house.

"Oh, uh, the front door was unlocked. I knocked a few times, but no one answered. I saw your car, so I knew you were home. When I walked in I saw that you were sleeping, and I didn't want to wake you."

Slowly, Kirsten's situation began to define itself. "Steve?" But which Steve was it?

Steve looked confused and made a gesture with his hands. "Yeah, it's me." He walked into the living room.

Kirsten leaned over and turned on a lamp that was next to the chair, spilling a soft glow into the corners of the room. She then placed her hand on her forehead, suddenly feeling the beginning stages of a migraine. "Sorry, I've been seeing things lately."

"What kind of things?" There was a clear vein of curiosity in his voice.

Kirsten didn't feel like talking about it so she shook her head, dismissing his question.

"Sorry, it's just that I've started seeing things too."

Her eyes shot up to face him before she could control it. "I don't want to talk about it now." Her voice was just above a whisper.

He nodded, acknowledging her request.

"What are you doing here?"

Steve caught the edge in Kirsten's voice and began backing away. "I'm sorry, if you want me to go . . . "

"No, it's just that I thought you were in Bermuda."

"I was."

The feeling had come back to her legs and she stood. "And?"

Steve smiled, but it was a lame attempt. "And I'm starving. Do you mind if I make you and Jess dinner?"

It was an awkward silence, the clanging of silverware against porcelain plates the only soundtrack. Steve had cooked up the best of what he could find in the cabinets, which wasn't much. Kirsten obviously had not gone shopping since James left. Pasta and roasted chicken- not exactly a gourmet meal, but compared to the empty boxes of microwave dinners that were littered around the overflowing trashcan, it was definitely an upgrade.

"What happened?" Kirsten finally asked, not all that interested in her food.

Steve waited until Jessica was looking down at her plate, twirling the pasta around her fork, before making eye contact with Kirsten. He moved his eyes over to Jessica real quick and then raised his eyebrows in a questioning fashion.

Water began to swell in Kirsten's eyes, and when she blinked a few were discharged into her pasta. Then she looked up at Steve and nodded that she understood. They'd wait to talk until Jess was in bed.

Steve took out the trash while Kirsten put Jessica to bed. When he walked back up the driveway, he took careful note of his environment, searching for signs of anything that might be out of place. The luminous glow from the streetlamps revealed nothing out of the ordinary, and he walked through the front door, locking it behind him. As he walked through the front foyer, Kirsten was walking down the stairs. She looked beautiful, Steve thought, and he suddenly felt a twinge of regret. His brother had chosen the better life while he spent his chasing vain ideologies and unsatisfying self images. As she walked past him, she forced a smile, and he wished, for the millionth time, that he had gotten married at some point in his life. He followed her into the living room and sat on the couch opposite of the chair she sunk into.

Kirsten thought Steve looked as if he was about to fall over and sleep for the next three years. Though he had taken a shower, he had not shaved, and the bloodshot eyes hadn't been affected either. His body language was almost exaggeratingly dramatic. He couldn't keep his shoulders up, or even his chin up. His eyes looked heavy, as if it took a conscious effort to keep them open. Though he was 51 years old, he had always looked like he was at least fifteen years younger. But not now. Kirsten spoke sympathetically. "What happened?"

His eyes drug upward until they rested on her gaze. "I didn't find anything new."

His voice betrayed the fact that there was much more to his story, and she didn't back down. "What happened?" she repeated.

He looked away from her, bringing his hand up to his head. "I don't know what I was thinking." Emotion suddenly began to manifest itself within a man she had never witnessed it in before. "I wasn't thinking." He looked up to the ceiling. "I thought that maybe if I tracked down the guy who was responsible, he'd take me to James. But there was nothing to find out." His voice began to shake, a sound not many had ever heard before. "He took off in the plane, and the plane never came back. If they made it to the island I was held on, then the SEALs would have found them."

"Did you find the man you were looking for?" she brushed a tear away with a thumb.

"Yeah."

"And?"

"And he knew only as much as we did." His watery eyes then met hers. "I don't think that I can stay here."

The statement took her by surprise. "Why?"

"It's a long story. The very reason I went down there in the first place . . . there were signs of a conspiracy, suspicious trades, and a line of money leading straight to the heart of it. So I went down to check it out. Anyway, it doesn't matter. One of the men responsible for the conspiracy was the same man who had me abducted and tried to kill James. He was a member of Bermuda's House of Assembly."

"Was?" Kirsten leaned forward.

"I killed him."

"You killed him? How? What . . . " Her thoughts became tangled.

"If the CIA learns of what I've done, which they will, then I'll most likely find myself in a lot of trouble. But if Britain finds out what I've done, then I'm dead. By either side, it doesn't matter. They'll use what I've done to stop the conspiracy, and then eliminate me to appease the opposition rather than give way to political unrest."

Kirsten's world spun around her until she was dizzy and her head was aching. "I need some aspirin." She got up and walked into the kitchen. When she came back in, Steve was asleep on the couch. She stood there staring at him, marking the vague resemblances he shared with his much younger brother. And she felt hope finally slip off her fingertips and disappear into a chasm below. As she raised the glass of water, her hand began to tremble, and water sloshed over the glass edge, falling to the carpet. She was staring at the mirror that hung mounted to the wall above the couch Steve was sleeping on. In it, she saw, not only herself, but a man's face watching her through the front window.

The face of the man in the mirror was a perfect resemblance of the face that was sleeping on her couch, just below the reflection.

She turned around, but there was nothing there. And, strangely enough, she suddenly felt a sense of relief at Steve's words, *I've been seeing things too.* Perhaps it wasn't just her. Perhaps there was something else going on here, and if it had to do with James, and it was still going on, then perhaps James was still alive. Or perhaps not. She took a drink of water, collapsed back into the chair, and fell asleep.

TWENTY-FOUR
Days of Noah

Arrows streaked through the air in multitudes, their mass so great they appeared as a single black, blurring cloud. The worshippers wasted no time in taking up arms and quickly began shooting at the mass of pure-blooded natives storming towards their temple. There was not one single native loyal to the gods of this place that was not trying desperately to defend their core of power. They pulled back on chords and released deadly arrows through the evening sky, sending enemy natives tumbling to the ground.

James was running behind Joshua, tempted to use him as cover. The arrows whistled as they streaked by, occasionally meeting an abrupt end with a sickening sound followed immediately by a cry of pain. Natives were falling down all around them, but once the archers were reached, James knew they would stand no chance against the swords being swung in pure-blooded fury.

The temple grew larger as their approach neared a climax. James, Joshua, and Chris fired a few bursts from their automatics, striking some of the archers and sending the rest diving for cover. At least that would preserve more of their friends. John had suddenly re-appeared and was running beside them, adding another level to his mysterious actions. There was certainly no time to question him now.

There were only fifty yards left to be covered before hand-to-hand combat would take over and the advantage would swing wildly away from the sky-people.

Chris jumped over a native that was struck by an arrow, falling down and almost taking his legs out from under him. Chris put a hand out to steady himself just as an arrow dug itself deep within the ground only two inches away from his outstretched hand. Another one screamed over his shoulder, just slicing the top layer of skin. He looked up, hoping that all the dark specks would be missing him when they plummeted to the ground. The native running beside him took an arrow straight through the Adam's apple and fell crazily to the ground. This only motivated Chris more, helping him find more energy than he felt he had. Only twenty yards now. He fired one last burst from his M-16 before throwing it over his shoulder. As four sky-people flew backwards, struck by his shots, he gripped his sword with two hands, readying himself for a battle lost in time.

The pure-blooded natives charged through the worshippers turned archers, cutting them down with remarkable precision. Most abandoned their bows and arrows, turning and fleeing, only those with swords standing their ground. The piercing noise of clanging swords filled the sky and thunder boomed overhead. Thirty seconds later, rain was falling heavily from the sky, washing blood away.

Jared grabbed the native's sword hand and kicked him in his exposed side, cracking at least two ribs. Then he spun him around by his hand, releasing him and sending him reeling into three other sky-people. Jared turned just in time to duck under a crazy swing by a huge bald man covered in scars. The man swung down. Jared side-stepped it and spun, bringing his sword up and around. But the massive native blocked it with ease and kicked Jared in the stomach, sending him, out of breath, to the wet ground. Another native came up from behind and thrust a spear straight at Jared, but Jared moved and the spear went through his shoulder instead of his head. He screamed, anger flashing fanatically in his eyes. He stood up, ignoring the huge native and concentrating on the one who had speared him. The sky-native had no weapon, it was sticking out of Jared's shoulder and straight up into the air. He began to back-peddle, Jared's face more than intimidating. Jared charged with a blood thirsty battle cry and sent the sky-person's head flying through the air. He stood there and enjoyed his revenge too long. When he turned, he was greeted by the monster native's sharp sword. It went straight through his side. Jared's eyes grew wide with the realization of defeat and failure. But he wasn't ready to roll over and die just yet. Before the sky-person could retrieve his sword, Jared took a few quick steps backwards, leaving the huge native without a weapon. Then Jared spun, bringing his sword up and around just as he did before. But now the sky-person had no sword to block the attack, and, out of reflex, he shielded himself with an arm. The arm fell to the ground, and Jared's next swing ended the mammoth's life. Jared stood, in the midst of the battle, and, for the first time, gained a sense of what was going on around him. Sky-people and pure-bloods were battling each other all around. Bodies were falling at an accelerated pace. Through the chaos- the blurred movements of shifting feet, attacking maneuvers, and the falling rain, Jared could make out the form of four men breaking away from the battle and charging the steps of the temple. Despite a spear sticking through his shoulder down into his chest and a sword protruding out of his back, he managed a faint smile. There was still hope after all.

Joshua charged up the steep steps, approaching the entrance way into the temple but also the two giants that guarded it. He could still hear James,' Chris,' and John's footsteps following close behind him. The steps were so huge that they were practically jumping up them, exhaustion and burning thighs tempting them to quit. As they got closer to the giants, Joshua pulled the shotgun from his back and pumped it with one hand, not dropping the sword. Then he threw it in the air, catching it by the handle, and prepared to fire.

The giants were enormous. They were covered in some sort of armor that resembled glass. It reflected everything around it. As James got closer, he could see himself and Joshua running in it- like it was made of tiny mirrors. The dark sky, the bloody battle below, and the jungle in the distance was all reflected in the giants' armor. Their eyes were black, set in a face carved from rock. Their massive arms led to huge six-fingered hands holding long, gleaming swords. The swords were not constructed from the crude metal the natives' were, rather these swords seemed to be made from glass or crystal, just like their armor. It was a futuristic contrast, the deeply tanned flesh protruding from behind glimmering glass-like armor. The two giants guarding the temple entrance was a scene stolen from many fantasy stories and even some cult sci-fi classics. Only the giants weren't rehearsing a script and acting a part. As they stepped forward and sliced the air with the gleaming swords, there was no mistaking their intent.

They all stopped dead in their tracks, just three steps below the towering evil, and looked at each other. The reflecting armor was more than troubling and it reflected the worrisome looks of the invaders.

Joshua raised the shotgun and aimed it at an ugly face. "There's one way to find out," he mumbled. He squeezed the trigger and a loud bang echoed off the temple and bounced off the nearby pyramids. The giant took half a step back. Blood began streaming down its armor. Its face was hidden behind a mess of torn flesh and blood, but its next step was a forward one. Joshua pumped and shot again. This time the shot struck the giant dead in the chest, but the armor only spider-webbed around the cracks the shot made.

"You gotta' be kiddin' me," came a disgruntled murmur from Chris' tightly pressed lips.

"Blow its head off!" screamed James as he prepared to take evasive maneuvers.

The bloody giant took one lazy step down towards them, the other stepping in front of the entrance. James ran to his left, Chris to the right, and Joshua jumped back down a step. John just stood there, mouth gaping wide, eyes fixed in a sensational state of both awe and terror. The giant ignored the fleeing prey and concentrated on the fear frozen stranger standing before it.

"Move, John!" James was screaming, but John wasn't showing any signs of comprehension or acknowledgement. James knelt and raised his assault rifle, all the while wondering why the other giant was just standing there watching. He lined up the giant's head and flicked the safety off.

Joshua fired from his hip, only some of the shot catching the top of the giant's head. He dropped the shotgun a bit lower, pumped, and fired again. This time the entire face disappeared in a fountain of red. But it kept advancing towards John.

A mere three seconds had passed since Joshua's second shot proved useless, and now the blood splattered armor of the giant was reflecting John's fear-stricken face in a variety of twisted shapes. The massive ungodly hulk was only a horrifying foot away from him, John's eyes locked in a trance, staring at his own contorted face in a reflection of death. Then, forcing himself to look up, he saw the towering beast raise its sword.

James squeezed the trigger, sending the distinct sound of automatic fire piercing through the rain and the intense battle below. The bullets struck their target and whatever was left of the giant's head was now lying five feet away from its feet. It stood, motionless, sword raised and waiting to be dropped onto the still-petrified stranger, until it finally began to wobble. Its knees buckled and the giant's mass began to lean forward.

John knew that he was about to be crushed, but he still couldn't bring himself to move. He watched in horror as his reflection grew larger as the reflective armor came crashing down on top of him. The last thing he saw before impact was his own pathetic wide-eyed expression of fear. Then darkness.

The other giant roared in a contorted mixture of surprise and anger before leaping high into the air. It landed in a kneeling position right between James and Chris, who were taken off guard by the sudden offensive move. The giant, remaining in its kneeling pose, swung the sword in an arc around its head.

James and Chris both ducked as the sword sliced through the air just above their heads. Joshua began pumping the giant with lead, showering the armor with a network of cracks, but apparently not much more. The giant rose to its feet, ignoring the shotgun's assault. It turned to face James, and James began backpedaling, but one of his feet got too close to the edge of the step and his foot slipped out from beneath him on the wet surface and he found himself flying backwards in the air.

Chris charged the giant's rear, bringing his sword down across the back of its knees. There was a gap in the armor there, and the giant threw its head back and wailed. That's when Joshua got in a perfect shot, striking the monster directly in the throat. Its chin fell limp against the cracked chest armor, and blood soon hid any trace of the reflective armor. Then it fell face first down the steps, continuing all the way down to the green grass, resting finally in a crumpled heap.

Chris and Joshua ran quickly to John and, with all of their might, were able to roll the giant off him. He had been crushed awkwardly between two steps, and they feared his back might be broken. They carefully positioned him lying down, horizontally, on a step.

"Where's James?" asked Joshua.

Chris wiped the water off his face and looked around. "I don't know, I didn't see what happened."

They both ran to the spot they had last seen him in.

James opened his eyes and a crazily disproportioned landscape was revealed to him. His mind tried to jump through all the hoops, to attain some grasp of comprehension, but the sight before him was too bizarre. And then he felt the pain explode in his head and blaze through his forehead. But with the pain came the realization of the last few moments, and he was now aware of his awkward position, upside-down staring up the temple steps. He rolled over onto his stomach, warm liquid running down his face and into his eyes and pushed himself up to his knees. Sitting there until he felt sturdy and the world stopped spinning, he brought his hand up and gingerly touched his wound. He winced and then observed his bloody fingers. He didn't remember hitting his head, but the evidence was only pointing to one thing. He staggered to his feet, suddenly aware of the peril they were in.

"James!"

James looked up, wiped the blood out of his eyes, and saw Chris and Joshua standing twenty feet above him. "Where's John?" His voice was forced.

"He's unconscious," yelled back Chris. "Are you okay?"

James began climbing back up the stairs, each step feeling as if his body was being mutilated by microscopic men inside of him. "Just great," he responded icily.

When he finally reached Chris and Joshua, Joshua demanded to take a look at his wound.

"You've got a pretty nice boo-boo there, chief. I think it might scar."

James forced a sarcastic smile. "Cute."

"We have to leave him." Chris interrupted and was nodding down at John.

James sighed, his head feeling like the vice it was in just turned another full revolution. "Let's go."

They ran up the last few steps and entered the temple.

The stillness was probably the most eerie factor. They found themselves standing in a corridor that stretched away from them and disappeared in a fuzzy perception. Torches flickered from the walls, but there were enough of them to supply a constant source of light so there were no shadows.

Chris cracked a crooked smile. "No one to welcome us? That's pretty rude."

James turned away from the long hallway and looked back through the entrance they had just walked through. Though he could see sheets of rain falling over the entrance and could just make out a section of the battle below, he thought it odd that there were no sounds to accompany the sights. He held a finger to his lips, signaling for Joshua and Chris to remain silent.

The quietness was definitely awkward, unnatural. Though the rain was pouring just a few feet away from them, thunder was rocking the evening sky, and a noisy battle was raging below, there was no sound at all. Nothing. The only thing that could be heard was the beating of their own hearts, other than that there was only the constant high-pitched ring that rang the ears in total silence.

"Can you feel that?" whispered Joshua.

James could feel it. There were strange vibes traveling through the hallway, and not just the vibes that made the hair on your neck stand, but actual literal vibrations humming off the rock walls.

"I don't like this." Chris double-checked his M-16, the sub-machine gun, and the automatic pistol he had tucked into his pants.

With a posing determination in his eyes, James began walking down the hallway, tiny sideways looks revealing the fear trying to hide behind the determination. "Come on, we don't have much time left."

They walked cautiously down the hall on soft feet, their weapons held high and ready. After walking fifty yards, doorways began appearing on both sides of the walls.

Joshua nodded his head in the direction of a doorway. "Should we check it out?"

James made a hand signal and Chris and Joshua immediately had their backs up against opposite sides of the doorway, James walking directly towards it. His trigger finger was shaking, sweat rolling down his face. He crouched low and prepared himself, but before he could throw himself through the doorway, Joshua held his hand out and grabbed him.

"Wait." He pulled James out of the doorway and next to him. "Look." He pointed to the entranceway. "There's no light."

At first James didn't understand what Joshua was talking about but then he noticed exactly what Joshua was seeing. There was no light coming from beyond the doorway, but also, there was no light from the hallway penetrating the doorway. It was as if a black curtain was stretched over it.

James nodded his understanding and released himself from Joshua's grip. He resumed his position in front of the entrance and slowly poked the barrel of the assault rifle into the darkness. The barrel disappeared.

"What the heck?" Chris walked away from the wall and to another doorway. Same thing. After checking four more, he ran back to James and Joshua. "They're all like this."

They hesitated, not sure how wise it would be to throw themselves into the unknown, but also realizing they had little choice.

"What do we do?" asked Joshua. His voice betrayed his willingness to comply with whatever the plan would be.

"We don't have much of a choice do we?" asked Chris.

James thought it a little odd that Chris seemed to want to jump through. "Man, you'd do anything to impress a broad, wouldn't you?"

Chris shrugged under the weight of the weapons strung over his back. "Hey, a story this heroic would be a great road to a pick-up line." He smiled. "That and the fact that I save her life. Come on, you have to like my odds."

Joshua raised a smug eyebrow. "You're weird."

But before Chris could answer, something exploded from the doorway and knocked them all onto their backs.

Not able to fully comprehend the force that knocked him onto his back, James tried desperately to catch his breath and focus his vision. The vibration noise was now an ear crushing hum, and James found himself clutching both ears, screaming in pain- screams that were lost in a sea of lethal sound waves. Blood began dripping from his ears and running down his wrists. It felt as if someone were trying to fit an ice-pick into his ears, and he swore they were about to explode. He cried out for help. "Jesus!"

The noise stopped. Joshua struggled to his feet and wiped the blood from his ears with his shoulders. Then he looked around. "What was that?"

Chris helped James to his feet. "What?" He couldn't hear anything but a constant ring in his ears.

Just then, Joshua thought he saw something at the end of the hallway. "Hold on." And before anyone could react, he was sprinting down the corridor, passing dark doorways all the way down.

"Where's he going?" James asked, steadying himself with one hand against the wall.

Chris shook his head. "I don't know."

And then the sound of footsteps behind them began growing louder.

"Something's coming!" yelled Chris, already aiming the M-16 down the hallway into the space they had already walked through.

A silhouette appeared running down the corridor towards them. James raised his rifle.

Joshua slowed to a stop, panting heavily, a mask of confusion contorting his face. "What the heck?"

James lowered the rifle, stole a cautious look over his shoulder off into the direction Joshua had run off in, and then eyed Joshua suspiciously. "Where exactly did you just come from?"

Joshua swallowed the lump in his throat and continued laboring to breathe. "I thought I saw something at the end of the hall, so I ran after it. Then you guys appeared just standing here."

Chris' eyes narrowed. "We didn't move."

Joshua looked behind him but saw nothing but an empty, torch-lit hallway. "I think someone's having fun at our expense."

"I really don't like this." Chris began looking at the walls differently, as if they would come alive and suck him in.

A new noise erupted from within the small confines of the bizarre corridor- footsteps. It bashed through the silence, vibrating back and forth off the endless walls, sounding like an army of bare feet.

"That noise is coming at us," stated Chris.

And then they appeared. Natives, sky-people, whatever- there were about twenty of them wearing red robes, walking straight for them.

James began backing up until his back hit something hard. He quickly turned around only to find himself staring at a wall. "You've got to be kidding."

Joshua and Chris backed into it as well.

"Where'd this come from?" yelled Chris. He turned around to face the army of natives coming for them like a stream of blood, their red robes shifting under the torchlight.

They dropped their swords and brought up their guns, aiming wildly at the dark faces cloaked in red.

"Fire!" James yelled. The sound of the automatic weapons was deafening in the small confines of the rock corridor, shells bouncing off the ground all around their feet. The hot lead was searing through the air, punching holes in the red robes. But that's all the bullets seamed to be doing. The crowd of robed natives continued unthwarted.

"What's going on?" Chris was keeping the 16 firing, leaning his shoulder into the reaction, keeping his aim steady. But nothing was happening.

Slowly, they ceased firing and let their smoking weapons drop beside them, able only to watch whatever was to come. As the natives grew closer, they were able to see what was beneath the bullet tattered red robes. There was no blood, there was no flesh- there was no anything. The robes were simply walking through the stale, smoky, hallway air.

"We're definitely not in Kansas now, man." Chris muttered through cracked lips, bracing himself for whatever horrible thing the flying robes had in store.

The ghostly figure in the front must have raised its arm, the sleeve elevating as if it were pointing at James.

"Oh-" James never had the time to complete the thought. He found himself elevated off the ground, his feet fifteen inches above the stone. The outstretched sleeve flung to the side, and James went in that direction too. He screamed as he was thrown into a dark doorway . . . and disappeared.

"James!" Chris yelled, but it was no use. He moved closer to Joshua, both of them leaning against each other, bracing for a similar fate.

They closed their eyes and were drowned in red fabric.

James opened his eyes. His head was throbbing. As his senses re-gathered, he noticed he was curled up in a fetal position, lying on a smooth, cool floor. Groaning in pain and dishevelment, he rolled onto his back, staring, spread-eagle, up into a bright light. He turned his head to his left and could see the assault rifle lying five feet away from him. He reached out for it, his fingers brushing the barrel.

It slid a few more feet away from him.

James blinked, comprehension being tossed around in a washing machine of logic. Ignoring the pain he felt surging through his body, he forced himself up onto his elbows. He studied the rifle, scrutinizing it suspiciously. Then he searched his environment, seeing no one around- only a glowing brightness. "This is getting ridiculous . . . " He leaned over and reached for the weapon, but it moved out from under his hand, and he missed it. The hairs on his neck stood up, his spiritual senses set ablaze, and he had to suppress a few nervous tremors that shook through his body.

Moving very cautiously, he was able to get to his feet. A few seconds later, his mind cleared. He suddenly began looking around for a point of entry, a doorway that he must have fallen through. But there was nothing around, only that strange glowing brightness. If there were walls, they were well hid behind the light. The only thing that James could be sure of was that he was standing on a hard surface that looked like glass. He took a step towards the rifle.

It moved away from him.

Fear began its process of transforming into a frustrated anger, and James ran towards it, diving across the slippery ground and reaching out for his weapon. But the assault rifle flew away from him, sliding all the way across the floor until it disappeared into the light.

James dropped his head against the ground, physically drained and now mentally at the end of his rope. The games were too much. He wanted it to end. He closed his eyes.

"Giving up already, James?"

James' eyes shot open with a sudden fire that burned every nerve-ending in his body. The voice seemed to come from all around him, and it was a voice that he immediately recognized.

"James Streen . . . we've met before. Do you remember?"

James still lay prone against his stomach. Daring to move his head, his eyes frantically searched for the source of the voice. His heart was beating so hard and fast, he thought he could start doing push-ups without the use of his arms. He swallowed, his throat and mouth desert dry.

"Come now, James, we had such a prosperous time before. I was hoping for a repeated pleasure."

It took a few moments for his words to come out, but he managed to stammer, "Who are you?"

The voice came back sounding distressed. "Oh my, James, we have already gone over this. Have you forgotten so soon?"

James grasped his head with his hands. "No. It was a dream . . . it was a dream-"

"Wishful thinking, I'm afraid. Our last meeting was as real as the air you breathe, James. Now, why don't you stand up, I'm growing bored of this prostrated fear that's keeping your face in the ground. I can hardly hear you."

"Leave me alone."

"I said, stand up." There was a razor sharp edge to the repeated demand.

James raised his head, which suddenly felt like it weighed a hundred pounds, and lazily swung his eyes back and forth. "I'm tired of your stupid tricks."

"I said stand up!"

The voice was so loud that it seemed to physically bombard him. He was lifted up off the ground and standing on his feet so fast, it took a few moments for him to realize what had happened.

"That's better, James." The voice was normal again.

"What do you want?" It came out just above a whisper.

"Come now, James, do not be shy. Speak up, for god sakes."

"What-do-you-want!" James screamed as loud as he could, but his voice didn't have the same surround-sound effect that the other did, it simply seemed to get lost, absorbed by the brightness.

The voice chuckled, and then the appearance of a man began to manifest in the effulgence. "James, it is not what I want from you, it is what I have to offer you."

James forced his eyes to rest on the figure that was now standing before him. It was the same figure that he had seen before. It had shape, but no characteristics. It was there- but it wasn't. James attempted to study the form, but that's all it appeared to be, a form. "Keep it."

Laughter came from the shaped head as it leaned back on its shoulders. "But you have not yet heard what it is that I have to offer."

"I know about your offers, one cursed all of mankind."

Suddenly the human form began to materialize into a green serpent. It hissed, its tongue flickering around James' feet. "Yessss, that offer wassss taken rather foolishly, it would sssssseem." And then, just like that, the serpent was a beautiful woman. "I can offer you a lot of things, James Streen." She ran a finger seductively down his chest, her hazel eyes reaching deep within him and summoning all his emotional elements. "No man can refuse this offer, James. None."

James turned his head, gasping in horror at what was happening inside him. "God-"

"Hey," her voice sounded like music from heaven and immediately began to soothe James' body. She took his face in her hands and looked into his eyes. "You're God isn't here. I am here." She leaned forward and kissed him.

Her lips were warm and seemed to melt on his. Every degree of resolve seemed to evaporate as her touch hypnotized his will. Then, in an instant, his will snapped back, bent but not broken. He pulled away from her and slapped her as hard as he could.

"Get off of me."

Her eyes narrowed, looking at him in a rageous unbelief. "Fine." Then she took on an image of a man. "How is this? Will this due?" He walked away from James, and then suddenly stopped, turning on his heel, hand on his chin. "You know, I think you rather enjoyed that."

James spit on the ground and wiped his mouth with the back of his hand. "Let me know when you're done screwing around."

The man smiled. He was dressed in a fine business suit, his hair slicked back, a mustache trimmed into points just at the corners of his mouth. "You do not know me, James." He motioned with his hand, which was suddenly holding a cigarette between two fingers. "I must apologize for misleading you before. I believe that I may have caused you to believe that I am . . . " He raised his shoulders and dipped his head down, moving his eyes sneakily back and forth. He finished his sentence in a sarcastic whisper. " . . . Lucifer."

Clenching his jaw tight, James answered, "That is what you had me to believe."

The man walked over to James and slapped him on the shoulder. "God, but you are a gullible character, aren't you?"

James decided it was time to get a move on with things. He wasn't scared anymore, and his heart rate had returned to normal. He was getting bored with all this drama. "A pretty interesting place you've got here."

The man tapped his cigarette and watched the ashes flutter to the ground. "You like it? It was no easy task, I'll tell you."

James snickered. "I bet."

He laughed. "I've been listening to you and your friends. I must admit, it has been pretty amusing."

"Really?"

"Oh yeah. I mean, the theories you people have come up with." He laughed and waved his hands. "Time travel!" He abruptly stopped laughing and became immediately serious, showing that everything was a mere act. "But, I must hand it to you, James, your theory on that particular subject I found to be rather profound." He took a long drag from the cigarette. "I give you an A for that one."

"So where exactly am I?"

The man flashed a warning smile. "Slow down, James. We're not best friends yet."

James' eyes nearly disappeared, only partially visible behind the narrow slits left by his eyelids. "Then can we please get to the point."

"Ah, yes, I was just about to address that, thank you. Sometimes I do allow myself to get sidetracked." He spun away from James, smoke escaping his lips and rising in the air. "Last time we talked, I educated you on the effectiveness of suspense. I needn't get into gory details about how we are running the world these days, do I?" He looked back over his shoulder at James and brought the cigarette back up to his lips. "You know, James, most of the world, even your fellow Christians, think that we only work through environments like this." He waved his hands at the formless light around him. "Like our little island we have here." He threw the cigarette onto the clear surface and smashed it out with his foot. "They only see us working in demonic and cultish scenarios. They don't believe that we could be involved with entertainment, music, gambling, drugs, money, sex, power . . . they refuse to associate us with the environment of spring-break, Mardi Gras or Cancun, and isolate us only to witches and sorcery. I mean, your Christian brothers and sisters are even more pathetic than the rest, James. They know about us, and yet they choose to remain blind to the things we poison their water with. You see, James, it's because they like what we offer, and they don't care about what it costs." The man laughed again. "Legalism, James. What a beautiful word. Say it with me, 1-e-g-a-1 -i-s-m. Notice the way it just glides off your tongue? Oh, no, James. I'm not talking about the legalism of the Jews that Paul addresses in Galatians and Romans. Oh, no, that legalism is almost extinct among true Christians today. I'm talking about this new legalism, this defensive terminology that you all use now to justify your, so-called, freedom." His lips spread into an evil grin. "Why does God put up with your stench- your pathetic, rebellious, hypocritical stench? You all abuse the grace He has given you by partaking of everything we provide the world with. You're no different than the heathens. You're all doing the same things, standing in the same lines. And whenever a good preacher comes along and preaches conviction, you all shout condemnation and have him run out of town riding on the tongues of all those mouths who gossiped him into bad character. You proclaim to have your 'freedom in Christ' and that justifies your compromise. You are all so damned ignorant. You don't even know what that freedom is." His laughter led into a long sigh. "But, that's the beauty of humanity, isn't it? You're all ignorant. Legalism, yes! Preach it! Shoot down the conviction of the Holy Spirit, misinterpret it as condemnation! Change the meaning of freedom to suit your fleshly desires! Do it, James! Do it! Isn't that why the Son of Man died? So that you would have the freedom to do whatever is to your liking under an umbrella of grace? Isn't that true freedom at the expense of God's blood?" He laughed and spun in a circle. "Oh, how wonderful. You people are so lost. There are but a few among you who truly see what's going on. Damn, I'm a genius! How about my culture? How about the way I direct it straight into your pathetic churches! You're all so blind. You've traded discernment for psychology, humility for self-esteem! The world, James, is under our control."

"You cannot touch God's elect." It was all that James managed to say.

"And who are they, James? Can you point them out, because I seem to have trouble telling the difference between my children and His these days."

"Is this why you brought me to this awful place? To share your views with me?"

A corner of the man's mouth lifted into a grin, and he looked down at the ground, thrusting his hands into his pockets. "No, James, of course not."

"Then can we please get to it soon?"

The man sighed. "Fine. I need you."

James blinked. "What?"

"A long time ago, I was once free to roam the earth. But I did something that God punished me for, something more horrible than even rebelling against Him."

"You tried to destroy the bloodline."

The man looked up, visibly shocked. “I am impressed. You know of Genesis six.”

“I’ve read it a few times. What does it have to do with me?”

“Oh, more than you could possibly know.”

James didn’t like the way that sounded, and his heart skipped a beat.

“Anyway, I was banned to this place. I have no power outside of it.”

“So what’s the bad news?” James asked.

“The bad news, James, is for you. You see, you are the one that is going to change all that.”

“And how do you think I’m going to accomplish that little feat when I can’t even get out of this stupid place myself?”

“You humans are so ignorant to the spiritual. You think reality is comprised only of what you can see. You know nothing of reality, James. Nothing at all. You were right, this place is not existing in the BC years, nor is it an alternate reality. You people watch too many of my movies.” He laughed. “Think of an onion, James. Think of its many layers. You see, realty is like an onion. But humanity only sees that brown skin, not even getting to the first layer of reality.” An onion appeared in his hand when he pulled it out of his pocket. He peeled off the brown skin, and it fluttered to the ground. “There goes your physical reality, James. What you have left is an entire world of layered realities- realities that humans refuse to believe exist. Not that I blame them, entirely. I mean, it’s not like God is making it obvious. But those of you who do stray close to the truth are so easy to lead astray. Parapsychology and all that nonsense . . . I’ll tell you, James, you are all a confused lot.”

“So this place is another layer of reality, existing at the same time as physical reality, yet within a different realm?”

The man dropped the onion and wiped a tear from his eye. “Stupid things always get to me.” He looked back at James. “Something like that. This is a physical reality, in a metaphysical sense. But I do not have the time to educate you on the principals of the spiritual world. You’ve seen enough by now to know that it is true.”

James didn’t even bother looking for the rifle, he knew it would do nothing against his enemy. Instead, he started praying. “Last time we talked you mentioned something about my son.”

“Whoa!” He held up his hands. “Hold on! You’re getting way too ahead of yourself. We’ll get to that.” He eyed James curiously. “Are you getting bored with me?” He waved his hands over his body. “Because I could change.” And then he did just that, until, standing in front of James, was Brian.

“You-”

He cut him off with a raised finger. “Hold it, James. You don’t want to swear now." He rubbed his eyes. "Now that I have your attention again, I'll continue."

James was thrown off balance by seeing Brian standing before him. Even though he knew it wasn't Brian, the visual perception of his good friend was toying with his emotions.

"As I was saying, I need your help. Now, I have access into your realm, but I'm powerless there. I cannot do anything. It's like watching a movie to me, 'look but do not touch.' It's been like that for a very long time, James. But one day that changed. Yes, I think I was more surprised than anyone, but about 300 years ago I got a grip on something within your world."

"What are you talking about? Aren't you supposed to be in chains?"

The man that looked like Brian shrugged. "Many of my fellow demons ended up there in Tarterus. Why I was sent to this place, I do not know. But I will prove that God made a mistake by allowing it, by freeing myself from this passive eternity."

"Right."

He snickered. "You mock me? You will not be laughing in a few minutes, Christian. Satan somehow sent me people, people from the physical realm. I do not know how and nor has he ever explained himself, but one day I had my own Adam and Eve. So I began my own insignificant Genesis account. And before long, I had a population of physical people in my metaphysical world. However, they were stupid and primitive. I could influence the world around them, but I could not directly teach them or educate them of my will. So you basically had the most severe case of human depravity without the demonic relationships."

"So your connection with the real world comes from the humans around you?"

"No, James. My connection with the real world came when I discovered that certain people granted me access into a physical existence within your realm. I had a limited amount of power, using these people as channels. I don't know why I hadn't thought of it thousands of years ago, but one day a revelation struck. I was roaming around one day, and bam! I found a little seed of mine."

James took a step back. "No. That's not possible."

He raised his eyebrows. "It isn't? Why not?"

"Because the flood destroyed your offspring."

"Ah, yes, the flood." He began walking in circles again. "If you would recall with me, James, Genesis chapter six, verse four. I believe it goes like this, 'There were giants in the earth in those days; *and also after that,* when the sons of God came in unto the daughters of men, and they bare children to them, the same became mighty men which were of old, men of renown.' You heard it yourself from the pure-blooded natives in this place. You've seen my giants first hand, and yet you doubt whether or not this is still taking place? This place has turned into a sort of workshop for me, James. An experiment. Think of me as a scientist, conducting top-secret experiments for my lord, Lucifer."

"Like the Nazis."

"Oh, I only wish I had been free enough to partake in that."

James didn't like the sudden vibes that he was receiving. Something in the atmosphere seemed to elevate- an unseen intensity was beginning to grow.

"Now, getting back to where I was before you interrupted- we were able to sneak a few more giants in there after the flood. Of course, we paid for it. Your God had us bound in darkness-"

James cut him off. "Except you."

"Yes, naturally. But you know what I've found, James? The people that I can use to exert my control are people still from those bloodlines. I brought the first here in 1687, and since then, we've just had a marvelous time. You see, I could control those people. After I had them take charge of my dumb islanders, they educated them with a language and with my will."

A lump began to rise in James' throat and sweat began to form on his brow. "You brought them here?"

He smiled. "Just like I brought you here."

James began shaking his head. "No . . . "

The image of Brian smiled. "I first met your brother, Steve, during the Vietnam war."

"No . . . "

"Yes. The nightmares you have? You were right about them too. They aren't just nightmares, they are memories- Steve's memories. The crop circle you saw here? The image in your head? That all came about through your brother. That little revelation that struck me one day? Your brother. I had found an access of power that centered around him, and it enabled me to spread my wings of influence in your world at that time. Or, more specifically, in the jungles of Vietnam. You've seen my work."

James took another step back, his prayers running scattered through his mind.

"Do you know what that means, James?"

Summoning some resolution, he spit back, "You're a liar."

He laughed, amused. "I know, we've established that. But mixing the truth in with the lie is so much more effective."

"Stop talking to me. Get-Away-From-Me!"

"Mr. Streen, you are not pure in your genealogy. And now, either you will help me, or your son will."

Joshua twisted the neck of the native until it snapped and he fell to the ground. They were coming at him from everywhere. Chris was nearby, fighting his way through them, trying to get to the entrance they had been thrown through. Joshua grabbed the knife-bearing hand of the next attacker, broke it, and threw him into the wall. Turning around in time to catch a shot to the face, he stumbled backwards and against the wall. He blocked the next blow and kicked the sky-person between the legs, dropping him immediately to his knees. Joshua then knocked him out with a roundhouse kick to the temple. Four natives jumped on him before he could get his stance prepared and he was tackled to the ground. They began punching his face, and he felt his nose break. Through blurred vision, he noticed the next fist coming down to strike him. He lifted his head into the punch and heard the native's wrist snap. He screamed and rolled off of Joshua. Then Joshua swung his feet around, taking out two of the natives' legs out from under them. Before the one native still standing could react to his sudden loneliness, Joshua brought his arms up over his head, planting his hands on the ground and pushing his lower body into the air. He wrapped his legs around the native's neck and twisted his torso, spinning the native to the ground, breaking his neck at the same time. He got back to his feet and wiped the blood out of his mouth, trying to see through the shadows who would be attacking next. When no immediate threat revealed itself, he began searching the ground for his weapons.

Chris felt his shoulder leave the joint and screamed as the large native tugged on his arm. He punched the native in the face as hard as he could, pain putting much of the force behind it. The native took a step back, stunned. Chris stepped forward and punched him in the kidney and then threw a palm into his chest, sending him stumbling backwards and falling on his back. He bent over and picked up the M-16 just in time to drain it into another charging group of blood-thirsty natives.

"So you see, I need you to help me."

"No, I don't see. I don't know what you're talking about!" James was growing frustrated and his head felt like it was going to explode. The room started to spin around him, his mind losing its grip on self-awareness.

"I used the Bermuda Triangle, as melodramatic as that may seem, to get you to this place where you can help me make the journey from this world," he spread his hands. "To yours."

"What do you mean you used the Bermuda Triangle?"

"Well, I use it quite often, really. It serves as a sort of gateway, if you would. You found the old English ship that came here in 1687, didn't you? And you found the *Milton Iatrides*. There's been a lot over the years."

James stuttered, his words not even making sense to himself. "Why?"

"Because I've been searching, James. I've been searching for people who have the blood of the Nephilim running through their veins."

Now James was struggling just to stand. "This doesn't make any sense."

Brian disappeared and turned into a grotesque demon, horns rising out of its head, saliva dripping off its teeth. "No, James, it makes perfect sense." The voice was hellish. "What I'm offering to you is something that none before could have accomplished." Its hoofed feet clanked on the ground as it walked closer to James. "I want you to be the Messiah."

James smiled, despite his clouded perception. "I believe the position is taken."

The demon smiled, revealing tiny sharp teeth protruding viciously from beneath swollen gums. "The position of Christ is taken. But not antichrist."

James chuckled. "This is the stupidest dream I've ever had," he muttered.

"This place has been entrusted to me by Lucifer, my king. I have recreated the Noahic dispensation, plus or minus a few details. Now, I am ready to transfer my creation over into your world."

James raised his head, realization finally taking a hold of him. "You're trying to bring about the end."

"My, you are a fast learner, James."

Its breath was so foul, James thought he was going to vomit.

"You are not the only one here who knows the Bible," it spat. "But as the days of Noah were, so shall also the coming of the Son of Man be. For as in the days that were before the flood they were eating and drinking, blah, blah, blah." It smiled.

"I think you've misinterpreted."

"Satan is coming to release me one day so that I can unleash this beautiful world of mine into yours. And then the prophecy will be fulfilled. Your world will experience what went on in Noah's day. And once your pathetic church is removed and the Holy Spirit no longer restrains us, your world will look just like this one."

"Aren't you forcing his hand by trying to escape on your own?" James wasn't hiding the icy edge to his voice.

"Yes, well, that stupid creature has taken far too long. If I can bring about the end, then I will do it without him."

"But you know how it ends."

The demon's eyes glared at him, yellow pupils penetrating his thoughts. "I know what your book says. But that is one prophecy that is going to change."

"I don't have time for this." James turned his back to the demon and began stumbling away.

The demon's voice caught his ears and stopped his feet. "You should see how much fun I'm having with your family."

The muscles in James' body tensed.

"If you will not help me escape this place, then maybe your son will."

"The antichrist is Jewish!" James shot back in a futile attempt to persuade himself.

"That's only one theory, James. Mine is a little different. My theory is that the antichrist will descend from a polluted blood-line. And, James, your blood-line is polluted."

"You're a liar."

"How else can you explain your being here? I brought you here, James. I couldn't do that unless there was an access of power resonating from you. And don't think it was one of your friends. I had discovered you when I discovered your brother a long time ago. Besides, I still have enough power from your brother and wife to scare the hell out of them in New York!" It laughed.

James surrendered. "Okay, fine. You want to use me to open some kind of portal to my world in which you and your experiment will crawl through? Where do we start?"

"It's not that simple, James. I wish it were, but it is not."

James groaned. "I knew it. You know what? I'm leaving." He continued stumbling away.

A three-fingered claw gripped James' shoulder, digging into the skin until blood began to flow. "You will do as I say."

James was confused. Confused as to why God was allowing this to happen, why he was even here, what he was supposed to do now. He even doubted if all this was really happening. It all sounded so absurd. Gateways and accesses to power? Layers of reality? He began speaking through a swarm of incomprehensible thoughts, spitting out the first random thoughts that inflected upon his brain. "You wrote the ransom letter. You knew I'd come. You were the man who told Lance's boss to put my brother on an island . . . "

The demon pulled its claws from James' shoulder, and James collapsed to his knees. "Well, it seems the only gateway from this world to yours is within that little area you've so appropriately called the Devil's Triangle." It turned and took a few steps away from James, its tail dragging on the ground behind it. "I couldn't just whisper commands into your ear, to make you take a boat or plane through the triangle. Imagine my surprise when your brother ends up so close."

James was on his hands and knees, trying to breathe, and spitting on the ground. "Why didn't you just use him?"

"I tried. But the little island they kept him on was just out of my reach. It took a storm to get you to stray into the right area. That's why I couldn't have Steve killed, he needed to be taken somewhere close to the triangle. And just my luck, those fools had a base of operations just outside of my reach."

"Why me?"

It shrugged and looked up into the light. "Call it your God's sovereignty, I guess. I've been waiting for an opportunity like this to come along for a very long time. Why it's you? You can thank your all-loving God for that."

"The pure-blood . . . "

"Ah, yes. The offspring of the first ones who have refused to subject themselves to my ways. Their bloodline is not tainted by my seed, their women hide from me. God must favor them, for I have searched for them almost a millennium."

James began crawling away from the demon. The demon didn't seem to mind, it just continued talking and walked beside him. He had enough information to fit all the puzzle pieces together now. The pyramids, the triangle, the crop circles . . . It all clicked now. And now, he just wanted to get out.

The demon spoke in a throaty voice. "You have enough information now to understand what is expected of you. Either you will comply, or I will kill you and will focus all my powers on bringing your son here to help me."

"You'll never get my son here."

It laughed. "Perhaps he will come to me."

James stopped crawling. "You can't honestly think my son is the antichrist."

"Why not? Someone has to be. Your son's got the blood I'm looking for."

Thoughts of escape began running frantically through James' head, but all they came to were locked doors. How could he escape from a place void of parameters? "Oh God, help me, please."

"What was that?" the demon asked.

James began crawling again, ignoring whatever the demon was saying. He had crawled for five minutes before his hand fell onto the assault rifle. The demon didn't notice. James kept crawling, silently moving the weapon along with him, trying to buy some time to come up with a plan. "Jesus . . . "

His eyes fell onto the surface beneath him and he saw his own reflection. But something else caught his eye. Looking past his reflection and through the floor, he noticed something below him, another room it appeared. Praying that it would work, he quickly got to his knees, bringing the gun up, and squeezed the trigger.

The demon laughed at the futile attempt of James' apparent intention. But the twisted smile was soon replaced by a fiery rage when it realized what James' intentions really were. Before it could react, James was gone.

TWENTY-FIVE
NEPHILIM

James found himself lying on his side staring at twenty barely clothed women. At first he thought it was another ploy, but then he noticed their physical conditions as well as the expressions they wore on their faces. He was in some sort of prison, its prisoners the captured pure-blooded women.

He tried to move and immediately felt a sharp pain in his side. His ribs were either cracked or bruised, he wasn't sure which. Rolling onto his back, he stared up into the hole he had created with his rifle. There was no light emitting from the hole, just darkness.

"Are you to save us?"

The girl's voice grabbed a hold of James' heart with two hands, squeezing the breath from his lungs and introducing a sympathetic sorrow he had never known before. He looked into the eyes of the one who had asked. Her eyes were coated with a layer of deadness, but there seamed to be a twinkle of hope that James was sure hadn't been there in a very long time. The girl's eyes told James more than she could ever convey with words, and they pulled James to his feet, drawing him to her.

"Help us, please." She was begging him, and he immediately decided that he would. Not knowing how was unimportant. He figured that these were the pure-blooded women, and that they were no threat to the pure blooded genealogy of the natives.

"Are there others?" he asked, wiping a dirty strand of hair from a bruised face.

Her swollen lips spread. "Yes. But they are with child."

"They're kept somewhere else?"

She nodded.

If any of them were pregnant, the child could be taken care of when born. James couldn't stand here and slaughter them all because one of them might be with child. "Okay, I'm going to get you out of here." He noticed that all the girls were chained to the wall. "Where is the key?"

She shook her head. "I do not know. A man comes down with it when it is time to . . . " she swallowed and a tear formed in her eye.

James put a hand on her shoulder. "It's going to be okay. There isn't going to be any more of that. I'm going to get you all out of here." He stood up, clutching his side, and looked around. Thankfully, the girls were all chained to the wall by the means of one long chain. It traveled through their crude cuffs and into the rings on the wall. All James had to do was break the chain and they would all be free from the wall. He looked for his weapon.

~~~

The corridor was littered with dead sky-people, blood flowing like a stream through the cracks in the rock floor. Joshua and Chris ran to the next entrance way and began shouting for James, but again they heard nothing in return.

"We don't have time for this!" yelled Chris. "The giants will be here any second. We need to-"

Joshua spun around to face Chris and cut him off. "To what? To cover every square inch of this place on our own, jumping through portals to God only knows where?"

The tension released from Chris as he let out a sigh and his shoulders dropped in surrender. "Then what do you want to do?"

"Stay alive as long as possible," he mumbled.

"You can make a run for the beach . . . "

Joshua shook his head. "I'm not leaving without James."

Chris smiled. "Seriously. What do we do now?"

Before Joshua could respond, the familiar pitter-patter sound of bare feet running on a stone surface caught their ears. They raised their weapons and stared into the far reaches of the corridor, waiting for the torches to illuminate their new adversaries.

The figures came into view and just before Chris squeezed the trigger, Joshua reached over and placed his hand on the barrel of the M-16, quickly lowering it to the ground.

"It's Jared." Joshua's voice was tainted with a sense of admiration.

"Are you sure?" asked Chris, still straining to see.

Before Joshua could answer, Jared was standing before them with thirty natives in his company. He was soaked in blood and there seemed to be a broken spear protruding from between his shoulder bones, yet he stood with a fire and zeal burning in his eyes. When he spoke, he spoke with conviction and steadfast purpose.
~~~

"Where is James?" he asked.

Joshua shook his head in frustration. "I don't know. He got thrown into one of these doorways." He pointed to one of the dark spots along the wall.

A look of despair briefly passed in Jared's eyes, but he took a breath and the look was gone. "No one knows where they go. It is a maze that many could get lost in . . . forever."

Chris stepped forward. "What do we do?"

"The natives outside are dead. I have a few men in other buildings. We wait now."

"Wait for what?" asked Chris.

"For the gods to reveal themselves."

James led the women down a corridor that looked exactly like the one he had been in before. He had found his rifle, Uzi, and his pistol and had shot the chain in two. Now they were running endlessly down the world's longest hallway. Five more minutes passed before James decided to grab a torch off the wall and set it on the ground. They continued running, leaving the torch to burn on the stony surface. Three minutes later they found themselves standing in front of the torch.

At that point James knew they would have to try one of the dark portals, otherwise they'd be running down this corridor for the rest of their lives. "Okay, I want everyone to go through the next entrance."

They nodded their understanding.

James stared into the portal, wondering what they would find on the other side. His body was racked with hesitation and doubt, but knowledge told him that this one was as good as any. He turned and faced the battered women. "Come on."

They bowed and cautiously walked forward, fear flickering in their eyes. But they obeyed and, one by one, they disappeared into the dark portal. After they had all gone through, James took one last look around and muttered a little prayer before throwing himself into the unknown.

Chris and Joshua were running beside Jared (half running with and half supporting his weakening frame) with the thirty pure-blooded natives following close behind when barely clothed women began falling into the hallway in front of them.

Joshua stopped running and forced everyone else behind him to do so too. "What?"

Chris raised the M-16 and instinctively rested his finger on the trigger.

But before anything else could happen James came out of nowhere and landed on top of the girls.

Leaving astonishment and relief behind, Joshua walked over to his friend. "So this is what you've been up to?"

Chris forced a smile. "You could have just told us you wanted them all for yourself. At least we wouldn't have worried so much."

James struggled to his feet and helped the girls to their feet. Then he saw Jared. From the looks of him, James couldn't believe he was still standing. "I believe these girls belong to you and your families."

Jared stepped close and examined them. And then a smile spread his lips. "Yes."

The girls looked unsure of how they would be accepted, ashamed that they had been caught. But when they saw Jared smile, they couldn't help but to feel relieved. The fear of rejection had died along with their captivity.

"How do we get out of here?" asked James.

Jared shook his head. "I do not know."

"Did you know about this place?"

Jared sighed in defeat and self-admittance. "No. The gods have created a maze. We cannot search the entire temple."

"So we concentrate on the giants?"

"Yes."

"So then let's find a way out of here." He turned and led the small army back down another corridor, contemplating which portal to jump through. He hadn't even taken five steps when one of the women reached forward and put a hand on his shoulder.

"This is the way." She was pointing to an entrance beside them.

James looked at her questioningly. "Are you sure?"

She nodded sheepishly. "Yes."

A native stepped forward and asked harshly, "How do you know this?"

In an instant her eyes transformed from shameful to aggressive. She looked straight into the native's eyes. "Because this is where they took us when they wanted us to bathe."

The native took note of the sharp tone in her voice and stepped back.

"Okay, then. Let's go." James nodded to Joshua and Joshua jumped through with Chris. After the hallway emptied into the portal, James jumped in after them.

Joshua hit the ground and grunted as the wind was knocked out of him. "There's got to be a better way of doing that."

Chris crashed down next to him and landed on his back. He moaned from the pain that suddenly erupted in his back where he'd been shot by Brian.

"You okay?" asked Joshua struggling to a standing position.

"Sure," he answered through clenched teeth, feeling the blood begin to flow down his spine.

Then the women began appearing. But they appeared standing up. There was no crash landing awaiting them.

"I knew there had to be a way . . . "

Chris held a straight face and nodded towards where the girls appeared. "You want to try it again? I'll wait."

A sarcastic grin evolved on Joshua's face. "Thanks. I'll wait until the next one."

The thirty pure-blooded natives did crash land in an avalanche of flesh. Then James landed on top of them.

Chris shook his head and looked at Joshua. "What do you think, a 2.1?"

James got to his feet and walked over to him. "Cute."

It was only then that Joshua began looking around their new location. It seemed they were in a big room. There didn't seem to be anything in the room, just an empty space chiseled from rock. "What is this place?"

A girl walked forward, her eyes taking in every detail of a place she did not like. Her voice sounded like it escaped a ghost. "This is where they rape us."

Chills ran up James' spine and a sudden exchanged glance with Joshua revealed he felt the same.

Chris stepped closer to the walls and noticed something scratched into the walls. But then he realized that they were not designs or words, but simple lines. Horror began bubbling within when he found a fingernail protruding from one of the scratch marks. He looked back at the girls and a tear began forming in his eyes as rage began festering within his body. "Where are the pregnant ones?" he asked in a choked voice.

"They stay in a special place where they are watched so that they do not kill the baby or themselves."

The answer was not what Chris was expecting and he brought a hand up to his mouth.

"I've seen enough," mumbled James. "Which way?"

One of the girls pointed into a dark corner of the room.

As they walked through the darkness, there appeared a light some distance away. "Is that the entrance?" asked Joshua.

The girl overheard his bewilderment and nodded.

"How did that happen?" James quickened his pace, closing the gap between the outside air. But something was wrong. He felt strange. He slowed down to a walk and Chris bumped into him.

"What is the matter?" asked Jared, anxious to get outside.

James looked around. "I don't know. Something's . . . "

And then they all knew. A sound of a million horrible screams rushed through the corridor and blew past them.

"What the . . . " Chris raised his weapon and swung it back and forth, frantically searching for something to shoot at.

Jared walked up beside James. "I think we should go."

James nodded, not taking his eyes off the ceiling, and agreed. "Yeah, I think you're right." Then he began to lead them quickly down the hallway again.

The temperature in the air dropped significantly in the next few seconds, and the corridor began to fill with visible breath coming from those breathing in it. James kept going, ignoring the vibrating and the screams. He felt like he was in a haunted house at an amusement park, only he knew that there would be no fake blood used in this act. As he got nearer to the entrance, he began to hear thunder pounding the atmosphere and saw lightening tearing through the sky in long branches of power. They were almost there.

A different kind of scream punctured the cold air and everyone turned around to see one of their fellow natives flying backwards down the hall, screaming in horror. Then another native was sucked out of his standing shock and drug violently along the stony ground, screaming until he disappeared into the darkness.

"Run!" James screamed. And they all obeyed. Ignoring the screams of the people in the back of the line being drug away by some unseen force, James, Chris, Joshua, and the remaining natives pushed themselves to run as fast as their legs would carry them. The entrance was just twenty yards away now.

Another scream. Joshua thought that one sounded much closer to him and he stole a quick glance over his shoulder. There were only twenty-five natives remaining, including the ten girls.

James threw himself out the entrance and into the driving rain, becoming soaked through in a matter of seconds. He jumped down the temple steps, careful to avoid slipping on them again. After going down three steps, he stopped and turned to make sure everyone had made it out okay. Joshua and Chris were trying to help the girls down the steps and the remaining fifteen natives were just emerging from within. The last pure-blooded native was half way outside when his forward momentum suddenly ceased, and he was fiercely snapped back inside the temple, his scream echoing off the corridor walls and fading into its depths.

"Oh no."

Joshua's voice managed to tear James' shocked stare away from the temple entrance and redirect it to another terrible sight. A tear slipped down James' face, indistinguishable in the rain. Lying on the step below them was John. He had a sword protruding from his chest, his eyes locked open and staring into the dark skies above. James heart sank so fast, he thought it had fallen out of him. He forced himself to swallow the lump in his throat. His mind grasped at empty space, searching for handholds of understanding, but finding nothing other than hopeless seas of shock. He was swimming through ink and trying to absorb the black waves with sheets of paper, hoping that the ink would somehow transform into a written explanation across the papers. And finally a thought struck a note and transferred his thwarted awareness to the fact that he still had three more friends to keep alive.

"I'm sorry, James." Joshua rested a quick hand on his shoulder before hopping down the next step. Chris and the natives followed, leaving James to stare in stricken grief at the man he once called uncle. James was pretty sure he would never see him again.

Joshua was half way down the temple when a huge gust of wind howled through the air and almost knocked him over. The rain was falling so hard now that it hurt. "What do we do?" screamed Joshua over what had to be a hurricane. But Jared stood transfixed, his people scattered around him the same. They were staring at something down below on the ground between the two pyramids. Joshua squinted in the rain, trying to see through the night, but all he could see was darkness.

And then a flash of lightening lit up the sky.

Chris tried to say something but nothing escaped his trembling lips. He took a step back.

James was kneeling next to John, praying. His faith suddenly seemed insignificant and even silly, and he did not hide his feeling from God. "God! If you want me to do something, tell me what it is!" He was on his knees, looking up into the sky, his arms outstretched, pleading. "Just tell me what You want from me! Do you want me to save these people? Do you want me to find Steve? Do you want me to live or die?" He screamed. "Tell me what You want me to do! I don't understand any of this nightmare You have me in! And my family! Was that all a joke? Were You teasing me? What's going to happen to them?" Then he fell onto his hands, silent. Thunder shook the temple and pounded his ears, but he didn't flinch. Finally, he began to whisper through strained vocal cords, "You need to help me out. I can't do this anymore. I can't take this. If there's something you want me to do, You're going to have to give me the strength to do it."

"James!"

Joshua's voice somehow transcended the wind and rain and made it to James' ears. He looked down to Joshua and didn't mistake the look on his face. Joshua was pointing to something below the temple. At first James couldn't see anything, but then a flash of lightening illuminated the stormy night. Standing below the temple, between the two pyramids, were giants- hundreds of them. And they did not look happy. James collapsed onto the step and leaned against the next one.

"God, I quit." He began to cry. "I can't do this." Then he stood up and shouted to the heavens. "We can't do this!" And then a voice cut through his protest. A voice James was becoming familiar with.

"I told you your God wasn't here, James."

James didn't even bother to look for the demon, instead he screamed out to God. "God! Are You here? Show us that You're in this place! Please!" Then time stopped. James moved his head back and forth, suddenly feeling like he was in a special effects segment of a sci-fi movie. Everything around him had stopped, frozen in time. Billions of rain drops hung suspended in air, the ones striking the ground paused in explosion. A bolt of lightening remained painted against the dark sky. James moved forward and walked down to Joshua and Chris.

"What is this?" asked Chris looking around.

"This is when God intervenes," James stated.

The three Christians studied the frozen natives who were leaning forward and preparing themselves to attack. The giants below were locked in twisted hatred, their mouths paused in open shouts of frustration and death.

James grabbed Chris and Joshua by the arm and pulled them close. "I think we need to pray."

So there they stood, three men gathered together in an evil land facing death, time stopped around them, God getting their attention. Then, suddenly, a hole began to tear open the sky. The darkness of night was peeled back as if it were a mere prop on a set of actors. A blinding brightness shone through the hole and engulfed everything. It was so radiant that James, Chris, and Joshua had to turn away and bury their faces from the brilliance. When they finally looked again, they could barely make out forms flying through the air, rushing towards the giants.

"Are those angels?" Joshua's voice was filled with awe.

James and Chris just stood in amazement watching the celestial beings emerge from the brightness.

"Oh my . . . " For the first time in his life, Joshua had a feeling of God's holiness. The brightness that seemed to engulf everything felt as if it was going to erase him. He dropped to his knees as an incredible conviction grabbed a hold of his heart and mind.

A story flashed through James' mind and brought his head up and shoulders back. Confidence and faith began burning within as he recalled, once again, the story of David's mighty men and of Jonathan and his armor bearer. And then God seemed to whisper a verse into his ear. It was that verse that sealed his purpose and rang out as clear as day in his soul. *"For there is no restraint to the Lord to save by many or by few."*

And just like that the light disappeared, the rain continued to fall, and lightning flashed through the sky to a chorus of thunder. The natives began moving down to the ground, but a huge gust of wind threw them all down.

Joshua stood up with a new motivated urgency charging through his veins. "I'll go find a tree to climb into and spend the rest of the Remington's ammo. You and Chris find a nearby spot to empty all the ammo you have into those things. Make sure our native friends don't turn on you and make sure they don't attack before you're done shooting. We'll kill them all in the weather." And then he turned and jumped down the remaining stairs, disappearing into the hurricane.

James had to run fast to catch up to Jared and stopped him from going any further. "Wait! You guys use your arrows from a distance!" It was hard to hear over the wind and rain, impossible when thunder sounded. "We're going to use our weapons! It's important that you don't get in the way of them! Do you understand?"

Jared nodded. "How will we know when to attack?"

James flashed a white smile. "When you hear our weapons stop."

Then James and Chris ran around to the other side of the temple and made their way down to the ground, using a pyramid for cover. They then turned up and sprinted into the woods, trying to ignore the trees that were bending almost to the point of breaking.

Joshua stared through the optical lens, seeing everything below him in a wash of green. Without the night-vision, there would be no way to see anything. He rested the cross-hairs over the head of a giant and began to squeeze the trigger when he decided better about it. The giants looked as if they were contemplating charging the temple and wiping out the natives. If he shot a giant in the front line, they might mistake the direction of the assault as coming from the natives, and then they would surely attack and wipe away any attempt that he had at avoiding pure-blooded casualties. He shifted the rifle to the back of the mass and shot a giant between its glowing green eyes. Joshua watched the drama of death play out on the giant's face. First there was curiosity, then doubt, then denial, then fear, then unbelief. The giant looked around for whatever it was that could have caused its injury. But another shot to the temple sent it into the mud.

Joshua had reasoned right. When the giant fell, the entire gathering turned their backs to the natives and examined their fallen comrade. Then arrows started to fall, striking them in the back. They turned, raising swords, and began to charge the temple. A disturbing noise that was their battle cry seemed to drown out the thunder and shake the ground itself. Joshua quickly took more shots at the advancing army as it began passing by him on the ground below. The wind was so strong that his aim was affected, and he had to take time to compensate before each shot. He dropped another giant, but it fell unnoticed by the others. It's all over, he thought.

But then the familiar sound of machine gun fire erupted from the other side of the clearing, by the other pyramid, and the giants abruptly stopped. Joshua watched through the lens as Chris and James' assault fanned across the multitude and filled the stormy air with showers of splattering blood. But none seemed to be falling. Joshua continued shooting.

Jared sighed in relief. He was sure that the giants were going to storm the temple and kill them all. But the loud weapons from the strangers distracted them and now they looked confused. Jared hoped they would split up. A few seconds later, his wish seemed to be granted.

James couldn't see anything. He just sprayed the area he knew was full of giants until his clip ran dry. Then he replaced it with another one and kept going. He would be out of ammo for the assault rifle in half a minute. "I'm almost out!" he screamed to Chris, who was finishing up his ammo for the 16.

A flash of lightening suddenly granted them a glimpse at their progress, and the half second window of vision was enough to linger in their heads for the next few minutes. Scores of giants were being moved unwillingly by the streams of hot lead that were coursing through their huge bodies. Thankfully, none of these giants seemed to be adorned in the armor the ones guarding the temple entrance were. The bullets were doing their job. However, the next flash of lightening revealed that none had fallen to the ground yet.

"Is this doing anything?" screamed Chris.

James dropped the empty assault rifle to the ground and took the Uzi off his back. "Keep shooting!"

Another bolt ripped through the violent skies.

"They're splitting up!" Chris yelled.

"Good! We might have a better chance if we can scatter them and spread them out into the woods!"

"What do you want to do?" Chris threw the M-16 to the ground and began shooting the assault rifle he had taken from John's dead body.

"Wait out the weather if we can!"

Chris shot him a doubtful look. "Those natives aren't going to stand much of a chance against them. Even if God grants us a miracle victory, what use is it if there's no one left to save?"

James continued firing the Uzi from his hip. He had already replaced the clip twice and was on his last one now. "I'm almost down to my pistol! We can't fight them with swords in an open field in the dark!"

A nearby tree cracked in half with the loud sound of exploding wood and was carried by the violent winds onto the field and rolled towards the giants.

"This is crazy! We need to find shelter!"

James shook his head in protest. "You said it yourself, if we wait then the pure-blood stand no chance!"

A bolt of lightening struck a tree across the field from them, and the fire was immediately put out by the strong winds and pouring rain.

"I hope that wasn't the tree Joshua was in," James said.

Chris grabbed James' shoulder. "I'm out of ammo. I've got two pistols and that's it. Joshua has the other assault rifle and the shotgun!"

"What about the other sub-machine gun?"

"I don't know!"

Then a defined 'click' noise signaled the end of the Uzi's onslaught. James dropped it and looked towards the temple. "I can't tell if they're still shooting arrows!"

"If the giants were splitting up, then maybe the natives changed plans!"

"I hope so! If they follow my orders, then they'll be attacking any second! That'll force us to join!"

"There's no way to tell how effective we were! We may not have hindered one of them!"

James was spitting mouthfuls of rain water out of his mouth and holding on to a tree, the wind trying to peel his face off. "Didn't Jared say there were more natives in the pyramids?"

Chris nodded. "Yeah!"

"Let's head towards them! Hopefully, Jared will do the same once he sees the giants are splitting up and scattering!"

"Yeah, assuming he could see!"

They headed back through the woods towards the pyramid, staying as low as they could, trying to dodge the pieces of debris they couldn't see blowing through the air like shrapnel.

Joshua took the scope off the rifle and let the rifle fall to the ground below him. He wiped away the blood that was running from his head due to a sharp stick that the storm had thrown at him. He managed to attach the scope to the assault rifle and brought it up to continue his work. But what he saw when he looked through the scope was not what he was expecting, and he almost fell out of the tree. Beyond the crosshairs, were twenty green giants running in his direction, glowing eyes staring right at him.

"Oh man." Joshua didn't even waste time trying to stop them from coming. He threw the assault rifle over his shoulder and began making his way down the tree. Half way down his foot slipped on a wet branch and he fell the rest of the way, bouncing off of branches for fifteen feet. He landed hard on his stomach and the air in his lungs was long gone. He gasped for air but none came. Clawing the mud around him, he struggled for just one breath, but his lungs seemed stuck together like plastic wrap. He rolled over onto his back, beginning to see bright spots in his vision, and cried out to God for His help. And then his lungs expanded and air came rushing back through his throat. "Thank You . . . thank You . . . " He got to his feet, also thankful that nothing seemed broken, and began running through the woods. He needed a place to hide.

When Jared noticed the giants breaking up, he immediately ordered all his men, and the women, to skirt around to the other side of the temple. Once they were on the backside, he ordered three of his men to escort the women to a safe spot where they could wait out the battle. They had disappeared into the jungle leaving Jared wondering if he'd ever see them again. One of the girls was his wife.

"Into the woods!" he cried to his men. "Break up and spread us apart! We wait until morning to attack!" Just as he finished his order, three giants came storming around the side of the temple stairs and began running for the group of natives. Jared grabbed three of his best men. "You stay with me!" Then he turned to the others. "Go and hide until morning! At first light, attack them with all strength and determination! Our future rests on you all! Now go!"

The natives only hesitated for a minute before responding and turning away from the three giants, leaving their leader and three brothers behind to die. They had just made it to the bottom of the temple when the three giants met with the four pure-bloods.

James felt his way to the pyramid's entrance, hoping there wouldn't be a small army of sky-people waiting for them. They entered the protection of the ancient structure, finding both protection from nature and seclusion. There was no one else to greet them. That wasn't to say that there weren't assassins lurking in the shadows waiting to overtake them though. James and Chris moved carefully through the dimly lit passageways of the pyramid.

"What do you think we'll find in here?" asked Chris, keeping his following distance as close to James as possible without walking on his heels.

James answered incredulously. "Is this a new game you've invented?"

Chris didn't answer but drew his two pistols. He noticed James didn't have the sword he was carrying before, and Chris couldn't remember what happened to his either. "Hey James, how we gonna' know which natives are with us?"

James didn't bother to turn and answer. "Rules of engagement. I guess we'll just have to react."

Chris didn't like that at all. It was just another complication dumped onto an already endless supply mounted against them. He searched the walls of the pyramid, wondering where the path they were on would lead.

Joshua was still running, despite the fact that the feeling had left his legs minutes ago. He could hear the giants crashing through the woods behind him, gaining on him. His breathing was shallow, his lungs arguing with his body, condemning it for subjecting them to this kind of stress. He slipped on a rock and landed on his face again. He ignored the pain, adrenaline his only power, and kept going, wondering if he stood any chance of making it. He had no goal, no destination. He was running blindly through the jungle in a hurricane being chased by twenty giants that were feeding off his fear. There seemed to be no escape. An impact across his chest sent his feet straight into the air and he landed on his back. If the ground wasn't deep with mud, he may not have gotten back up. The nearing sound of blades slicing through trees spurred him to move again, and this time he ducked below the fallen tree. He was being blasted by jungle debris on every side. Sticks, thorns, stones, branches, even animals were being thrown at him by the powerful winds. He knew it was only a matter of time before a gust caught him and lifted him off his feet, breaking his back against a tree. He had to get out of the jungle. He had to get to the shore. And then a plan struck him just as lightening struck a nearby tree.

There in the center of the room was some sort of decorated coffin set on display. Candles were littered throughout the whole room, the walls adorned with artwork.

"I wonder who this guy was," questioned Chris, offhandedly, while studying the drawings illuminated by the candles.

James walked close and ran his fingers over the marble lid. He replayed the demon's conversation in his mind but came up empty as to who could have been so important. Then he looked at Chris.

Chris turned to face James just in time to catch the look on his face. "What?"

"I . . . " He stopped and laughed. How could one put this in words without sounding crazy? "When I disappeared in the temple, I ended up having a conversation with this . . . demon."

Chris' brow furrowed.

"You're not going to understand, but this demon, or whatever, is attempting to transfer this world of his into ours."

"Okay," he stated in confusion.

"There's a verse in the Bible that suggests that when the Lord comes back, the times on earth will be just like the times of Noah. Now, whether or not that means the details of Noah's day or just the fact that the people were self-consumed and not perceptive of God's warnings of a flood, scholars argue. But the things we see in this place are things that the book of Genesis talks about."

"The giants?"

James nodded. "Yeah. In Hebrew they are called Nephilim."

"Oh."

"This demon thinks that the antichrist will come from the bloodline of the Nephilim."

"So that's why it's producing so many? Trying to find one that falls from its momma' with a pitchfork?"

"Actually, no. From what I gather, it thinks the antichrist will descend from the bloodline of the Nephilim in our world. This world and everything in it has nothing to do with ours. It wants to change that by finding a relative of the original Nephilim and get him into this place. It thinks that with a descendant of an original Nephilim here from our world, it will have the key to opening a portal in which it can transfer its Noahic army into our world, led by the antichrist and bring about the end."

Chris scratched his head. "I see. So, the Bermuda Triangle . . . "

"It's been searching. Remember the strangers that come here? That Jared told us the gods want? That's why. It's looking for a very specific person."

A look of realization flashed in his eyes, and he eyed James suspiciously. "The ransom note?"

James nodded. "It thinks that I have the blood of the Nephilim."

"Do you?"

James laughed sarcastically. "I don't know, Chris. How should I know? You know any family trees that go back 6,000 years?"

"Are you what it wants?"

James shook his head. "No. I'm a Christian. It tried for Steve, but it miscalculated. So in an act of desperation, it set me up, and now it's suggesting that my unborn son may be the person it's really looking for to free it from this place."

"Oh."

The doubt in Chris' voice was not foreign to his own feelings. "I know. This is all so crazy."

"But, if it's trapped here, how did it discover you and set you up?"

"Apparently, the way it discerns which humans are descendants of the forbidden union is according to its degree of power centering around the individual."

"So these people act as a power source in our world?"

James stifled a yawn, suddenly feeling exhausted. "It told me that it has no influence in our world, it can only witness the passing of time, like watching a movie. But it told me that when it gets close to one of these 'unpure-blooded' people, a small degree of influence opens."

"You think if I turned you in, it'd let me go back to earth?"

James laughed politely. "If I thought that would work, I'd have turned myself in a long time ago."

There was suddenly a sound that captured both their eyes and drew them to the center of the chamber. It came from the marble coffin.

"What was that?" Chris asked, fearing the implication of his own question.

James walked closer to the coffin. "I don't know." And then the marble lid began sliding away from the coffin. James jumped back, fear erasing any thought of exhaustion.

"Should we go?"

James moved his head away from the opening coffin and stole a quick glance down the corridor that they had taken to reach the chamber. It was dark. Only five minutes ago torches lit the entire way. Now those torches were out. "I don't think so."

Chris couldn't imagine why not and imitated James' deductive reasoning, hoping he would understand the conclusion. When he saw the dark corridor he understood.

"Whatever comes out of that thing is not going to be nice." James took the safety off his pistol, wondering if it would make a difference.

Despite the tension buzzing in the air, Chris managed a wiry smile.

"Really? I was under the impression that really nice dead people stepped out of opening coffins."

Before James could respond, something to his right caught his eye, and he knew, even while turning, that there was nothing there but the stone wall. The hair on his neck stood straight. It was becoming a new style.

Though James had most of his back to it, Chris was facing it and watched it come straight out of the wall. His heart leapt in his chest and then bewilderment wrestled it. Standing before them in the chamber was a man wearing a business suit, a mustache fashionably trimmed to the corners of his thin and tightly pressed lips. There was an evil smile pulling at one side of the mouth, and the eyes seemed taunting.

"Hello, fellows." The man raised his hand and directed the attention back to the center of the room. "May I introduce Martin?"

The man had distracted James and Chris from the opening coffin and, now returning their attention to it, they were horrified to see a skeleton sitting upright from within it.

Joshua was retracing the path they had taken to get to the temple. He had already passed two of the villages they had wiped out and was fast approaching the next. Making sure the giants stayed on his trail made things much more problematic as one bad spill could have them on top of him before he could recover. But in order for his plan to work, they had to be chasing him.

Through the hurricane, he could make out the sound of rushing water and knew he had found the stream, now an overflowing river. He ran towards the sound until he reached the newly made edge. The rushing waters had knocked out a lot of land, expanding its width. Joshua looked back through the pouring rain, waiting to get a glimpse of the giants. Lightening lit up the sky and he saw the giants just thirty yards away. And they saw him. Joshua jumped into the raging waters.

The man laughed at Chris' response to the skeleton. "This is the man who helped me start it all." He shook his head and lowered his voice. "Obviously, he's dead." Walking closer to James, he smiled behind hopeful eyes. "So I need a replacement."

"Just use one of your Nephilim," stated James.

"No, no, it must be a person within your realm of reality, a true descendant of the bloodline."

Chris' fingers were itching on the triggers of the pistols, and he was waiting for an excuse to use them.

The business-clad demon noticed. “Do not even think about it, Christopher Roberts.”

Chris hesitated, not sure what kind of behavior the situation called for. And then the man before him changed into a dragon-like creature, breathing smoke and walking on talons.

“So your little experiment could only go so far with Martin. Once he died, you were left with nothing to do but play with your own creation.” James was no longer intimidated by the demon’s vast array of images.

“I need a power source that I can channel through to directly interact.”

“You said that the natives had no language until you could teach them.”

“That is true.”

“That’s not what they told us.”

“They had a primitive dialogue based on sounds. Their writing was more of an art class. The fools sounded like apes. It was a beautiful thing when English Martin here showed up.”

James looked at Martin, who was beginning to develop a coating of skin, and asked, “Who was he?”

The dragon made a noise that was figured to be a laugh. “He was the leader of a cult group called *The Community of the Beast.* He was very effective in his day. It was very hard to get him here.”

Chris was very confused and couldn’t take his eyes off of the regenerating skeleton. He stammered through his question. “Why are you telling us all this?”

The dragon shifted into another image- the image of the girl that came from the *Milton Iatrides.* There was a pleasurable gleam in her eyes as she noticed Chris’ horrified response. “No doubt you have a million of your American movies playing through your mind. Well, to dispel that thought, I will just say this: there is nothing that I can tell you that would change anything. I am spiritual, you cannot kill me, so I am in no immediate danger. There is nothing you could do with the information that would bring harm to me. No, Christopher, I tell you the truth because watching you die with confusion in your eyes is not as satisfying as watching you die in hopelessness.”

Chris raised the gun, it was trembling in his grasp. “Stop it.”

James attempted to warn Chris of the futile threat, but it was too late, Chris had fired three shots at the girl. She shattered into a swarm of dust and disappeared. They looked around the room, searching for it to reappear. But the only thing they saw was a man standing before them, a man that had died 300 years ago.

“Either you will help me, or your son will. Do not think that you can stop my armies, it is useless to resist. Death is your only other option." The voice rebounded off the walls and then faded away.

"You may have missed the angels that just showed up," responded James with an edge in his voice.

Laughter erupted and echoed off the stone. "Angels? Chosen angels? They do not come to this place, James. I am sorry, but you are on your own. In the meantime, I will leave you to get acquainted with an old relative."

Then Martin took a step towards them and his lips pulled into a thin, blood-thirsty, grin. He threw his hand up, and they were thrown backwards, tumbling down the corridor and into blackness. As they came to a stop and attempted to regain their bearings, they could hear the sound of walking feet growing eerily closer. They could also hear Martin's evil laugh traveling through the humid air, coming to get them.

Joshua was on his hands and knees, fighting to crawl into the wind. He imagined his pants would be ripped off his body any second and his eyes blinded by the pelting sand. The ocean was a fierce display of powerful chaos, waves thundering against the land and tearing apart the beach. The *Milton Iatrides* was still firmly imbedded in the beach, its mammoth proportions still held trapped due to the years of persistent tides. The waters were raging around it though, waves exploding against her body and rushing over what deck was still visible. Joshua knew he would be taking a huge risk at trying to board her, but it was his only chance. He crawled to the surf and forced himself to his feet, pushing himself against the wind like he was pushing a lineman at the scrimmage line. Thunder exploded the exact instant a bolt of lightening ripped through the sky and reflected off the sadistic waves below. Joshua saw the twenty footer right before it curled over and crashed into the water, creating another wave that flew over his head and engulfed him in tropical waters, propelling him back in vertigo towards the beach. The wave threw him into the ground without remorse and the wind was knocked out of him once again. The next wave was merciful and carried him up onto the beach where he fought to regain his breath.

With fatigued agony, he wiped wet sand off his face and peered at the tree line through the wall of rain and darkness. And lightning allowed him to see the shapes of large people exiting the jungle. He stumbled back to his feet and ran towards the ocean with everything he had, screaming at the top of his lungs, and threw himself into the rage. He disappeared below the surface and attempted to swim towards the freighter without being tossed around at the exterior, but his theory was fatally wrong. The strong riptides and undertows were working together in an insane effort to destroy the ocean's floor, and Joshua was flung about like a rag doll. Reflexively, he opened his eyes, but saw nothing but complete darkness. He reached out towards the ground, but he felt nothing but water and knew he had no idea which way the surface was. He began to see flashing light in the corners of his vision and his lungs burned for air. He couldn't believe he was going to die like this, drowning in the ocean. But then again, he thought, that's what should have happened to begin with. And then he was thankful for the longevity of his life and the salvation he had discovered since. He opened his mouth, prepared to take in a torrent of salt water in his body's last attempt to discover air when he was thrown into the submerged railing of the ship. He ignored the pain that electrocuted his body and grabbed onto the railing, new hope suddenly pushing his body past the limits of normalcy. He didn't know how long he was under water, but he knew that at no time as a SEAL had he come even close to matching it. He pulled himself upward until his head broke the surface and inhaled all the air he could, swallowing a wave at the end. He vomited into the waters and held on to the railing as tight as he could, the ocean tenaciously pulling the rest of his body away from his tight grip.

He finally made it onto the flooded deck and pulled himself towards the entrance to the ship using a firm hold on the rail. He squeezed through the open doorway and made his way into the dark depths of the flooding ship. Finding a narrow corridor, he un-shouldered the shotgun and slid down a wall, sitting on the wet and tilted floor. He pumped the shotgun and pulled the box of shells out of the cargo pocket of his ragged pants. He rested the gun in his lap, aimed towards the tiny corridor in front of him and, for the first time in a while, concentrated on breathing. His large chest was rising rapidly over his eager lungs. He leaned his head back against the ship's body and waited.

The dead Englishman, Martin, was having his way with James and Chris. Of course it helped that he was exhibiting supernatural powers and seemed unfazed by any attack that was mustered by the two Americans.

James was being held above the possessed man and soon found himself sailing through the air and fast approaching the stone wall. He crashed into it and fell into a heap.

Chris dodged an arrogant knockout blow, stepped into Martin, and thrust his open palm into the man's Adam's apple. Martin choked and struggled to grab his neck, but Chris broke his nose with a straight shot before he could react. Martin stumbled backwards, but Chris wasn't planning on granting him recovery time. He stepped into Martin again, kicking him between the legs and striking him in the chin with an uppercut as he collapsed to his knees. Martin blacked out and fell to his side.

James struggled to his feet, a wide smile on his face. "Wow."

Chris shook his hand, his knuckles stinging. "Dead freak." He turned around to face James but stopped when he saw a shadow stretch across the wall and come up behind him. He had just enough time to brace for the impact.

James pulled out his pistol and shot Martin in the head as Chris slid by him on the floor. But if Martin had felt any pain, he ignored it. The blood that was running down his face made it to his lips, and he glided a tongue over them, smiling.

James grabbed Chris and pulled him to his feet. "Come on, we're leaving!"

But just before they started their getaway, they were lifted into the air and suspended. The unseen force turned them around so that they were facing Martin. He had a sword in his hand.

"What do we do?" asked Chris, desperately.

"Pray."

Martin began walking closer to them, twirling the sword in his hands. The gleam of the blade, from reflecting torchlight behind him, matched the gleam in his eyes.

"Out loud!" shouted James.

"What?"

"Pray out loud!"

Chris shook his head and scrambled his mind to react. "Oh God," he stammered, his words etched together in ignorant knowledge. "Please save us from this enemy that is taunting Your children! Use us as Your instruments to deliver the people from the works of darkness . . . "

James began praying too.

Martin suddenly slowed in his approach, suspicion and uncertainty replacing arrogant pride. His eyes began shifting about the room as if he detected another unseen presence.

" . . . And God, I pray that You teach me how to live! Give me a second chance at life! I thank You for dying for me! I don't know much, but I know that the cross has power over hell, and now I ask You to reveal that in a physical way!"

They both fell to the ground, suddenly released by the invisible force.

Martin screamed, ignoring his fears, and charged with sword held high.

Chris ran towards the man, still praying. Martin swung the sword downward, aiming to cut Chris in half vertically. But Chris anticipated the move and side-stepped the attack, thrusting a side-armed punch to the throat. Continuing to move with his momentum, Chris then swung his other arm around, and bent it around Martin's neck, pulling his feet out from under him.

"And God, I pray that you make that beautiful girl from the boat fall in love with me!" Then he lifted his foot and brought it down as hard as he could on Martin's neck, a sick sound echoing in the pyramid. "And God, one more thing. I pray that Martin doesn't get up again."

And then, right before their eyes, Martin's flesh disintegrated off old yellow bones, leaving a skeleton lying on the ground.

James bent over, took a firm hold on the skull, and yanked it off the vertebrae. Then he threw it against the wall, shattering it into a hundred pieces. He wiped his hands together and mumbled, "Amen."

They came thumping through the small corridors of the old freighter, squeezing their bodies closer to where Joshua sat waiting, blood-thirsty battle cries echoing off the ship and mixing terrifyingly with the hurricane attempting to swallow the rest of the *Milton Iatrides*.

Joshua waited until he could smell them before firing the shotgun. The first blast caught the leading giant in the neck and the second separated it. It crumpled to the ground, the frenzy of the others pushing and trampling it, desperately trying to squeeze by. Joshua didn't stop firing until he had to reload. As his shaking hands slid shells into the bottom of the shotgun, the giants were beginning to tear apart the three huge corpses that blocked the corridor before them. Their frustration made Joshua get to his feet and run down the corridor, putting more distance between him and the monsters that wanted to rip him apart limb by limb.

The obstacle was cleared and the remaining giants were running again. Joshua aimed the shotgun and blew apart the face of the first, and, as it dropped, fired three shots into the wall of muscle that was pushing past the corpse. Again there was a pile-up in the small corridor and again the giants had to make their way through it. But this time Joshua didn't run. Instead, he replaced the shotgun with the assault rifle and switched it to AUTO. He held down the trigger, aiming at the mass of fighting flesh squeezing through the confined space of rusted steel. The hallway lit up with bright flashes and shadows were cast disfigured all over the place. Hot shells bounced off the walls and floor while a steady stream of lead sunk into the mountain trying to squeeze past itself. Blood and flesh was splattered all over the corridor by the time the last bullet in the magazine was spent. Joshua quickly replaced it with his last, pulling it from his back pocket, and ran deeper into the ship. It was too dark to tell whether he was heading for the aft or the stern, and he could recall no great distinguishable sight that would have told him before. The sound of enraged giants followed him all the way through the hallway and down the ladder.

The first giant stepped over the hole, attempting to use the ladder, but Joshua sprayed enough lead upward that the massive giant let loose his grip on the metal rungs and plummeted to the ground at Joshua's feet. After two more giants met the same fate, they stopped coming. They would have to find another way to get to Joshua. And, since Joshua's assault rifle had run out of ammo, he couldn't be more relieved. He sat against the ship's steel, keeping the ladder within reasonable distance, and closed his eyes. Somehow, fear, adrenaline, and fatigue had struck a deal, and his world slowly dissolved into blackness. Thoughts of the giants returning were quietly executed as sleep welcomed him with arms open wide.

Though the thoughts racing through Chris' head were far from the pyramid, there was at least some degree of fascination born from the images his eyes beheld. His mind tried to grapple two different thoughts at the same time, his mind pulling his brain one direction while his emotion was strongly pulling it in another. The process was confusing and overwhelming.

"This is incredible." James' tone of voice displayed that same sense of incredulous awe that seemed to have become the normal way of talking.

Chris agreed, trying to steer his mind to James' comment and away from the woman he was sure was in danger. Even though he had no tangible evidence to back him up, he swore that the demon interpreting itself as the girl was directly aimed at him- a message. All that Chris wanted to do was get to her, but even if he could make it to her alive, he still didn't know where she was.

James moved the torch over the painted wall. After searching the pyramid in its entirety, they had found one other room. The fact that it was empty had struck James' curiosity and he was soon attempting to discover the room's purpose. He had found it written on the walls under torchlight. Some kind of hieroglyphics was drawn all over the wall, and, though they were in a foreign form of expression, since they were more pictures than words, it was simple to understand the message it was meant to convey.

"It looks like a recreation of Genesis." James moved the light to a better position, illuminating the artistic timeline. He pointed to two figures that seemed to be drawn having intercourse, a dozen figures sketched below them signifying the multiplying of their seed. "Adam and Eve . . . begot sons and daughters . . . "

Chris moved closer to examine the crude portrayal of the beginning. "Isn't there supposed to be a special tree or something? Didn't Adam and Eve eat an apple they weren't supposed to?"

James moved the light back and forth, his eyes searching frantically. "Yeah, but I don't see any record of a fall or something that would have introduced the state of this evil."

"Then I guess it's not Adam and Eve?"

"Let's see if . . . " He moved down the wall. The next images were of people working and constructing make-shift huts, killing animals, and fighting each other.

"Life goes on," stated Chris, dryly.

James continued walking. If his conversations with the demon could be trusted, then during this whole time it was unable to directly influence the people. But the next image showed a boat on the shore with a group of men walking on the water. "Interesting," James mumbled.

"There's your introduction to evil."

"Look at the way they're walking on the water. A symbol of deity or power?" He continued on to an image that portrayed the group of men teaching the people. By the mouths being exaggerated and their tongues depicted as moving, it was clear that what the men were teaching them was a language . . . A language both Chris and James knew to be English.

Now Chris began to focus on the history, wondering how far it could have gone and wondering when it could have been recorded. "Whoever did this had to have done it after the fact. It's all done in the same format despite a recorded language shift."

James nodded. "And who would start recording a beginning that had no significance?"

Chris swallowed the lump in his throat and wondered what exactly they were going to find on this wall.

"Look," said James.

The wall suddenly took on a weird look, almost a psychedelic look, portraying deified figures coming from the sky and commanding the people. But the group of men from the boat were no longer in the pictures.

"Where'd they come from?" asked Chris.

James was too struck to answer. He stared at the images of these glowing men forcing women into having sex with them. Then, beneath them, were drawn giants.

"Wow." Chris grabbed James' hand and moved it to his right, shedding more light onto the wall.

Next was a collage of pictures depicting crop circles, more sex, giants building something that was probably the temple, and also a small group of men throwing spears at the glowing figures. But the next art work showed the rebels being chased by the giants, who had chains extending from their necks up and into the hands of the flying deified men. And then everything was scribbled, as if the person recording the history was in a rage while they were drawing. The people were portrayed as chaotically killing each other and raping each other. The picture was disturbing.

James side-stepped along the wall, revealing more of the mysterious history with the torch, and Chris followed close by, peering over his shoulder.

"More boats." Chris was pointing over James' shoulder.

"This was definitely an aftermath portrayal." James concluded this by the fact that the boats were presented next to each other. An ignorant concept of airplanes was also sketched. As the flame moved, the scene played out. People looked to be running from the boats and planes and into the jungle as men floating in the sky seemed to be chasing them. The next act looked like a meeting between the same people that came from the boats and planes and one of the flying men. But then the flying man points to the ground with an angry expression and the next scene is of all those men having their heads cut off by men in loincloths. There was another sketch scribbled underneath that whole scene that included figures eating with a person from the boat underground. Then they escort him into the woods where they bow to the floating man and the floating man shoots lightening at the man from the boat. James knew that was the scenario Jared had described to them.

The light danced on the end of the torch and the room shifted in an array of twisted shadows, eerily accompanying the artistic portrayal of an evil record. The next drawing showed seven men on the beach. The next presentation of them was at a crop circle. Then one of them was in the crop circle.

The paint was peeling and faded at this part, but there was no mistaking it. The seven people were back together on the beach, and they were all carrying guns.

"Oh man." James brushed his hand over the paint but only removed a layer of dust.

Chris stared at the hand print that James left in the dusty picture. "You don't think . . . "

James moved along the wall.

"It is." Chris began looking around the room, feeling the familiar touch of his pistols under his fingers.

James hurried to the end of the room, the torch flickering violently as the air fueled it. And there they were.

Portrayed on the ancient wall were two figures, one holding a torch, staring at a wall inside a pyramid. But it was the countless sketched giants that were surrounding the pyramid, hiding in the nearby woods, that made James drop the torch.

TWENTY - SIX

FINAL BATTLE

The rain slowed and the clouds parted, allowing the rising sun to shine across the shattered land. The hurricane's violence had escalated throughout the night and into the early morning, smashing the island without remorse. Trees were scattered all over the terrain, fields of grass smashed and beat into the water that now covered them. Not one hut had survived and even the more sturdy log cabins now lay in a mess of logs. The jungle looked as if God had gone through it with a giant weed-whacker. Dead sea life was piled on the sand at the jungle's edge.

Bodies of natives and giants were strewn across the broken landscape. The fury of the wind had either crushed them into fixed objects or pulverized them with flying debris. But there were those who had made it through the nightmare alive, and they began to regroup and prepare for the next stage in this battle for survival.

Joshua's eyes fluttered open, but only darkness greeted them. As his body awoke, he struggled for a firm grasp on the handles of recollection, attempting to recall with clarity what his mind was disorienting with fatigue. Once a firm hold on self-awareness was finally gained, the recollection that came with it drove him to his feet and up the rusted ladder.

The ship was completely dark, and Joshua had to use the end of the shotgun to feel his way through its steel passageways. Forgetting the path traveled, he wandered aimlessly through the old freighter, looking for signs of daylight. Though awake with adrenaline pumping, his mind was still miles from a place of complete control. And the darkness that pressed him from every angle did not help formulate a degree of management. Also running confused in his mind were the giants he had failed to kill. His senses were blazing in anticipation, waiting to hear a sound that would signal their terrifying presence. But then something about that thought struck a chord, and the note it sounded stopped Joshua in his tracks. His brain began to swim through the vague details of the night before, assuming the day had changed over, and he recalled dead giants littering the cramped corridor. He also remembered the giants that had fallen down the ladder and immediately knew that they were not there when he had woken up. He turned and ran, as fast as perpetual blindness would allow, back the way he had come. Reaching the bottom of the ladder, he concluded what he had feared- they were gone. A new zeal for daylight accompanied him up the ladder this time.

The darkness toyed with the concept of passing time and made minutes feel like hours. After what seemed like days, Joshua found himself in a room littered with all kinds of debris floating in the few inches of water that was swallowing his feet. He bent over and grabbed a hold of a floating object. He immediately recognized it as a book. Standing up, he walked to the closest wall and felt a tipped bookcase lying on the ground. He wished he had a flashlight. And then his memory smacked his brain and cursed his stupidity. He slammed his fist into the wall, realizing that he had left the night vision scope attached to the empty assault rifle which was still at the bottom of the ladder. He would have to go back and get it.

He swore another day had passed before he was back in the same room with the night scope. He switched it on and the room suddenly became visible in a wash of green. Books and clothes were floating in the water, the dressers and shelves that had once contained them, overturned. Joshua examined the room, not sure what he was looking for, but knowing as soon as he saw it.

He sloshed through the water and bent over a small table that was knocked onto its side. The drawer was half way open, but no water had seeped in to destroy its contents. Joshua opened the drawer and pulled out the black book.

Holding the pistol out in front of him, his left hand clasped around the bottom of the handle to steady it, James cautiously exited the pyramid. He walked bent low to the ground, sweeping his aim back and forth. Chris followed out after him with two pistols in hand, wrists crossed. They had anticipated being surrounded by giants as the picture had portrayed, but, as of yet, there was no sign of anything other than debris spread over a landscape that was painted under a calm sunny sky.

"This is kinda' freakin' me out," whispered Chris as he took note of the stillness that seemed louder than the hurricane the previous night.

James walked by him and into the woods. "Come on."

They ran through the woods until they came upon a pile of spent shells.

Then they cast their gaze out across the same field where the giants had gathered together the night before. There were no Nephilim bodies lying amidst the clutter of broken branches and other jungle debris.

"You can't be serious." Chris stepped out onto the field that he knew had been covered by streams of deadly hot lead, yet there was nothing to prove it.

A sudden twinge of hopelessness sank James' heart into his stomach, but before he could dispel it, an arrow whistled through the air and stabbed the tree beside him. He turned and dove to the ground seeking shelter from the trees. Chris dove to the jungle floor right beside him. "Did you see where it came from?" he asked Chris.

Chris shook his head, no.

They both strained to see across the field and into the opposite tree line, but saw nothing.

"I don't see anything." James couldn't ignore the strange feeling that was buzzing in his sub-conscious.

It was dead still. Not a bird sang out, not an insect breathed. There was only a steady light breeze that toyed with the shattered leaves littering the field. Time seemed to slow down in the sense that any conscious thought seemed drugged and lethargic. There was something in the air that felt different, that felt . . . strange.

"I don't like this," whispered Chris, wiping the sweat off his brow.

James peeked out from behind the tree he was leaning against, but saw nothing but the tattered field under a partially cloudy sky.

And then the ground began to shake.

Standing to his feet, Chris held onto the tree to steady himself, unable to imagine what was causing the earthquake.

James was too confused to think, he merely reacted by searching for that same cause Chris was unable to imagine.

And then it revealed itself with the incredible sound of a battle cry.

James and Chris both turned at the same instant to see an army of natives pouring through the trees, running straight towards them. They were running with fire in their eyes and mad determination in their long steps. Blades of all sorts were raised, ready to be washed with the blood of the enemy. James and Chris just weren't sure who that enemy was.

"Are they sky-people?" asked James, squinting.

"I have no idea," replied Chris, taking a step back and clicking the safeties on his pistols.

James didn't know what to do, he was stunned with surprise, his feet held fixed to the ground with indecision. And, before he could react, the natives were on top of them, waving razor sharp swords and spears, screaming in a bloodthirsty chorus of insane rage. There was nothing James or Chris could do. They were both dead.

But the mass of natives passed by them, running instead for something else beyond and leaving them behind untouched and catching their breath.

All that Chris could see was a dark blur moving all around him, the natives moving so fast that his hair was moving with the breeze they created with their velocity. But not one had even taken notice of him.

James opened his eyes as the sound of thunder faded into the distance and the earth stopped shaking. He spun around to see where the army was running to and what he saw dropped his jaw in terrible astonishment.

The mass of natives were half way across the field when, out from the opposite woods, another army appeared, materializing from behind the broken jungle. This army was filled with natives too, but handfuls of giants were scattered throughout them.

James watched in stunned fascination and horror as both armies raced to meet each other in a violent conflict of death and pain. They crossed the empty space that separated them with such speed that bodies were sent flying into the air upon impact. And then the sound of clanging metal and screams of pain drowned out the morning sky.

Never before had James or Chris witnessed such awful, brutal warfare. The modern practice of advanced weaponry was cleaner and more proficient when it came to killing than the crude edge of a sword. It was unimaginable, the gore. It almost seemed as if it were raining blood. The intensity in which the men fought was unmatched. They fought with an insanity motivating their fighting, blind rage swinging and hacking at anything that moved.

The giants weren't even immune to the furiousness of the pure-blooded natives' desire for survival. Their legs were hacked out from under them and they disappeared beneath falling swords. But the war was not lopsided in favor of the pure-blooded. There were enough giants to wreak havoc throughout the ranks of the rebelling natives. They swung huge swords, cutting groups of natives apart- both their own and the pure-blooded together.

"What do you want to do?" asked Chris.

James didn't seem to hear him. He just watched, transfixed, as the horrific scene played out before him.

"James?"

He finally turned his head away from the bloodbath and locked eyes with Chris. "Do we have a choice?"

Chris knew there was little other option. If the pure-blooded natives lost the battle then their own survival would be cast into serious doubt. Though the odds were stacked high against them, the sight of the angels descending from the sky nurtured a hope that was beyond reason. He nodded, took a deep breath, and took off towards the battle that filled the field, praying the whole exhilarating way.

James followed after him, pistol in one hand, while swinging Martin's sword in the other. A voice kept repeating in his head, " . . . By many or by few."

Joshua finally found daylight pouring through the doorway leading to the deck. He thanked God and began approaching the outside air, eager to escape the old freighter that seemed to him more like a tomb. Expecting some sort of trap, Joshua threw himself through the entranceway and flew into a tuck and roll, bouncing to his feet with shotgun raised. But there was nothing there to greet him.

He looked around the ship, noticing that more of it seemed visible. The huge freighter had been massively uncovered, revealing at least 20% more of her deck. Clear calm waters washed over the extent of the *Iatrides,* massaging and cleaning parts of her body that had been covered by sand for at least twenty years. His gaze was drawn upward to the gray clouds scattered throughout an otherwise blue sky. The sun was almost finished with her climb into afternoon status, and there was a nice calm breeze blowing across the tropical land. But then Joshua turned to face that land and was more than shocked at what he saw.

The beach looked like a scene from a post-apocalyptic movie. The beach had receded far into the ocean, leaving behind a fleet of partially buried ships and planes to bathe and rust in the early morning sun.

Joshua closed his gaping jaw and trotted over to the side of the deck, observing the panorama view of what he knew to be the ships and planes that had disappeared without a trace within a very specific area of the Atlantic Ocean. Old propellers from WWII planes were protruding out of the sand next to the very distinguishable body of an A-6 attack bomber. Joshua also noticed pieces of multiple DC-3 planes scattered throughout the museum of missing vehicles. Freighters, steamers, coasters, pleasure yachts, and even what appeared to be the hull of a submarine were distinguishable from the protruding deck of the *Milton Iatrides.*

A sudden sense of sorrow washed over Joshua, and he was no longer fascinated, but sickened. Had he been an archeologist discovering some great mystery surrounding the fate of men thousands of years ago, perhaps it would have been different. But the mere fact that he was looking at jets and pleasure yachts placed him into a situation not more than a few years past at most. Some of the men that were piloting those ships and planes were still question marks within the hope-centered hearts of their families. It was not a gloried discovery, it was a horrible truth discovered. The fate of thousands had been lost in this same place that Joshua and his friends were fighting to liberate. He wondered how the people had suffered, how they had died. Had they seen the things they had? How far did they get before a pure-blooded native sold them out?

He shook his head and erased the thoughts, deciding, instead, to rejoin James and Chris. He slid down the deck and hopped over the railing, landing in the sand. Once he reached the tree line, he took one final look at the graveyard of lost ships and planes that had baffled and terrorized so many people. Then he turned and sprinted through the jungle, wondering where the giants had gone to and hoping James and Chris would be alive to find.

The Nephilim stood head and shoulders above the swarm of people moving about them, their huge swords cutting down men like wheat. The battle raged as if the fate of the world was to be decided, as if heaven and hell were both invited to the same plot of land. Ferociousness amplified the air, men sweating, bleeding, fighting, and dying, pouring their last breaths into an effort to crush their enemy. The armies were well matched and, though not numbered among the greatest ever assembled, they were just big enough to paint an epic scale.

James and Chris shot at any native that attacked them. There was no time to take confusion into consideration, if someone threatened them, they killed them. There was no time to think about it or reflect on the choice. There was only enough time in the battle to react. They could only hope in retrospect that they were not eliminating pure-blooded natives in their haste.

Chris shoved off of a pure-blood and swung around, avoiding an attacking blow from somewhere within the crushing crowd. He brought both pistols up and squeezed off a few shots, lifting a charging native off his feet. Chris felt someone running up behind him and swung around again, shooting a native who had his sword raised and ready to fall. There were so many men pressing in on him, he thought he would suffocate before being crushed, but then an intense pain erupted at the small of his back. Reflexively, he arched his back and screamed, turning to see the blood covered native that had slashed him. Before Chris could raise a gun, another native ran past in a blur, leaving Chris' attacker headless. But there was no time to think about it. A hard shove from behind threw Chris into the middle of two men doing battle. Their swords had just missed him. He fell at their feet and watched as the one native stabbed the other through the chest. The dead native collapsed next to him. The native still standing then pulled his sword up over his head and thrust it straight down into the ground where Chris' head had just been. But Chris was already swinging his feet around, and he kicked both of the native's feet out from under him. Chris jumped on top of him, but the native was able to get his foot up into Chris' chest, and he threw him over his head. Chris came out of his tuck and roll just in time to duck another blow from another native. Chris shot him and returned his focus back to the other native that was just getting back to his feet. Chris shot at him but missed, hitting nearby natives instead. The native charged straight into Chris' left hook, and he spun to the ground unconscious.

James was being equally pressed, resorting to dropping his shoulder and ramming into masses of people, hoping he didn't feel sharp metal slide through him in the process. He was swinging his fists ferociously, striking at anyone who got within arm's reach. He had been slashed twice already, his thigh erupting blood and his side split open. But he kept fighting with a tenaciousness he had never before known. He reached out and grabbed a native by the hair and spun him into the sword of a pure-blood, while in the same movement bringing his leg up and down in an axe kick, breaking another attacker's nose. He quickly dropped to the ground as two blades cut through the air above him with a *woosh.* He shot the one native, rolled over to his other side, and shot the other. As he was lying on the ground, he cast his gaze out across the battlefield, through the sea of legs and raining blood, and noticed the piles of corpses that were beginning to fill the area. He got to his hands and knees before noticing an especially large set of legs walking straight through the crowds of smaller. Dead bodies fell to the ground beside them as a path was carved. Quickly rising to his feet, James looked out through the chaos and saw the tall form of a vicious looking Nephilim walking straight for him, the natives in his way meeting a quick end.

Chris crossed his arms and shot two sky-people that were charging him on opposite sides, but he had only enough time to drop the empty pistols before throwing himself out of the way of a launched spear. He landed on top of a bloody corpse whose expressionless eyes were locked open staring into his. Chris shuddered, grabbed the native's sword, and got back to his feet. He connected swords with another native, noticing the giants in the background making their way closer to him.

The giant swung at James, its huge sword taking three heads off that were in the way. James ducked under the blow as the three dead natives toppled to the ground around him. He didn't hesitate but rammed his sword into the belly of the towering giant. But the giant didn't seem to notice. It pulled the sword out and threw it back at James who had to move quickly out of its way. There were plenty of swords littering the battlefield by now, and James had no trouble finding another one. He brought it up to defend another blow by the giant, but the force in which the giant swung, pushed James' own blade back against his body, cutting deep across his chest. He then wisely decided that he wouldn't try to block the giant's blows.

The giant swung again and almost took off James' arm. James stabbed it through the leg. It only laughed. James staggered backwards in shock and picked up two more swords. The giant didn't seem to care how many swords James had. The giant quickly reached out and grabbed James by the throat, lifting him off the ground, crushing his neck. James knew that if he didn't do something in the next few seconds, he was dead. The giant brought the sword back, preparing to run it through the man hanging in his grip.

Chris saw James' situation just in time. He cut down an archer that had been running nearby, and took his bow and arrows. He lined up the giant in his sights, praying that the arrow would find is target. He pulled back on the chord and released.

The giant was just beginning to thrust its sword into James' chest when an arrow struck it in the back of the neck. The arrowhead protruded through the other side, causing it to gag. James used the split second to play his only option. With all the might he could muster, he flung both swords up across the giant's wrist, and, like scissors, they cut all the way through. The giant screamed as James fell to the ground. Two seconds later the giant fell.

Chris sighed in relief before an incredible pain exploded in the back of his leg. Turning around, he found himself standing face to face with a child, its face disfigured with wretched ugliness. An evil smile beamed with satisfaction across its face. It was holding a bloody knife. Chris put another arrow into the bow and shot the little creature in the chest. It died with a twisted smile on its twisted face.

James was exhausted, his arms numb. He had used his last amount of strength to swing both swords around and dismember two more attackers. Now he had to drop a sword and control one with both hands just to get it up over his head. He began wandering away from the battle, closer to the tree line. His mind was not working clearly anymore, exhaustion terminating his reason. Finally, he reached a tree and fell against it. Sitting there and fighting to stay conscious, he realized that his exhaustion was largely due to the extreme blood loss his wounds had made provision for. Darkness began to close around his vision when a giant began walking towards him out of the dust of battle. He appeared like an apparition, emerging from a distorted background. Its eyes were alive with fire, its long black hair blowing in the breeze. It carried no sword, but a seven foot axe. The blade and handle was sticky with blood.

James tried to move, but his body did not respond. He could only watch as the massive giant walked closer, the axe in its hand growing larger.

Again, Chris just happened to catch the scenario out of the corner of his eye. Only this time, there was nothing he could do. Shooting an arrow at the giant would be futile considering the range in which he would have to shoot, and there was also the fact of the giant's back already being full of arrows. Despair grabbed Chris' heart, and he decided to run for it anyway. Ignoring the pain that came surging through his leg with every step, he ran like a mad man through the remaining crowds of fighting natives, pushing them away and cutting them down. It seemed as if he were moving in slow motion, and he realized that James was about to die.

James decided that he would spend his last thoughts thanking God for the opportunity to serve Him and to pray for his family. And then it was only Kirsten that filled his mind. A tear slid down his cheek as a strange smile spread across his lips. He recalled a CS Lewis quote that went, "The pain now is part of the happiness then." And he thanked God for the happiness he had been blessed with, for his wife and his family. Then he closed his eyes as the blade of the axe came crashing down to meet him.

Suddenly, there was a strange noise of sticks breaking and plants bending as something exploded out of the woods behind him. James opened his eyes just in time to see a blur pass in front of him and strike the giant. His mind struggled to keep his eyes open, and he could only see in part what was happening. Two men were standing in front of him, attempting to defeat the massive giant.

James blinked. There were two faces peering down at him. His mind grappled with the sight while their words slowly made their way to his ears.

"James, can you hear me?"

It was Edward and Mahalalel. James smiled, nodding. "Yes." His voice sounded as if it had escaped a mouthful of sand, his tongue dry and stuck to the roof of his mouth.

"Don't talk," commanded Edward. He was wrapping a piece of the giant's skirt around James' leg.

"Here." Mahalalel pulled a thread out of his own shirt and handed it to Edward.

Edward shook his head. "I need a needle."

Mahalalel stooped over the giant and pulled an arrow out of its back. Then he ripped one of the feathers from it. "Use this." He handed it to Edward.

It was crude, but there was enough of a point for it to work. Edward began stitching James' arm with thread and a feather.

No one noticed that the giant was still breathing.

Joshua was running through the severe aftermath of the hurricane, coming up on the second destroyed village when a sudden dark feeling reached out and grabbed him. He continued running though, ignoring the sound of something crashing through the woods behind him. A gorilla pounding past him caught his eye and he watched in fascination as it ran away from him.

Then a bird flew past his head flying in the same direction. A swarm of insects came next. Joshua turned around to see what was going on and only saw a dark cloud hovering over the land, animals of all kinds running towards him and ultimately past him. The situation was strange, and he wondered if a fire had started somewhere in the jungle.

After a few more minutes and another hundred animals running or flying past him, he noticed the reflection of the cloud in the river he was running beside. Perhaps it wasn't a cloud. He slowed to a stop and turned around, wondering if it was smoke. But what he saw wasn't smoke. He wasn't sure what it was. He took a step closer, peering with curiosity at the darkness that was swallowing the sky, chasing every living thing out from under it. And then he noticed that it wasn't just the sky that was being affected by the unrolling blackness. The landscape was also turning dark, not the darkness created by a cloud covering the sun and casting a shadow. This darkness was pitch black, as if it were erasing everything it came across, leaving nothing behind but the space that part of the globe once filled.

Joshua stood in awe for a few more seconds before his brain began transmitting to his legs. It was getting close enough now that Joshua could see its actual effect on the land. He watched as it swept eerily over a cliff not four hundred feet away. As the pitch black veil washed over it, it left behind a scene from a nightmare. The cliff and surrounding land was left stripped of color, of clarity. Instead, the land and sky looked like the negative of a picture, the trees unmoving, and a few birds caught suspended in flight. It was as if this dark entity stole everything it passed over, leaving behind a mere skeleton of what once was.

A panther almost knocked Joshua over as it flew past him, its legs pounding the ground in desperation. He turned and ran, a man in the midst of a hundred different animals all knowing that to get caught in the darkness would be fatal.

"How are you holding up?" asked James.

Edward shook his head. "Fine. I wouldn't be much of a help in battle, probably get myself killed in a few seconds, but what's the difference?"

James swallowed with great effort. "The women?"

"They're fine." He looked back at the battle which had begun to slow down. Then he turned to face James again. "James . . . " Their eyes met. "I want you to know that I believe what you were saying . . . about God and all. I can only hope that John comes to believe it too."

"John's dead, Edward."

After a few awkward seconds passed, Edward's eyes dropped to the ground, the news stunning his brain. "Where's everyone else?" His voice was hoarse now, choked with controlled emotion.

"Lance is dead. I haven't seen Joshua since last night, and Chris is out there somewhere."

Mahalalel stepped forward. "Jared?"

James closed his eyes. "Haven't seen him since last night."

Edward sat silent for a few moments, his mind trying to figure a way to introduce itself to tragic adjustments. When he finally spoke, it was with a tear. "Are you sure your God can save me, James?"

James opened his eyes and looked very deliberately into Edward's. "Yes. He's your only hope."

Then there was a strange sound, and Edward's face began to pale.

James' mind was so fatigued that he couldn't comprehend what had happened. Edward stretched out his hand and laid it on James' shoulder, and that's when James noticed the blade of an axe protruding from his chest.

A tiny drop of blood rolled off Edward's bottom lip. He squinted in pain and the knowledge of death, but a burning sense of awareness was glaring through his eyes. There was an extraordinary glimmer of hope that outlined his pupils, as if he knew that his life was not over, but just beginning. He whispered with his last struggling breaths, "Thank you." Then his hand fell off James' shoulder and he fell sideways into the ground.

James sat in shock, unable to place together the sudden consequences of what had just happened. He tore his wide eyes off Edward's body and laid them on the giant that was struggling to get to its feet.

Mahalalel fainted before he could finish picking up the sword, his wounds nowhere close to freeing him from their power.

Chris was almost there. He had slowed to a jog after seeing Edward and Mahalalel explode from the jungle behind James and drive spears into the attacking giant. But he seemed to be the only one that noticed the giant still moving. So he sprinted, but there was nothing he could do to stop the giant from getting to its knees and swing its axe into Edward's back. He screamed in raging fury, his wrath only moving his legs faster. The giant was just standing up when he jumped up and off a fallen tree that was lying fifteen feet behind the beast. He threw himself high into the air, and came down with a mighty swing onto the giant's neck. Chris landed on the ground a full five seconds before the giant's head did.

There was no remorse, no second guessing. Chris was furious. He let his burning eyes absorb Edward's body, not able to believe that he could have been taken away so fast. He resisted the urge to obey blind rage and go on a suicidal attack into the remaining army of sky-people.

"Funny, isn't it?"

James' detached voice annoyed Chris whose chest was pumping hard. "Funny?"

"Yeah. We all go looking for my brother in Bermuda, and here we are dying in a land of giants and flying saucers . . . " His face twisted with a lazy grin. "I guess if you're gonna' die, what difference does it really make. How, when, where . . . it doesn't matter." He was almost delirious and barely holding on to consciousness.

"Come on, James. We don't have time for this." Chris pulled him to his feet and half dragged him back into the field, leaving the body of their friend and an unconscious Mahalalel behind.

"Animals . . . "

Frustration had Chris grinding his teeth, and he ignored the arrow that flew past his head, instead wondering what to do with James who was now a burden. But then Chris saw them too. He thought that James was hallucinating when he mentioned animals, but he was right. There were hundreds of them pouring out of the jungle and running across the battlefield. Tigers, panthers, monkeys, and an array of other jungle animals just kept running, not noticing the raging battle, the fresh blood and meat, or even the obstacles they created. They ran, crawled, flew, and hopped as fast as they could.

Chris had seen this before.

Joshua burst through the tree line along with a gorilla and a tiger, but they were faster than him and far past in a few seconds. He looked back over his shoulder and saw nothing but darkness creeping closer. It stretched out, reaching for him with long black fingers. He knew it was only a matter of time before he was engulfed and submerged into a world much more disturbing than the one he was running through. He spotted James and Chris struggling through the battlefield only thirty yards away and decided that he would die with them.

There was no suggestion of form in the utter blackness, it simply spread its amorphousness throughout the sky and ground. Like an invading army of locusts, it consumed everything, leaving behind a freakish skeleton of reality. But then even that was ripped into the sky. The strange image of trees and jungle life frozen in inverted colorlessness was pulled upward into nothingness. It looked as if a huge vacuum was opened and was moving above the island, sucking up everything into it: trees, animals, plants, dirt, rocks, mountains, clouds, even the air itself seemed to be swept upward, evaporating into non-existence. Reality itself was being peeled away, the very concept of the island being erased by a more dominant reality . . . a spiritual one.

"That's what I saw on the beach the first day." Chris was holding James upright, watching in helplessness as the black curtain closed in on them. He barely gave any attention to Joshua, who was running towards them, barely escaping the epic reach of what could only be evil.

James sluggishly took note of the battle behind them. The sounds that accompanied war had faded, and he was surprised to find both pure-blooded and sky-people standing transfixed, staring at the impending blackness. They forgot each other, and self preservation threw away any thought of a victory. They all began to take steps backward, ignoring the piles of dead comrades all around them.

"But I don't remember that." Chris was pointing behind the spreading plague at the island being sucked into the sky.

Through pain and wicked fatigue, James' mind was still able to process the bizarre sight that looked more like something from an LSD inspired 70's music video. "The physical is being erased . . . "

"What do you mean?" asked Chris.

"Reality in its truest form is not what you and me see, it's what we can't see. The eternal reality is a spiritual one, this one is only home to mortal physicality." His eyes pounded the ground, and he wondered what it would be like on the other side. "This reality is only kept in existence by the mind of God. Atoms, molecules . . . It's all subjective in a broader realm. Our state is slave to the one that keeps us alive."

"So if that thing is sucking up our reality, where does that leave us?"

James smiled a tired and defeated smile, eyes looking up into the perpetual blackness that was almost on top of them. "I don't know, Chris. Maybe our fleshly bodies will be sucked into a spiritual vortex just like the rest of the island, but no spiritual force can take our souls. They belong to God. If this thing kills us, then we'll be in heaven before we realize we've died."

Chris' eyes dropped heavily to the ground. "But I don't want to die yet . . . "

Before James could answer, Joshua was diving at their feet and the wall of darkness was sweeping over them.

It was the strangest thing they had ever experienced. The only thing that could come even close to the experience was the detached, yet realistic feel of a dream. It was as if they were outside themselves, yet not, floating in a void surrounded by jungle wallpaper. The jungle was in a different place, yet they could see it all around them. It almost had the appearance of being a collection of cardboard props, one dimensional and behind fogged glass. Their feet sunk below the grass as if it were a mere projection.

Joshua tried to get to his feet, but he couldn't push himself off of anything, there was nothing solid, and his hands went straight through the ground. He stared at his greenish hands, moving them around on the other side of the grass. It was as if the ground and the trees and everything but themselves were only a mere image being projected by a movie projector. He moved his hand to touch a nearby tree, and his fingers passed straight through it. He looked up to James and Chris who seemed to be experiencing the same awe he was overwhelmed with, yet they looked more as if they were in a dream state too.

There was no attempt to speak to each other, no acknowledging another's presence. It was everyone's own dream.

Chris turned to look behind him, his head moving in lethargic slow motion, and watched as more of the landscape turned into a hologram. The other living creatures that were captured in the dark blanket stood frozen. Birds were suspended in flight, their wings paused where they had been when overshadowed. Tigers and monkeys were stopped in a dead run. It was bizarre, the feeling that Chris had. It was like a weird dream- there was no reason to feel the way he did, but something about the situation was terrorizing. He reached out to grab James, to see if he shared the same concern, but his outstretched hand went straight through his shoulder. He jerked it back real quick, his heart pounding in his chest. James didn't even seem to notice. Chris thrust his hand into James again and was horrified to see his hand inside what he thought had to be a holographic image of James. He pulled it out and hesitated. Finally, he cautiously placed his hand on his own stomach, and it passed through.

And then he looked up and noticed the jungle being sucked into the unseen above.

Like an aftershock, the ripple traveled through the transparent world, sending the entire visible world into upheaval. The trees were dislodged from their rooted homes and sucked into the air, the dirt that once covered them accompanying the ascent. Everything was lifted into the sky as if an invisible tornado was vacuuming up reality itself.

James could only cover his face in a futile attempt to hinder the force of impact. He would have screamed, but it happened so suddenly that he didn't have time. In that fraction of a second, confronted with his own fragile existence, he wondered if he would be thrown upward with the rest of the world, or if the things beneath his feet would just tear through him as they were pulled up from under him.

But there was only a flash, a blur of color that passed briefly before his eyes. The entire world had passed straight through him and left him behind. He turned and saw the invisible force continue to suck up the island like a lawnmower. He could see natives running away and suddenly stop, suspended in a state of limbo within the arms of darkness. Birds and animals surrounded them. But then, as the scene was pulled out from under them and ripped into the sky, they went with it. James took a quick look around and made sure

Joshua and Chris were still with him and wondered why they had not been sucked up as well.

Then an incredible darkness washed over them, exploding from nowhere and wrapping them within its power. Vertigo was immediately a factor. There was no north, south, east, or west. There was no up or down, no left or right. There was only complete and utter darkness, pitch black. It was a haunting feeling, not being able to tell whether your eyes were opened or closed.

Without being able to feel himself at all, and not being able to see himself or anything else, Chris felt as if only his conscious was alive, departed from his body, departed from the world.

And then the blackness faded, and he was able to see that his body was still visibly present, if not physically. James and Joshua were still close by.

A deep hue of red began spreading throughout the darkness like dye in water. It clouded the nothingness and brought with it another horror- a horror that would have stopped the heart of any physical man . . . but Chris wasn't so sure he was a physical man anymore.

James knew what was happening and recalled his thoughts on it. What he always had imagined as being the most horrible and terrifying thing one could witness was being unveiled for him now. All the evil, all the supernatural powers, all the perverseness that they had witnessed in this place was only a small reflection of what they were about to see. And James prayed he could take it.

The curtain was pulled back and another realm revealed- a realm invisible to human eyes and doubted by many of the same. Coming into full view was the spiritual realm- the realm of demons and angels. But there were no angels.

Joshua screamed so loud, he imagined his vocal chords disintegrating within his throat. It was a nightmare a million times worse than anything he had ever seen before. A dark invisible hand gripped his heart and squeezed until he felt paralyzed with fear, completely subject to those hoards of hellish creatures that were flying in wispy streaks about his head. They looked like ghosts, long tails of indistinguishable light trailing from behind twisted and horrid faces, no distinguishable bodies otherwise. There was a noise that pierced the reddish sky, the same sky that enveloped everything as far as eye could see. Shrieks of disdain and blasphemies curled the blood and paled the face. Joshua closed his eyes as a face resembling a bull with man's features flew towards him. But those ghosts weren't the only entities occupying the space now glowing red from what seemed to be a distant fire. There were also more physically attributed creatures- creatures with hoofed feet and man's chests. Long curled horns protruded sickeningly from within huge bald heads and wrapped around their ears. They had black eyes, serpent-like tongues, and tiny jagged teeth. Blisters were festering all over their bodies and releasing a horrible stench, pus oozing from numerous sores. There were thousands of them, if not millions. They were spread as far as the eyes could see.

"Welcome to the real world, James Streen." The familiar voice seemed more horrible now than before.

James couldn't be sure if the words were audible or if he simply knew them in his mind. He looked through the hellish scene, shaking uncontrollably, and saw nothing speaking.

"Do you think that you can bring a stop to this, natural man? Reveal your power within my realm, within the realm of reality, and I shall bow before you in submission!"

The voice seemed to have a strange power to it, as if it were draining the very life out of him. Fear was in place as James, a mere man, found himself tossed behind the scenes. The true evil that generated only glimpses of itself on earth was staring at him. Scared to death took on a new meaning for James, a very literal new meaning. The way he felt when someone jumped out and scared him in a dark house was amplified eternally and prolonged inevitably. It was the worst feeling of scared shock he had ever known and it wasn't going away.

Chris was also experiencing the same sensation. Fright spread and infected his mind without release, elevating itself to an unbearable level of intensity. He feared hell. And it looked as if its gates were opening.

"Join me, James. I will make you more powerful than you could ever imagine. You will be like God."

The initial shock and even its sustaining power was beginning to fade just enough to allow him to think. He answered within his mind, not bothering to shout out. "You don't have that power to give. And since when are your offers bent on humanity's best interest?"

"I will not argue. It is your last chance. Give me your soul, let me use you to bring about the end, or I shall use your son to do what you will not."

"My soul is not yours, and it is not mine. My soul is God's. If you want it, then take it up with Him."

"You fool."

"You can't erase us from your little workshop as you are them." He looked out into the dark red hue that stretched into darkness, and then, barely visible, was still the traveling shroud, lifting the island into the sky, natives going with it and disappearing. "You can't kill us. We are under someone else's protection. You can't erase our souls or send them to the grave. We are Christ's, and He defeated you when He broke the power of sin and death!"

At the mention of 'Christ,' every disgusting creature dispersed and disappeared for a few seconds before reappearing. James smiled. "This war is over."

The voice came back through the void of consciousness. "Perhaps, but I want you to know that I will be watching you every second of your life. The intimate moments with your wife, I will be watching. Your son's birth, I will be there. On his third birthday, I will help blow out the candles. High School graduation, I will cheer beside him. I will fight for him. I will be his father, and I will bring him to me, and he will be the one who I use to bring about the end of the earth."

James knew that the demon was right. There was nothing he could do as a physical man to influence anything within the spiritual realm. So he would ask someone else to do it. He began praying, exercising the only spiritual weapon available to him.

The veil of darkness continued to spread over the land. Like a tidal wave, it consumed and destroyed everything it came across. Natives and animals were still running from it, trying with every ounce of remaining strength to live a few seconds longer.

And then the heavens opened.

A huge ray of glowing whiteness shot down from the sky like a beam of light. It was blinding to look at, glory radiating from the heavenly hosts that were descending through it. The stream of light stood in the way of the approaching darkness, providing a barrier separating the evil tide from those still alive. It stretched east to west until disappearing into both horizons. The dark flood struck the wall of light and stopped. It swam back and forth over the brightness, looking for a crack or some other way through, but there was no leak in the heavenly dam. The evil shadow stretched its long fingers in desperate attempts at penetrating its awesome obstacle, leaving exhausted natives, and even giants, to stop running and watch in amazement the scene before them. There was no darkness anymore. A huge wall of blinding light was all that could be seen, as if the sun itself had fallen to the planet and continued to shine in all its glory. The natives turned from the sight, blind and confused.

James noticed that the demons suddenly became aware of another presence. They all seemed to focus their attention in one direction, and James turned to see what it was that was behind him. Something was there, but it was too far away for James to tell exactly what. He squinted, ignoring the hordes of hellish creatures screaming past him and rushing into the direction he was peering in. Though his senses were berserk, his mind completely malfunctioning at what it was trying to comprehend, he still knew what was happening. The dark reddish hue was getting lighter, brightness entering from one general direction, the demons racing to confront it.

Though his eyes were still locked wide with shock, Chris' mind began to function again. It was still slow, sluggish in lifting the sights to comprehension, but sanity and self-awareness were making strides at relevance again. The most horrific thing he had ever seen in his life was beginning to change. There was light poking through the dark hues like rays through mist. They pierced the dark confines and scattered the nightmare. No longer was evil omnipresent but sanctioned to quadrants ever shrinking in the glorious light that was sweeping through its influence. As Chris watched the spiritual scene unfold before him, he couldn't believe what his eyes were actually viewing. It was another world, blinded to the physical one he thought he had known so well. He realized, in as much as a partial insanity allows, that he had a back stage pass to reality. And he knew that it would be a performance he would never forget.

The light clashed with the darkness, and the darkness was erased as it always is in the presence of light. The hoards of demons clashed with their old brothers, the celestial beings that chose not to rebel against the Most High. They fought, eternal bodies versus eternal bodies, in a way indiscernible and unclear. The spiritual forces collided in horror and brilliance, the war raging, the fate of the island and everyone on it hanging in the balance. But James knew that the outcome of the battle was already determined, that the King of the army wasn't simply hoping His soldiers could pull it off. He knew Who it was that was really controlling the battle. And that knowledge was more than enough to convince him of the outcome.

And the outcome was determined swiftly. In fact, the entire string of events had happened so quickly that it would be a matter of confusion as to whether or not time itself had even passed. It was a strange experience, one that would defy one's concept of time and reality. For both seemed completely subjective within the realm they were witness to, blending together in an undefined mixture of events. It felt as if the entire scene started and ended at the same time, the passing of events only discerned by the mind's eye and not in any chronological layout externally. If time did not stop, then it took on a different form. The fact that events did seem to be played out would suggest a passing of time, but James, Joshua, and Chris would all agree that something was strangely and fundamentally different. It felt like a weird dream, detached and odd yet making perfect sense, everything happening at once, yet chronologically so.

James was thanking God for the intervention, watching as demons were beat back by figures too bright to discern. The deep red hues were mostly a light pink now, the brightness swallowing most of it and chasing the rest into the corners of the spiritual realm. The battle seemed over.

A loud sound suddenly echoed through the brightening void, capturing the attention of everything within it. Appearing from out of the now distant darkness was a figure that became more recognizable as it approached. It swayed back and forth with each step, dragging a long tail behind it- though there seemed to be no floor on which to drag it on.

"No!" The figure screamed and then began yelling things in another language. The sound of its wretched voice complimented its horrific appearance. It stood eight feet tall, its face pale white, huge horns protruding straight out from the sides of its head like an ox. Red eyes glowed over a big nose, a large ring piercing it. Its mouth was a cave of stalagmites, saliva dripping from the many sharp teeth. The body was covered in mucus giving it the appearance of just being born. Its waist met a reptile's pair of legs that stretched down to razor sharp claws. A pair of dragon-like wings was folded high behind its head.

It screamed again. "My creation no one will steal from me!" It began walking closer to James, flickers of flame dancing from its mouth. "I will kill you."

James turned away from the monster and tried to escape, but he was only running to stand still. There was no ground under his feet to run on, his legs beating helplessly against nothingness. It didn't matter what he knew now, it didn't matter whether or not he thought God was going to rescue him, his emotional side of humanity was overloaded and stretched to breaking point as the sight of the approaching demon transcended human capabilities. His mind malfunctioned, crazy fear detaching reason from being. He continued to run nowhere as the demon came nearer.

Joshua watched on in utter terror and helplessness. The demon's wings spread and began beating the empty space, somehow moving the creature quickly towards James, who was trying as hard as he could to gain one inch in his desperate flailing.

The hellish creature soared past him, twisting at the waist and coming around to face him. It opened its mouth to speak and its mouth was overflowing with maggots and worms. They crawled and slithered through its teeth, dropping down its face and into the bottomless reality of the spiritual realm.

"I brought you here to this place, my place. This has been my prison since the flood of Noah, and I brought you to liberate me from it. You will free me from this passive existence or I will kill you. This is your last offer." It spat saliva, mucus, and worms with its horrible voice. "You are my seed, I am your father."

James had stopped struggling, suddenly very alert and very calm. He knew that he was not alone in this place. "You are not my father, you damned creature! How can you think that you can force God's hand at bringing about the end? The date is set, and your eternal stupidity has cost you more than your soul. This place is no longer yours!"

The creature spread its wings with a furious cry, fire erupting from its mouth and nostrils, its claws flexing, clutching empty space. Ghosts and other spiritual creatures circled around it, as if it was summoning them. The sight was terrible, the entire realm seeming as if it would tear apart at the furious tantrum put on by the angry demon.

James gasped as the demon brought back its hand, black claws glimmering under red light, and prepared to take off his head.

It swung with a ferocious and deafening cry, sending ripples rolling through the reddish hues and into the unseen expanses.

James closed his eyes.

There was a loud noise and a flash of light that spread throughout the void, the image of trees, clouds, and the rest of the island briefly flickering through the brightness. Joshua and Chris shielded their eyes from the impact and the explosion of lights that resulted.

James slowly opened his eyes, his head screaming with a deafening ringing sound. The demon's hand was barely visible in the brilliance of glowing light, another hand holding it at the wrist. It was painful to look upon, but James looked over the sight as long as he could stand it. There, standing before him and holding the wrist of the demon, was a figure clothed in light. It was hard to make out any features, but he thought he could see the outline of wings emerging from within the glow.

Then the most unbelievable thing that James would ever experience happened. The angel turned his head away from the demon and cast his gaze onto James. James would have collapsed had gravity been a property within this realm, the look from those eyes, beautiful- yet terrifying. They beamed with clarity and purity, cutting hard through James' features. And then they softened.

"Servant of the Most High God, child of His Majesty . . . " His voice sounded like an orchestra. It was authoritative yet comforting, and it overpowered every other noise. "No longer are you a slave to this world or this fiend. Go and give God glory." Then the angel turned back to face the demon. He thrust his other hand around its neck and the creatures flying about its head dispersed and disappeared.

"Hello, Brother," said the demon with a sarcasm covering his words like the maggots covering his teeth.

The angel did not smile, did not return the sarcasm. He simply muttered, "Once upon a time . . . " He lifted the demon into the air and said, "Your abominations will be tolerated no longer. You are no longer free to move about this place and dictate your awful will. Behold, Lucifer has brought his children to this place and now the Lord brings His. This place is no longer yours."

The demon snickered under the angel's grip. "He cannot stop the end.

My creation will be claimed and the world will once again know the days of Noah."

The angel nodded with patience. "Yes, so shall the coming of the Son of Man be. But you are nothing but a puppet."

Fire raged within the dark eyes of the demon as it made one final attempt at lunging for James. But the angel withstood the attack and struck it with a flaming sword. The demon and its fallen companions screamed out in agony and the red hues disappeared with them in a brilliant flash of light.

When the light finally faded, James, Chris, and Joshua could just make out the jungle's landscape being replaced. It almost seemed magical, as if someone were rewinding the events of the raptured reality- trees, dirt, clouds, rocks, and everything else were streaming back down from the sky and falling back into the place they had existed before. Everything was being replaced just as it was before the dark tide swallowed it.

There was no sign of a darkness spilling over the sky, only a bright sun shining through scattered clouds and washing over a weather-beaten jungle. A group of pure-blooded natives were slowly getting up while the remaining sky-people were attempting to make a run for it. The lifeless bodies of Nephilim were scattered throughout the jungle, presumably falling dead when the demon had been conquered.

With two eyes traveling in sketchy precaution, James attempted to let himself adjust to the natural scene around him. He grabbed his left wrist with his right hand and was reassured when he could feel it. He lifted his foot up and stepped hard into the ground- it was solid.

Joshua walked up behind him along with Chris, and there they stood, not saying a word, their eyes taking in the world around them. Not one of them knew what to say, what could be said. The wonder and awe, the torment and the horror, had left them in a sense of fear and reverence. For the next moment of time, they stood still, reflecting on what they had witnessed, and could only wait for the sensation to fade. A steady breeze blew through their hair and they squinted under the sun's bright rays. Trees swayed in the wind, and birds flew through the air as if nothing had happened. But something was different. And the three men wondered about it, each lost in a thoughtful meditation, questions and answers being formulated, prayers being said. They groped for a knowledge of how to handle this incredible revelation . . . the supernatural. Tears began falling.

Finally, Joshua turned his head, his eyes slowly grazing the jungle and finding the remaining natives. No one else that had been sucked up into the vortex seemed to have been returned, and the only remaining sky-people were being defeated by pure-blooded warriors. Joshua's lips spread and his voice was found, though barely audible. "Praise God," he whispered. "Praise God."

TWENTY-SEVEN

VOYAGE: ONE LAST HOPE

:::: *A WEEK LATER*

A new world had been discovered, a world without fear. No longer were giants running through the woods, crop circles appearing in the morning, or the gods descending in their cloud cars. There were no shadows of evil left to torment the pure-blooded natives, no more sky-people to kill or enslave them. The air was lighter, the sun brighter, and the island full of colorful life. For the first time in their lives, the natives were enjoying their existence.

"So what will happen to the gods?" Mahalalel had asked. Evidently, he had not been destroyed by the demon because he had believed the small amount of truth he had been exposed to. His soul was protected and now he was trying to understand this new faith James was speaking of. In answer to his question, James had told him that the demons or 'the gods' will always be there, but as long as his people did not invite them into their lives, they would be powerless to do anything but watch them live peaceful lives. "Evil is manifested in those ways by inviting the demons. They cannot come into you and control you uninvited," James had said. He then tried to explain to Mahalalel that the place was under a new government- no longer was evil in control.

All in all, the last week had been a week spent recovering from injuries and getting the food and rest their bodies needed, answering questions the natives had, and preaching Jesus Christ to them. Nearly all of the remaining natives chose to give their lives to this loving God James told them about. It was a glorious time. But it was also a sad time. Jared's body was found where it was last seen on the steps of the temple. They carried his body and all the slain bodies back to the beach and burnt them. While the natives were mourning the deaths of so many of their friends and family, James was left to deal with the deaths of Brian, Edward, John, and even Lance, beginning to think of his family as well.

The women walked around freely, no longer in danger of being abducted. The smiles that were shining on their faces canceled out the price of freedom and brought smiles to all those who observed them. No longer did the race have to live their lives in hiding. Their dream was realized, the prophecy fulfilled. God had given them a hope and He had delivered in His time.

There was one specific girl who found herself in the constant company of one of the strangers, and whether she liked Chris' company or not, Chris didn't care. He had followed her everywhere for the last week trying to make her fall in love with him. And, after a week, they shared a common look in their eyes.

James closed the Bible that Joshua had found in the *Milton Iatrides* and looked up into the sky, noticing the frolicking of a few tropical birds beneath large puffy clouds. He was sitting with his back against a tree, his feet buried under the warm sand. He closed his eyes, listening to the sound of the ocean and the frolicking birds, and began to pray.

A shadow falling across him opened his eyes.

"I think she's ready." Joshua was smiling. He was referring to the *Polymer III* long distance yacht that they had found on the beach the day after the battle. Though most of the ships that had been washed up or uncovered were damaged and in pieces, a few seemed completely intact. The *Polymer III* was one of them.

James looked up to Joshua, squinting into the blinding light coming from behind Joshua's head. "Can you take a step to your right?"

Joshua moved over. "How's that?"

James could see again, Joshua's head now blocking the circle of light. "That's better."

"When do you want to do this?"

James cast his eyes across the landscape, deep in thought. "You sure you want to? This is a pretty beautiful place now, and we'll probably end up dying out in the middle of nowhere if we go."

Joshua placed his hands on his hips and looked up into the sky, taking a few seconds to think it through. "Yeah." He shook his head. "I want to go back." Then he looked back down at James, his brow raised. "Don't you?"

James smiled. "Oh yeah." He thrust out his hand, signaling Joshua to help him up. Joshua lifted him to his feet with ease.

"How are you feeling?"

James flashed a grin. "Like a few giants just jumped me."

Joshua laughed. “You’re looking better. There doesn’t seem to be any infection.”

James shrugged and began walking. “I’m fine.”

As they made their way to the natives who were busy building houses, above ground for a change, they noticed Chris and the girl walking hand-in-hand towards the beach.

“Oh, man.” Joshua shook his head. “Can you believe that?”

James smiled, but it was a forced smile. Sadness gripped his heart one more time, because he knew that Chris would not be able to get her to leave with them.

“Hey Chris!” Joshua called out.

Chris spun his head and acknowledged Joshua and James, changing his direction and pulling his new love along behind him. He walked up with a huge smile beaming on his face. “What’s up?”

James couldn’t believe it. The girl was beautiful, he couldn’t blame Chris for that, but she seemed more than just beautiful. Her eyes sparkled with a timid sense of awe that turned to adoration when they swept over Chris. She was hiding in his shadow, peeking out from behind his broad shoulders. She trusted him . . . she loved him . . . James couldn’t believe it. He knew that she had responded to the gospel, and he silently thanked God for His graciousness.

“You just about ready?” asked Joshua.

Chris’ smile faded and his eyes dropped to the ground where he was swirling his foot in the sand. When he looked back up, there was a tear forming in the corner of his eye. “I’m not going back with you.” His voice cracked half way through, and he had to repeat himself.

“What do you mean?” asked Joshua.

Chris turned and looked at the beautiful woman that was hiding behind him. “I can’t leave her. She’s everything I could ever want. I’m not going to walk away from her.”

“Bring her with you, she has a family that would be more than happy to find out she’s alive.”

“You can’t promise me that you guys will make it. I can’t ask her to leave her home, to follow me into possible death just because I’m used to a different reality.”

A tear slid down James’ cheek and he choked a bit before clasping a hand on Chris’ shoulder. They looked at each other for a moment, two brothers replaying all the adventures and all the great times. Then they fell forward and embraced.

“I don’t want to keep you two.” James took a step back. “But later on, I need to talk to you.” He held up the Bible and Chris understood.

"Okay." He smiled and turned, leading the girl to the sands of the beach.

As James watched them walk away, he answered Joshua's question. "We'll leave tomorrow."

Mahalalel was watching Lud's body being carried to the beach. It had been discovered a few hours before by a boy collecting firewood.

"He believed in you," he told James.

"He seemed like a remarkable man."

"He was." Mahalalel's weary eyes found a woman sitting alongside the jungle, crying silently into her hands.

"Who's that?" asked James.

"That is Jared's wife. She was one of the women you rescued from the temple. Jared died saving their lives."

"Will she marry again?" he asked.

"I cannot say. Maybe someday."

"I'm leaving tomorrow with Joshua." He tried to see the response from the corner of his eye, but it almost seemed as if Mahalalel didn't hear him.

"Will they ever come back again?" His voice was serious, his eyes set on the horizon.

"No, not in your lifetime."

Mahalalel looked over at James. "What does this mean, not in your lifetime?"

"You are God's children now, the one true and living God's. He loves you, and He will take care of you. As long as your people believe and worship Him, there will be no room for evil to operate."

He sighed. "I have so many questions."

"I know. Chris is going to stay with you, if that's all right. I am going to give him the Bible Joshua found. All your questions can be answered in there."

A smile spread his lips. "Your friend, I think, likes my sister, Deborah, very much."

James acted surprised before he even thought about hiding it. If Mahalalel thought that the girl was his sister, then it would be Chris' place to tell him the truth if he found it necessary. "Yeah, I think he does."

"Is that why he stays?"

"Yeah."

"He wants to marry her, does he?"

James couldn't keep the grin off his face. "I think so."

Mahalalel seemed to think about that for a little bit. "You will not stay?"

He shook his head. "I have my own wife and daughter that I will try to get back to."

"Do you miss them?"

"More than I ever thought possible."

"I will pray to your loving God and maybe He take you to her."

"He's your loving God too."

Mahalalel turned away from James, a big smile lighting up his face. "Yes, He is."

"Mahalalel, I have just one question. What ever happened to Tahhowson?"

The smile faded from his face. "We found that he was the leader of those of my people who were taking the strangers to the gods. He was making peace with the sky-people by turning people like you over to them."

"Do you know if any survived?"

"We never saw them again."

"Tahhowson didn't want to be delivered by the strangers you dreamt about?"

He wagged his head. "He did not believe."

They both stood watching the sun begin its descent over the waves.

The next morning the *Polymer III* was floating in shallow waters after being pulled from the beach. It took just about every native to help, but they pulled it into the water with shouts and hollers from those cheering them on. There was no gas in it and the radio seemed dead so they built huge oars, using the propellers from a plane as paddles. It sat bobbing gently up and down with the current, but whether it was an inviting sight or not was still to be determined.

"I can't believe it." Joshua was staring at the yacht.

James smiled. "It sure beats using the seaplane's skids as canoes."

"Yeah, maybe."

"Are you ready?"

"I think so. Have they finished loading the food and water?"

"Yeah, there's a month's worth for two people if we ration."

Joshua looked around the island again. "We haven't really talked about this, but what if home isn't out there?" He shifted his gaze back over the ocean.

"There's no way I can live here knowing my family is out there. I can't live my life without trying. You don't have to though; you can stay here with Chris."

Joshua seemed to think about it for a while. Then he shook his head. "No, I have family who need to hear what you've told me about Jesus. I'm going with you."

Chris walked up to them from behind and joined them in the shallow surf. "It's crazy, isn't it? The way things ended up? Us saving these people and all . . . "

"It sure is." James put his arm around Chris. "Don't forget the things I wrote down for you last night. It's very important."

Chris laughed. "Just call me Pastor Chris Roberts for now on."

The night before, James had given him a crash-course in hermeneutics, trying to explain to him how to interpret the Bible. Though there were a ton of things that Chris would have benefited from learning, for himself as well as for the natives, with the aide of the Holy Spirit, James believed he would do just fine. There were no televisions and liberal messages to pollute a population here. No advertising and marketing, no music and television to promote vanity and worldliness, and no secular supremacy trying to blot out God from the minds of the people. There were no distractions, and James trusted that God would use Chris to lead these people closer to Him.

Deborah came up from behind Chris and leaned against his back. Chris wrapped his arm around her as he stared at his two friends. "Man, I'm gonna' miss you guys."

James' jaw grew tight and his eyes began to fill. "We'll meet again someday."

Now Chris' eyes grew damp. "I'll be looking forward to it." Then he looked down at Deborah. "Well, maybe not at first . . . "

James and Joshua laughed.

"Thank you, James. For sharing Christ with me. None of this would have meant anything without Him."

"It never does." James gave him a huge hug and they held it for a while, knowing that they would never see each other again on this planet.

"When you get back, if you wouldn't mind telling my sister what happened . . . She won't believe you, but tell her anyway. Tell her about Christ, and tell her I love her."

James released his hold on him and took a step back. "I will. You make sure you read that Bible, a lot. And make sure you love her more than you love yourself." He nodded towards Deborah and a tear escaped. "I always thought I'd-" He started over. "Well, I never thought I'd see you married, but . . . " He swallowed the rock in his throat. "Listen, you just tell your kids about their uncle James, all right?"

"You bet. You tell that wife of yours to take care of you."

"She does."

Joshua stepped forward and embraced Chris.

"You take care of yourself, man." Joshua pounded him on his back.

"I will. Maybe someday you'll have a family of your own, and then we can all get together."

Laughter came with shed tears.

James wiped his eyes with the back of his hands and sighed. "Man, I can't believe this."

Then Deborah stepped forward and hugged James and Joshua. She looked up into their eyes and said, "Thank you." And then a tear slid down her soft face.

By now every native was lining the beach waiting to see them off. Mahalalel walked over to them and thanked them again. Even he shed some tears. There was both laughter and crying coming from the crowd as they prepared to watch their heroes float over the horizon.

After the final goodbyes were said, James and Joshua began walking out to the boat. Once reaching it, they pulled themselves up and prepared for their journey. Five minutes later, they were drifting in open water, putting distance between them and the island.

"I just can't believe everything we've been through," Joshua was saying. "How long has it been since we got to Bermuda?"

James never took his eyes off the island. "I don't know. A month, maybe more . . . "

Joshua stood next to him staring at the fading land, replaying all its horrifying events back over in his mind. "So long," he whispered and gave a courteous wave.

"It's over." James could still see Chris and Deborah standing in the water, waving.

"Almost."

They kept their eyes on the beach until it disappeared over the horizon, the natives and Chris never to be seen again. They thought about their other friends that had fallen there and a strange sadness began to wash over them.

Chris wiped the tears away with the back of his hand and squeezed Deborah's hand tighter. "God, please let them make it." And then he turned and followed the rest of the natives back to their new chores, his bride-to-be walking beside him.

:::: ON THE WATER

Sunshine lit up the clear waters around them like solar panels, blinding light reflecting back into the cloudless sky. The gentle waves hit the bow of the *Polymer III* and exploded with a splash. Joshua and James were pulling at the oars that they had fastened to the back sides of the boat. They spent an hour at a time before resting for two. It didn't feel like they were making any progress, but who could really tell? There were no distinctions by which to judge, only endless water in all directions.

Joshua lifted the oar into the boat and wiped the sweat from his forehead. He looked up into the blazing sun, feeling like one of those cowboys portrayed in the old western movies who saw mirages in the desert. His body was shiny with sweat, his dark skin feeling even more cooked than it had the last three days.

"You look terrible." James was laughing from across the boat.

Joshua shot him a dirty look that only made James laugh harder. His face was covered in what was beginning to look like a full-grown beard, his body growing thinner every hour spent under the relentless fireball. His wounds were closed but still fresh. He looked like a prisoner that had just escaped a forty year captivity.

"You don't look so hot yourself, buddy." He managed a faint smile and stood up, walking into the cabin.

James lifted the oar into the boat and looked over the side. His reflection stared back at him, and he realized that Joshua looked better than he did. A beard covered his face as well, and he had ugly scars developing all over him. His skin was charred and some of the muscle that once covered his body was missing and unaccounted for. "I need a vacation."

Joshua overheard him from the cabin. "You and me both."

Three days had come and gone since they left the island and no sign of land, boats, or planes.

"What are you going to do if we get back?" asked James.

"I'm going to take a shower, put on a nice pair of clothes, and go eat a steak at a nice restaurant."

"How do you think the adjustment will be?"

Joshua sighed. "I don't know, James. How can life be the same after seeing all that we've seen? I wonder if there will be a day I go to sleep when I don't se all that playing over in my mind."

"Yeah, and we won't be able to get anyone to believe us, so it's not like we can share the experience."

Joshua laughed. "We'll be giving each other phone calls in the middle of the night making sure we aren't dreaming."

"It's going to take a while, I think. But, it probably won't be too long before all of this just seems like it was a really weird dream."

"Except Chris not being there."

"Yeah, and John, Edward, and Brian."

Joshua lay down on one of the benches inside the cabin and closed his eyes. James remained sitting under the sun, his thoughts in New York and watching his wife.

Two weeks passed. They had made a mistake in the rationing and the food was almost gone. Water wouldn't last another week. The horizon never offered a shape other than that of the formless and endless rolling waves. No vessels of any kind spotted the seascape, no traces of land appeared in the distance.

"Well, it was a nice run." Joshua couldn't hide the sound of failure in his voice.

"I'm not ready to die yet," James responded.

Joshua laughed. "I'm not either, but it doesn't seem to be up to us."

The endlessness of the ocean pressed in on them and injected a severe sense of hopelessness. They were like tiny ants on a stone cast into the middle of the Sahara.

But still they prayed, hours at a time, begging God to deliver them and to give them strength. But also mixed in with their requests were prayers of thanksgiving and praise. Their sense of reality began to stretch above and beyond their own desires and a peace started to resonate within them. Whatever God's will was, it was the perfect plan- that was the truth they were beginning to act on.

Hours later, the sun disappeared in another glorious sunset, and darkness was soon blotting out everything. Clouds had begun to cover the sky so there was no moonlight to reveal the separation of water and sky. Nothing was discernible, only the sound of the waves slapping the yacht and the wind traveling over the waters was noticeable.

Then it began to rain.

James and Joshua were huddled together in the cabin. They were silent, their eyes watching the glass as water pounded against it. Thunder echoed and lightening lit up the sky, giving just enough light to reveal the mountainous waves attempting to flip their boat. They were soaking wet, and they knew the boat had to be close to giving up her buoyancy. This is it, they thought. All they had to do was wait for that one wave that would sweep them from the boat and take them to a watery grave.

The *Polymer III* was tossed around on the fingers of the ocean like it was a toy. It was a miracle that she hadn't sunk yet. Every time she would pass over a wave, her bow would sink into a void until the next rolling wave would crash into the vacant spot, attempting to force the bow beneath the ocean.

Once, the yacht had tipped so far to one side that James and Joshua were thrown against the wall so that their feet weren't even on the ground anymore. Then another wave countered and caught the yacht as it was tipping and threw her back to center. James and Joshua fell from the wall and onto the ground, striking their heads on something in the process. As they passed into unconsciousness, they reached out and grabbed each other, seeking some degree of comfort knowing that they weren't going to die alone.

James' eyes opened. The familiar feel of a rocking boat helped orient himself and he struggled to his knees. Joshua was beside him, and James checked his pulse. He was breathing.

After surveying the yacht, James had discovered that the food and water had either been swept overboard or destroyed by the crashing waves the night before. He sat on the boat and stared out over the water, his mind tired of thinking about death. Instead, he let his stoic stare settle on the bouncing water, squinting into the reflecting light.

Joshua walked out of the cabin. "I can't believe we're still afloat."

James shrugged. "The food and water is gone."

Joshua didn't respond.

After a few seconds passed and Joshua hadn't said another word, James turned to see what he was doing. He was standing still, staring up into the clouds.

"You okay?" James asked.

He only pointed up into the sky.

James followed Joshua's finger into the depths of the sky and immediately shot to his feet.

Contrails.

James wasted no time. "Help me look for flares!"

Joshua followed him back down into the cabin, and they began going through cabinets and drawers. Nothing.

Suddenly Joshua stood up. "Try the radio!"

"It's dead, we tried it before," James argued.

Joshua ran back onto the deck and into the wheel house. "There was no transmission. Did you check the power though?"

James answered, "No."

Joshua worked on the radio, and he soon heard static. He looked at James and smiled.

James could hardly contain himself. He ran back onto the deck and began searching the horizon for signs of ships, planes, or land.

"Mayday, mayday, this is the *Polymer III.* Can anyone hear me?"

Nothing.

He switched frequencies and continued repeating his message while James continued searching the seascape and the sky.

He was just about to give up, to collapse in defeat, when a voice came back over the radio.

"*Polymer III, this is Dutch Treat, what is your emergency? Over.*"

Joshua looked up from the radio and yelled to James. "James! We're saved! We're saved!"

James came running into the wheel house and embraced Joshua, jumping up and down and laughing with shed tears.

"*Polymer III, this is Dutch Treat, do you copy? Over.*"

As Joshua reached for the radio, the hair on James' neck stood up straight.

Joshua noticed. "What is it?"

James shook his head. "It can't be."

"What?"

"The *Dutch Treat* went missing in the Triangle."

Joshua forced a chuckle. "Stop it."

James' eyes were set swimming with fear. "I'm serious."

Joshua shot him a sideways glance and picked up the radio. "*Dutch Treat,* we are stranded afloat with no food, water, or gas."

"*What are your coordinates? Over.*"

Before Joshua could answer, James grabbed the radio out of his hand. "*Dutch Treat,* what year is it?"

There was a pause on the other end and then a confused voice asked, "*Excuse me?*"

"The year!" James yelled.

"1974."

Joshua and James looked at each other, their bodies tingling with unbelief.

James woke up with a start and was relieved to find Joshua still trying to raise someone on the radio. "That wasn't a very funny dream."

But when Joshua turned around, he had two horns protruding out of his head and a serpent-like tongue flickering from behind jagged teeth. His eyes glowed red and a tail was wrapped around one ankle.

"Hello, James Streen." The voice came from the radio, and it was the same familiar voice that James had tried to forget. "Did you really think that you could get away?"

Joshua walked closer, flashing his clawed hands, saliva dripping off his chin.

Joshua was shaking James by the shoulders trying to get him to wake up. "James! Wake up!"

James was screaming and twitching in response to something that he was seeing in his dreams.

Joshua slapped him in the face. "Wake up, James!"

James opened his eyes and yelped in surprise to see Joshua on top of him. He scrambled backwards and away from him.

"Relax, man. You're having a nightmare."

James looked around the deck of the boat, searching for the creature he thought was hiding somewhere close by.

"It's okay, James. You were just having another dream." Joshua walked back to the radio that was spitting static into the air and let James recover. Joshua was getting tired of these nightmares they were having, and he wondered if they would ever recover from their experience with the supernatural.

"Sorry," James mumbled, rubbing his head.

"Like I said, we'll probably be calling each other in the middle of the night." He then repeated his message over the radio.

"Do you think-"

"*Polymer III, this is the USS Miami, we read you.*"

At first James and Joshua just looked at each other, not able to comprehend the noise that just came from the radio.

"*Polymer III, do you copy?*"

"Answer them!" yelled James, snapping out of it.

Fumbling with the receiver, Joshua finally managed to reply. "Oh man, are we glad to hear you! We're stranded afloat with no gas. We need to be picked up."

"Polymer III, what are your coordinates?"

"Uh, this vessel isn't equipped with GPS equipment, and the compass doesn't appear to be working. It's cracked."

"Your signal is getting stronger, so we're going to assume we're moving towards you. We're going to initiate a search. Hang in there, Polymer III, we're coming for you."

"Thank you, we'll be waiting."

James smiled and thanked God. Joshua screamed a loud, "Yahoo!" and the two embraced and jumped for joy.

"We're going home!"

:::: *HOME*

Driving through New York in the back seat of a taxi cab proved to be one awkward experience for James. Though it was his home and he had grown up driving in cars- the sight of traffic, street signs, flashy cars, and people walking around talking on cell phones was almost too much for him to handle all at once. He just couldn't comprehend that he was back, that any of the past month and a half had taken place. He felt disoriented and confused, realities mixing and blurring together in his mind.

Joshua was on his way back home too. The two had said their goodbyes and promised to call sometime during the week. James told Joshua to get his hands on a Bible and to find a good church. Joshua said he would.

After being asked for the hundredth time how they ended up adrift in a boat that had been missing for twenty-three years and what happened in Bermuda, they were more than ready to get out of the Naval station. A few men in black suits showed up and started asking James about Steve, and he was growing very annoyed. When people started asking about the seaplane, they decided that it was time to make an escape. Jumping out a bathroom window, they climbed into the back of a passing truck. Waiting for the opportune time, they abandoned the truck and ran down the street. They managed to grab a taxi and took it out of state.

After eating at a diner, the fresh set of clothes given to them by the Navy helping their appearances, they decided to split up and head for home.

As the taxi grew nearer to his house, James couldn't stop the feeling of butterflies in his stomach. He knew that Kirsten must be an emotional wreck, convinced that he was dead, and he couldn't wait to see her face when he walked through the front door. He couldn't believe he was actually going to see her again. A tear rolled down his cheek and he thanked God for the millionth time.

He paid the driver with some pretty beat up bills, not able to comprehend how his wallet had stayed in the back pocket of the pants he had worn for the last month and a half, and shut the door. As the taxi pulled away from the curb, James stood, empty handed, in front of his house. Except for a few neglected landscaping chores, the house was exactly as he remembered it. His BMW was still sitting in the driveway with a pair of bullet holes in the windshield. He sniffed the fresh air and the scent of upstate New York as a breeze blew by. His sea legs hadn't gone away yet and walking was still awkward, but he didn't really notice. He was standing at the front door before he knew it.

He pushed the door open and walked in. The feeling was overwhelming, and he prayed he wasn't dreaming. He thought for sure that he would never see this scene again. There was no noise coming from any of the downstairs rooms so he began walking quietly up the stairs. Jessica's door was open so he stuck his head in, but it was empty. He checked the clock hanging on the wall. It was 1:30. He guessed she was over one of her friends' houses.

He walked down the hall and towards the bedroom. The door was opened just a crack, and he could see the form of a woman lying in the bed.

His heart skipped a beat.

Very quietly, he opened the door and stepped into the room. She was even more beautiful than he had remembered. Her eyes were closed, and the sad expression painted on her face gave James a twinge of guilt for putting her through this whole mess. He approached the side of the bed, using every ounce of self control not to run and pick her up.

Kirsten felt the presence of someone watching her and she opened her eyes. But what she saw, she did not comprehend. Her dead husband was standing beside her, smiling.

Their gaze was locked on each other, volumes of feelings and emotions being translated through watery eyes. Neither one could do anything but remain transfixed in astonishment, the person before them stirring up such an emotional storm that words couldn't be uttered. Kirsten's eyes were spitting tears, the look of unleashed joy resonating from behind them, yet there was a hesitant look there as well- she didn't know if he was real.

"Hey, Baby." James reached down and stroked her arm.

His voice and his touch set her senses blazing and she sat straight up. "Is it you?" She was crying uncontrollably, wrestling to get out of the bed and onto the floor. "Is it really you?"

James helped her up, taking notice of how pregnant she was and how attractive she was. "Yes, it's me."

"Oh! It can't be! It can't be! Is it you?" She nearly tackled him onto the floor and was holding him so tight, he was having trouble breathing.

"It's me, Baby. I'm home." He squeezed her back and they just held each other for a while, crying, saying nothing. Then she spasmodically ran her hands all over his face and head, trying to convince herself of his presence. He held her face in his steady hands, waiting for her to calm down. But she wasn't. She continued weeping, not knowing what she wanted to do with him, to hug him or kiss him, or just look at him. So she fitfully went back and forth between all three. James ran his hands through her hair, gazing into her eyes, wanting to erase all the torment she had been through. They were both hysterical, not knowing how to convey what they were feeling. The tears that were making the wood floor slippery just didn't seem to be enough. The sporadic and desperate kisses didn't seem to say it all, either.

Finally, she began to settle down and she pulled her head back and looked up into his eyes. "I don't even know what to say . . . I thought you were dead."

He stroked her cheek, wiping away tears with his thumb. "I love you."

A few more tears escaped and fell to the floor as she embraced him again. "I love you so much."

"It's okay now." He kissed her forehead, wetting her hair with his tears. He rocked her back and forth in his arms, treasuring the feel of her against him. It was a feeling he thought he would never know again.

"Jess is over a friend's house," she stammered.

"How is she?"

She stepped back again. "She was in denial. I tried to be strong for her but . . . " Her sentence was choked off by sobs. She buried her face in his chest.

"It's okay," James repeated. The emotions inside of him felt as if they were going to blow him apart.

Their lips met in a sweet union serenaded with salty tears and relentless emotion. Finally, their feeling seemed to have found an outlet, and they relaxed in each other's arms, their lips still locked, the messages still being sent. After a full two minutes, their lips separated, and their eyes met. Smiles spread across their faces and they embraced again.

The love they both thought would never be realized again was suddenly back, and the emotion in the room would have collapsed the house had it been more than metaphysical or spiritual. They did not leave the room for the rest of the day.

"Oh, Steve's back."

James rolled over and looked at her, a dumbfounded look on his face. "What?"

Kirsten smiled. "He just showed up one day. He went back to Bermuda looking for you but got into some trouble and now he's lying low."

The information paralyzed his brain for a few minutes. He had completely given up on his brother, and had honestly forgotten about him since seeing Kirsten again. After his mind was able to compute that information, he leaned closer to his wife and kissed her again. He smiled as he looked into her deep blue eyes. "Kirsten . . . " he whispered.

She tilted her head in curiosity and lifted it up under her hand. "James. . ."

James sighed. "I don't know how to tell you what happened."

"I don't want to know yet."

He ran his fingers over her soft face. "So much happened . . . "

"I can tell. You're covered with scars, and you're about thirty pounds skinnier."

James smiled. "Will you accept a skinny James Streen for a while?"

A mischievous grin painted her lips. "Oh, I guess I could put up with it for a little while."

"Good. Just don't roll over in the middle of the night, you might break me."

She hit him and laughed. "You jerk!"

They laughed and kissed again.

Tomorrow the world would have to be faced and many things would have to be explained to so many people. He would get to see Jessica, whom he was dying to see, and maybe he would see Fred and George too. But right now, he didn't care if tomorrow didn't come for a month. The clock read 2:30 A.M., and he and Kirsten were still talking about the past month and a half. She told him about all the strange events that took place in the house, and Fred and George's investigation, about the letter . . . And he told her an edited version of what happened to him. He left out the parts about what the demon said about their son. He didn't want her to know about that. But he told her about the giants and the natives, and how God used them to save the pure-blooded people. He also told her about Chris, about his decision to stay behind, and that he, Joshua, and Edward all accepted the Lord. But when she remembered to tell him about the design left on their daughter's bed that was discovered by Fred, James couldn't help the sudden skip of his heart, for she described to him the same image that was portrayed in the crop circles. But he quickly recovered and let the occasion for elaboration pass. Why dwell on it? That's exactly what the enemy wants.

"I can't believe you're home," she whispered.

"Neither can I."

"I didn't think I could live without you. I didn't know what I was going to do."

He held her tighter in his arms. "Shhh . . . I'm here, and I'm not going anywhere." He kissed her forehead.

At 4:15 A.M., they finally fell asleep.

The morning came, and James found himself staring at Kirsten, studying her sleeping body as he had since the day they were married. Her face was glowing and her hair was spread across the pillow. She looked like an angel- a large angel, but an angel. And it wasn't a figure of speech, for James had seen an angel.

He stroked her face.

There were no nightmares that plagued his mind while he slept. No Vietnam dreams, and no dreams about the island. It was the first peaceful sleep he had in a long time.

He leaned over and gently pressed his lips against Kirsten's temple. Then he quietly got out of bed and got dressed. He was down the stairs just in time to answer the door. When he swung it open, Jessica was standing there, looking up into his eyes. At first, she didn't seem to understand, and then, she lunged forward and wrapped her small arms around his waist. James picked her up and held her tight, more tears running down his face.

"Everyone said that you were missing," she cried.

"I'm home now, Honey. It's okay." He was rubbing her back, letting her sob over his shoulder.

"Please don't leave us again, Daddy."

"I won't, Baby. I won't."

He carried her up the stairs and into their bedroom.

Kirsten woke up just in time to see her husband walk through the bedroom door with Jessica in his arms. She smiled, emotions being stirred again at the sight of how tightly Jess was clinging to James' neck.

James laid Jess on the bed next to Kirsten so that she was in the middle of her parents.

Kirsten rolled over and embraced James, an all loving look shared between them. Jess was squished in the love sandwich. They all laughed.

James reached for Kirsten's hand and squeezed it tightly. "Thank you, Jesus."

Jessica repeated his prayer. "Thank you for bringing back my daddy, Jesus."

Kirsten smiled. "Amen." Then she leaned over Jess and kissed her husband.

EPILOGUE
A Year Later

James was holding his son, Christopher Streen, in his arms. He was a tiny baby, undersized for his age, but so was his father at the same age. His blue eyes were an express image of Kirsten's, his hands and feet belonging to James. Already, he was beginning to reveal mannerisms that would mark his personality. James brushed back his black hair.

Joshua walked through the room on his way to the kitchen from the bathroom. "Hey, you want a drink or something?"

James looked up from his chair and smiled. "Yeah, sure. I'll take a Coke."

"One Coke for daddy, comin' right up."

James looked over to the couch and winked at Kirsten and Jess who were watching *Marry Poppins* on the television. The sound of laughter came from the kitchen, and James tried to angle his head around the doorway to see what was going on. "Hey, what's going on in there?"

Joshua stuck his head out from around the corner, whip cream smeared on his face. "Uh, nothing." Then he disappeared and there was more commotion.

"You guys better behave yourselves!" James teased.

Joshua and Amy came out of the kitchen with whipped cream spread over their faces and their arms around each other's waists.

"For the record," Joshua was raising a finger. "We are a very well behaved couple and-"

Amy grabbed his side and he bent over, slapping her hand away.

"Stop it!" He grabbed her back and she screamed.

"Stop grabbing my fat!" she screamed.

Joshua rolled his eyes and exchanged an understanding look with James. "Fat . . . The girl weighs ten pounds, and she thinks she's fat." He looked at her. "What am I going to do with you?"

The 5'9" brown-eyed girl he met at the Baptist church seven months ago looked into his eyes. "You could marry me."

The remark caught him so off guard that he stood stunned for a few seconds, not knowing how to reply. She just continued to stare into his eyes, waiting for some kind of response.

"You want to?" he asked.

"Is that your proposal?"

"What? No. I mean . . . " He held up his hands. "Hold on, back up. You actually wouldn't mind marrying me?"

Amy flashed a crooked smile. "Oh, I don't know, Josh, I'm sure I could always wait around for someone better to come along."

Joshua's face dropped.

"But I'd be waiting an awfully long time, and I would like to have kids at some point."

Joshua smiled. "Hey, the idea is wonderful. How 'bout we pray about it, and then I'll pretend to surprise you at a later date?"

She wrapped her arms around him. "Can't wait."

James and Kirsten laughed.

"You sure you know what you're doing, Amy?" James asked.

"Hey!" Joshua shouted.

"What? It's only fair to warn her."

"Nobody warned me about you," Kirsten shot at him from across the room.

James looked down into Chris' brown eyes. "Can you believe the way your mother talks to me?"

He laughed and waved his hands, sticking tiny fingers into his father's mouth.

Kirsten and Amy were cleaning up the kitchen and Jess was asleep on the couch. Chris was upstairs sleeping in his crib.

"Do you ever think about it?" Joshua looked away from the TV and turned his attention to James.

James looked him in the eyes. "I think about Chris. I wonder what he's doing. I pray for him all the time."

"Do you think he's okay?"

"Every time I hear of another plane or boat missing in the Triangle, I can't help but to wonder what's going on."

Joshua looked out the window. "You don't give any thought to what that thing said about your boy, do you?"

The truth of the matter was that James did. Every time he looked at Christopher, he heard the words the demon had spoken to him. "It's a stupid feeling. It doesn't mean anything. I know that God is in control, that the demon can't just take him, but I still get this weird feeling inside when I look at him. It's stupid, but the feeling's there."

Joshua leaned back against the cushion on the couch. "It doesn't even seem like it all happened."

"I know. Every time I think I've put it out of my head, I get another call from the Bureau, the Navy, Coast Guard, scientists, New Age fanatics, or someone from John's family. Or Brian or Edward's."

"Have they stopped asking you questions about the *Polymer III* yet?"

"Yeah, they seem to be over that. I must admit, from their vantage point, us showing up in a boat that disappeared in 1980 is a bit odd. The wife of the owner posted a $25,000 reward just for information about him, and then here we come in his boat 23 years later . . . "

Taking a sip from his glass, Joshua moved his gaze from the window to the ceiling. "There's one thing that's been bothering me."

"What's that?" asked James.

"Yeah, the *Milton Iatrides* traveled through the triangle from New Orleans in 1970, but it was last reported being right off the hub of Brazil."

James seemed to think about that for a while. "I've thought about it too. I don't understand it."

Joshua finished the contents in his glass and stood to his feet. "Do you mind if I look around in your library?"

James nodded. "Knock yourself out. I'm going to take Jess up to bed."

Joshua made his way from the living room to James' study, pausing to listen to Kirsten and Amy's whispered conversation coming from the kitchen. He smiled at the mention of his name and thought of how wonderful life had been since getting back from the island- or whatever it was. His life in Christ was more than he could have ever imagined, and he regretted not pursuing the truth sooner.

He had moved to New York, five minutes from James, and met Amy at their church. He had begun to thrive in the Word and in his fellowship with other Believers, the discipline that formed him into a SEAL shaping him into a new kind of soldier- a soldier for Christ. And he considered it no small matter. The words that were spit from the demon's mouth had sparked a fire within James' heart and had eventually reached his own. The way the demon perceived Christians was not entirely off the mark. The world was changing and the Christians seemed to be changing right along with it, generally speaking. Holiness no longer seemed to be a matter of concern within the church. There seemed to be a love for the things of the world and a tolerance for the sin that the Bible condemns. These things convicted James in a way that caused him to change his own life and then to begin spreading the message of sanctification and holiness to those around him. Too many of God's soldiers were being entertained in the enemy's camp, and James knew that if a revival was to take place, it would be through the pursuit of holiness. Change would have to occur. The demon was right, it was getting hard to tell the difference between the children of God and the children of the devil. And how could the light shine and attract the attention of those Christ would seek to draw to Himself when those He desires to use are having problems shining through the secular fog they bathe in? It was a new mission for James and it soon became a mission for Joshua as well. With such severe discipline habits, Joshua couldn't understand how so many people could give in so easily to so many temptations, eventually finding themselves desensitized to the voice of God. He thrived at the Christian life, at crucifying the flesh and forsaking self. His training had taught him that anyone can surrender, it takes no great person to give in to something, but it's the resisting, the fighting and climbing that proves who one is. He was called to obey and he served His King with severity. He did not take the grace he was given lightly, it was a serious matter to him, and to serve Christ in return was his reasonable service.

He searched over the names of all the books, running his finger across their letters. James had developed quite a collection of books concerning the Bermuda Triangle, UFO's, Atlantis, ancient civilizations, and giants. Joshua recalled his own studies, and facts began to mix with his own experience, trying to find a middle ground. Both Joshua and James had personally seen the briefs available for inspection from civil investigating authorities. The National Transportation Safety Board in Washington D.C. was one of their first stops. There they were able to read over the one or two page accounts of known facts concerning the disappearance of planes within the Bermuda Triangle- a startling number that never made the newspapers. They also talked to members of the Seventh Coast Guard district, which has jurisdiction over the Triangle, and were told that in no search conducted by them, for any airplane or boat reported overdue and then missing, has a body ever been recovered. Even in events where the vessel may be found, it is always found deserted or ditched in shallow water with the ignition key removed and the doors tightly closed- but no sign of the pilot, ever. Further investigation led them to discover that over 120 vessels that disappeared had been equipped with emergency position-indicating radio beacons, which are designed to be activated when they float free of a sinking ship, or emergency locator transmitters, which are jettisoned from an aircraft fuselage upon impact. These transmitters are able to broadcast for days, even weeks, and yet none seem to have ever been released by those vessels and planes vanishing in the Triangle's mysteriousness whereas they seem to have no problem functioning in the rest of the world's oceans.

Their studies revealed a great mystery surrounded by exaggerations and insane theories, but they discovered enough to know that something was happening there, had been since it was called "Sea of Doom," "Graveyard of the Atlantic," and "Sargasso Graveyard" back in the 18th and 19th centuries. The term 'triangle' hadn't been used until 1952. The infamous Flight 19 and other accounts of bizarre occurrences within the triangle had captured the interest of the two people there and back again. Radio transmissions of pilots complaining about compasses going haywire, objects appearing in their paths, forcing them to change course, sudden appearances of fog, and other strange reports added to the mystery. The Triangle had claimed over 1,000 disappearances in the past twenty-five years alone. They could only wonder if the demon was responsible for them all.

There were many theories out there attempting to explain the phenomena, theories stretching from one extreme to the other. Magnetic opposition, mass quantities of methane gas released from the ocean's floor, space-time vortices, UFOs, black holes, top secret government testing, and even power crystals from the ancient civilization of Atlantis have been blamed for the mysteries surrounding the Devil's Triangle. Was there truth to any of it? Before the events of last year, Joshua would have laughed at the question. Now, he was seeking the answer himself.

"You know what's interesting?" James voice interrupted his thoughts.

"What's that?"

"The names, Jared, Mahalalel, Seth, and Lud . . . Names recorded in the genealogy of Genesis chapter five, right around the time of Noah."

Joshua paused. "That's kinda' weird."

"Yeah, I thought so."

"I was just thinking about the Triangle," Joshua said.

James walked up beside him. "I've been thinking about a lot. Genesis six and the verses in Jude . . . The Nephilim and the fallen angels . . . " He shook his head. "I was reading this one guy that was saying he thought that UFOs were the souls of the Nephilim, the spiritual part of their existence." And then he laughed. "And then I was reading this guy who said that the giants in chapter six were only genetic anomalies, nothing more. That 'the sons of God' doesn't mean angels but the 'sons of Seth.'"

"I don't know about that one." Joshua pulled out a book entitled *Angelology*. "I think we've seen a side of reality most never witness."

James stared out the window that was above the bookcase. "Do you ever wonder if there's an island out there, just sitting in the Atlantic with pyramids and natives and . . . Chris?"

"Everyday."

"It's a spiritual world, this physical reality is only its clothes," James mused.

Joshua put the book back in its spot and waved his hand over the whole collection. "Pyramids, crop circles, aliens, giants, Atlantis, the Triangle, demons and angels . . . "

"It's a mystery, but it's a spiritual one."

"And yet we have all the spiritual revelation we need right here." Joshua picked up a Bible off the top of the bookcase. "One day we will see Him face to face."

"'But as the days of Noah were, so shall the coming of the Son of Man be. For as in the days before the flood, they were eating and drinking, marrying and giving in marriage, until the day Noah entered the ark' . . . "

Joshua let the thought tingle his brain. "The days of Noah . . . "

"So evil that only one family escaped God's judgment."

Joshua turned and looked at James. "Tell me the truth, do you get scared?"

He shrugged. "All that we've been through can't be explained. I wrestle with that. Sometimes it drives me crazy, not knowing where we were or how we got there . . . All these crazy ideas start swimming through my mind, these theories I read about start to taunt me. A portal to Atlantis? Time travel? The demon's words, 'my workshop,' what it wanted to introduce to our world . . . It all gets to me at times."

"Do you think that's how the end will come?"

James shook his head. "I don't know. We have a physical perception based on man's actions and the result of those actions, but what is actually taking place in that unseen world behind the scenes? I don't think I want to find out again. Instead, I'll just trust that God is in control and whatever Satan has up his sleeve, it's already been pre-approved by God to meet His ultimate end. Sure, Satan can bring hell onto earth, but that will only lead to his destruction and the new heaven and earth. It's all in His hands, I have to let go of it or I'll drive myself insane."

"It's just that I can't get some of that stuff out of my head . . . the faces on those creatures . . . I see them sometimes in a reflection from a mirror or in the corner of my eye . . . I just can't seem to forget about them."

"Me neither. But perhaps it's a scar worth having. After seeing evil, it's easier to spot it in camouflaged packages. Even if it does come with a bow."

"I was looking over some history books the other day, reading some of the ancient civilization's records of cloud cars and all that stuff. It's all so bizarre."

James put his arm around Joshua and spun him back towards the kitchen. "Yeah, it is. But then I pick up His Word and I look into Kirsten's eyes, and you know what? Things don't seem so bizarre anymore." He patted Joshua on the back. "Why don't we see how our women are doing?"

Joshua raised his eyebrows. "No complaints from me."

They walked out of the library just as the front door opened and Steve walked in.

"Hey, Guys." He shut the door and moved forward to shake hands.

"You're late," said James.

"I know. I got another phone call as I was walking out the door."

Steve had struck a deal of sorts with the government agencies once the whole conspiracy was considered destroyed. Because it seemed to fall apart due to Steve killing Mr. Alexanders, the agencies let him off based on the agreement that he would disappear from government business and live a low-key life not attracting attention. Steve was more than happy to accept the offer, and he was spared imprisonment or consequences worse than that. Every once in a while he would get a phone call or an investigator trying to sniff him out, but all he had to do was make a phone call and the problem would be taken care of. He had adopted a new life, a simple one, and as long as he bothered no one, no one would bother him.

James directed both him and Joshua into the kitchen.

Amy caught the sight of Joshua coming through the doorway out of the corner of her eye and quickly stopped what she was saying in mid-sentence, blushing to make it more obvious.

"What was that?" Joshua came up from behind her and massaged her shoulders.

"Nothing."

Kirsten gave James a kiss and then gave Steve a hug. "I didn't know if you'd make it."

Steve smiled. "Come on, and miss this get-together? This is church for me."

Though he still wasn't willing to turn his life over to Christ, he was beginning to notice a difference in his family and friends, and he was asking a whole lot of questions lately. And James was just fine with that.

Kirsten shot him a look. "Church ain't gonna' get you to heaven." She then retrieved ice cream out of the freezer as they all sat around the table.

"Yeah, yeah . . . " Steve rolled his eyes. But there was something there, something that hadn't been there before his little train ride back to Virginia, after he saw something that he couldn't explain. He knew that he would have to confront the questions that he seemed to be asking himself sooner or later, and, in truth, he wanted to. That's why he liked coming over to his brother's house. He may put on the 'whatever' show, but inside, he was desperate for what they had. He knew he wouldn't be able to hold out much longer.

The five friends sat around the kitchen table eating ice cream and telling stories. After the dishes were empty and the table cleared, they all played a game.

James squeezed Kirsten's hand under the table as he looked over the faces that surrounded him. God was gracious, He was truly gracious, he thought. It was a scenario he would have never dreamt possible a year ago. He was stranded in an evil world, hunted by enemies, disturbed by evil spirits, convinced that his brother was dead, that he would never see his child born, and that he would leave his wife a widow with two children. Though he was forever grateful that God had other plans- that was the fact, God had other plans. And they involved him still being alive along with the people surrounding him. He couldn't wait to find out what those plans were.

Kirsten lost and Amy comforted her as James and Steve argued over who should have won. Joshua laughed as he watched the drama unfold, wondering if he and Amy had a future much like James and Kirsten. He hoped so.

James stared at Christopher, his son who he named after a great and wonderful friend, a friend that was out there somewhere, though there was no certainty as to where. James knelt beside the crib, taking Christopher's tiny hand in his, and he began to pray. Tears fell to the floor as words of thanks and words of petition were offered to the heavens. He prayed so earnestly that Christopher would grow up to be a man of God, set apart and on fire for the one true King. He felt the same way about Jessica but had shed fewer tears over her. Perhaps it was because he still feared the promise made by the demon, though he didn't believe it. Another irrational fear, he thought.

He wiped his eyes and stood up, staring at his sleeping one year old son for another five minutes. "Lord, he is yours." Then he turned and started to walk out of the room, but there was a figure standing in the doorway that made his heart jump through his chest. The figure was covered by a shadow, and James took a step back, his mind paralyzed with fear.

"Are you coming to bed?"

Kirsten stepped out of the shadow and into the room.

"You scared me to death." James said, trying to catch his breath.

"I'm sorry. I like watching you pray for our son."

He followed her down the hallway but stopped to peek into Jessica's room. After being confident that all was well, he worked on catching up with Kirsten who was already in their room. By the time he entered, she was already in bed.

"Tonight was nice," she said.

James climbed into bed next to her. “Yeah, it was. Can you believe Amy put that on Joshua like that?”

Kirsten laughed. “I thought Joshua was going to pass out.” She wrapped her arms around his neck and brought his head down to hers. She kissed him lightly on the lips before he kissed her back.

Suddenly, the demon’s words came crashing through James’ mind. *“I’ll be watching . . . ”*

As Kirsten ran her hands through his hair, he smiled. “Let it watch.”

Kirsten look at him funny. “What?”

James smiled. “Nothing.”

Then he kissed her.

THE END?